Naturopathic Standards *of*
Primary Care

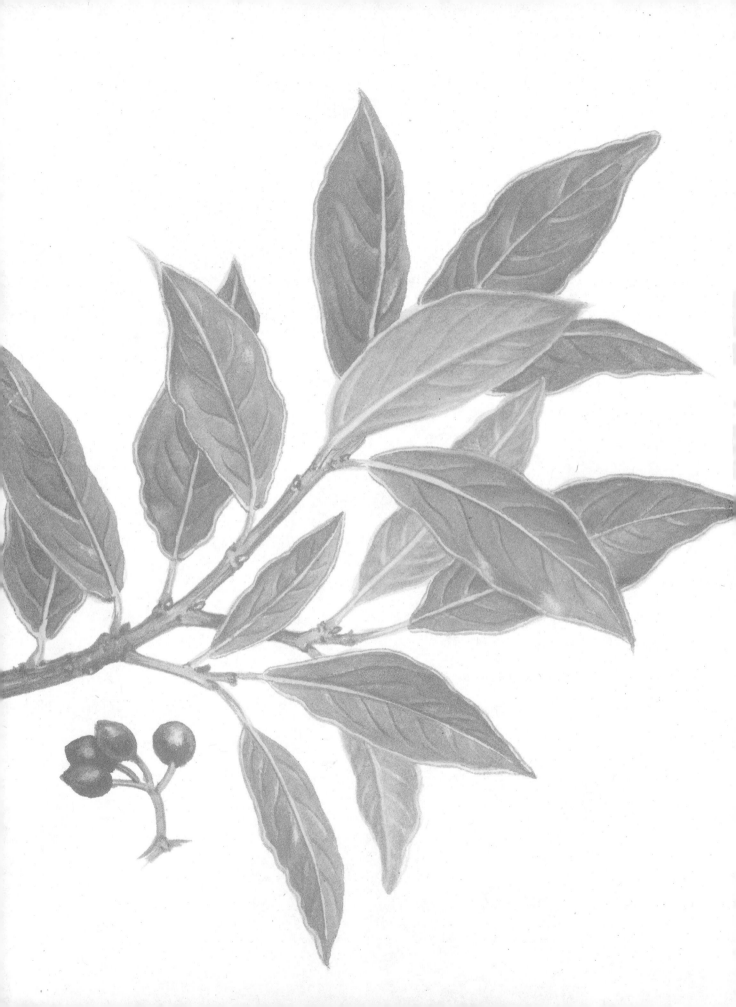

Naturopathic Standards of
Primary Care

Shehab El-Hashemy, MBChB, ND

CCNM
PRESS

Dedication: This book is dedicated to my mentors and teachers at The Canadian College of Naturopathic Medicine, the many naturopathic physicians from whom I continue to learn, the dedicated cadre of primary care instructors of CLE 303 – and to my students for their feedback and critical thinking that undoubtedly shaped the evolution of this book.

Acknowledgments: The author would like to thank Dr Nick De Groot, BSc, ND, Dean of Clinical Education at The Canadian College of Naturopathic Medicine (CCNM), for his ongoing support to this project; Dr Aubrey Rickford, BA, ND, Associate Professor of Asian Medicine & Clinic Faculty at CCNM, for his valuable input in the Hypertension module; Dr Philip Rouchotas MSc, ND, Assistant Professor of Nutrition at CCNM, for writing the Dyslipidemia module; Dr Jasmine Carino, ND, Associate Professor and Clinic Supervisor, for feedback on content and references; Bob Hilderley, Executive Director of CCNM Press, for his unwavering attention to detail in editing this manuscript.

Disclaimer: The medical and health information presented in this book is based on the research, training, and professional experience of the authors, and is true and complete to the best of their knowledge. However, this book is intended only as an informative guide for those wishing to know more about medicine and healthcare; it is not intended to replace or countermand the advice given by the reader's personal healthcare provider. The publisher and the authors are not responsible for any adverse effects or consequences from the use of information in this book. It is the responsibility of the reader to consult a qualified healthcare professional regarding personal care.

The author of this book has taken every effort to ensure that all information contained is accurate and complies with NABNE, AMA, and CMA guidelines and accepted standards at the time of publication. Due to the constantly changing nature of all medical sciences and the possibility of human error, the reader is encouraged to exercise clinical judgment and incorporate new information that becomes available with continuing research. In particular, the reader is advised to check the manufacturer's published monographs of all prescription and non-prescription agents (pharmacological, botanical, nutritional, and homeopathic) before administration.

ISBN 1-897025-17-3

Edited by Bob Hilderley. Designed by Sari Naworynski.

Printed and bound in Canada.

Published by CCNM Press Inc., 1255 Sheppard Avenue East, Toronto, Ontario, Canada M2K 1E2 www.ccnmpress.com

CONTENTS

Acronyms & Abbreviations

Examination Boards & Licensing Bodies

MCCQE	Medical Council of Canada Qualifying Examination
MCC	Medical Council of Canada
NABNE	North American Board of Naturopathic Examiners
NBME	National Board of Medical Examiners
NPLEX	Naturopathic Physicians Licensing Examination
USMLE	United States Medical Licensing Examination

Regulatory & Professional Associations

AANP	American Association of Naturopathic Physicians
AMA	American Medical Association
BDDT-N	Board of Directors of Drugless Therapy – Naturopathy
CAND	Canadian Association of Naturopathic Doctors
CMA	Canadian Medical Association
RCPSC	Royal College of Physicians and Surgeons of Canada

Health Assessment

#	fracture
AAA	abdominal aortic aneurysm
AAL	anterior axillary line
Abx	antibiotics
AD	Alzheimer's dementia
ADLs	activities of daily living
AP	anteroposterior (imaging)
A&O x 4	alert & oriented to person, place, time, and date
A/O, A&O	alert and oriented
A&P	auscultation & percussion
Asx, ASX	asymptomatic
Ausc, auscul	auscultation
A&W	alive and well (in family Hx)
BP	blood pressure
CA	chronological age
CABG	coronary artery bypass grafting
CAD	coronary artery disease
C&A	conscious and alert
C&S	culture and sensitivity
CC, c/o	chief complaint, complains of

CKD	chronic kidney disease (previously termed CRF)
DOB, D/B	date of birth
DU	diagnosis undetermined
Dx, diag	diagnosis
DDX	differential diagnosis
Ex	examination
F	female
FH, FHx	family history
FOD	free of disease
F/U, FU	follow up
FUO, FWS	fever of unknown origin, fever without identifiable source
h/o	history of
H&P	history and physical
Ht, h	height
Hx, H	history
IADL	instrumental activities of daily living
IBW	ideal body weight
IPPA	inspection, palpation, percussion, auscultation
IQ	intelligence quotient
LAD, LAO	left anterior descending, left anterior oblique (coronary)
LRT	lower respiratory tract
LWD	living with disease
M	male
MA	mental age
MCI	mild cognitive impairment
MHx, MH	medical history
MMSE	mini mental state examination
NAD	no apparent distress/ disease, no acute distress, nothing abnormal detected
N/C, NC	no complaints
NED	no evidence of disease
NKA	no known allergies
NKDA	no known drug allergies
norm	normal
NVS	neurological vital signs
P	pulse
PA	posteroanterior (imaging)
P&A, P/A	percussion and auscultation
palp	palpation

PE, PEx, PX	physical examination
PERRLA	pupils equal, round, react to light & accommodation
PH	poor health
PMH, PMHx	past medical history
PMI	past medical illness, point of maximal impulse (cardio Ex)
PPHx	previous psychiatric history
Px, prog	prognosis
Pt	patient
R, RR	respiration, respiration rate
RAD, RAO	right anterior descending, right anterior oblique (coronary)
RPO	right posterior oblique
R/O, RO	rule out
ROS	review of systems
RVC	responds to verbal commands
Rx	prescription
SOAP	subjective, objective assessment, plan
SONP	soft organs non palpable
S/S	signs & symptoms
Sx	symptoms
UT, UTI	urinary tract, urinary tract infection
T	temperature
TPR	temperature, pulse & respiration
Tx, tr, treat	treatment
UCD, UCHD	usual childhood diseases
U/O, UO	under observation
URT, URTI	upper respiratory tract, upper respiratory tract infection
UT, UTI	urinary tract, urinary tract infection (commonly refers to lower UTI)
VS, v/s	vital signs
WDWN	well developed, well dressed, well nourished
WNL	within normal limits
Wt	weight
X&D	examination and diagnosis
y, yr	year
y/o	years old

Naturopathic Standards of Primary Care is not designed to provide primary care practitioners with static 'cookbook medicine' that is imposed by some guideline generating authority. Rather, it is designed to present and critically appraise the reasoning behind current best practices (medical, naturopathic, surgical, and otherwise), external evidence, and patients' preferences to allow for the generation of contemporary standards of care. In this manner, clinical guidelines for primary care practice are subjected to a flexible approach that informs the practitioner of available supporting evidence.

This book is also designed to expand basic problem-solving skills and to extend them beyond pattern recognition and differential diagnosis list generation to a systematic process of symptom/sign recognition, cost-effective laboratory investigation, procedural diagnosis, proper follow-up, and case management in primary care settings. At the practicing naturopathic physician level, problem solving emphasizes looking for many possible solutions under the circumstances and empowering the patient to choose the best of several options. Such problem solving skills will often involve handling business, legal, and occupational challenges in addition to standard medical issues. Naturopathic Standards of Primary Care is a compilation of mutually exclusive modules that are provided as pieces of the clinical reasoning puzzle.

Primary care is sanctioned by almost all naturopathic regulatory bodies as a critical skill required of naturopathic physician registrants and is thoroughly examined in the Naturopathic Physician Licensing Examination Step Two (NPLEx II). Providing a bridge between conventional and alternative medicine, naturopathic doctors are carving a niche for themselves as healthcare professionals capable of discussing the effectiveness and limitations of treatments within their scope of practice, in reference to medical, surgical, and other available alternatives. That is why a considerable effort was exerted to present naturopathic primary care standards in conjunction with those of the American Medical Association (USMLE II) and the Canadian Medical Association (MCCQE).

The primary objective of this publication is thus to provide senior naturopathic medical students, new practitioners, and retraining naturopaths with a basic guide to navigate 'uncharted waters' in the field of primary care. Obviously, as your navigational skills are further developed, such a guide will function as an avenue for critique, re-evaluation, and subsequent revision.

> Primary care is sanctioned by almost all naturopathic regulatory bodies as a critical skill required of naturopathic physician registrants.

As a secondary and more practical objective, almost all of the information presented is established by the North American Board of Naturopathic Examiners (NABNE) as requisites for successful performance in the Naturopathic Physician Licensing Examination (NPLEx II). You may use this text to prepare for your naturopathic clinical board exams. Each applied clinical skills module comprises questions derived from NPLEx II, USMLE II, and MCCQE, with comprehensive yet concise answers provided to assist you with this examination and to serve as a clinical handbook in your primary care practice.

Certainly, the presentation of material in this book reveals my interests, background, and biases. Nevertheless, I trust that you will find a balanced and current handbook, which brings forward my fascination with the role of naturopathic primary care physicians as licensed practitioners of preventive health care and carriers of the torch of good outcome-based medicine.

Shehab El-Hashemy, MBChB, ND

PRIMARY CARE PRINCIPLES

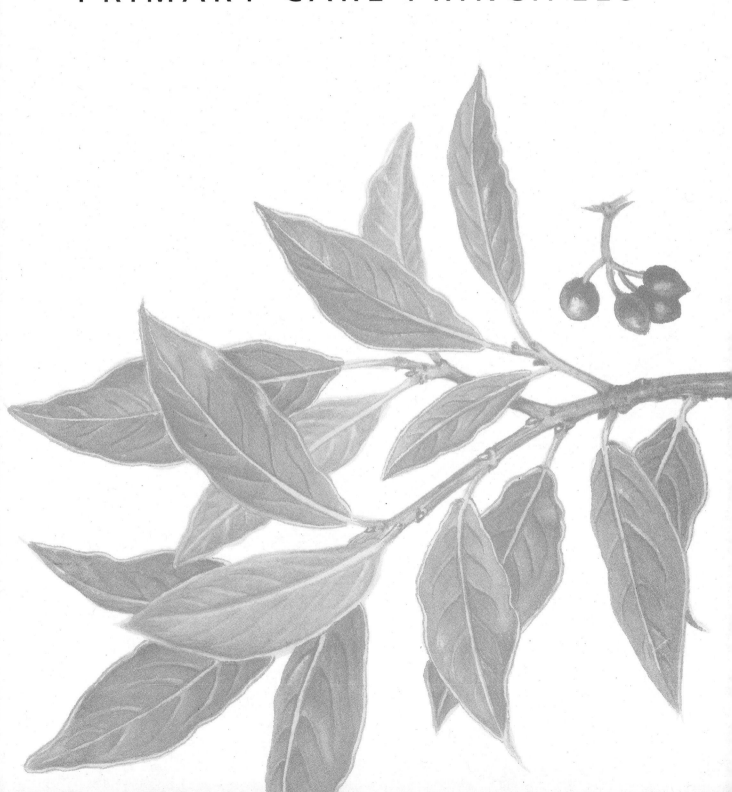

Primary care practice continues to place ever-increasing demands on contemporary healthcare professionals. In the not so distant past, decision making at the level of the primary-care physician was simply based on recalling a memorized algorithm or part of a didactic lecture. In this manner, one simply practiced the way one was taught. Views regarding disease processes, diagnostic beliefs, and treatment expectations took generations to evolve. However, in our era of rapid global information exchange, the revision of traditional views, beliefs, and expectations is occurring at an astoundingly accelerated pace.

Peer-reviewed publications pave the road for pioneers to reshape the landscape of healthcare policy and practice. At any given time, there are approximately 44,000 clinical trials being conducted, which fuel the generation of some 700 monthly systematic reviews that ultimately affect current practices in conventional, complementary, and alternative medicine. To complicate matters further, there are many reputable organizations, regulatory bodies, professional societies, advisory panels, and government-appointed task forces that issue significantly variable guidelines for the practice of primary care.

For example, in recent years, naturopathic physicians may have confronted the following questions in their practice:

Peer-reviewed publications pave the road for pioneers to reshape the landscape of healthcare policy and practice.

- Should I prescribe *Hypericum perforatum* for severe depression?
- What about S-Adenosyl-Methionine with bipolar II disorder?
- Can hypertensive patients safely stop their medications if they modify their lifestyle?
- Can dietary measures outperform pharmacological agents as primary interventions for hypercholesterolemia? What about diabetes?
- What could an abnormal laboratory test result mean?
- What is a relevant and complete physical examination of a case of frequent sore throats?
- What type of diet induces remission in an IBD flare up?
- Should I recommend vitamin E for patients with atherosclerosis?
- Am I obligated to report infectious diseases to public health? What about adverse reactions?
- Should I stop prescribing L-Arginine for peripheral vascular insufficiency?
- What is the side effect profile of natural hormone replacement?
- Would any of the above issues affect the way I obtain informed consent in my practice?

Consider how the traditional opinions held by naturopathic primary care providers regarding these questions have changed over the last few years. Our attitude and clinical judgment that is pertinent to the practice of naturopathic primary care appear to be changing in light of our growing body of knowledge. Primary care clientele and, to some extent, regulatory bodies expect and, at times, demand higher-level-cognitive processing of available information geared toward assessment and case management. This is the expectation and the demand this book will enable you to meet as a primary care naturopathic physician.

SCOPE OF PRACTICE

Various naturopathic medical regulatory boards have defined primary care, distinguishing the scope of this practice from co-treatment and consulting treatment. For example, the regulatory board of naturopathic medicine in Ontario (BDDTN, 2004) defines these three practices provided by naturopathic physicians as follows:

- **Primary Care Management:** The "provision of patient's overall healthcare management including the monitoring of all treatments in progress with other providers as appropriate."
- **Co-treatment:** The "treatment of a patient in concert with the doctor providing primary care management of the patient."
- **Consulting Treatment:** The provision of "a second opinion or ancillary care for a patient whose primary care management is being provided by another doctor."

Among these three scopes of practice, naturopathic physicians have traditionally concentrated on co-treatment and consulting treatment, often foregoing primary care management either due to lack of familiarity with the legal requisites of primary care practice or failure to receive adequate academic training and clinical mentorship. This publication will thus focus on these issues to encourage naturopathic medical students and practitioners to add requisite primary care competencies to their repertoire of services.

STANDARDS OF PRACTICE

Naturopathic doctors in most regulated jurisdictions are expected to adhere to published standards of practice (SOPs) that outline aspects of care delivery and service to the patient and community.

These standards of practice serve two major functions: they identify the responsibilities and scope of practice of naturopathic doctors, and they are used in disciplinary and judicial functions to evaluate the actions of naturopathic doctors. The two types of standards that apply to licensed naturopathic doctors are either Basic or Case Specific SOPs.

Basic Standards of Practice

Regardless of the scope of practice of the naturopathic doctor (primary care, co-treatment, or consulting treatment), the following standards are considered basic:

The naturopathic doctor will …

> Naturopathic doctors must comply with local and regional laws in the conduct of their practice.

1. Have knowledge of and comply with the laws and regulations governing the practice of naturopathic medicine in the jurisdiction of practice.
2. Provide a level of care consistent with each patient's individual condition.
3. Actively consult and/or refer as appropriate to other health professionals when the patient condition so warrants.
4. Treat each patient with respect and human dignity regardless of the individual's health condition, personal attribute, national origin, handicap, age, sex, race, religion, socioeconomic status, or sexual preference.
5. Respect the patient's right to privacy by protecting all confidential information.
6. Deal honestly with all patients, colleagues, public institutions, and legal bodies, and refrain from giving any false, incomplete, or misleading information.
7. Report any healthcare provider whose character or competences are deficient or who is grossly negligent or reckless.
8. Maintain clear and adequate patient-care and billing records for at least 7 years after the patient's last visit.
9. Formulate an assessment/diagnosis to a level consistent with the patient based on knowledge, training, and expertise of the naturopathic doctor and the technology and tools available to the profession.
10. Advise the patient regarding significant side effects from the treatment plan.
11. Monitor each patient at a level consistent with the degree of management being exercised.
12. Refrain from providing primary care management for any patient where the relationship with the patient (such as family member, close personal friend) would serve to interfere with the doctor's objective judgment.

Case Specific Standards of Practice

The following case-specific standards are considered a guide for the development of standards for particular incidents or presentations:

1. The scope of the doctor's practice (primary care management, co-treatment, consulting treatment, or expert testimony) shall be identified.
2. The scope of the problem (complaint, specific naturopathic medical modality) and all other pertinent data, such as history, diagnosis, other pertinent data, shall be identified.

3. The body of knowledge to be used in assessing the problem shall be identified.

4. All management plans should address the entirety of the presenting condition.

5. Diagnosis should be derived from an appropriate body of knowledge that is applicable to the problem, with no possibility of conclusions being drawn out of context.
   - Sources of information used to derive management decisions must be generally accepted by the naturopathic profession.
   - Universally acceptable sources of information include textbooks, journals, information taught in naturopathic medical schools, and recognized expert opinions in the naturopathic community or in the specialty area in question.
   - As with other all other healthcare professions, reliable information sources, expert opinions, and testimony from outside the naturopathic profession are also acceptable.

6. When required, regulatory bodies shall render disciplinary and/or judicial decisions to ensure:
   - Protection of the public and the public interest from risks of physical or mental harm, misrepresentation, inappropriate billing not consistent with fair and accepted practices, full disclosure of treatment and its effects, appropriateness of referral, etc.
   - Compliance with all applicable laws.

UNIFYING IDEALS OF PRIMARY CARE PROFESSIONALS

In addition to these standards, almost all healthcare professionals engaged in rendering primary care services (medical doctors, naturopathic doctors, nurse practitioners, and extended care nurses) agree on the following guiding principles of conduct:

1. Will be committed to wellness and the prevention of disease.
2. Will acquire and apply good knowledge of local community services.
3. Will collaborate with other health providers for the benefit of their community.
4. Will advocate for public policy to promote health.
5. Will promote continuity of patient care and respect patient-physician relationships.

They also agree upon a basic level of competency for primary care practitioners:

1. Will be able to recognize importance of diagnosis of serious life-threatening illnesses.
2. Will be able to diagnose and manage diseases common to their community.

WHEN SHOULD NATUROPATHIC DOCTORS REFRAIN FROM PROVIDING PRIMARY CARE SERVICES?

The following standards of practice were adopted by the Ontario regulatory body of naturopathic medicine in 2004. Although these guidelines are considered universal by most practitioners, the reader is advised to review local or regional standards of practice for clarification.

The naturopathic doctor will refer and/or seek consultation when …

1. A life-threatening situation occurs or is suspected.
2. Diagnosis or treatment is not within the scope of naturopathic practice.
3. Diagnosis is required but cannot be confirmed with the training and technology available to the naturopathic doctor.
4. Treatment requires expertise or technology not available to the naturopathic doctor.
5. Response to treatment is not adequate or the patient's condition deteriorates.
6. Second opinion is desired.

> Primary care practitioners will commonly refer their patients to or seek advice from other healthcare providers.

REFERRALS AND CONSULTATIONS IN PRIMARY CARE

Primary care practitioners will commonly refer their patients to or seek advice from other healthcare providers.

Common reasons for consultations and referrals
- Advice (on diagnosis or treatment, for medicolegal purposes)
- Specialized evaluation skill (specialized laboratory tests, specialist scope of practice, mental health evaluation)
- Specialized treatment skill (specialized treatment, failed treatment approach, mental health counseling)
- Patient or third-party request (regulatory body standards, insurance guidelines)

Referrals

A referral is request that another healthcare provider accept the ongoing treatment of a patient. It implies that the accepting provider will be independently and continuously managing at least one significant health problem a patient may exhibit.

Consultations

In contrast, a consultation is a request for management guidance from another healthcare provider. It implies that the primary care provider will receive advice on diagnosis and management, but will retain decision-making and continuity of care obligations. Consultations may be informal (a.k.a. curbside consultations) or formal where patients are sent to other providers for in-depth evaluation.

Formal Consultation Requests

In order to respond to a presenting question, the consultant should be supplied with adequate, relevant, and succinct patient information. A good formal consultation request is based on the following criteria:

- Name and age
- Summary of current concern
- Related health history
- List of medications
- Summary of pertinent family and social history
- Summary of related physical findings
- Results of any diagnostic tests
- Results of previous consultations with clear specifications of the:
    1. Question that you need answered; or
    2. Problem that you wish to have evaluated; or
    3. Aspect that you want to be treated.
- Urgency of response
- Any patient's preferences or values that may affect the response.

Formal Consultant's Reports

Ideally, consultant or specialist reports should include:

- Purpose of consultation as understood by the consultant
- Findings of the consultant's history and physical exam
- Results of any diagnostic tests
- Any treatment provided
- Patient's response to any treatment
- Consultant's assessment or opinion regarding the topic of consultation
- Further treatment recommended
- Further consultations recommended
- Urgency of recommendations
- Summary of instructions given to the patient
- Concluding statement regarding whether consultation is considered complete or consultant's desire to see the patient in the future

Coordination of Care

During consultations or referrals to specialists, the primary care provider must coordinate the patient's care to avoid delays in treatment (falling through the cracks), iatrogenic morbidity, duplication of effort, waste of financial resources, needless tests, and risk of litigation. When several providers are involved in a specific patient's care, someone has to be clearly in charge of coordination (usually the primary care provider). This coordinator must document and follow up on all communications with consultants and secondary care providers.

STRUCTURE OF ENCOUNTERS IN PRIMARY CARE SETTINGS

In primary care settings, the chief task of the physician is promptly to establish a management plan that is appropriate for the resolution of the present complaint (that is, figure out what is going on then acting accordingly). The structure of the encounter is a systematic task list that enables the physician to obtain a story that ultimately leads to proper assessment, treatment, and follow-up.

Many students and perhaps a few practitioners express concern that time constraints of daily practice are not conducive for gathering a "complete" history, ordering a "complete" battery of laboratory evaluations, and performing "head-to toe" physical examinations before implementing a treatment plan. Indeed, part of succeeding in a primary care practice depends on your ability to work within operational constraints, such as reasonable visit durations and cost. In other words, if someone comes to you concerned about bloody diarrhea, you must be able to formulate an effective management plan by the end of the patient's encounter. Below we shall discuss strategies that will enable you to become comfortable with diagnostic uncertainty and provide such time-sensitive, cost-effective, safe, and effective treatment plans within typical and realistic practice parameters.

In private practice, you will rarely have more than 60 minutes to do a history and physical. Thus, every question or item on your physical exam has to count. The true clinical challenge for the naturopathic doctor is to ask those questions and do those items on a physical examination that will most directly and effectively sort out likely hypotheses, and screen for impairment in related organs or systems that might reasonably be involved. During follow-up visits, a complete understanding of the patient's story can be obtained.

> In primary care settings, the chief task of the physician is promptly to establish a management plan that is appropriate for the resolution of the present complaint.

Acute versus Chronic Presentations

In acute presentations, a more focused approach is required since one is often faced with time sensitive decisions that have to be made (for example, starting rehydration therapy, prescribing provisional treatments, ordering diagnostic tests, consulting with specialists, or sending the patient to the emergency department). Once this complaint-oriented approach is completed, the physician adopts an efficient management plan and can proceed into obtaining a more complete historical database, filling-in the gaps, addressing secondary concerns, and engaging in preventive healthcare, which, in turn, will lead to better patient care.

Data Gathering Methods

At the student level, the following time-honored sequential data-gathering format represents the launching pad for problem solving:

> Biographical data → Source and reliability → Reason for seeking care → Present health or history of present illness → Past health history → Family history → Review of systems → Functional assessment → Physical examination

Experienced problem solvers, however, collect required information in a fluid and efficient conversational format that varies considerably depending on the patient's chief concerns. They tend to focus on specific problems, recognize patterns, synthesize provisional impressions, ask questions with high sensitivity (to exclude suspicions) and specificity (to support suspicions), and gather relevant data. In this fashion, the diagnostic reasoning process dictates the format of the doctor-patient interaction. In other words, knowledge of disease processes, clinical reasoning, and evidence-based management guidelines allow problem solvers to identify quickly the underlying cause of illness within the time constrains of daily practice.

Data Gathering Forms

A number of data gathering forms are used routinely in primary care practice, including the following:
- Comprehensive Health Assessment
- Physical Exam Checklist
- Functional Assessment
- Past Medical History (PMH)
- Family History (FH)
- Social History (SH)
- Review of Systems (ROS)
- Cognitive Status Examination
- Depression Questionnaire
- CAGE Questionnaire

PRIMARY CARE PROVIDER'S TASK LIST

Regardless of your choice of data-gathering or data-recording format, the level of competency required of primary-care physicians with regards to episodic interactions can be defined as follows:

1. Identify important cues in the patient's story (Basic Health Assessment):
* Demographic information (gender, age, occupation, residence)
* Symptom analysis
* Functional assessment
* Patients' belief or understanding of their symptoms (and impact on their daily life, family members, and lifestyle)
* Routine vital signs (temperature, pulse, heart rate, blood pressure, weight, height, last menses, smoking status, and recreational drug use).

2. Understand and perform Advanced Health Assessment techniques:
This process focuses on constructing management plans based on "best evidence" that will leave little doubt in the problem-solver's mind:
* Determine what additional questions need to be asked.
* Ask complaint-specific questions to assess patient's risk for certain differential diagnoses.
* Determine what needs to be examined.
* Perform physical examination maneuvers that are suggested by the chief complaint.
* Perform physical examinations appropriately.
* Make selective observation of fine detail during physical examination.
* Selectively requisition high yield (or gold standard) diagnostic/laboratory work-ups.

3. Apply clinical reasoning to test differential or competing diagnoses:
* Identify presenting patterns in light of the doctor's knowledge of known presentations.
* Identify absence of findings that are "sensitive" markers of certain conditions (use a "rule-out" strategy).
* Identify presence of findings that are "specific" markers for certain conditions.
* Recognize your own diagnostic limitations if any, and involve other practitioners in the evaluation plan when indicated.

4. Manage the presentation:
* Discuss diagnostic impression and available treatment options with the patient in order to empower them to choose an effective and practical treatment option.
* Design follow-up plans to ensure resolution of condition and compliance of patient with treatment plan.
* Revise diagnostic hypotheses based on patient's response to initial treatment (no matter how confident you are in your diagnosis, no theory is beyond the threat of disproof).

> The use of data-gathering forms, electronic and printed, is on the rise. However, no form can capture the skill of an experienced primary care provider.

- Coordinate care and disseminate of information among healthcare providers within the patient's circle-of-care.

INTENTIONAL INTERVIEWING
Interpersonal Skills

Honesty and sincerity are the best traits a naturopathic physician can display to inspire cooperation and compliance (heart speaks to heart). If you are a student doctor, introduce yourself as such and tell the patient that you will be sharing your findings with an attending physician. You may also mention that you are working as part of a clinical team with the mandate to provide the best care possible. As a gesture of your respect to the patient, you may also ask them how they wish to be addressed.

Interviewing Skill
Open-ended Questions

The effectiveness of your questioning technique relies heavily on how you use open-ended questions (*Tell me about your abdominal pain?*), empathy (*It sounds like you are experiencing a lot of pain*), verbal cueing (*Uh-huh or I see*), encouragers (*Stitching pain!*), summarizing (*So this pain started yesterday night, you feel this stitching abdominal pain every few hours, it wakes you up at night and does not seem to be getting any better – is this correct?*).

Close-ended Questions

When the open-ended strategies are exhausted, you may use more direct close-ended questions, which allow you to test your provisional hypothesis (*Does the pain improve after a bowel movement?*). However, avoid leading (*Is it stitching or stabbing in character?*), multiple, or judgmental questions and comments.

Confidentiality

If the patients report sensitive information of psychosocial, sexual, or emotional nature, they need to be assured of their confidentiality, though you should be aware of the situations where confidentiality would not be upheld, such as your legal obligation to not harm others ("duty to warn"). These requirements may vary by jurisdiction of practice, but generally include situations of suspected child abuse, communicable diseases, disclosure of credible intent to harm someone, or when ordered by a court.

Listening Attentively

Listening without interruption is another interviewing skill that will convey to your patients the feeling that they are attended to. Silence, when used deliberately, may also allow your patients to gather their thoughts and formulate a meaningful answer to your question.

Summarizing

After each major line of questioning, you should again summarize your findings and check with the patient to ensure that no important information was missed. You should also verify information that you think is relevant to the patient's presentation by asking for rationale *(How did you come to know that you are allergic to echinacea?)* or documentation *(Can I take a look at your prescription to check dosages?* or *What were the results of the stress test? Can I obtain a copy?)*.

Medical Jargon and Acronyms

It is wise to use language that the patient can easily relate to. If your patients have a medical background, it is unlikely that they will misunderstand you. Otherwise, if you have to use medical terms, then explain them in a manner that is appropriate to the patient's level of education and background.

Transitions

It helps when doctors explain to their patients what information they seek and why. If patients appreciate the necessity and relevance of the information you need, they will likely cooperate and may even expand on certain aspects that were not mentioned before. For example, you may transition between the history of present illness to past medical history by saying, *Now that I have a good description of your concerns, I am going to ask you a few questions about your past health history and family history, because this information will help me identify if there are health risks that may be related to your symptoms.*

Delivering Information and Counseling

Again, the information you provide to your patients should be clear, concise, and appropriate to the patient's level of education and background. Because there may be a power differential, the patient should feel that you are non-judgmental and sincere. Be aware of your body language, for example, when your patients tell you that they consume nothing but doughnuts, coffee, burgers and cola! If you want to suggest a change in lifestyle, an alternative to judgmental behavior is to check with patients if they are ready to receive such advice.

Professional Behavior

Thus far, you have been direct, thorough, sensitive, and honest with your patients. Of equal importance for fostering mutually respectful doctor-patient relationships is not to give premature diagnoses or false reassurances. If the presentation challenges you (if no provisional diagnosis can readily be identified), you should tell your patients that you are not sure of the diagnosis and that you will do your best to figure it out.

In most jurisdictions, naturopathic physicians are required to provide this information explicitly to their patients. For example, the Province of Ontario

> The information you provide to your patients should be clear, concise, and appropriate to the patient's level of education and background.

regulatory board (BDDT-N) requires that naturopathic physicians share their diagnostic impression, evaluation strategy, and follow-up plans with their patients. This is considered to be an important part of obtaining informed consent.

Doctor as a Teacher

Your ability to educate your patients effectively relies on their understanding and processing of the information they already have. For example, you may ask your patients to explain to you what they consider to be safe sex practices, and then proceed to affirm their practices and address any misunderstandings. To know what it is you need to teach, you may pose hypothetical situations, ask if the patient has additional questions, or ask for a demonstration of particular technique (for example, stretching exercises or use of a peak flow meter).

Closure

At the end of the encounter, you should clearly explain your management plan to the patient:

1. What are you going to do? Schedule diagnostic tests, for example, or make referrals, prescribe provisional treatment, etc.
2. What do you want the patient to do? Make lifestyle changes, for example, or avoid strenuous exercise, go to an occupational therapist, go to the hospital if the situation gets worse, etc.
3. Schedule the time of your next appointment.

FOCUSED HEALTH HISTORY IN PRIMARY CARE

Initially, your attention should be directed towards the patient's reason for seeking care. An efficient approach is to start with open-ended questions and employ facilitative verbal and/or non-verbal communication skills.

Information gathered regarding the History of Present Illness (HPI) should include onset, duration, frequency, character, setting, intensity, aggravating & ameliorating factors, associated symptoms, and the patient's belief or perception regarding their symptoms (why?).

Include relevant Past Medical History (PMH), Family History (FH), Social History (SH), allergies, habits (for example, use of alcohol or drugs), and sexual history (if appropriate to presentation).

REVIEW OF SYSTEMS (ROS)

Go through a complaint-oriented Review of Systems (ROS) as indicated by the presenting symptom. For example, if the chief complaint is abdominal pain, then GI, pulmonary, genitourinary, musculoskeletal, and psychosocial ROS should be explored during your initial encounter.

In some efficiency driven practices, medical practitioners may resort to pre-printed intake forms to collect a patient's entire history (HPI, PMH, FH, and ROS). However, Paul Cutler, author of *Problem Solving in Clinical Medicine* (1998), strongly discourages healthcare practitioners from relying on printed intake forms or computer intake procedures. A primary reason for doctors to take the history is to build rapport and get to know their patients. Experienced physicians are interested in the patient's body language, verbal tone, mood, facial expression, and peculiar reactions in addition to answers to their questions. No machine or printed form can possibly capture such content, which often significantly changes the problem solving focus or the direction of the entire doctor-patient encounter.

Conducting the Physician-Led ROS

Explain to your patient that you will be asking some questions that will help you with your assessment. Remember to use language that is appropriate to the patient's education and background. Record details of positive and relevant negative answers in your chart. A time-saving strategy is to tell your patient that you will "rhyme-off whole sections", and then ask them if they identify with anything that you mentioned. This memory aid for review of systems may be helpful.

FUNCTIONAL ASSESSMENT

Functional assessment encompasses the following criteria:

Activities of Daily Living (ADL)

This is the capacity of the patient to eat, bathe, go to the toilet, dress, groom, move about the house, transfer from bed, transfer from toilet, and control bowel and bladder. Assess as independent or dependent.

Instrumental Activities of Daily Living (IADL)

These are instrumental capacities, such as cooking, cleaning, using telephone, writing, shopping, doing laundry, taking medications/supplements, using public transit, walking outdoors without getting lost, managing money, independent travel out of town, and driving. Assess as independent or dependent.

Nutritional State

This includes body weight, recent weight gain or loss, 24-hour diet recall, BMI or waist-to-hip-ratio, alcohol/ cigarette/ marijuana/ cocaine/ amphetamines/ heroin/ barbiturates/ caffeine/tea/cola use, and any perceived substance dependency.

Self-Concept and Esteem

This includes personal beliefs regarding education, financial state, appearance, belief system, and methods of self-care.

> Experienced physicians are interested in the patient's body language, verbal tone, mood, facial expression, and peculiar reactions in addition to answers to their questions.

REVIEW OF SYSTEMS

System	Details
❏ *General Health Status:* Weight gain or loss, weakness, fever, chills, sweats, or night sweats.	
❏ *Cardiovascular:* Retrosternal pain, palpitations, cyanosis, dyspnea on exertion, orthopnea, nocturnal dyspnea, nocturia, edema, known murmurs, hypertension, coronary artery disease, anemia, last ECG or other heart tests.	
❏ *Respiratory:* History of asthma, emphysema, bronchitis, pneumonia, tuberculosis; shortness of breath, chest pain, wheezing, cough, sputum (colour/ amount); hemoptysis, toxin or pollution exposure.	
❏ *Gastrointestinal:* Appetite, food sensitivity, dysphagia, heartburn, indigestion, abdominal pain, discomfort, sour eructation, nausea, vomiting, hematemesis, history of abdominal disease, flatulence, recent change in bowel movements, stool characteristics, constipation, diarrhea, black or gray stools, rectal bleeding, rectal itching, hemorrhoids, fistula, use of antacids or laxatives.	
❏ *Skin:* History of eczema, psoriasis, hives; pigment or color change, change in a mole, excessive dryness or moisture, pruritus, bruising, rash or lesion, amount of sun exposure, use of sun tan lotion.	
❏ *Hair:* Recent change, texture in change or loss.	
❏ *Nails:* Recent change in shape, color, or brittleness.	
❏ *Head:* Frequent or severe headaches, head injury, dizziness, syncope, or vertigo.	
❏ *Eyes:* Change in vision, blurring, blind spots, eye pain, diplopia, redness, swelling, watering, discharge, glaucoma, cataracts, date of last vision test or glaucoma test.	
❏ *Ears:* Earache, infections, discharge, tinnitus or vertigo, hearing loss, hearing aid use, exposure to noise, and method of cleaning ears.	
❏ *Mouth and Throat:* Mouth pain, frequent sore throat, bleeding gums, toothache, lesion in mouth or tongue, dysphagia, change in voice, hoarseness, tonsillectomy, use of chewing tobacco, smoking, change in taste, daily dental care, last dental checkup.	
❏ *Neurologic:* History of seizures, stroke, fainting, blurring of vision, black outs; recent weakness, tic, tremor, coordination problems or paralysis; recent numbness, tingling, memory problems, nervousness, mood change, depression; history of mental illness or hallucinations.	

System	Details
❏ *Neck:* Pain, limitation of movement, lumps, swelling, enlarged and tender nodes, goiter.	
❏ *Breast:* Pain, lump, nipple discharge, rash, history of breast disease; axillary tenderness, lumps or swelling; breast self-examination, last mammogram and results.	
❏ *Peripheral Vascular:* Limb coldness, numbness, or tingling; swelling of legs; discoloration of hands or feet, varicose veins, intermittent claudications, thrombophlebitis, ulcers, long term-sitting or standing, crossing of legs at knees, wearing support socks.	
❏ *Urinary:* Recent changes, frequency, hesitancy, straining, urgency, nocturia, dysuria, polyuria, oliguria, narrowed stream, cloudy urine, dark urine, hematuria, incontinence, flank pain, groin pain, suprapubic pain, low back pain, last DRE or PSA; history or urologic disease, kidney stones, UTI, or BPH; measures to avoid UTIs, use of Kegel exercises after childbirth.	
❏ *Male Genital:* Penile or testicular pain, sores, lesions, penile discharge, lumps, hernia, testicular self-examination.	
❏ *Female Genital:* Age at menarche, last menstrual period, cycle and duration; amenorrhea, menorrhagia, premenstrual pain, dysmenorrhea (primary or secondary), intermenstrual spotting; vaginal itching, discharge, age at menopause, menopausal symptoms, post-menopausal bleeding.	
❏ *Sexual Health:* Presently in a relation involving intercourse? Aspects of sex satisfactory to you and partner? Recent changes or concerns, dyspareunia (for female), changes in erection or ejaculation (for male), use of contraceptives, contact or history or STDs (gonorrhea, herpes, Chlamydia, venereal warts, HIV or syphilis).	
❏ *Endocrine:* History of diabetes, polyuria, polydipsia or polyphagia; thyroid disease, intolerance to heat or cold, change in skin pigmentation or texture, excessive sweating, changes in appetite and weight, abnormal hair distribution, nervousness, tremors, history of hormone therapy.	
❏ *Musculoskeletal:* History of arthritis, gout, joint pain, stiffness, swelling, deformity, limitation of movement, noise with joint movement; recent muscle pain, cramps, weakness, gait instability, incoordination; low back pain, disc disease; physical exercise pattern.	
❏ *Hematologic:* Bleeding tendency, bruising, lymph node swelling, history of blood transfusion; exposure to toxic agents or radiation.	

Activity and Exercise

This includes pattern of typical day, exercise regime (type, amount, warm-up, type of stretching, monitoring of body's response to exercise), and leisure activities.

Coping and Stress Management

You may ask patients to describe the stresses in their life, including recent changes, and their methods to relieve stress.

Environmental Concerns

Safety of residential area, adequate heat and utilities, access to transportation, involvement in community services, perceived hazards at home or workplace (asbestos, inhalants, lead paint, chemicals, repetitive motion), use of seatbelts, and travel/residence in other country.

Perception of Own Health

You may ask the patient to define good health, their view of their current health, health concerns, and health goals, as well as their expectations in seeing you.

Depression

If depression is suspected, you should inquire and record your observations regarding the following:

* Does the patient admit to suicidal or homicidal ideation?
* Does patient have a plan?
* Has patient ever acted on this plan?
* Is there any inappropriate blame or guilt?
* Is there any psychomotor retardation or agitation?
* Is there blunted or labile affect? What about diurnal mood variation?
* What about sleep pattern? Any difficulty falling asleep, mid-sleep-cycle awakening, or early morning awakening?
* Is there loss of appetite? What about recent weight gain or loss?
* Does the patient experience loss of mental concentration ability?
* Is the patient able to temporarily forget the depression? Which activities alleviate poor mood?
* Has the patient abandoned social contact?
* Is there any loss of pleasure in previously pleasurable activities?
* Does the patient have hope for the future?
* What are the patient's current or recent stressors?
* Does patient feel able to influence the external environment?

COGNITIVE STATUS EXAMINATION

If there is a need to assess a patient's cognitive status, the standard Mini-Mental State offers a complete and easily conducted cognitive function evaluation.

Chart total Mini-Mental State score along with level of consciousness: alert, drowsy, stupor, or coma.

Abstract Reasoning Assessment

If you need to test abstract (higher-function) reasoning ability you may use proverbs and ask the patient to explain them to you. For example, if you ask a patient to explain the proverb *Don't put all your eggs in one basket*, you may get a concrete answer, such as "If you put a lot of eggs in one basket, they will break," or an abstract one, such as "To reduce risk, one should distribute his investments in more than one project."

PHYSICAL EXAMINATION IN PRIMARY CARE

If after taking a good history and generating the differential diagnosis list, you should develop an appreciation of what may be causing the presentation. You may then choose from various physical examination procedures.

- Hypothesis-driven physical examinations: These are aimed at narrowing down your list of possibilities or confirming your clinical impression.
- Complete head-to-toe physical examinations: These may need to be used if the history is complex or vague and you are left without a workable list of differential diagnoses.

Notwithstanding, if a hypothesis-driven physical examination is employed in the initial encounter, a complete physical examination should still be completed in subsequent encounters to elaborate possible complications of the patient's primary problem or to screen for unrelated coexisting problems.

> If a hypothesis-driven physical examination is employed in the initial encounter, a complete physical examination should still be completed in subsequent encounters to elaborate possible complications.

Physical Examination Tips

1. Wash or sterilize your hands before touching the patient. Better yet, do it in front of the patient.
2. Never examine the patient through clothing, such as socks, t-shirts, bras, or undergarments.
3. Determine a logical sequence for your intended PE; then follow this sequence in an organized manner.
4. Explain to your patient what it is you are about to do and why before commencing with the examination. For example you may say, *Your lower abdominal pain may be caused by problems in your digestive, urinary, or genital tract. To figure it out, I'll need to examine your chest, abdomen, genitals, and rectum. Is that all right?*
5. When you disrobe the patient, use serial exposure to preserve the patient's modesty.

Cognitive Status Examination

Function	Instructions	Score
Orientation		
1. What is the date today (year, season, date, month)?	Ask specifically for omitted parts.	(/5)
2. Where are we (country, city, clinic, floor)?	One point for each correct answer.	(/5)
Registration		
Ask patient to repeat a series of three objects after you.	The first repetition determines the score.	(/3)
Name three objects (e.g., lemon, coin, chair), take one second to pronounce each object, then ask the patient to repeat the series.	One point for each correct answer.	
Attention and Calculation		
Serial 7s. Ask patient to begin with 100 and count backwards by 7. Stop after five subtractions (93, 86, 79, 72, 65) OR Ask patient to spell "world" backwards (dlrow =5, while dlorw=3).	Score the total number of correct answers.	(/5)
Recall		
Ask patient if they can recall the three objects you previously mentioned.	Score 0-3	(/3)
Language		
1. Show patient 2 objects (necktie, pen) and ask them what they are?	Score 0-2	
2. Ask patient to repeat one sentence after you "no ifs, ands or buts."	Score 0-1	
3. Give patient a piece of paper and tell them to "take paper in your right hand, fold in half, and put it on the floor."	Score 0-3	
4. Give patient a piece with the following sentence written on it: "Close your eyes." Ask patient to read and do what it says.	Score 1 point if patient closes their eyes.	
5. Ask patient to write any sentence for you on a piece of paper. See if sentence is sensible and contains subject and verb.and punctuation.	Score 0-1 disregard grammar and punctuation	(/9)
6. Ask patient to copy a design of intersecting pentagons (each side should be about 1 inch)	Score 0-1 disregard rotation or tremor.	
	Total Score	(/30)

6. If you feel it is important to perform breast, genital, or rectal examinations, explain the reasoning to your patients and obtain their consent.

7. Prepare your environment so that all necessary tools for your intended examination are readily available – clean and ready medical instruments, charged batteries, specula, thermometer/lens covers, gown, table paper, tongue depressors, cotton swabs, gloves, lubricants, and tissues.

8. If you ask the patient to change positions, offer to assist because this may be difficult for some patients.

9. If your patient expresses acute distress or pain during the PE, acknowledge this and strive to make the patient more comfortable.

PRINCIPLES OF PROBLEM SOLVING IN PRIMARY CARE

The history of knowledge is filled with intellectual milestones, which, to some extent, influence the way we currently think, argue, and express our ideas. The following prominent thinkers undoubtedly have affected the way we reason in contemporary naturopathic and medical circles: Fu Hsi, Shen Nung, Thales, Democritus, Empedocles, Hippocrates, Pythagorus, Plato, Aristotle, Diocles, Herophilus, Erasistratus, Celsus, Galen, Avicenna, Paracelsus, Aquinas, Bacon, Copernicus, Vesalius, Harvey, Descartes, Galileo, Kepler, Gilbert, Newton, Bacon, Hume, Thomson, Hahnemann, Darwin, Einstein, Lindlahr, and Lust (and the legacy continues). Indeed, most contemporary problem-solving strategies bear close resemblance to Frances Bacon's (1561–1626) quest to "Rid the mind of all preconceptions," the experimental method of Galileo Gallilei (1564-1642), and Isaac Newton's (1643–1727) principles of reasoning.

Problem Solving Strategy

1. Acquire information from patient's history and physical examination.
2. Evaluate and group derived information into a well-defined list of problems.
3. Generate a list of hypotheses (based on probability, decision trees, independent research, or database searches).
4. Test your hypotheses systematically (further questioning, examination, testing, following a hunch, consultation or referral),
5. Assume hypotheses that cannot be disproved are true until other more accurate ones displace it. That is, no theory is considered above the threat of disproof.

> Although this problem solving strategy may appear to be time consuming, it is indeed required to resolve complex presentations that do not point toward a single key clue.

Although this problem solving strategy may appear to be time consuming, it is indeed required to resolve complex presentations that do not point toward a single key clue. Furthermore, this is the logic we need to apply in order to solve clinical puzzles, consistently and reliably, especially ones that are either new to the primary care provider or peculiar and unanticipated.

References

Cutler P. Problem Solving in Clinical Medicine – From Data to Diagnosis. 3rd ed. Baltimore, MD: Lippincott Williams & Wilkins, 1998:14, 25-36.

Dains J, Baumann L, Scheibel P. Advanced Health Assessment & Clinical Diagnosis in Primary Care. 2nd ed. Philadelphia, PA: Mosby C.V. Co. Ltd., 2003.

Jarvis C. Physical Examination and Health Assessment. Student Laboratory Manual. 3rd ed. Philadelphia, PA: W.B. Saunders, 2000:29-43.

MiniMental LLC. Mini-Mental State: A Practical Method for Grading the Cognitive State of Patients for the Clinician. Journal of Psychiatric Research 1998;12(3):189-98.

Ontario Board of Naturopathic Medicine (BDDT-N), 2004. Policies and Guidelines. Toronto, ON, 2004.

The Personal Health Information Protection Act (PHIPA, 01 November 2004) is the privacy legislation that governs the manner in which personal health information may be collected, used, and disclosed within the healthcare system in Canada. For further information on PHIPA beyond the scope of this document, please visit the web-site of the Information Privacy Commissioner at www.ipc.on.ca.

In the United States, you should consult the documentation guidelines for evaluation and management (E&M) developed by the American Medical Association (AMA) and Health Care Financing Administration (HCFA) at www.hcfa.gov.

SOAP CHARTING

As a self-regulating profession, naturopathic doctors are expected to follow accepted professional standards for recording notes in patient files. SOAP charting is one of these standards. SOAP is an acronym for subjective (S), objective (O), assessment (A), and plan (P).

Standard SOAP charting is important for legal purposes. In most jurisdictions, SOAP charting is a cornerstone of many of the Quality Assurance (QA) programs that are required of regulated professions.

Standardized charting is also necessary for effective communication among healthcare professionals. Upon reviewing a patient file, another healthcare professional (ND, MD, RN, RN-EC, DC) should be able to understand easily what has taken place with regard to patient care. SOAP charting is a flexible tool that can be adapted for use in most styles of practice, including those focusing on traditional Chinese medicine (TCM) or homeopathy.

Good charting will provide the practitioner with a tool to guide assessment, goal setting, treatment planning, progress tracking, and treatment plan modification. It reminds the practitioner what has been done and guides what should be done next.

Charting Guidelines

Style

All chart entries must be dated and signed by the physician. All chart entries must be made in black or blue ink. Chart entries must be neat and concise while representing a summarized reiteration of what took place with regards to patient care. All charting corrections or changes should be performed as follows:

> Good charting will provide the practitioner with a tool to guide assessment, goal setting, treatment planning, progress tracking, and treatment plan modification.

- Draw one line through the entry to be changed. The corrected entry should still be legible.
- Write the new entry beside the old entry.
- Initial the change.

Content

Each chart should have the following components: a subjective (S) history, objective (O) physical examination, assessment (A) and diagnosis, management plan (P), and future plan (FP). Note that within the SOAP format, there are variable styles of presenting this required information.

SOAP CONTENT

S: Subjective History: Information you have been given before seeing the patient if relevant + history of presenting complaint(s) + past medical history + family history + relevant ROS + social history.

O: Objective Physical Examination: Data that you inspect, palpate, measure, auscultate, or observe. Indicate only pertinent positive and negative findings relative to the patient's presentation.

A: Assessment or Clinical Reasoning: Problem list → DDx list → Ruled-out list → Likely or Presumptive Diagnosis:

- **Problem List (Assessment):** Different definitions of patient problems in the outpatient setting and their use in patient assessment and management have been described since this convention began in the 1960s. At our clinic, we recently adopted the system designed for use in family practice described by Rakel in *Essentials of Family Practice* (1998;96-97). Rakel defines a problem as "anything that requires diagnosis or management or that interferes with quality of life as perceived by the patient. It is any physiologic, pathologic, psychological, or social item of concern to either the patient or the physician."

    These "problems" can be anything of concern either to you or to the patient, be it anatomic (hernia), physiologic (undiagnosed jaundice), a previous diagnosis, a sign (central edema), a symptom (dysuria), economic concern (financial stress), social problem (family discord), psychiatric condition, physical handicap, abnormal lab or imaging finding, or risk factor (smoking). The criteria are far more inclusive than those of a "diagnosis."
- **Diagnosis (Assessment):** This is where you summarize your clinical reasoning based on the preceding steps. This aspect of assessment is perhaps the most important part of the chart. It may be as simple as stating a particular diagnosis when you are fairly certain about it. When a doctor considers

the diagnoses likely but not certain, a "working" or "presumptive" diagnosis should be used. Diagnostic rational should be included in situations where it would not be easily inferred. Remember that every stated differential diagnosis (DDx) requires a corresponding action in the plan. This is true even when the action is to watch and wait).

Sample Clinical Reasoning Chart

Problem List	DDx List	Ruling out criteria
HPI	Acute bronchitis	Unlikely by history & PE
CC1 Chronic cough	Pneumonia	Unlikely by PE (chest is clear to
CC2 High blood pressure		P&A) + no fever or hyperventilation
	Congestive heart failure	Class III CHF unlikely by history
Med History:		and physical exam. Maybe class II
Vasotec 10 mg bid		CHF consider echo
	TB	Possible - Rule out by CXR &
Family History:		Mantoux if persistent
Diabetes, Hypertension	COPD	Unlikely by PE & Spirometry
	Cough due to Med S/E	Likely (onset with a recent dose
Diet & Lifestyle:		increase of Enalapril)
Poor diet, sedentary lifestyle	Essential hypertension	Likely
	Secondary hypertension	Unlikely by ECG and chem panel
ROS:	Stage 2/Moderate HTN	Yes
Fatigue, heartburn, weak	Malabsorption syndrome	Explore by trial ttt
and vertically-ridged nails;	Malnutrition	Likely due to poor diet
SOB with moderate exercise;	Increased risk for DM II	Yes
two-pillow orthopedia	Increased risk for CAD	Yes
	TCM - Yin & Yang	Likely Zang fu presentation &
P/E:	imbalance	pulse
Transient wheeze; BP 160/190	TCM - Liver fire	Unlikely by presentation & pulse
Screening Labs:	No anemia, infection, or hematological dz	
CBC WNL	No dyslipidemia	
Lipid panel WNL		

Sample Diagnosis

1. Cough due to Med S/E - ACEI Enalapril
2. Stage 2 Moderate (Essential) Hypertension
3. Malnutrition
4. Yin & Yang imbalance
5. Risk factor Assessment: Increased for type 2 DM + CAD
?? stage II CHF; TB

P: Plan: All actions recommended or prescribed during the patient's visit should be noted. Remember that the plan must contain an action corresponding to your assessment (again even if the action is to do nothing).

- Include instructions for diet or lifestyle modification or intervention; any medication (herbal/botanical, homeopathic, neutraceutical, or prescription).
- Where possible, charted prescriptions should include dosages in terms of metric measurement (mg/grams) as well as posology "3 caps t.i.d."
- Important side effects that patients were informed about and what they were instructed to do if they occur.
- Therapeutic application or self-treatment.
- Laboratory testing or imaging.
- Therapeutic order and naturopathic principles that have guided the plan.

FP: Future Plan: This section should include your intended management plan, including follow-up frequency, phone consults, consultations, referrals, and other aspects of coordination of care.

Sample Patient Intake Chart

Patient's Name: _D.V._   **Doctor's Name & #**: _Jane Dow # 885621_
Supervisor: _Dr Adams ND_   **Date**: _____

S: History: Information you have been given before seeing the patient if relevant + History of presenting complaint(s) + Past medical history + Family history + relevant ROS + Social history.

The patient is 40-yr-old male who comes in with a complaint of upper chest "discomfort" for the last 3 months. The discomfort is primarily brought on by exertion and is worse if the weather is cold. Occasionally, he feels similar discomfort when walking or doing heavy work. It has occurred twice when he was upset. He describes the "discomfort" as a steady pressure. It is not affected by breathing or position. It is alleviated by stopping his exertion. He currently gets the "discomfort" 2-3 X/wk. He came in today because three days ago, he awoke at 1 AM with a similar pain but it was severe and radiated to his neck. He sat up for a few minutes and it went away. Since the event, he has not had sex with his wife for fear of pain and wife discovering his "problem."

PMH - He has been told that he has "borderline" hypertension 5 years ago but never addressed it. A routine ECG was normal a year ago.
FH - Father died of cancer at age 72, but also had coronary artery disease.
ROS - He does not report shortness of breath at rest, dizziness or light headedness. He does not know his cholesterol, does not watch his diet, and does not exercise.
Diet - Mainly fast food, doughnuts and coffee.
SH - Has smoked 1ppd X 20 years. He does not consider his job particularly stressful.

O: Physical Examination: Data that you inspect, palpate, measure, auscultate, or observe. Indicate only pertinent positive and negative findings related to patient's presentation.

On PE, Pt is well dressed, well nourished, and is in no acute distress. He does not display much emotion.
BP 140/90
Neck - no venous distension.
Heart - regular rhythm, no murmurs.
Lungs - clear to percussion and auscultation.
Chest wall - no tenderness over rib cage or costochondral joints.
Abd - no tenderness, bowel sounds present, no hepatomegaly or splenomegaly.
Extremities - no peripheral edema, peripheral pulses +2 equal bilat.

A: Assessment or Clinical Reasoning: Problem list → DDx list → Ruled-out list → Likely or Presumptive Diagnosis

Problem List: Complete list of significant concerns include HPI, Meds, FH, ROS, diet, P/E, labs	**DDx List:** Include all possible causes of current presentation	**Ruling out criteria:** Rule out unlikely DDx based on your intake, P/E, problem list and DDx list
HPI	Acute miocardial infarction	Unlikely from remitting Hx
Chest Pain - progressive anginal pain with exertion and emotions upset; 3 months, SOB on exercise, Nocturnal dypnea, orthopnea	Aortic dissection	Unlikely from history and P/E
	Coronary artery insufficiency/ stable angina	Likely need stress ECG to confirm
	Pulmonary embolus	Unlikely from history and P/E
	Pneumothorax	Unlikely from history and P/E
FH - Cancer and CAD - Father	Congenital coronary anomalies	Unlikely from age of onset
	coronary artery spasm	Maybe, stress ECG is needed to rule out
ROS - does not watch is diet No exercise, smoker, does not know cholesterol level	Myocarditis	No fever, murmur, or friction rub
	Aortic stensis	Unlikely since Radial pulses not diminished
Diet - Poor diet - fast food & Doughnuts	Mitral regurgitation or prolapse	No murmurs
	Dysrythmias	No tachycardia or irregularity
SH - Sedentary lifestyle Limited stress	Psychogenic origin	No hx of stressful events
	Precordial catch syndrome	Unlikely from age of onset
P/E: Bp 140/90	Non-coronary chest pain	Maybe, consider if cardiac stress test is negative for CAD
	Increased risk of CAD	Yes
	Sedentary lifestyle	Yes
	POOR DIETARY HABITS	Yes
	stage 1 hypertension	Yes

Diagnosis: In order of likelihood. Write no more than five likely or provisional Dx.

1. Coronary artery insufficiency with fixed stenosis and angina
2. coronary artery spasm
3. stage 1 Hypertension
4. Non-coronary chest pain - GI or MS
5. Lifestyle factors - smoking, Poor diet, sedentary lifestyle, no exercise

P: Management Plan: In order of importance, include immediate plan and, diagnostic workup (required and cost-effective). Write no more than five entries.

1. *Cardiac stress test + Echocardiography*
2. *CBC*
3. *Lipid profile*
4. *Encourage smoking cessation*
5. *Lifestyle counseling*

Follow-up:

Comprehensive Health Assessment Form

Date of Visit: _____

Chart Record #:_____

Telephone: (home) _____ (business) _____

Provider: _____

Language _____ Interpreter present: ☐ Yes ☐ No

Patient Name: _____

Address: _____

Date of Birth: _____ Age: ____ Gender: ☐ Male ☐ Female

Informant/Relationship: _____

Reliability: ☐ Adequate ☐ Inadequate

History of Present Illness

_____
_____
_____
_____
_____
_____
_____
_____
_____
_____
_____
_____
_____
_____
_____
_____
_____
_____
_____
_____
_____
_____
_____
_____
_____
_____
_____
_____
_____
_____
_____
_____
_____
_____
_____

Past surgical History/Trauma/Hospitalization

☐ T & A: ☐ Appendectomy: ☐ Cholecystectomy:
☐ Hernia repair: ☐ Hysterectomy: ☐ Laparotomy:
☐ Cesarean section: ☐ Biopsy:

Other/Details:

Allergies

☐ Drugs   ☐ Environmental   ☐ Foods   ☐ Latex   ☐ IV Contrast

Details:

Reproductive History

Menstrual: _____ Age at menarche _____ LMP _____ Interval _____ Duration _____ Flow _____
☐ Regular ☐ Irregular ☐ Cramping ☐ Intermenstrual Bleeding ☐ PMS
Obstetrical: G _____ T _____ P _____ A _____ L _____ Complications: _____
Menopause: Age _____ Abnl Bleeding: _____ Symptoms: _____
Hormones: ☐ ERT ☐ HRT ☐ topical _____ *Contraceptives:* _____
Sexual Activity: ☐ same sex ☐ opposite sex ☐ abstinent ☐ single partner ☐ multiple partners ☐ > 4 lifetime partners
STD hx: _____

Concerns:

Past Medical History

☐ HTN ☐ Asthma/COPD ☐ Seizure Disorder ☐ Breast Disease ☐ DM ☐ GERD ☐ Renal Disease ☐ Anemia
☐ CVD/CAD ☐ Hepatitis ☐ Thyroid Disorder ☐ Transfusions ☐ CVA ☐ Osteoporosis ☐ Bleeding Disorder
☐ Psychiatric ☐ CA ☐ Arthritis ☐ Infectious Disease ☐ Childhood Illnesses

Other/Details of Above:

Medications

☐ OTC ☐ Vitamins ☐ Supplements/Herbals ☐ Prescriptions

Social History

Marital Status: ☐ Single ☐ Married ☐ Domestic Partner ☐ Divorced ☐ Widowed
Cohabitants: _____   *Children:* _____
Education: _____   *Occupation:* _____
Interests/Activities: _____ *Exercise:* ☐ Aerobic ☐ Weights _____
Diet: ☐ Balanced ☐ Calcium _____ *Sleep/Rest:* _____
Caffeine: ☐ No ☐ Yes cups/day _____   *Tobacco:* ☐ No ☐ Yes PPD ___ # Years _____ Quit Year _____
Smoking in home: ☐ Yes ☐ No _____ *ETOH:* ☐ Yes ☐ No ☐ Daily ☐ Weekly ☐ Monthly # drinks ___
Recreational Drugs: _____ *Support Systems/Coping Skills:* ☐ Adequate ☐ Inadequate

Family History

☐ *Family History Unknown*
Father: _____   *Mother:* _____
Siblings _____   *MGF:* _____
MGM: _____   *PGF* _____
PGM: _____   *Other:* _____
Cultural/Religious Influences: _____

Health Maintenance History

Exam	Last Date	Results	N/A	Refused	Exam	Last Date	Results	N/A	Refused
Pap Test					Dental				
Mammogram					Vision				
SBE/TSE					Hearing				
Stool guaiac					Lipid Profile				
Flex Sig/ Colonoscopy					FBS				
CXR					PSA				
ECG					PPD				

Immunizations (dates):					Safety:				
Td		MMR/titers	Hep B	Polio	☐ Seatbelt Use ☐ Cycling Helmet ☐ Sunscreen				
Varicella vaccine/chickenpox					☐ Occupational ☐ Smoke Detectors ☐ Housing				
Influenza		Pneumovax			☐ Domestic Violence ☐ Firearms				

Review of Systems

☐ **General:** ☐ fever ☐ chills ☐ night sweats ☐ fatigue ☐ unexplained weight loss ☐ weight gain

☐ **Skin:** ☐ pruritis ☐ rash ☐ hair loss ☐ worrisome lesion ☐ pigment change ☐ moles ☐ sweating ☐ dry skin ☐ nail change

☐ **HEENT:** ☐ headache ☐ dizziness ☐ earache ☐ hearing loss ☐ tinnitus ☐ vision change ☐ eye pain/sensitivity
☐ excessive tearing ☐ eyeglasses/contact use ☐ glaucoma ☐ rhinorrhea ☐ nasal congestion ☐ post nasal drip ☐ sinus pain
☐ nosebleeds ☐ hay fever ☐ sore throat ☐ mouth sores ☐ hoarseness ☐ toothache ☐ bleeding gums ☐ dentures

☐ **Breast:** ☐ pain ☐ lumps ☐ discharge ☐ history of breast disease ☐ implants

☐ **Pulmonary**: ☐ cough ☐ sputum ☐ hemoptysis ☐ SOB ☐ pain with respiration ☐ wheezing ☐ cyanosis

☐ **CV:** ☐ chest pain ☐ palpitations ☐ DOE ☐ orthopnea ☐ PND ☐ diaphoresis ☐ syncope ☐ heart murmur ☐ leg edema

☐ **PVD:** ☐ claudication ☐ varicose veins ☐ phlebitis ☐ coldness of hands/feet ☐ leg ulcers

☐ **GI:** ☐ dysphagia ☐ heartburn ☐ change in appetite ☐ food intol ☐ nausea ☐ vomiting ☐ hematemesis ☐ abdominal pain
☐ bloating ☐ flatulence ☐ diarrhea ☐ constipation ☐ melena ☐ jaundice ☐ dark urine ☐ BRBPR ☐ change in BM
☐ hemorrhoids ☐ hernia

☐ **GU**: ☐ dysuria ☐ urgency ☐ frequency ☐ hematuria ☐ nocturia ☐ polyuria ☐ suprapubic pain ☐ flank pain
☐ incontinence ☐ lesions

♂ ☐ hesitancy ☐ dribbling ☐ decreased force stream ☐ testicular pain ☐ testicular mass/swelling ☐ penile discharge
☐ erectile dysfunction

♀ ☐ vaginal itch ☐ abnl vaginal discharge ☐ vaginal dryness ☐ dyspareunia ☐ sexual dysfunction ☐ abnl vaginal bleeding

☐ **Endocrine:** ☐ polyuria ☐ polydipsia ☐ polyphagia ☐ heat/cold intol ☐ tremor ☐ lump in throat ☐ unexplained wt change
☐ hair changes

☐ **Heme:** ☐ anemia ☐ easy bruising ☐ swollen glands ☐ bleeding of skin/mucous membranes ☐ freq infections ☐ allergies
☐ delayed healing

☐ **MSK:** ☐ joint pain (location _____) ☐ stiffness ☐ restriction of motion ☐ swelling
☐ erythema ☐ bony deformity ☐ myalgia ☐ muscle cramps ☐ weakness ☐ antalgic gait ☐ back pain

☐ **Neuro:** ☐ focal weakness ☐ paralysis ☐ numbness ☐ tremor ☐ seizure ☐ syncope ☐ gait disturbance ☐ memory loss
☐ aphasia

☐ **Psych:** ☐ anxiety ☐ panic attacks ☐ depression ☐ mood changes ☐ irritability ☐ nervousness ☐ decreased libido
☐ eating disorder ☐ sleep disturbance ☐ suicidal thoughts ☐ impaired judgment ☐ hallucinations ☐ confusion

Comments/Details:

Physical Exam

Vitals

Ht _____ Wt _____ Temp _____ Resp _____ Pulse _____ BP (upright) _____ (supine) _____

Visual Acuity

Right _____ / _____ Left _____ / _____   Corrective lenses: ☐ yes ☐ no

N = Normal A = Abnormal (Check appropriate box)	N	A
1. **General Appearance**: age • LOC • nutrition • development • mobility • affect • speech • hygiene		
2. **Skin**: hydration • color • texture • hair • nails • lesions		
3. **Head**: shape • size • symmetry • scalp • TMJ • lesions		
4. **Eyes**: lids • conjunctiva • sclera		
Extraocular muscles		
Visual fields		
Pupils: size, reaction to light and accommodation		
Fundi		
5. **Ears**: pinna • canals • TMs • hearing		
6. **Nose**: patency • nares • sinuses • nasal mucosa • septum • turbinates		
7. **Mouth**: lips • gums • teeth • mucosa • palate • tongue		
8. **Throat**: pharynx • tonsils • uvula		
9. **Neck**: ROM • symmetry • palpation • thyroid • trachea • carotids • jugular veins • lymph nodes		
10. **Breasts**: size • symmetry • skin • nipples • palpation • nodes		
11. **Chest/Lungs**: excursion • palpation • percussion • auscult		
12. **Cardiac**: PMI • palpation • rate • rhythm • S1 • S2 • murmurs • gallops • bruits • extra sounds		
13. **Abdomen**: appearance • bowel sounds • bruits • percussion • palpation • liver • spleen • flank • suprapubic • hernia		
14. **Anorectal**:		
Perianal		
Digital rectal		
Stool guaiac		
Prostate exam		
15. **Female Genitalia**: perineum • labia • urethral meatus • introitus		
Internal: vaginal mucosal • cervix		
Bimanual: vagina • cervix • uterus • adnexa		
16. **Male Genitalia**: penis • scrotum • testes • hernia		
17. **Lymph Nodes**: cervical • subclavian • axillary • inguinal • other		
18. **MSK**:		
Back/Spine: ROM • palpation		
Upper Extremity: ROM • strength • palpation		
Lower Extremity: ROM • strength • palpation		
19. **Peripheral Vascular**:		
Upper extremity: pulses • appearance • temp		
Lower extremity: pulses • appearance • temp		
20. **Neurologic**: cranial nerves • motor • sensory • cerebellar • reflexes • gait • mental status		

Document Abnormals (by number)/Comments

_____

_____

_____

_____

_____

_____

_____

_____

_____

_____

_____

Lab/Studies

_____

_____

_____

_____

_____

_____

_____

Assessment and Plan

_____

_____

_____

_____

_____

_____

_____

_____

_____

_____

_____

_____

Periodic Heath Screening Plan

Exam	Performed	Scheduled	N/A	Refused
Breast Exam				
Mammogram				
Pap Test				
Prostate exam				
Testicular exam				
Digital rectal with guaiac				
Sigmoid/Colonoscopy				
Bone Density				
PPD				

Health Counseling

(Check if discussed; describe any intervention)
☐ Smoking cessation _____
☐ Alcohol / Drug use _____
☐ Diet / Weight _____
☐ Vitamins / Calcium _____
☐ Periodic Dental / Vision care_____
☐ Exercise / Sleep _____
☐ Sun exposure _____
☐ Seatbelts / Helmets _____
☐ Stress / Family issues _____
☐ Safety: Weapons / Domestic Violence _____
☐ Sexual issues / risks _____
☐ Contraception _____
☐ Living will / Power of attorney _____

Other

Lab/Studies Ordered

☐ CXR   ☐ Lipids   ☐ Creat/BUN   ☐ HbA$_1$C   ☐ ECG   ☐ CBC/diff   ☐ LFTs   ☐ TSH
☐ Electrolytes   ☐ FBS   ☐ UA/UC
☐ Other:

_____   _____
Provider's Signature   Date

Primary Care Performance Assessment

This performance standard reflects the expected level of competency required of primary care naturopathic physicians in clinical practice.

Practitioner: _____ Date: _____ Evaluator: _____

Competency Index			
Not Competent	Below Average	Average	Above average
1	2	3	4

Evaluation Criteria	Competency Index 1- 4	Total Points
1. Identify important cues in the patient's story (Basic Health Assessment):		
1.1 Demographic information (gender, age, occupation, residence)		
1.2 Symptom analysis		
1.3 Functional assessment		
1.4 Patient's belief or understanding of their symptoms (and impact on daily life, family members and lifestyle)		
1.5 Routine vital signs (temperature, pulse, heart rate, blood pressure, weight, height, last menses, smoking status, and recreational drug use)		
Section Total (out of 20)		
2. Understand and perform Advanced Health Assessment techniques:		
2.1 Determine what questions need to be asked. Asking complaint-specific questions to assess patient's risk for certain differential diagnoses.		
2.2 Determine what needs to be examined		
2.3 Perform physical examination maneuvers that are suggested by the patients overall presentation		
2.4 Selective observation of fine detail during the examination (where applicable)		
2.5 Selective requisition of cost-effective/m high-yield laboratory work-ups (where applicable)		
Section Total (out of 20)		

Evaluation Criteria	Competency Index 1- 4	Total Points
3. Learning process and application of clinical reasoning skills:		
3.1 Appreciate the presented and implied tasks of the case		
3.2 Recognize own knowledge limitations if any, identify learning issues, acquire new knowledge to meet the assigned task		
3.3 Identify absence of findings that are 'sensitive' markers of certain conditions. Identify presence of findings that are 'specific' markers for certain conditions		
3.4 Identify presenting patterns in light of the patient's knowledge of known presentation		
3.5 Revise diagnostic hypotheses based on self-directed learning		
Section Total (out of 20)		
4. Management of the presentation:		
4.1 Discuss diagnostic impression and available treatment options with the patient in order to empower them to choose an effective and practical treatment option.		
4.2 Design appropriate management plans that ensure resolution of condition and compliance of patient with treatment plan.		
4.3 Identify and utilize community resources that may assist in resolving the presentation (where applicable)		
4.4 Involve other practitioners (consultation and/or referral) in the evaluation or management plan (where indicated)		
4.5 Design appropriate follow-up that ensures resolution of condition. Coordinate care and dissemination of information among healthcare providers within the patient's circle-of-care.		
Section Total (out of 20)		
5. Assessment of group: Includes evaluator's subjective assessment of strengths and weaknesses and suggestions for improvement.		
•		
•		
•		
•		
Section Total (out of 20)		
Competency Assessment Total Score (out of 100)		

EVALUATION OF CHARTING PRACTICE

Not only teachers and students of primary care but also naturopathic physicians and allied healthcare professionals might find this form useful for periodically evaluating charting practices in a clinical setting.

Quality Competent	Poor	Below Average	Average	Above Average	Total points
Clarity (legibility, precision of language, neatness)	1	2	3	4	
Organization (logical, focused, internally consistent)	1	2	3	4	
Accuracy (complete, concise, relevant)	1	2	3	4	
Analysis (synthesis, problem list, appropriate DDx, clinical reasoning)	1	2	3	4	
Management (appropriate for the resolution of presentation)	1	2	3	4	
				Out of 20 points	
Evaluator's Feedback:					

The following are some laboratory evaluations commonly requested by primary care naturopathic physicians, with a brief explanation of their clinical value.

Test	Used clinically to detect or rule-out	
EKG or ECG	Ventricular hypertrophy, coronary artery disease, rhythm disturbances, and electrolyte imbalance.	
Holter monitor	Paroxysmal rhythm disorders, functional impairment, and confirm panic attacks.	
CBC	Anemias, infections, hematologic disorders.	
Ferritin	Iron deficiency anemia, hemochromatosis, liver disease.	
WBC w/diff	Infections (detection and management), inflammatory disorders, bone marrow disorders, response to therapeutic agents (drugs, botanicals, supplements), response to toxins.	
Platelet counts	Bleeding disorders, aplastic anemia, leukemia, ITP, SLE, infectious mononucleosis.	
PT	Extrinsic clotting pathway defects, liver disease, vitamin K deficiency, warfarin therapy.	
PTT	Intrinsic clotting pathway defects, hemophilia, SLE, heparin therapy.	
BUN/creatinine	Uremia, chronic kidney disease.	
sPotassium	Chronic renal failure.	
ALT	Hepatocellular disorders, hepatitis, cirrhosis.	
ALP	Obstructive jaundice, cholecystitis, pancreatitis.	Impaired liver function: these tests are often referred to as liver function tests (LFTs).
AST	Hepatocellular disorders, hepatitis, cirrhosis.	
Bilirubin	Obstructive or functional impairment of liver, nausea.	
GGT	Hepatocellular disorders, hepatitis, cirrhosis.	

Laboratory evaluations are requested by primary care physicians to confirm, rule out, or detect diagnoses.

LDH	Liver, heart or kidney disease.	Impaired liver function: these tests are often referred to as liver function tests (LFTs).
Albumin & total protein	Edema, ascitis, chronic renal failure.	
Amylase	Pancreatitis	Cholecystitis with or without obstruction.
Lipase	Pancreatitis	
Urobilinogen	Hemolytic anemia, hepatocellular jaundice	
Vitamin K	Bleeding disorders, liver disease, deficiency.	
Ammonia	Cirrhosis	
Imunoglobulins	Hayfever, rashes, urticaria, hives.	
Spot Urinalysis	Urinary tract infections, diabetes, occult hematuria, nephrotic and nephritic patterns.	
24 hour urine protein	Nephrotic disease, postural proteinuria, chronic kidney disease.	
Urine microscopy	Glomerulonephritis, gout, kidney stones.	
FBS, HbA1C	Diabetes (detection and monitoring).	
OGTT	Borderline diabetes, gestational diabetes.	
Serum Lipids	Dyslipidemias, (detection and monitoring), familial hypercholesterolemia.	
Electrolytes	Renal insufficiency, congestive heart failure.	
TSH, T4	Clinical and subclinical hypothyroidism and hyperthyroidism.	
Stool O& P	Parasitic infections on the GI tract.	
Gram stain	To support a diagnosis of bacterial infection.	
C&S	To identify causative bacterial pathogen and its antimicrobial sensitivity.	
Pap smear	Cervical dysplasia screening.	
Fecal Occult Blood	Colon cancer screening, small GI bleeding, anemia.	
Serum B12	Macrocytic anemias, alcoholism.	
PSA & ratio	Prostate cancer screening.	

NATUROPATHIC AND EVIDENCE-BASED MEDICINE

The philosophy of naturopathy can be traced to the era of Hippocrates (460-377 BCE). However, the concept of curing illness via natural means was developed further as a result of newfound interest during the 18th and 19th centuries when practitioners such as Vinzenz Priessnitz (1799-1851) and Sebastian Kneipp (1821-1897) established comprehensive hydrotherapeutic interventions to cure many health conditions. The principles and practice of this *Naturheilkunde* (German) were subsequently introduced to the United States by Kniepp's protégé, Benedict Lust (1870-1945), who coined the term naturopathy.

Naturopathic medicine embraces the belief that health is influenced by each individual's inherent healing ability (*vis medicatrix naturae*). In this paradigm, disease is viewed empirically as a direct result of ignoring or violating the general principles of health. Historically, these principles have been defined as comprising internal and external environments. Traditional naturopathic practitioners thus aimed to correct and stabilize these environments as primary interventions to ward off disease.

From a technical perspective, modern naturopathy or *Naturheilverfahren* can be defined as an eclectic system of healthcare, which integrates elements of alternative and conventional medicine to support and enhance self-healing processes. The different therapeutic interventions and modalities vary according to the jurisdiction of practice, but generally include the historical crafts of herbal or botanical medicine, hydrotherapy, dietetics, exercise, and meditation. In some jurisdictions, the practice also includes clinical nutrition, homeopathy, spinal manipulation, iridology, acupuncture, pharmacotherapy, minor surgery, life-style counseling, and traditional Chinese medicine.

Naturopathic medicine has been described as a science and an art. Proponents of evidence-based practices argue that in cases where unbiased evidence exists, science should prevail. Clinical practice is also an art, attending to characteristics of individual human beings. Naturopathic medicine takes into account individual attributes in the context of available evidence.

To a large extent, contemporary naturopathic practitioners have shored-up traditional naturopathic empiricism with the principles of evidence-based medicine to diagnose and manage health conditions. Evidence-based medicine (EBM) can be contextually defined as "an approach to practicing medicine in which the clinician is aware of the evidence in support of clinical practice and the strength of that evidence."

> To a large extent, contemporary naturopathic practitioners have shored-up traditional naturopathic empiricism with the principles of evidence-based medicine to diagnose and manage health conditions.

Evidence-based care combines (1) the best available external evidence, (2) the naturopathic doctor's clinical expertise, and (3) the patient's preferences when making decisions about their healthcare.

1. EXTERNAL EVIDENCE

EBM practices translate into adopting the habit of making selective, efficient, patient-centered "searches" for evidence and then incorporating quality findings into everyday practice.

External evidence includes research from the basic sciences and, in particular, patient-centered clinical research into the accuracy of diagnostic tests (including the clinical examination), the markers used for making prognoses, and the effectiveness and safety of treatments, whether for therapy, prevention, or rehabilitation. This external clinical evidence may invalidate previously accepted practices and replace them with new ones that are safer and more effective, with better outcomes.

External evidence is based on verified research information on specific cohorts of patients. Selection criteria for entry into these research studies are often rigid. By design, these clinical trials can only analyze a fraction of a problem or situation that may exist in clinical practice. Conclusions relating to trial cohorts are assumed to hold true for other cohorts that appear to be similar. For example, a particular patient in your practice may exhibit multiple pathologies that render her unlike any other patient in published studies. Is the available "evidence" valid for that particular patient? There is no means to know the answer for certain, only a means of deducing one empirically.

2. CLINICAL EXPERTISE

External clinical evidence can inform but never replace clinical expertise. This expertise even decides whether the external evidence is relevant to the patient at all. To illustrate this point, consider that only 20% to 37% of conventional medical practices are indeed evidence based (Imrie, 2002). The balance of accepted medical practices are based on empiricism. This is the process of learning from daily observation and experimentation rather than theory (for example, give aspirin and observe effect on reported headache) via inductive philosophy (conclude that aspirin relieves headaches). Such empirical knowledge passes from one generation of physician educators to the next. Through this process, the knowledge is upheld, refined, or altogether rejected by the next generation. The traditional Chinese medical doctrine is an example of the empiricist school of thought.

Rather than embarking on the impossible task of reading every report on every medical advance, the doctor interested in EBM learns to be more focused. EBM practices translate into adopting the habit of making selective, efficient, patient-centered "searches" for evidence and then incorporating quality findings into everyday practice.

The clinician also needs to be conscious of the limitations and possible dangers of following external evidence slavishly. For example, the use of intravenous diuretics in acute pulmonary edema has evolved without any formal randomized controlled trial evidence because the application of a trial comparing such intervention with a placebo would be considered unethical. In this case, ignoring clearly successful interventions because of lack of randomized controlled trial (RCT) evidence would simply be illogical. In addition, collating evidence for uncommon conditions (or side effects) is difficult and may not allow for adequate analysis (think Cox II inhibitors). Though EBM-friendly evidence is important, the limitations of adopting austere approaches must be recognized.

Many naturopathic or complementary and alternative medicine (CAM) interventions are difficult to blind or have no satisfactory placebos because they rely on "complex effects" that are a crucial part of the healing process (Kleijnen, 1994). Ted Kaptchuk, author of *The Web that Has No Weaver* and research fellow at Harvard's Center for Alternative Medicine Research, suggests that the most important role for CAM could be to bring these effects into the forefront of medicine. Randomized controlled trials attempt to cancel out variable factors, such as the therapeutic setting, the personality of the therapist, the amount of time given to patients, and even the very words spoken to them. Instead of being hidden within the placebo arm, these should be disentangled and systematically studied so that their therapeutic benefits can be harnessed by all involved in the provision of health care (Chaput de Saintonge, 1994). It follows that the art of both conventional and complementary medicine and the "complexity of caring" is difficult but not impossible to study (Dixon M, 2000).

3. PATIENT'S PREFERENCES

Patient preference is paramount to the concept of patient-centered care and yields to individualized management plans that foster compliance. For example, your expertise may lead you to believe that acupuncture will most likely relieve a particular patient's sub-acute low back pain. If this patient is afraid of needles or simply does not prefer this approach, he will likely not comply with the treatment plan. In practice, patients may not volunteer their preference – and the therapeutic relationship may ultimately suffer. Where comparable options (this applies to evaluation and treatment) exist, it is imperative to incorporate your patient's unique preferences to inspire compliance and collaborative responsibility.

It follows that naturopathic best practices can be defined as a merger between a rich body of empirical knowledge, clinician expertise, good quality external evidence, and preferences of patients to arrive consistently at appropriate management plans.

PROBLEM-BASED LEARNING

Evidence-based medicine is an active process that attempts to enhance the physician's expertise by applying external evidence and patient's preferences.

> Naturopathic best practices can be defined as a merger between a rich body of empirical knowledge, clinician expertise, good quality external evidence, and preferences of patients to arrive consistently at appropriate management plans.

Evidence-based medicine is, therefore, a process of life-long, problem-based learning. This process may involve:

1. Identifying a clinical question or need for inquiry.
2. Efficiently tracking down the best evidence with which to answer the question.
3. Critically appraising the evidence for validity and clinical usefulness to withstand your own scrutiny.
4. Applying the results in clinical practice.
5. Evaluating performance of the evidence in clinical application.

In applying standards of external evidence to primary care practices, terminology and questions about the quality of the evidence and the validity of the test are very important, as stressed by the chief medical examination boards: USMLE, MCCQE, and NPLEX.

EVIDENCE EVALUATION TERMINOLOGY

Basic scientific concepts and terms are used in evaluating test validity and study quality.

- **Test Validity**: the *accuracy* of a diagnostic test. In other words, does the test measure what it claims to measure? For example, Candida Questionnaire versus actual candida overgrowth, Depression Questionnaire versus clinical depression, MAST versus alcoholism, etc.

- **Test Reliability**: the precision, reproducibility, or consistency of any diagnostic test. If a test is reliable, then it will provide the same score if two different people administer the same test. As a primary care clinician, you should be aware of the reliability of the routine tests you use in your practice (for example, CBC, PAP smear, mammogram, PCD examinations, function tests) or anything that is used to guide your clinical reasoning process.

- **Incidence**: the number of new cases of a disease in a unit of time = absolute (or total) risk of developing a condition.

- **Prevalence**: the total number of cases of a disease (new and old) at a specific time.

- **Attributable Risk**: the number of cases of a disease attributable to one risk factor (for example, lung cancer and smoking).

- **Relative Risk**: compares the disease risk in people exposed to or harboring a certain factor with the disease risk in people who are not. This value can only be calculated form experimental or prospective studies.

- **Clinically Significant Relative Risk**: any value other than 1 is clinically significant. When a person's RR is 1.5, they are 1.5 times more likely to develop the condition in question; alternatively, if a person's RR is 0.5, they are half as likely to develop something.

- **Odds Ratio**: a less desirable method of estimating the relative risk. This value can be calculated from less rigorous studies.

> As a primary care clinician, you should be aware of the reliability of the routine tests you use in your practice or anything that is used to guide your clinical reasoning process.

- **Standard Deviation**: a feature of normal or bell-shaped distributions: 1 SD holds 68% of the values, 2 SD hold 95%, and 3 SD hold 99.7% of the values.
- **Mean**: average value.
- **Median**: middle value.
- **Mode**: most common value.
- **Normal distribution**: a distribution of values where the mean = median = mode.
- **Skewed distribution**: a distribution where the data do not follow the normal bell-shaped curve.
  - a. Positive skew: an excess of high values = the tail of the curve is on the right (mean > median > mode).
  - b. Negative skew: an excess of low values = the tail of the curve is on the left (mean < median < mode).
- **Correlation coefficient**: measures to what degree two variables are related (ranges from -1 to $+1$)
- **Confidence interval**: this is the acceptable threshold for studies to be accepted by the medical community. A confidence interval of 95% indicates that the mean of the entire population is within 2 SD of your experimental mean.
- **P-value**: the chance that data were obtained by error or chance. The acceptable threshold for studies to be accepted by the scientific community is 5% or less. P-value of < 0.05 is the cutoff for statistical significance.

QUALITY OF EVIDENCE

The following table of questions is derived from objectives set by three examination boards: USMLE, MCCQE, and NPLEX.

1. What are the differences in the quality of evidence?	Source

Evidence Ranking: Medical evidence has been ranked from highest to lowest quality and desirability as follows:

1. Experimental studies
2. Prospective studies
3. Retrospective studies
4. Case series
5. Prevalence surveys
6. Expert opinion
7. Individual case reports

MCCQE
USMLE

2. What is an experimental study?	Source

Experimental Study: tend to be regarded as the 'gold standard' because they compare two equal groups, in which one variable is altered and its effect (if any) is measured. Experimental studies use double blinding and well as matched controls to ensure accurate data.

MCCQE
USMLE

3. What are prospective studies?	Source

Prospective Studies: also known as observational, longitudinal, cohort, incidence, or follow-up studies. Generally, a sample is divided based on the presence or absence of a risk factor; the groups are then followed over time to see what diseases they develop. You can calculate relative incidence from this type of study (for example, smokers have a higher incidence of cancer of the lung, oral cavity, esophagus, larynx, pharynx, bladder, kidney, pancreas, and cervix).

MCCQE
USMLE

4. What is a retrospective study?	Source

Retrospective study: case-control studies, in which population samples are chosen after a certain fact, based on presence (cases) or absence (controls) of disease. Retrospective studies can be used to calculate an odds ratio, but not true relative risks or incidences.

MCCQE
USMLE

Source

5. What are case series studies?

MCCQE
USMLE

Case Series: describes the clinical presentation of people with a certain disease. This type of study is good for extremely rare diseases or a new strain of a virus, and often suggests the need for a retrospective or prospective study.

Source

6. What are prevalence surveys ?

MCCQE
USMLE

Prevalence or Cross-sectional Surveys: look at the prevalence of a disease and the prevalence of risk factors. When used to compare two different populations (cultures, countries, socioeconomic groups, or age groups), such surveys may suggest a possible cause of a disease.

Source

7. How is the sensitivity of a test defined? What are highly sensitive tests used for clinically?

NPLEX
USMLE
Moore,
2001

Sensitivity: the ability of a test to detect disease (the # of true positives divided by the # of people with the disease). Tests with high sensitivity are used clinically for disease screening. Remember from lab Dx the acronym SNOUT (a SeNsitive test rules OUT a suspected condition).

Source

8. How is the specificity of a test defined? What are highly specific tests used for clinically?

NPLEX
Moore,
2001

Specificity: the ability of a test to detect non-disease or health (the # of true negatives divided by the # of people without the disease). Tests with high specificity are used clinically for disease confirmation. Remember the acronym SPIN (a SPecific test rules IN a suspected condition).

Source

9. What is positive predictive value (PPV)?

NPLEX
USMLE

Positive Predictive Value: a calculated value that tells you the likelihood that a patient has the disease when a certain test is positive (the # of true positives divided by the total number of people with a positive test).

10. How do the concepts of sensitivity, specificity, and predictive value affect interpretation of any diagnostic test result? A Bayesian 2x2 table is used for illustration.

		Disease in a community		Property	Formula
		(+)	(-)	Sensitivity	A/(A+C)
Test results	(+)	A	B	Specificity	D/(B+D)
	(-)	C	D	Positive predictive value - PPV	A/(A+B)
* A = true positives B = false positives C = false negatives D = true negatives				Negative predictive value – NPV	D/(C+D)
				Odds Ratio	(AxD)/(BxC)
				Relative Risk	[A/(A+B)]/ [C/(C+D)]
				Attributable Risk	[A/(A+B)]- [C/(C+D)]

Source

NPLEX
Moore,
2001
MCCQE

11. What would an abnormal test result mean?

Source

Moore,
2001

Abnormal Test Result Interpretation:
1. Patient is sick.
2. Patient is well, but a statistical outlier.
3. Patient is well, but is not of the age, sex, or race group of the reference range population.
4. Patient is well, but is carrying out a proscribed activity, such as jogging or eating, before the sample was obtained; *or*
5. Population reference range may not be the healthy reference range.

Thus, an abnormal test result may indeed be an indicator of health. That is why we recommend a clinical reasoning process based on preponderance of evidence, not just an isolated piece of data or information.

12. Is there any single test that can rule in or out a particular disease?

- No. There is no single test that exhibits sufficient SNOUT or SPIN. Even if you have a wonderfully sensitive and specific test in the 95% range, by definition 5% of normal individuals will exhibit abnormal results. So the number of "false" findings is proportional to the number of tests used. Of course, if you subject a patient to a barrage of tests (a.k.a. a panel), you are bound to find some abnormal findings there. But does the finding mean anything? Lofgren (2004) mentions that 64% of normal individuals will exhibit at least one abnormal result on a standard blood chemistry panel composed of 20 individual tests. In this case, it is indeed abnormal for anyone to have a normal "screening" by the chem-20 panel.
- Several tests in combination give you increased sensitivity (but lower specificity). To increase specificity, you need to apply tests in a sequence, for example:

> ↳ Hb shows up low on a CBC (maybe anemia, maybe not)
>> ↳ Request ferritin or TIBC (rule out iron deficiency). If ferritin high suspect anemia of chronic disease or thalassemia
>>> ↳ Request Hb electrophoresis (rule out thalassemia)

13. What subtypes of bias may exist in a clinical study?

Bias Sub-types:
- Nonresponse bias: When people do not return printed surveys, phone calls, or return for follow-up visits.
- Lead-time bias: Due to time differentials. For example, screening tests that claim to prolong survival compared with older survival data when in fact the difference is due only to early detection, not to improved treatment or longer survival.
- Admission rate bias: When an experimenter compares outcomes from two patient populations, in which diagnostic inclusion criteria are not the same (for example, a higher rate of mortality may be due to tougher admission criteria rather than efficacy of treatment).
- Recall bias: When people inadvertently over- or underestimate risk factors because they cannot remember exactly.
- Interviewer bias: Occurs in the absence of blinding, when a scientist inadvertently categorizes an outcome "significant" in the case group and "not significant" in the control group.
- Unacceptability bias: When people do not admit to deleterious or embarrassing behavior to please the interviewer.

References

Bouchert A. USMLE Step 2 Secrets. Philadelphia, PA: Hanley & Belfus Inc., 2000.

Naturopathic Physician Licensing Examination Part II (NPLEx II) Blueprint. Portland, OR: North American Board of Naturopathic Examiners (NABNE), 2004.

Molckovsky A, Pirzada KS (eds.). The Toronto Notes 2004: Review for the Medical Council of Canada Qualifying Exam. Toronto, ON: Toronto Notes Medical Publishing Inc., 2004.

Chaput de Saintonge DM, Herxheimer A. Harnessing placebo effects in health care. Lancet 1994;344:995.8.

Dixon M, Sweeney K. The Human Effect in Medicine: Theory, Research and Practice. Oxford, UK: Radcliffe Medical Press, 2000.

Edzard E , Pittler MH, Stevenson C, White A. The Desktop guide to Complementary and Alternative Medicine: An evidence based approach. London, UK: Mosby, 2001:50-55, 61-64.

Imrie R. The evidence for evidence based medicine. Complement Ther Med 2002;8:123-26.

Kaptchuk TJ. Powerful placebo: The dark side of the randomized controlled trial. Lancet 1998;351:1722.5.

Kleijnen J, de Craen AJM, van Everdingen J, Krol L. Placebo effect in double blind clinical trials: A review of interactions with medications. Lancet 1994;344:1347.9.

Lofgren RL. Principles of preventive maintenance and test selection. Mladenovic J (ed.). Primary Care Secrets. Philadelphia, PA: Hanley & Belfus, 2004.

Moore R. Hematology Laboratory Diagnosis. Hamilton, ON: McMaster University Press, 2001.

Sackett DL, Rosenberg WMC, Gray JAM, Richardson WS. Evidence-based medicine: What it is and what it is not. BMJ 1996;Jan 13;312:71-72.

Sackett DL, Rosenberg WMC, Gray JAM, Richardson WS. Evidence-based Medicine: How to Practice and Teach EBM. New York, NY: Churchill Livingstone, 1997.

Recommended EBM Resources with Naturopathic Content

ACUBRIEFS

http://www.acubriefs.com

Acubriefs was established and is supported by a grant from the Medical Acupuncture Research Foundation (MARF). Its purpose is to make the most comprehensive database of English language references on acupuncture available online. Access to the database is free.

AMED: Allied and Complementary Medicine Database

http://www.bl.uk/collections/health/amed.html

Compiled by the British Library, AMED is a literature database, in the English language, in the field of allied and alternative medicine. It offers information from different countries, especially from Europe. The database contains bibliographic data, keywords, and abstracts since 1985. Subjects covered: Acupuncture, homeopathy, hypnosis, chiropractic, osteopathy, rehabilitation, herbalism, holistic treatments, Chinese medicine, occupational therapy, physiotherapy, podiatry.

Agency for Healthcare Research and Quality (AHRQ)

http://www.ahrq.gov

The Agency for Healthcare Research and Quality (AHRQ) produces a range of publications and electronic information products that are available to users through different channels and a variety of formats. This is a well-sourced database of Clinical Information, Evidence-based Practice, Outcomes & Effectiveness, Technology Assessment, Preventive Services, and Clinical Practice Guidelines.

American Indian Ethnobotany Database

http://herb.umd.umich.edu/

Subjects covered: Foods, drugs, dyes and fibers of native North American peoples.

ARCAM and CAMPAIN

http://www.compmed.umm.edu./Databases.html

The Center for Integrative Medicine at the University of Maryland has developed, and regularly updates, two bibliographic databases: The Arthritis and Complementary Medicine Database (ARCAM) and the Complementary and Alternative Medicine and Pain Database (CAMPAIN). These databases are compiled from regular comprehensive electronic and hand searches of scientific literature sources world-wide. The Cochrane CM register is searchable here as well. Access is free.

Biomed Central

http://www.biomedcentral.com/

Over 100 OPEN ACESS journals covering all areas of biology as well as conventional and complementary medicine (free).

CABI - CAB ABSTRACTS

http://www.cabi-publishing.org/
AbstractDatabases.asp?SubjectArea=&PID=125
Subjects covered: Human health and nutrition, animal sciences and veterinary medicine, plant and agricultural sciences, and the management and conservation of natural resources. More than 9,000 serial journals in more than 50 languages are scanned, as well as books, reports, and other publications.

CAMLINE

www.camline.org/
Canadian website on evidence-based CAM.

CAM on PubMed

www.nih.gov/nccam/camonpubmed.html
The National Centre for Complementary and Alternative Medicine (NCCAM) and the National Library of Medicine (NLM) have partnered to create CAM on PubMed, a subset of NLM's PubMed.

Chalmers Research Group

http://www.chalmersresearch.com/epi6188/CAMdbs.pdf
Databases with CAM content from the Chalmers Research Group, Children's Hospital of Eastern Ontario Research Institute.

CINAHL

http://www.cinahl.com/
CINAHL contains references to journal articles, healthcare books, nursing dissertations, selected conference proceedings, standards of professional practice, educational software and audiovisual materials in nursing. Subjects covered: Nursing and allied health.

Cochrane Library – including Cochrane Collaboration CM Field

http://www.cochrane.org
http://www.compmed.umm.edu/Cochrane/
The Cochrane Library consists of a regularly updated collection of evidence-based medicine databases, including The Cochrane Database of Systematic Reviews. The systematic reviews provide high quality information to people providing and receiving healthcare, and those responsible for research, teaching, funding and administration at all levels.

FreeMedicalJournals.com

http://www.freemedicaljournals.com/
The Free Medical Journals Site was created to promote the availability of full text medical journals on the Internet.

Global Health

http://www.cabdirect.org/
CAB HEALTH brings together the resources of the Public Health and Tropical

Medicine (PHTM) database and the human health and diseases information extracted from CAB ABSTRACTS since 1973. It contains foreign language journals, books, research reports, patents and standards, dissertations, conference proceedings, annual reports, public health, developing country information, and other difficult to obtain material. Subjects covered: communicable diseases (including HIV/AIDS), tropical diseases, parasitic diseases and parasitology, human nutrition, community and public health, and medicinal and poisonous plants.

HerbMed

http://www.herbmed.org

HerbMed, produced by the nonprofit Alternative Medicine Foundation, is a categorized, evidence-based resource for herbal information. It includes hyperlinks to clinical and scientific publications and dynamic links for automatic updating.

Herb Research Foundation

http://www.herbs.org/index.html

HRF provides a search service from their specialty research library containing more than 300,000 scientific articles on thousands of herbs.

Hom-Inform

http://www.hom-inform.org/

Hom-Inform is a database of literature references to homoeopathy, with key terms and some abstracts, provided by the British Homeopathic Library.

IBIDS

http://ods.od.nih.gov/Health_Information/IBIDS.aspx

International Bibliographic Information on Dietary Supplements (IBIDS) is produced by the Office of Dietary Supplements at the National Institutes of Health. It is a database of published, international, scientific literature on dietary supplements, including vitamins, minerals, and botanicals.

Intramedicine

http://www.seeq.com/popupwrapper.jsp?referrer=&domain=intramedicine.com

Intramedicine is oriented to professional pharmacists and patients and provides a Chinese herbal database.

MANTIS

http://www.healthindex.com

Manual, Alternative and Natural Therapy is a database for healthcare disciplines not covered by major biomedical databases. The MANTIS Database is a sizable source of osteopathic, chiropractic, and manual medical literature.

Natural Standard

http://www.naturalstandard.com

Natural Standard is a database founded by clinicians and researchers to provide high quality, evidence-based information about complementary and alternative therapies. It is primarily oriented to clinicians and pharmacists. Subjects covered: Alternative and complementary medicine.

Phytobase
http://www.gamed.or.at/archiv/bm/informationsdienste/phyto.htm
Phytobase is a database of literature on toxicology, pharmacology (pharmacodynamics, pharmacokinetics), therapeutic uses for natural compounds, and isolation of natural compounds from plant material. Phytobase indexes 140 scientific journals published worldwide and currently includes spproximately 20,000 records from 7,800 publications. The language of the database is German.

PsycINFO
http://www.apa.org/psycinfo/
PsycINFO includes journal articles, books, book chapters, dissertations, and government reports in professional and academic literature in psychology and related disciplines. Subjects covered: medicine, psychiatry, nursing, sociology, education, pharmacology, physiology, linguistics and other areas.

PubMed
http://www.pubmed.org
National Library of Medicine's search interface to access the 10 million citations in MEDLINE, and Pre-MEDLINE, and other related databases.

The Richard and Hinda Rosenthal Center for Complementary and Alternative Medicine
http://www.rosenthal.hs.columbia.edu
Founded in 1993, this center builds bridges between diverse therapeutic traditions and modern medicine.

The Research Council for Complementary Medicine
http://www.rccm.org.uk/static/Links_CAM_databases.aspx?m=11

Tropical Plant Database
http://rain-tree.com/plants.htm
Each plant file contains taxonomy data, phytochemical and ethnobotanical data, uses in traditional medicine, and clinical research from Raintree Nutrition, Inc, Austin, Texas.

APPLIED CLINICAL SKILLS

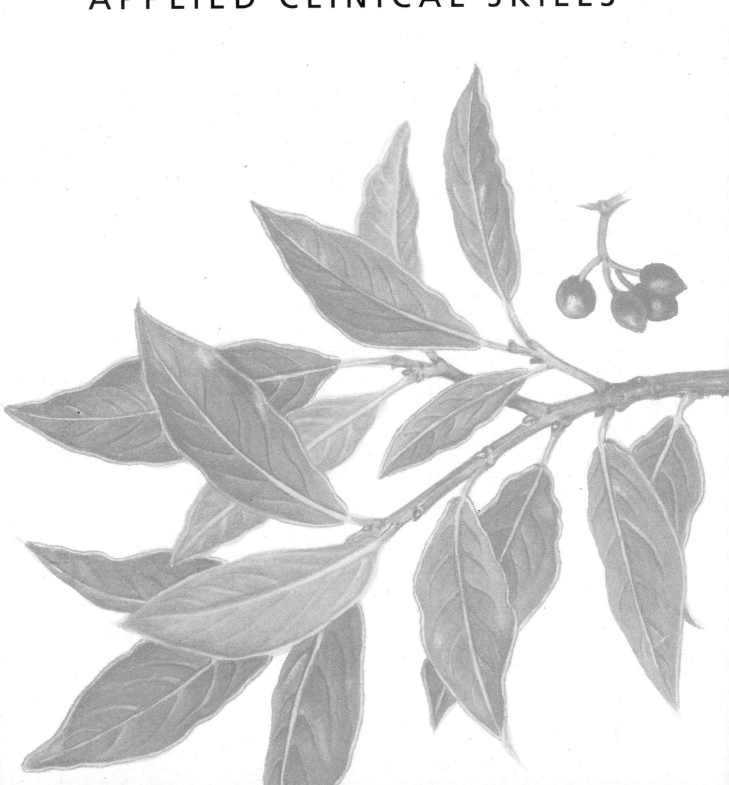

PREFACE

This clinical guide offers a series of mutually exclusive modules that develop the basic knowledge of body systems and medical conditions, clinical reasoning strategies, and therapeutic management skills needed in naturopathic primary care practice. Each module represents a body of knowledge of a system – for example, cardiology – and provides diagnostic and treatment protocols for significant conditions – for example, hypertension. To foster prompt clinical reasoning, direct Socratic-style questions are posed. These are the kind of questions naturopathic medical students will face during their clerkships, clinical rotations, board examinations, and, ultimately, practice of naturopathic primary care. Signs and symptoms and diagnostic criteria are presented in systematic lists to check off. First-line naturopathic treatment approaches are discussed in convenient charts for handy clinical reference. The first-line treatment approach, which encompasses empirical and research-based naturopathic doctrine, is referenced and critiqued in a clear manner that enables clinicians to utilize and individualize naturopathic best practices to suit their needs. Conventional treatment approaches are also described, and emergency conditions are identified.

To enable the development of competency in the assessment and management of primary care presentations, care has been given to ensure that each module presents current research and complies with the standards of relevant medical boards and associations. The three principal bodies referenced are the study guides for NPLEX (II), USMLE, and MCCQE (II) licensing examinations:

NPLEX (II): North American Board of Naturopathic Examiners
North American Board of Naturopathic Examiners (NABNE), Naturopathic Physician Licensing Examination Part II Blueprint and Study Guide. Portland, OR: NABNE, 2005.

USMLE (II): National Board of Medical Examiners
Bouchert A. USMLE Step 2 Secrets. Philadelphia, PA: Hanley & Belfus Inc., 2000.

MCCQE: Medical Council of Canada
Molckovsky A, Pirzada KS (eds.). Review for the Medical Council of Canada Qualification Examination. Toronto, ON: Toronto Notes Medical Publishing, 2004.

Also referenced are guideline-generating international and national medical associations, such as the World Health Organization, Center for Disease Control, US Preventive Health Services Task Force, and Canadian Diabetes Association, as well as evidence-based trials, literature reviews, and expert opinion.

These primary practice guidelines, primary evidence (trials) citations, secondary sources (reviews), and published expert opinion are included as abbreviated references in the "Source" column of each module, followed by full references at the end of each module. Common conditions for primary care are presented here; in future editions, other systems will be addressed, including conditions in gynecology, endocrinology, geriatrics, and pediatrics.

In sum, this section of *Naturopathic Standards of Primary Care* functions to prepare naturopathic medical students for their licensing board examinations by posing typical exam questions with well-reasoned answers, and offers the naturopathic primary care practitioner with a convenient clinical handbook for common presentations.

CARDIOLOGY

ELECTROCARDIOGRAM

MYOCARDIAL INFARCTION AND ISCHEMIA

HEART MURMURS

THROMBOSIS

STROKE

CONGESTIVE HEART FAILURE

COR PULMONALE

CARDIOMYOPATHY

CARDIAC ARRHYTHMIA

CONGENITAL HEART DEFECTS

PEDIATRIC CONDITIONS

HYPERTENSION

DYSLIPIDEMIA

ELECTROCARDIOGRAM

Source

Hamption, 2003

1. What is an ECG?

Electrocardiogram (ECG): records the electrical activity of the heart. Various pathologies cause specific changes in the trace. The ECG is not a flawless diagnostic tool. A patient with an organic heart disorder may have an apparently normal trace, whereas a perfectly normal individual may show nonspecific abnormalities. ECG findings must be placed within the patient's clinical context. In naturopathic primary practice, ECGs may be used to screen for cardiac abnormalities where indicated (e.g., chest pain, hypertension, and COPD).

Atrial depolarization: The P waves represent atrial depolarization. The PR interval is caused by the slow propagation of the depolarization through the AVN; this allows time for the ventricles to fill. PR is measured from the start of P to the start of R. Once the depolarization reaches the ventricles, conduction must be fast. The impulse passes though the following hierarchy of structures:

AVN → Bundle of His → Right then Left bundle branches → Anterior fascicle of the left bundle branch → and finally the Posterior fascicle of the left bundle branch.

Ventricular depolarization: This is recorded as the QRS complex. In practice, the Q, R and S waves are not always present. The Q wave is defined as any initial downward deflection. The R wave is defined as any deflection upwards. The S wave is defined as any down deflection that is not Q. The T wave is the repolarization.

2. How do you read an ECG?

Reading an ECG: Pattern recognition develops with time, but in the beginning, a methodical approach is needed. The diagnosis of the normal electrocardiogram is made by excluding any recognized abnormality. (If you are not familiar with ECG interpretation, start with any current self-study ECG workbook. The following instructions are intended to provide a concise reference only and should not be relied on in clinical decision making.)

1. **Rate and Rhythm:** Sinus rhythm is the normal rhythm of the healthy heart in adults. In children, sinus arrhythmia is a variant of normal, resulting in a reduced rate on inspiration.
   - Abnormalities of rhythm can be divided into bradycardia, tachycardia, or irregular rhythm.
   - There are three pathological irregular rhythms: atrial fibrillation; second degree heart block; and ectopic beats.

2. **Cardiac Axis:** The cardiac axis is the predominant direction of ventricular depolarization. Determination of the axis is useful in the diagnosis of:

- Right ventricular hypertrophy (when the axis is >90 degrees).
- Left anterior hemiblock (when the axis is <-30 degrees).

3. P waves: The P wave is caused by the depolarization of the atria and is altered by atrial pathologies. Of note are the defective P waves caused by atrial hypertrophy:

- P pulmonale (RA hypertrophy): P pulmonale are big, tall, peaked P waves on ECG. They are associated with lung disease.
- P mitrale (LA hypertrophy): P mitrale is an ECG finding of a P wave shaped like an M. It is indicative of a hypertrophied left atrium (think mitral stenosis or LVF).

4. PR interval: The reference range for the PR interval is between 0.2 sec (5 small squares) and 0.12 sec (3 small squares). The PR interval represents the time taken for activation to pass from the sinus node, across the atrium, through the AV node, into the Purkinje system, and finally to activate the ventricles.

- PR interval prolonged: In first-degree heart block, there is a delay in the conduction pathway from the sino-atrial node to the ventricles. This is illustrated on an ECG as a PR interval of greater than 0.2 seconds. A finding of first-degree heart block may have no pathological significance. However, it may be a sign of underlying disease.
- PR interval reduced: A short PR interval is defined as being shorter than 0.12 seconds (3 small squares on standard ECG recordings).

5. QRS complex: The duration of the QRS complex is between 0.08 seconds (2 small squares) and 0.12 seconds (3 small squares).

- A wide QRS is seen in ventricular conduction delays and ventricular ectopic beats.

6. QT interval: This interval is measured from the start of the QRS complex to the start of the T wave. In the normal adult it should be between 0.33 and 0.43 seconds.

- Prolonged QT interval in excess of 0.45 seconds is associated with ventricular arrhythmia, syncope, and sudden death.
- Shortened QT interval may be due to hypercalcaemia or digoxin toxicity.

7. ST segment: These represent a baseline between QRS and T. Changes in the ST segment are often associated with cardiac pathology:

- ST depression:
  - Indicates myocardial ischaemia
  - May be associated with the discomfort of angina
  - Rest leads to a reversal
  - Not a sign of infarction
  - May be caused by hypokalemia
- ST elevation:
  - An upwardly convex and elevated ST segment indicates acute myocardial infarction or variant (Prinzmetal's) angina; the affected leads indicate the area of affected myocardium.
  - An upwardly concave, elevated, and widespread ST segment indicates pericarditis.
  - ST reciprocal change: Reciprocal change describes the phenomenon where ST depression observed in leads opposite an infarct zone is caused by the infarct and do not indicate remote ischemia.

8. T waves: These represent repolarization of the heart, and undergo temporary or permanent change secondary to cardiac conditions.

■ T wave inversion: T wave inversion is a feature of myocardial infarction and angina.

   ● In ventricular hypertrophy, there may be T wave inversion in the leads that look at the respective ventricle (i.e., V5, V6, II, and VL looking at the left ventricle; and V1, V2, and V3 looking at the right ventricle).

   ● Digoxin administration causes T wave inversion, particularly with sloping depression of the ST segment.

■ **Tall T waves**: T waves may be lengthened or made taller by electrolyte imbalances, especially hyperkalemia.

■ **Small or flattened T waves:** These may be caused by: ischemia; thick chest wall, or emphysema; pericardial effusion; cardiomyopathy or myocarditis; constrictive pericarditis; hypothyroidism; hypoadrenalism; hypokalemia; and hypocalcemia.

MYOCARDIAL INFARCTION AND ISCHEMIA

3. How is chest pain managed?

Source

NPLEX
MCCQE
USMLE

Chest Pain Management: In primary practice (as well as on NPLEX II), the first task when a patient complains of chest pain is to make sure it is not due a life-threatening condition. Rule out myocardial infarctions (MI) and myocardial ischemia (angina) as causative factors for the patient's complaints. An MI (heart attack) is never treated in an outpatient facility, be it allopathic or naturopathic.

Age under 40: A patient under the age of 40 with no known heart disease, strong family history, or multiple risk factors for coronary artery disease (CAD) is unlikely to have an MI.

Risk Factors: Physically fit patients, consuming a healthy diet, who are without cardiac risk factors and whose HDL is high, are not likely to have heart attacks.

Character of Pain: The pain associated with MI is usually neither sharp nor well localized. If the pain is reproducible on chest palpation, the cause is in the chest wall. Additionally, if the pain is related to certain foods or eating habits, it is usually gastroesophageal in origin.

■ Notwithstanding, many primary care providers still opt for an ECG and possibly one or more cardiac enzyme assessments (such as Creatine Kinase–MB fraction, troponin I, or Lactate Dehydrogenase) to make sure that a heart attack has not occurred.

4. What findings on ECG should make you suspect an MI?

Source

NPLEX
MCCQE
USMLE

ECG Signs of MI:

■ Flipped or flattened T waves

■ ST segment elevation (ST depression = ischemia, while elevation = injury)

- Early segmental development of significant Q waves
- With these readings → Call an ambulance to take patient to ER immediately.

Source

NPLEX
MCCQE
USMLE

5. What is the character of pain in MI?

MI Pain Characteristics:
- Crushing or pressure sensation.
- Poorly localized substernal pain that may radiate to shoulder (particularly in men), arm, or jaw.
- Lasts for at least half an hour and is not reproducible by palpation.
- Pain is relieved by nitroglycerin in angina but not in MI (since the damage of infarction is irreversible).
- 25% of MIs are without chest pain, especially in patients with diabetic neuropathy. Instead there is CHF, shock, or confusion. This is often seen in geriatric patients

Source

NPLEX
MCCQE
USMLE

6. What other clinical findings would suggest a MI?

Other MI Signs and Symptoms:
- Diaphoresis
- Anxiety
- Tachycardia
- Tachypnea
- Paleness
- Nausea and vomiting
- A large MI may cause CHF, with secondary distention of neck veins and bilateral pulmonary rales (in absence of pneumonia symptoms); S3 or S4 heart sound; new murmurs; hypotension and/or shock.

Source

NPLEX
MCCQE
USMLE

7. What characteristics of the patient history indicate a diagnosis of MI?

Risk Factors:
- History of angina
- Previous chest pains
- Murmurs; arrhythmias
- Risk factors for coronary artery disease (CAD)
- Hypertension
- Diabetes
- Medications, such as digoxin, furosemide, or cholesterol lowering drugs (this means that patients have CAD risk factors)

Source

NPLEX
MCCQE
USMLE

8. What are the common noncardiac causes of chest pain?

Non-Cardiac Causes of Chest Pain:
- Gastroesophageal reflux disease (GERD) and peptic ulcer disease (PUD): There is usually a relation to certain foods (spicy, chocolate), smoking, or lying down. Pain is relieved with antacids or milk. Patient's with PUD usually test positive for *Helicobacter pylori.*
- Chest wall pain: Costochondritis and bruised or broken ribs cause well-localized and reproducible pain on chest wall palpation.
- Esophageal problems: Achalasia or esophageal spasms are difficult differential diagnoses. One has to rely on negative findings of the MI work-up and often refer for barium swallow or esophageal manometry.

- Pericarditis: This is easier to ascertain because there is usually a viral upper respiratory infection (URI) prodrome; ECG shows ST elevation; erythrocyte sedimentation rate (ESR) is elevated; and a low grade fever is present. Sitting forward often relieves this type of pain.
- Pneumonia: This is even easier to differentiate because patients will have pleuritic pain (see Pulmonology module), cough, fever, and/or sputum production.
- Aortic dissection: Memorize the following: STAR (Severe, Tearing, And Ripping) pain that may radiate to the back (rule out pancreatitis).
- There is strong association with Marfan's syndrome (tall, thin, double-jointed patients) and blunt chest traumas.

9. What is stable angina and how is it managed?

Source

NPLEX
MCCQE
USMLE

Angina: strictly means that the heart is temporarily not getting enough oxygen.

Stable Angina Signs and Symptoms:
- Pain on exertion that is relieved by lying down and resting for a while.
- Pain is described as a squeeze or pressure behind the chest wall.
- Pain may radiate to shoulders, neck, or jaw.
- Pain lasts for less than 20 minutes and is relieved by nitroglycerin.
- Often shortness of breath, diaphoresis, and or nausea.

Management:
- Prudent naturopathic management would follow best practices (above) and opt for an ECG and possibly one or more cardiac enzyme assessments (such as Creatine Kinase–MB fraction, troponin I, or Lactate Dehydrogenase) to make sure that an MI has not occurred.
- ECG will not be remarkable unless performed during the acute attack. Everything else will be WNL.

10. What is unstable angina?

Source

NPLEX
MCCQE
USMLE

Unstable Angina: a worsening of the condition of stable angina (i.e., frequency is increased).

Signs and Symptoms:
- Enzymes will be normal, but the ECG will show ST depression.
- Pain will last longer than 20 minutes, and will not be relieved by nitroglycerin.
- Pain will often begin at rest.
- If these signs and symptoms are present → Refer to ER.

11. What is variant or Prinzmetal's angina?

Source

NPLEX
MCCQE
USMLE

Variant or Prinzmetal Angina: rare condition, caused by coronary artery spasm.

Signs and Symptoms:
- Onset not related to exertion
- Normal enzymes
- ST elevation
- Responds to nitroglycerin.

Treatment: This is conventionally treated with calcium channel blockers to reduce arterial spasms. → Refer to GP or ER.

Source

NPLEX

12. What is the first-line naturopathic treatment for stable angina?

Naturopathic Treatments for Stable Angina

1. Minimize obstacles to healing
- Lifestyle: Ideally, no smoking, alcohol, or caffeine. Implement a medically supervised aerobic exercise plan (start with short walks).
- Stress: Stress management (relaxation/yoga/Qi gong/behavioral therapy) 30 minutes 3X per week.
- Diet: Reduce or eliminate saturated fats, hydrogenated oils, cholesterol, fried foods, simple carbohydrates, and food sensitivities. Increase consumption of fiber, onions, garlic, vegetables, and cold-water fish.
- Risk factors: Address underlying hypertension, diabetes, or obesity if applicable.

2. Clinical nutrition
- Coenzyme Q10: 150-300 mg q.d. Reduces frequency of angina by 53%; increases exercise tolerance.
- L-carnitine: 500 mg t.i.d. Heart ischemia induces its deficiency; improves angina; and allows myocardium to be more efficient in oxygen utilization.
- Magnesium citrate: 200-400 mg t.i.d. Dilates coronary arterioles; improves myocardial energy production; reduces peripheral vascular resistance. S/E: osmotic diarrhea with higher doses.

3. Botanical medicine
- *Crataegus oxyacantha:* "solid extract" 100-250 mg (standardized to 10% procyanidin content) t.i.d. Excellent cardiac tonic; interacts with enzymes to enhance myocardial contractility.
- *Ammi visnaga:* 100 mg (standardized to 12% khellin content). Effective at relieving angina symptoms; similar in action to calcium channel blockers. S/E: may cause nausea and vomiting.

Pizzorno, 1999

HEART MURMURS

13. What are functional heart murmurs?

Functional Heart Murmurs: only systolic murmurs (you would be able to tell if you are taking the pulse at the same time) may be functional or flow murmurs.

Signs and Symptoms:
- Grade 2/6 (slight) systolic murmur over the aortic area.
- No chest pain, dyspnea, syncope, cyanosis, or edema.
- Normal chest radiograph and ECG results.
- Usually no other remarkable physical findings or positive family history for cardiac disease.

Management: This is a finding of no significance, which you will need to explain carefully to the concerned patient.

14. Which adventitious heart sounds are considered normal?

Normal Heart Sounds: Heart murmurs are exhibited by almost everyone sometime during their life. As a general guideline, those murmurs occurring without any evidence of cardiovascular abnormality are considered innocent normal variants. Murmurs are classified based on their timing and duration:
- Normal murmurs include functional systolic murmurs of children and young adults; mammary soufflé late in pregnancy and during lactation; and aortic systolic murmur of older age.
- S2 physiologic splitting on inhalation is considered benign or normal.

15. What are common abnormal heart sounds?

COMMON ABNORMAL HEART SOUNDS

Auscultation	Other Findings	Diagnosis
Mid systolic click (usually) + late systolic murmur	Squatting *decreases* murmur, while valsalva increases it.	Mitral valve prolapse
Harsh systolic murmurs heard over aortic area that radiates to carotids.	Squatting *increases* murmur, while valsalva decreases it. Left ventricular hypertrophy, angina, heart failure, and syncope.	Aortic valve stenosis
Pan-systolic murmur that radiates to axilla	Left ventricular hypertrophy, pulmonary hypertension.	Mitral regurgitation

Auscultation	Other Findings	Diagnosis
Early diastolic murmur and S3 sound (resembles the rhythm of 'Tenn-es-see'); best heard at the apex.	Left ventricular hypertrophy and dilation.	Aortic regurgitation
Late diastolic murmur and opening snap; best heard at the apex.	Atrial fibrillation, pulmonary hypertension.	Mitral valve stenosis
S4 sound (resembles the rhythm of 'Ken-tucky'); heard just before S1.	Old age, increased resistance to ventricular filling.	Atrial Gallop

■ It is good practice to take carotid pulse while listening to heart sounds. Murmurs that occur during the pulse are systolic and vice versa. S1 (LUB sound that is best heard on the right of sternum) is made when the AV valves close at the beginning of systole. S2 (DUB sound that is best heard on the left of sternum) is made when semilunar valves (aortic and pulmonic) close at the end of systole.

Source

NPLEX
MCCQE
USMLE

16. What is the general guideline for endocarditis prophylaxis?

Endocarditis: Antimicrobial prophylaxis is considered when a patient has a known valve disease or prosthetic valves and is scheduled for surgery (dental procedures too). The idea is simple – destroy the *Staph. aureus* & *epidermidis* and *Streptococcus viridans* before the autoimmune cascade starts (again).

THROMBOSIS

Source

17. What are the risk factors for deep venous thrombosis (DVT)?

NPLEX
MCCQE
USMLE

Deep Venus Thrombosis Risk Factors:
1. Surgery (orthopedic, pelvic, or abdominal)
2. Malignancy
3. Immobilization
4. Pregnancy
5. BCPs
6. Deficiencies in anticlotting factors (e.g, antithrombin III)

Source

18. What is the clinical presentation of DVT?

NPLEX
MCCQE
USMLE

DVT Signs and Symptoms:
■ Hallmark is unilateral leg swelling (pitting edema), intermittent claudication, pain and/or Homan's sign (in only 30% of DVT cases).
■ Palpable cords imply superficial thrombophlebitis but not DVT.

Diagnosis:
■ Recommended diagnostic test remains Doppler ultrasound or impedance plethysmography of leg veins.

- When the diagnosis is not clear, the invasive venography is resorted to.
- If DDx edema → Refer to ER if you suspect DVT.

19. Can superficial thrombophlebitis cause pulmonary embolism (PE)?

Source

NPLEX
MCCQE
USMLE

Superficial Thrombophlebitis: Superficial thrombophlebitis (palpable clot cords + erthyma + edema + pain) is localized to superficial veins and is not considered a cause of pulmonary embolism.

Treatment:
- Naturopathic treatment and pressure stockings are effective at controlling or reversing the condition.
- Conventional treatment usually involves NSAIDs.

20. What is the prognosis of DVTs?

Source

NPLEX
MCCQE
USMLE

DVT Prognosis: DVT can cause pulmonary embolism (PE) and ascending thrombosis, requiring systemic anticoagulation therapy.

Treatment:
- IV Heparin is used to initiate treatment, then oral warfarin is used for at least 3 months.
- Naturopathic treatments may be used as adjunct or alternative treatment after the condition has stabilized.

STROKE

21. Can DVT lead to a stroke?

Source

NPLEX
MCCQE
USMLE

DVT and PE: DVT can cause PE, but not stroke, because lung arterioles will act as a filter for circulating emboli. However, in the extremely rare occasion that a patient also has a patent foramen ovale or ventricular-septal defect, this argument would not hold true.

22. What are the symptoms and causes of PE?

Source

NPLEX
MCCQE
USMLE

PE Signs and Symptoms:
- Classical presentation is sudden shortness of breath (due to loss of alveolar gas exchange), tachypnea (to compensate for the loss), and chest pain. → Refer to ER immediately.
- May exacerbate into lung infarction with hemoptysis, hypotension, or death.
- Ventilation/perfusion scan will show the area of diminished blood flow.
- Chest X-ray (CXR) rarely shows peripheral pleural opacities.

Causes:
- PE may follow DVT, delivery, or long-bone fractures.
- Divers who ascend too quickly (or who take flights a couple of hours after a series of deep dives) may also develop multiple air embolism (bends) as well as PE. The pulmonary arterioles act as filter to circulating emboli (e.g., thrombi, amniotic fluid, fat, or air).

CONGESTIVE HEART FAILURE

Source

NPLEX
MCCQE
USMLE

23. What are the hallmarks of congestive heart failure (CHF)?

Congestive Heart Failure Signs and Symptoms:
- Fatigue dyspnea
- Ventricular hypertrophy (ECG)
- Cardiomegaly (CXR)
- S3 or S4 sounds on cardiac physical examination

Source

NPLEX
MCCQE
USMLE

24. How are right and left CHF distinguished?

RIGHT VS. LEFT VENTRICULAR FAILURE

Right Ventricular Failure

Peripheral edema; jugular venous distension; hepatomegaly; ascites; and /or cor pulmonale

Left Ventricular Failure

Orthopnea (sleeps on more than one pillow or sitting up); nocturnal dyspnea; and bilateral rales over base of lungs.

- In practice, it is usually both ventricles that are failing.

25. How is CHF classified and treated?

Acute CHF: an abrupt disruption of circulation and ventilation. The common example is extensive myocardial infarction secondary to coronary atherosclerotic artery disease (CAAD).

Chronic CHF:
There are four stages of CHF, according to the New York Heart Association:
- Stage I: Symptom free at rest
- Stage II: Symptom free at rest + dyspnea on moderate physical exertion
- Stage III: Symptom free at rest + dyspnea on minor physical exertion
- Stage IV: Symptoms exist at rest (peripheral edema and dyspnea)

Conventional Treatment: Acute CHF is commonly treated on an inpatient basis with oxygen, diuretics, and positive inotropes. Chronic CHF is treated on an outpatient basis with sodium restriction; ACE inhibitors (first-line agents that reduce mortality rates); and diuretics. Advanced cases are treated with digoxin and vasodilators.

Naturopathic Treatment: Recommended for Stage I and II, but only as adjunctive therapy for Stage III and IV.

26. What is the first-line naturopathic treatment for chronic CHF?

Source

NPLEX
MCCQE
USMLE

Naturopathic Treatment for CHF Stage I and II

Approach: Naturopathic treatment is recommended for Stage I and II, but only as adjunctive therapy for Stage III and IV.

1. Address underlying cause
- Reduce hypertension.
- Lose weight if obese.
- Implement a medically supervised aerobic exercise plan (start with short walks).

2. Dietary measures
- Encourage a healthy diet.
- Emphasize whole plant foods.
- Restrict sodium intake.
- Avoid refined, processed, and fatty foods.

3. Clinical nutrition
- L-carnitine: 300-500 mg t.i.d. for at least 6 months. Improves exercise tolerance by 16% to 25% and ventricular ejection fraction by 12% to 13%.
- Coenzyme Q10: 150-300 mg q.d. for at least 3 months. Clinical studies documented significant efficacy in improving CHF symptoms and quality of life.
- Assess and treat deficiencies in magnesium, thiamine, and arginine.

Pizzorno, 1999

4. Botanical medicine
- *Crataegus oxyacantha:* 'solid extract' 100-250 mg (standardized to 10% procyanidin content) t.i.d. Used alone for early stages; combine with conventional treatment for advanced stages. Improves cardiac efficiency and work capacity.
- *Selenicerius grandifloris* (positive inotropic and negative chronotropic, Nervine) and *Convallaria majalis* (considered as a safer alternative to Digitalis) should be considered.

Saunders, 2000

COR PULMONALE

Source

NPLEX
MCCQE
USMLE

27. What is the definition and presentation of cor pulmonale?

Cor pulmonale: right ventricular enlargement secondary to primary lung disease (the ventricles try to increase output to overcome the imposed resistance).

Causes:
- COPD and PE
- Other less common causes include primary pulmonary hypertension and sleep apnea.
- Clinical findings may include tachypnea, cyanosis, clubbing, parasternal heave, and distinct S4 sound (over right side) in addition to signs of pulmonary disease.

CARDIOMYOPATHY

Source

NPLEX
MCCQE
USMLE

28. What is a cardiomyopathy? How is it classified?

Cardiomyopathy: a term used to denote a group of primary myocardial diseases that cannot be related to coronary atherosclerosis, hypertension, valvular disease, infections, or congenital heart disease. Cardiomyopathies are considered diseases for which heart transplantation and surgical repair are recommended.

Classifications: Cardiomyopathies are classified on the basis of clinical and pathological features into three groups:
- Dilated
- Hypertrophic
- Restrictive

The most common is dilated cardiomyopathy, a systolic disorder, where progressive heart failure is caused by hypertrophy and dilation of all four chambers of the heart. This is mostly an idiopathic condition, but a minority of cases may be due to alcohol, viral myocarditis, and drugs, such as doxorubicin.

Source

NPLEX
MCCQE
USMLE

29. What are the causes of restrictive and constrictive pericarditis?

Restrictive Pericarditis: amyloidosis, sarcoidosis, hemochromatosis, and myocardial fibroelastosis may lead to restrictive cardiomyopathy. These are diagnosed by histological examination of a ventricular biopsy.

Constrictive Pericarditis: characterized by dense fibrous connective tissue that encases the heart (restricting diastolic expansion). This can be corrected by removing the abnormal pericardium. It is often idiopathic, but may follow suppurative or caseous pericarditis. Clinical signs will include a 'pericardial knock' (an early diastolic sound that represents the sudden cessation of ventricular diastolic filling imposed by the rigid pericardial sac) or S4 sound. Of course, a ventricular biopsy will not indicate any pathology.

31. Which cardiomyopathy is likely in a young athlete who passes out while exercising?

Source

NPLEX
MCCQE
USMLE

Hypertrophic Cardiomyopathy: often an autosomal dominant trait, this is an idiopathic condition, where ventricular hypertrophy reduces cardiac output (diastolic dysfunction). This condition is treated conventionally with beta-blockers and calcium-channel-blockers to allow the ventricles more time to fill. Strenuous exercise should be avoided in such cases.

CARDIAC ARRHYTHMIA

32. What ECG abnormalities indicate cardiac arrhythmias?

Normal ECG "lead II" tracing for comparison:
- Normal rhythm, called sinus rhythm, is paced from the sinoatrial (SA) node.
- The heart rate for normal sinus rhythm is from 60 to 100 beats per minute.
- Sinus rhythms show a normally oriented P wave before each QRS complex.

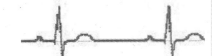

Sinus Tachycardia:
- Normal P, QRS, T, rate > 100.
- Usually no treatment is recommended.
- Treat the cause.

Sinus Bradycardia:
- Normal P, QRS, T, rate < 60.
- Usually not treated.
- Atropine is used is used in severe and symptomatic cases.

Premature Ventricular Contractions (PVCs):
- Wide QRS, unrelated to P wave.
- Usually not treated.
- Lidocaine is used in severe and symptomatic cases.

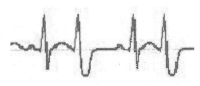

Ventricular Tachycardia (VTAC):
- Bizarre, wide QRS, no P wave, rate >100.
- Emergency condition.
- Immediate Lidocaine administration is needed.

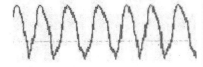

Ventricular Fibrillation (VFIB):
- Chaotic waves.
- Emergency condition.
- Defibrillate immediately.

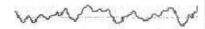

Premature Atrial Contraction (PAC):
- Premature P wave, irregular P-P interval.

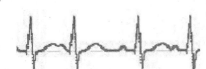

First-degree Heart Block:
■ Long PR interval.
■ No medical treatment is recommended.
■ Beta-blockers and calcium-channel-blockers are contraindicated.

Second-degree Heart Block:
■ Mobitz type I: increasing PR interval until a QRS complex is dropped.
■ Usually benign but pacemaker or atropine if severe.
■ Mobitz type II: multiple P waves, but when beats are conducted PR intervals are unvarying (pacemaker).

Third-degree Heart Block / with Idoiventricular (escape) Rhythm:
■ Bizarre QRS, slow rate 20-40.

Hypercalcemia:
■ Short/absent ST segment.

Hyperkalemia:
■ Tent-shaped T wave.

Digitalis effect:
■ Scooping ST segment

Asystole:
■ Flatline.

Atrial fibrillation/flutter: random electrical activity in the atrium, with ventricular beats occurring irregularly. Acute cases are 'cardioverted' with quinidine or direct current cardioversion. Chronic cases need effective anticoagulation (since atria are acting like egg-beaters), then cardioversion. Naturopathic treatment is recommended to prevent relapses. Relapses require digoxin and sustained warfarin.

Source

MCCQE
USMLE

32. What endocrine disease is suggested in sinus tachycardia or atrial fibrillation?

Hyperthyroidism or Thyroid Storm: may be indicated with presentation of sinus tachycardia or atrial fibrillation.

Source

NPLEX
MCCQE
USMLE

33. How does Wolf-Parkinson-White (WPW) syndrome present?

Wolf-Parkinson-White Syndrome: a subtype of atrial flutter. The classical example is a child who becomes dizzy/SOB/syncope after playing, and then recovers completely with no lasting effects.

Signs and Symptoms:
■ Atrial flutter is a fairly organized back-and-forth motion of electricity within the atria.
■ The rate of atrial depolarization is typically 300 beats per minute.
■ Usually every other atrial beat is blocked in the AV node, resulting in a typical ventricular rate of 150.
■ With increasing AV block, the rate may slow to 50, 75, or 100 (if the rate is regular, it will be some fraction of 300).
■ In WPW syndrome, atrial beats will be conducted 1:1, resulting in a ventricular rate of 300.

CONGENITAL HEART DEFECTS

34. What are the common congenital heart defects?

Source

NPLEX
MCCQE
USMLE

COMMON CONGENITAL HEART DEFECTS

Defect	Characteristics
Ventricular septal defect (VSD)	Most common heart defect. Pan-systolic murmurs are heard next top sternum. Most cases will resolve without intervention. Associated with Down syndrome, fetal alcohol syndrome, and maternal toxoplasma, rubella, cytomegalovirus, or herpes infections.
Tetralogy of Fallot	Most common cyanotic heart defect. Tetra=four: VSD, RVH, pulmonary stenosis, and overriding aorta. It is important to note that children with this condition often squat after exertion. This habitual squatting is termed tet spells.
Patent ductus arteriosus	Constant 'machine-like' murmur in upper left sternal border. Dyspnea and possible CHF. The defect needs to be closed – indomethacin (sclerosing agent) and/or surgery are recommended. Associated with maternal rubella infection.
Atrial septal defect	Asymptomatic until adulthood. Fixed split S2 and palpitations. Most atrial defects do not require surgical correction.
Coarctation of the aorta	Upper extremity hypertension only. Systolic bruit over upper/mid back. Associated with Turner's syndrome.

PEDIATRIC CONDITIONS

Source

NPLEX

35. What are normal heart rates for children?

Normal Pediatric Vital Signs:

- Heart rates >100 are normal.
- Respiratory rates >20 are normal.
- Consult developmental charts for age-specific vital sign parameters.

Source

NPLEX
MCCQE
USMLE

36. What changes occur in the circulation as a neonate adapts to extrauterine life?

Circulation at Birth:

1. First breaths inflate the lungs → decreased pulmonary resistance → enables blood flow to pulmonary arteries (instead of the monopoly that the ductus arteriosus had thus far).
2. Clamping of the umbilical cord → increases left ventricular pressure → functional closure of foramen ovale.
3. The resulting increased oxygenation of the blood → inhibits prostaglandin production in the ductus arteriosus → gradual atresia of the ductus arteriosus.

HYPERTENSION

Source

NPLEX
MCCQE
USMLE

37. What is hypertension?

Hypertension:

- Blood pressure average >140/90 mmHg, measured on *two or more separate occasions taken over a period 4 weeks* (two measurement rule). It follows that you should not initiate treatment until you have followed this two-measurement rule.
- Isolated elevation of either systolic or diastolic also warrants this diagnosis. For example, 145/60 mmHg and 115/95 mmHg.
- The most common cause of death among untreated patients of hypertension is the same as for the general population – coronary artery disease (CAD).

DIAGNOSTIC GRADES AND STAGES:

Grading	Staging	Persistent systolic or diastolic blood pressure
Optimal	Normal	<134/84
High-Normal	Stage 0	135-139/85-89
Mild	Stage 1	140-159/90-104
Moderate	Stage 2	160-179/105- 114
Severe	Stage 3	180-209/115-119
Urgent	N/A	>210/ 120

- Individuals with high-normal BP are at increased risk for major cardiovascular events (coronary, cerebral, and renal disease as well), according to the Framingham Heart Study.
- Hypertension is the number-one modifiable risk factor for strokes and is a major risk factor for coronary, cerebral, and renal disease. Lowering BP significantly decreases incidence of heart disease, myocardial infarctions, atherosclerosis, renal failure, and dissecting aortic aneurysms.

38. Are there any exceptions to the two-measurement rule?

Source

MCCQE
USMLE

Two-Measurement Rule: The reason for adopting the two-measurement rule is to account for normal daily fluctuations in BP (around 30 mmHg). However, most resources indicate exceptions to this rule:
- If BP is >210/120 or if end organ damage is present (see below).
- During pregnancy, where pre-eclampsia *may* be the cause of hypertension. Presentations suggestive of pre-eclampsia (proteinuria, edema, and progressive hypertension in a pregnant female) warrant prompt referral to an OB/GYN specialist for primary management.

39. What is a hypertensive urgency versus a hypertensive emergency?

Source

MCCQE
USMLE

Hypertensive *urgency:* BP > 210/120 mmHg without symptoms.

Hypertensive *emergency***:** BP > 210/120 mmHg with symptoms of end-organ damage. Examples include: acute left ventricular failure, chest pain or angina, MI, encephalopathy (headaches, confusion, papilledema, mental status change, vomiting, blurry vision, dizziness, and/or seizures), and acute renal failure.

Treatment: Both conditions require immediate treatment, but the latter is more worrisome. Treatment usually involves one of the following medications:
- Nitroprusside
- Nitroglycerin
- Labetalol
- Diazoxide

40. What causes hypertension?

Source

USMLE
NPLEX
MCCQE

Hypertension Causes:
- Approximately 90% to 95% of hypertension cases are considered idiopathic, multifactorial, or essential hypertension.
- The remaining 5% to 10% are due to secondary causes.
- Approximately 8% may have underlying primary aldosteronism.

Source

MCCQE
USMLE

41. What are the most common secondary causes of hypertension?

SECONDARY CAUSES OF HYPERTENSION

Young men	Excessive alcohol intake (stop using alcohol) if it causes hypertension.
Young women	Birth control pills (stop using the pill) if it causes hypertension.
Both genders	Renal artery stenosis (listen for bruit, request arteriogram for diagnosis). Treatment is simple balloon dilatation.
Elderly	Renal artery stenosis from atherosclerosis (diagnose as above).

Source

MCCQE
USMLE

42. What are other less common causes of secondary hypertension?

Pheochromocytoma: wild swings in blood pressure with diaphoresis and confusion. A history of the five Ps (high BP, head pain, palpitations, perspiration, and pallor). Confirm with testing 24-hour urine sample for catecholamine degradation products (i.e., metanephrines, venyl mandelic acid, and homovallinic acid).

Polycystic kidney disease: flank mass, family history (autosomal dominant pedigree), elevated serum creatinine, and blood urea nitrogen (BUN).

Cushing's syndrome: moon face, buffalo hump, central obesity, peripheral wasting. Test 24-hour urine sample for free cortisol or request a dexamethasone suppression test.

Conn's syndrome: aldosterone secreting adrenal tumor. Look for high levels of aldosterone, low renin, hypokalemia, metabolic alkalosis, and/or adrenal mass on CT.

Coarctation of the aorta: hypertension only in upper extremities, unequal pulses, radiofemoral delay, and rib notching on CXR (associated with Turner's syndrome). Angiography establishes this diagnosis.

Renal failure: from any cause. In children, be alert for post streptococcal glomerulonephritis.

Source

MCCQE
USMLE

43. How often should you screen for hypertension?

Hypertension Screening:
- Ideally, everyone should be screened every year starting at the age of 18.

Source

MCCQE
USMLE

44. What laboratory evaluations should be ordered in every hypertension diagnosis?

Hypertension Work-up:
1. Urinalysis for protein, glucose, and blood.
2. Assessment of serum levels of creatinine, potassium, glucose, calcium, and uric acid.
3. Lipid profile.
4. ECG to exclude coronary artery disease (CAD), left ventricular hypertrophy (LVH), and myocardial deterioration.

45. What is the first-line treatment for non-urgent hypertension?

First-line Treatment for Nonurgent Hypertension:
- All resources recommend that the first-line treatment should always be lifestyle modifications.
- Pharmaceutical and /or botanical medications should *only* be started after a 3 to 6 month trial of lifestyle modifications.

Lifestyle Modifications:

- Stop alcohol and tobacco consumption.
- Start the Dietary Approaches to Stop Hypertension (DASH) diet:
  - Eat a menu consisting of low-fat dairy, reduced saturated fat, high-fiber whole foods, increased fruits, vegetables, and nuts (expect average reduction of 11.4 mmHg systolic and 5.5 mmHg diastolic in first 11 weeks).
- Restrict salt and caffeine intake.
- Reduce weight (modest loss of weight of 10% or so can normalize blood pressure on its own).
- Decrease stress.
- Increase physical exercise (aerobic activity for 30 to 40 minutes at 70% of patient's Heart Rate Maximum (HRMAX) at least three times per week.

46. What are the first-line medications for the treatment of hypertension?

Source

USMLE
MCCQE
CPS

Harrison

JNC VI

First-line Medications for Treating Hypertension: Four classes of drugs are used as first-line therapy. Choice depends on the individual patient and the medical presentation.
1. Diuretics (Thiazide, Loop, or Potassium sparing)
2. Beta adrenergic receptor blockers (beta-blockers or BB)
3. Angiotensin converting enzyme inhibitors (ACE inhibitors or ACI)
4. Calcium antagonists

Class	Examples	Specific Indications	Side Effects and Contraindications
Diuretics	Hydrochlorothiazide (Esidrix), Furosemide (Lasix), spironolactone (Aldactone), combination diuretics (Diazide)	Elderly, Black; CHF, central or peripheral edema.	S/E electrolyte imbalance (low serum potassium, calcium, magnesium), B vitamins depletion; C/I pregnancy, gout, and osteoporosis.
Beta Blockers	Atenolol (Tenormin), Acebutolol (Sectral), Metoprolol (Lopressor), Propranolol (Inderal)	Young, Caucasian; CHF, angina, previous MI, senile tremor, tachycardia and migraines.	C/I in diabetes (suppress symptoms of hypoglycemia), asthma, COPD, pregnancy, peripheral arterial disease (claudication), any heart block.

Class	Examples	Specific Indications	Side Effects and Contraindications
ACE Inhibitors	Captopril (Capoten) Enalapril (Vasotec) Lisinopril (Zestril) Ramipril (Altace)	Young, Caucasian; CHF, diabetes; impotence with other hypertension medications.	S/E electrolyte imbalance, neutropenia; C/I pregnancy, renovascular hypertension (may case acute renal failure).
Calcium Antagonists	Verapamil (Isopten) Diltiazim (Cardizem) Nifidepine (Adalat) Ailodipine (Norvasc)	Elderly, Black; angina, migraines, arrhythmias, tachycardia, Raynaud's syndrome, peripheral arterial disease.	C/I heart block (verapamil or diltiazim only), sick sinus syndrome, pregnancy.

- Treatment with a diuretic or a beta-blocker is the first-line pharmacologic strategy recommended by the Joint National Committee VI because they are the only agents that have been shown in clinical trials to reduce mortality.
- Angiotensin-converting enzyme (ACE) inhibitors are first-line agents for congestive heart failure (they seem to reduce mortality rates).
- In diabetes, ACE inhibitors slow progression to nephropathy and neuropathy.
- Angiotensin receptor blockers (ARB) are used when patients do not tolerate ACIs well (e.g., Losartan Potassium "Cozaar" and Telmisartran "Micardis").

Safety Caution: Hydralazine (Apresoline) and Methyldopa (Aldomet) are considered safe for pregnant women and women of reproductive age, while Labetalol (Normodyne) is gaining acceptance. Remember that magnesium sulfate (or citrate) lowers blood pressure.

Source

Stamler et al, 1987

47. Can patients with hypertension stop their medication by changing their diet?

Hypertension and Diet: According to the 4-year Hypertension Control Program (HCP) trial, 39% of hypertensive patients successfully discontinued their medications when they followed basic nutritional intervention, which was defined as:

- Weight loss
- Salt restriction
- Alcohol avoidance

If these measures are combined with the DASH diet, a physical exercise program, and stress reduction measures, impressive outcomes may be observed. Such modest lifestyle changes can produce substantial cumulative effects.

48. What is the first-line naturopathic botanical treatment for hypertension?

Source

NPLEX
TNM

Mashour,
1998

Saunders,
2000

Silagy and
Niel, 1994

Naturopathic Botanical Treatment for Hypertension

Botanical	Contraindications	Drug Interactions	Side Effects	Overdose
Crataegus spp.	Pregnancy	Potentiates digitalis, convallaria, and cardiac glycosides.	Nausea	Fatigue, diaphoresis, rash on hands
Piscidia erythrina	None known	None known	None known	Bradycardia, hypotension, paralysis
Viscum album	Pregnancy and lactation	Inhibits vasomotor medullary center and vagus nerve. Cholinomimetic	Lightheadedness, orthostatic hypotension	N&V; bradycardia, hypotension, vertigo, liver toxicity, central coma
Leonarus cardiaca	Pregnancy	None known	None known	N/A or None known

- **Allium sativum:** Allicin in *Allium sativum* (garlic) exhibits moderate blood pressure lowering effect in hypertensive patients. The recommended dose is 1-2 cloves of garlic q.d. or 300 mg dried extract t.i.d.

- **Selenicerius grandifloris and Convallaria Majalis:** For stable CHF patients, *Selenicerius grandifloris* (positive inotropic and negative chronotropic, nervine) and *Convallaria majalis* (considered as a safer alternative to digitalis) should also be considered.

49. What is first-line naturopathic clinical nutrition treatment for hypertension?

Naturopathic Clinical Nutrition Treatment for Hypertension

Source

NPLEX

Marz, 1999

Patki, 1990

Maizes, 2002

Ferrara, 2000

Fish oil for the heart, 1987

Digiesi et al, 1992

Nutritional Recommendations	*Rationale*	*Dose (where applicable)*
Restrict sodium and increase potassium intake	As the extracellular level of potassium increases, the sodium-ATP pump is activated, which causes a decrease in intracellular sodium. This is correlated by an average reduction of BP of 12-16 mmHg. Daily potassium intake and/or supplementation of 1.5-3 g decrease blood pressure about half as much as drug therapy.	Ideal K:N ratio is 5:1. Recommend fruits and vegetables relative to dietary intake.
Magnesium Citrate	Magnesium acts as a natural calcium channel blocker in clinical studies. It prevents calcium from entering vascular smooth muscles and subsequent vasoconstriction.	400-800 mg q.d. Watch for osmotic diarrhea.
Olive oil	Monounsaturated fatty acids (MUFA) in olive oil were shown in Ferrara's Mediterranean diet randomized crossover trail to reduce systolic BP by 6-8 mmHg.	Based on dietary intake.
Fish Oil	Approximately 60 clinical trials indicate that omega-3 fatty acids found in fish oils, such as eicosapentaenoic acid (EPA) and docosahexanoic acid (DHA), are effective in lowering BP. Both EPA and DHA inhibit prostaglandin synthesis in platelets and blood vessels, while EPA additionally suppresses production of thromboxane A2. Studies have shown average cumulative reduction of 10 mmHg in BP.	1-5 tsp q.d. (3-6 g q.d.)
Coenzyme Q10	Double-blind studies have indicated statistically significant average blood pressure reduction of 10.6-19.5 mmHg after 4-12 weeks of use. Coenzyme Q10 is especially indicated where there are other cardiovascular complications.	100-300 mg q.d. in divided doses, with meals.

Nutritional Recommendations	Rationale	Dose (where applicable)	
Vitamin C	Retrospective studies show an inverse correlation between vitamin C intake and blood pressure.	Based on dietary intake.	Simon, 1992
Pyridoxine (vitamin B-6)	One small trial indicated modest reduction of both systolic and diastolic BP with oral administration of vitamin B-6.	5 mg/kg q.d.	Ayback et al, 1995
Bonito protein extract	Bonito (a type of tuna) contains an oligopeptide that exhibits significant ACI activity. Three clinical trials indicate blood pressure lowering effect of at least 10 mmHg systolic and 7 mmHg diastolic without the usual ACI side effects.	Typical dose is 500 mg (isolated peptides) t.i.d.	Fujita et al, 2001

50. What are the suggested management plans for hypertension in outpatient clinics?

Mild Hypertension Treatment (systolic BP 140-159 or diastolic 90-99 mm Hg):
1. Rule out secondary causes of hypertension.
2. Perform blood chemistry, urinalysis, lipid profile, and ECG.
3. Implement first-line dietary and lifestyle modifications for 3 to 6 months.
4. After 6 months: Re-evaluate presentation and need for adjunct treatment (clinical nutrition and/or botanical medications) for another 6 months.
5. If condition improves, re-evaluate annually.
6. With no improvement after the above 12-month period, refer to family physician for co-management.

Moderate Hypertension Treatment (systolic BP 160-179 or diastolic 100-109 mm Hg):
1. Rule out secondary causes of hypertension.
2. Perform blood chemistry, urinalysis, lipid profile, and ECG.
3. Implement first-line dietary and lifestyle modifications and adjunct clinical nutrition measures for 3 to 6 months.
4. After 3 to 6 months: Re-evaluate presentation and need for adjunct botanical medications for another 3 months.
5. If condition improves, manage as above.
6. With no improvement after the above 6 to 9 month period, refer to family physician for co-management.

Severe Hypertension Treatment (systolic BP 180-195 or diastolic 110-119 mm Hg):
1. Rule out secondary causes of hypertension.
2. Perform blood chemistry, urinalysis, lipid profile, and ECG.
3. Implement first-line dietary and lifestyle modifications, adjunct clinical nutrition measures, and botanical medications for 1 to 3 months.
4. After 1 to 3 months: Re-evaluate presentation and need for medical treatment.
5. If condition improves, manage as above.

6. With no improvement after the above 1 to 3 month period, refer to family physician for primary management.

Urgent Hypertension Treatment (systolic BP greater than 195 mm Hg or diastolic greater than 120 mm Hg): Refer to inpatient facility or to the emergency department.

Source

NPLEX

Macioca, 2001

Wong et al, 1991

51. From a Traditional Chinese Medicine perspective, what are the differential Zang-Fu syndromes for hypertensive presentations? Do you know how to differentiate among these distinct presentations?

TCM and Hypertension: The following generalization is included to stimulate thought integration, rather than limit one's perception to a selected pathology:

- Liver Fire
- Liver Yang Rising from Yin Deficiency
- Phlegm-Damp stagnation of the Middle Warmer
- Yin and Yang imbalance

A comparative review of Chinese traditional and Western medical approaches to the treatment of mild hypertension has been published, with accounts of controlled trials that address the role of TCM in the management of hypertension.

DISLIPIDEMIA

Contributing author: Philip Rouchotas MSc, ND

Source

NPLEX
MCCQE
USMLE

52. Why are lipid levels important clinically?

Clinical Importance:

- Dyslipidemia (a.k.a. hyperlipidemia, hypercholesterolemia, or 'high chlesterol') is one of the main known modifiable risk factors for atherosclerosis, a systemic inflammatory disease of the vascular system, which accounts for roughly half of the deaths in North America.
- The course of atherosclerosis leads invariably to coronary artery disease (CAD), cerebrovascular disease (CVD), and peripheral vascular disease (PVD).
- Atherosclerosis is the most important cause of permanent disability.

Source

NPLEX

Bugarelli, 2002

53. What are classic risk factors for atherosclerosis and CAD?

Classic Risk Factors: The following risk factors are additive with respect to overall risk of significant atherosclerosis and coronary heart disease. Patients with three or more risk factors have over 700% incidence of CAD compared with similar cohorts. Note that HDL levels > 60 mg/dl negate one risk factor (it is that protective).

- Low HDL < 35mg /dl
- Hypertension
- Diabetes mellitus
- Smoking > 10 cigarettes/day

- Physical inactivity
- Family history of early MI

Bugarelli, 2002

Novel Risk Factors (gaining acceptance):
- Elevated triglycerides
- Low TC:HDL ratio
- Elevated homocysteine
- Elevated C-reactive protein (CRP)
- High serum fibrinogen
- Lipoprotein a (LPa)
- Apoprotein A-1 and B-100 LDL particle size Interleukin 6 (IL-6)

54. What clinical findings would possibly indicate hyperlipidemia?

Source

NPLEX
MCCQE
USMLE

Reliable Clinical Signs of Hyperlipidemia:
- Xanthelasma
- Eruptive and tendinous xanthomas
- Corneal arcus
- Lipemia retinalis (retinal blood vessels appear pink instead of red)
- Obesity

55. How often should you screen for hyperlipidemia?

Hyperlipidemia Screening: No single protocol is universally accepted, but the following practices are the most widely followed:
1. National Cholesterol Education Program (NCEP) recommends comprehensive screening of all adults 20 years and older with a fasting lipoprotein profile (which is total cholesterol, LDL, HDL and TG) every 5 years.
2. US Preventive Health Services Task Force recommends a more reserved screening program:
   - Class A: men 35 years and older and women 45 years and older – screen via testing total cholesterol (TC) and HDL cholesterol every 5 years.
   - Class B: men & women 20 years and older with known risk factors – screen via testing TC and HDL cholesterol every 5 years.
3. Canadian Diabetes Association recommends yearly screening with a full lipoprotein profile for all adults with diabetes.

56. What are lipoproteins?

Source

NPLEX
MCCQE
USMLE

Lipoproteins: lipid transporters, composed of cholesterol (or cholesteryl ester), triglycerides (TG), phospholipids, and apoprotein. The two major classes of lipoproteins are:
- TG-rich: chylomicrons and very low density lipoprotein (VLDL)
- Cholesterol-rich – low density lipoprotein (LDL) and high density lipoprotein (HDL)

57. What is reported on a complete lipid panel?

Source

NPLEX
MCCQE
USMLE

Lipid Panel Report:
- TC value
- LDL-C value

- HDL-C value
- TG value
- TC: HDL-C ratio
- LDL-C : HDL-C ratio

Source

Depres,
2001
Wolfret,
2004

58. Is LDL-C a predictor of disease risk?

LDL-C Risk Factor: LDL-C levels have been reproducibly correlated to increased risk of heart disease, stroke, and death:
- Levels greater than 3.9 mmol/L typically predict increased risk of disease of approximately 50%.
- Current evidence also suggests that a mere 1% decrease in LDL-C is associated with about 2% decrease in risk of coronary heart disease.

Source

USMLE

59. How is LDL cholesterol calculated?

LDL Level Calculation: LDL levels are usually calculated based on other plasma lipids measurements (this is done for economical reasons). After direct measurement is obtained for TC, HDL, and TG, LDL is estimated using the following equation:

$$LDL = TC - (HDL + TG/5)$$

This calculation is accurate, provided TG levels do not exceed 400 mg/dl. LDL levels can also be directly measured if specifically requested, but this is not routinely done in practice.

60. Should patients fast before lipid profile testing?

Pre-test Fasting:
- Although TC and HDL will not be significantly affected by recent food consumption, TG levels will change dramatically.
- Because routine LDL-C is calculated based on TG level, estimation of LDL-C requires a fasting sample.

Source

ATP III,
2004

61. What are the most recent guidelines of the ATP III for lipid-lowering interventions?

ATP III Intervention Guidelines: The Adult Treatment Panel III (ATP) of the National Cholesterol Education Program (NCEP) established management guidelines in 2001, and then revised them in 2004 due to the subsequent reporting of five large clinical intervention trials utilizing statin therapy.

1. Regardless of the method employed (e.g., lifestyle changes, statins, niacin, fibrate), the recommended target of therapy is:

Category	Target LDL - C level
Moderate risk patients	LDL-C < 130mg/dL
High risk patients	LDL-C < 100 mg/dL
Very high risk patients	LDL-C < 70mg/dL

2. Therapeutic lifestyle changes remain an essential component of the treatment of dyslipidemia.

3. Cholesterol-lowering drug therapy is recommended in high-risk patients. This category now includes diabetic individuals. It is also proposed that elderly individuals benefit from lipid lowering therapy regardless of presenting LDL-C levels.

4. Individuals with elevated triglyceride (TG) levels in addition to elevated LDL-C levels are candidates for addition of fibrates to statin therapy.

5. When LDL-lowering drug therapy is employed in high-risk or moderately high-risk persons, it is advised that intensity of therapy be sufficient to achieve at least a 30% to 40% reduction in LDL-C levels.

Intervention Review:

- The NCEP established dietary guidelines as first-line interventions for the management of mild to moderate dyslipidemia in low to moderate risk individuals. The magnitude of efficacy of these interventions has been reproducibly demonstrated as 8% to10% reduction in LDL-C levels.

APT III, 2004

- A recent systematic review summarized 97 human intervention trials which cumulatively included over 137,000 subjects in intervention groups and over 138,000 subjects in placebo groups. Relative risk for overall mortality was as follows; N-3 fatty acids 33% reduced mortality risk; statin 23% reduced mortality risk; niacin 4% reduced mortality risk; fibrates 0% reduced mortality risk.

- Number needed to treat (NNT) for statin was found to be 228. Translation - in order to prevent one death, 228 people needed to be treated with statins for 3.3 years.

- In primary prevention trials, fibrates increased mortality. Number needed to harm (NNTH) was 132. Translation - one additional death occurred for each 132 people taking fibrates for 4.4 years.

62. What is the Portfolio Diet for lowering LDL-C? How does it compare to the NCEP diet and drug intervention?

Source

Jenkins, 2002, 2003

Lamarche et al, 2004

Portfolio Diet: Dr David Jenkins is credited with the creation of the Portfolio diet, which is based on the hypothesis that combining various foods, each independently known to reduce LDL-C levels, would produce a magnitude of efficacy far superior to previous dietary strategies. The Portfolio diet is a meat-free diet (fish is an exception), which also restricts high-fat dairy products, and includes:

- Viscous fibers (e.g., oats, psyllium, okra,eggplant): 20 g per day
- Soy protein (e.g., soy milk, burgers, deli meats): 20 g per day
- Raw almonds: 28 g per day
- Plant sterol fortified margarine: 2000-3000 mg plant sterol per day

Efficacy: Recent studies of the Portfolio diet included three treatment groups. One group received the NCEP diet for cholesterol lowering; the second group received the NCEP diet plus therapeutic dosage of statin medication; and the third group received the Portfolio diet. The interventions have reproducibly demonstrated the following:

Treatment Group	Outcome
NCEP diet	8% reduction in LDL-C levels
NCEP diet plus statin drug	30% reduction in LDL-C levels
Portfolio diet	30% reduction in LDL-C levels

Source

Jenkins, 2002, 2003

Despres et at, 2001

63. What dietary recommendations can further increase the efficacy of the Portfolio Diet?

Portfolio Diet Enhancement: This diet was designed to demonstrate that "foods found in every-day grocery stores could deliver a large magnitude regarding lowering of LDL-C." To demonstrate this critical endpoint, researchers had to limit confounding variables by adhering to the following parameters:

- Subjects were prevented from losing weight by designing diets that are calorically equivalent to their pre-trial diets.
- Subjects were instructed to maintain current levels of physical activity and exercise was not encouraged.
- All aspects of the Portfolio system had to be derived from commonly consumed foods.
- No supplements of any kind were permitted.

Since clinicians are not bound by the above experimental parameters, the following strategies can be easily incorporated to enhance the magnitude of efficacy of the program:

Lakka et al, 2004

Varady et al, 2005

St-Onge et al, 2003

Devaraj et al, 2004
Madigan et al, 2000
Perona et al, 2004
Ferrara et al, 2000

Harris, 1997
Sitori et al, 1998
Stark et al, 2000
GISSI-Pre-venzione, 1999

1. Caloric restriction in any individual presenting with a BMI of greater than 25 (BMI calculated as weight in kilograms divided by height in meters squared). This intervention has demonstrated a reproducible benefit on lipid levels.
2. Low to moderate intensity exercise (like walking). A safe and effective exercise prescription is 50% to 60% of maximum heart rate (maximum heart rate = 220 minus age) four to seven times per week. This intervention has consistently demonstrated a lipid lowering effect.
3. Replace 'plant sterol fortified margarine' with a plant sterol supplement. Dose: 1500 mg per day (500 mg t.i.d., with meals). Sterol supplementation has demonstrated reproducible reduction of 10% to 14% in LDL-C.
4. Eliminating margarine would render the diet an exceptionally low-fat diet (which is known to adversely affect lipid levels). As an alternative, substitute the margarine with two tablespoons of extra virgin olive oil. The oil should be consumed raw. This intervention has been shown to reduce LDL-C levels by approximately 12%. As a side effect, it has been shown to reduce blood pressure and fasting blood glucose in diabetic individuals.
5. Inclusion of a fish oil supplement adds further benefit to the intervention. Fish oil has minimal effects on LDL-C (potentially even increasing LDL-C by 2% to 5%). However, fish oil profoundly decreases TG and significantly increases HDL-C levels. The therapeutic dose of fish oil should be no less than 2000 mg EPA/DHA combined per day. Fish oil should be consumed with meals because this increases absorption by as much as two-fold.

Source

NPLEX
MCCQE
USMLE

Despres, et al, 2001

64. Will these interventions address the more significant concern of TC:HDL-C ratio?

TC:HDL-C Ratio: Elevations of the TC: HDL ratio predict increased incidence of CAD by up to 140%. The most powerful predictor of an elevated TC:HDL-C ratio is being overweight or obese – namely, increased visceral adipose tissue (VAT). Caloric restriction, combined with exercise, results in significant decreases in VAT. Implementing caloric restriction plus exercise directly addresses the underlying cause of an increased TC:HDL-C ratio.

65. What medications are used in the treatment of hyperlipidemia?

Source

NPLEX
MCCQE
CPS
USMLE

HYPERLIPIDEMIA MEDICATIONS
Four classes of drugs are used: HMG-CoA reductase inhibitors, fibrates, bile-acid binding resin, and niacin.

Class and Examples	Mechanism of Action	Efficacy & Side Effects (S/E)
HMG CoA Reductase Inhibitors (Statins): Atrovastatin (Lipitor) Fluvastatin (Lescol) Lovastatin (Mevacor, Altocor) Pravastatin (Pravachol) Simvastatin (Zocor)	Widely used; reversibly inhibit 3-hydroxy-3-methylglutaryl coenzyme A reductase; considered first-line therapy for treating high levels of LDL cholesterol resistant to dietary control.	Can lower cholesterol by up to 35%; shown to decrease mortality risk by up to 23%. S/E: elevation of transaminases (AST, ALT), reversible myositis (with elevation of CPK), GI disturbances, nausea, headache, fatigue, insomnia, and rash.
Fibrates: Bezafibrate (Bezalip) Ciprofibrate (Modalim) Gemfibrozil (Lopid)	Fibric acid derivatives are used in hypertriglyceridemia that is unresponsive to dietary control; stimulate lipoprotein lipase; decrease TG; increase fatty acid oxidation in liver and muscle; and may decrease VLDL production.	Ineffective in patients with elevated elevated cholesterol but normal TG; may lower TG from 20-50% and increase HDL by 10-15%; not shown to decrease mortality risk. S/E: Myositis like syndrome (especially if renal function is impaired), GI disturbances, dermatitis, impotence, headache, dizziness, and blurred vision.
Nicotinic acid: Nicotinic acid (Niacin) Extended-release Nicotinic acid (Niaspan)	Inhibits VLDL production and thus LDL; stimulates lipoprotein lipase; decreases TG; increases HDL cholesterol; and decreases plasma fibrinogen.	Flushing side effect limits niacin's use; may lower TG by 20-50%; has been shown to reduce incidence of CAD; reduces mortality risk by 4%. S/E: flushing, dizziness, headache, palpitations, nausea, vomiting, and pruritus.
Bile-acid-binding resins: Cholestyramine (Questran, Prevalite) Colestipol HCL (Colestid)	Basic anion exchange resins that prevent enterohepatic recirculation of cholesterol by binding bile acids in the intestine; especially useful when high LDL is the main finding.	Not absorbed systemically; have been shown to decrease mortality from CAD; relieve pruritus associated with biliary obstruction. S/E: GI disturbances are common, may aggravate hypertriglyceridemia, and interfere with absorption of fat-soluble vitamins and other drugs.

Source

NPLEX

Hu et al, 1997

Ascerio et al, 1999

Mattson et al, 1985

Bugarelli, 2002
Harper et al, 2001

Rispin et al, 1992
Gore et al, 1994

Hanaki et al, 1993

67. What is the first-line naturopathic clinical nutrition treatment for dyslipidemia?

Naturopathic Clinical Nutrition Treatment for Dyslipedemia

Recommendation	*Rationale*
Avoid eating saturated fatty acids (SFA), trans fatty acids, and undesirable polyunsaturated fatty acids (PUFA)	**Saturated fats:** very high in cholesterol content and consumption. Directly associated with increase risk of heart disease, as well as chronic degenerative diseases. SFA sources are primarily fried foods, animal and dairy products. **Trans-fatty acids**: increase LDL and decrease HDL. Associated with the highest risk of heart disease. TFA sources are margarine (some brands are TFA free), shortening, hydrogenated vegetable oils, snack foods (most brands), and deep fried foods. **Polyunsaturated fatty acids:** typically contain omega-6 fatty acids, tend to lower HDL, and promote production of inflammatory mediators and prostaglandins. Undesirable PUFA sources are corn oil, safflower oil, and cottonseed oil (used in processed food products).
Eat food sources of monounsaturated fatty acids (MUFA) and omega-3 fatty acids	**Monounsaturated fatty acids:** lower total cholesterol and LDL, but do not affect the level of HDL. Food sources are olives, olive oil, avocado, almonds, and cashews. **Omega-3 fatty acids:** promote production of anti-inflammatory prostaglandins, prevent heart disease, and inhibit clot formation. Reduce risk of sudden cardiac death, arrhythmia, and hypertension. Food sources include cold-water fish (e.g., salmon, herring, mackerel, sardines, kippers), flax oil, and walnuts.
Increase fiber consumption	**Fiber:** in 88% of fiber interventional studies, a significant reduction in cholesterol was shown. Oat bran, oat meal, and konjac root glucomannan seem to provide the best cholesterol lowering effect, followed by psyllium and flax.
Supplement with coenzyme Q10 (CoQ10)	**CoQ10:** depleted in patients who are taking statin drugs. CoQ10 an essential compound in mitochondrial oxidative phosphorylation, which has been demonstrated to be a strong lipid antioxidant that helps reduce symptoms of angina and improves exercise tolerance in patients with CHF. The typical supplemental dose is 100-300 mg q.d., in divided doses, with meals.

Recommendation	Rationale	
Supplement with B vitamins	**B vitamins:** A deficiency in folic acid, vitamin B-6, and/or vitamin B-12 impairs the conversion of homocysteine (a derivative of methionine) into cysteine. Elevated plasma homocysteine levels above 10 mcg/dl is an independent risk factor for heart disease and peripheral artery disease. Supplementation with B complex vitamins has been shown to reduce this elevated risk by reversing hyperhomocystenemia.	Ubbink et al, 1993

67. What is the first-line naturopathic botanical medicine treatment for dyslipidemia?

Naturopathic Botanical Medicine Treatment for Dyslipidemia

Botanical	Evidence and Side effects	Dose	
Allium sativum	Consumption of 1-2 cloves of garlic daily has been shown to reduce total cholesterol by 9-12 % and help lower blood pressure in randomized trials. The evidence is not clear regarding prepared garlic supplements.	1-2 cloves q.d. or 300 mg dried extract q.d.	Bierenbaum, 1993
Monascus purpureas	In a large clinical trial, Chinese red yeast rice demonstrated reduction of total cholesterol by 16%, reduction of LDL by 21%; and elevation of HDL by 15 %. Red yeast rice is a traditional Chinese food that exhibits HMG-CoA reductase inhibition, which is partly due to its high content of lovastatin. As with all statins, there is a potential for elevation of liver transaminases, reversible myostis, and depletion of coenzyme Q10.	1.2 g b.i.d.	Heber et al, 1999
Commiphora mukul	Gugulipid is the resin from the Indian myrrh tree. Randomized trials demonstrate a 10-12% reduction in TC, 25% reduction in LDL, 27% reduction in TG, and 16-20% elevation in HDL without significant side effects. There is a theoretical concern with patients on anticoagulants because they may potentiate their effects.	500 mg t.i.d. (5% guggulsterone)	Pizzorno & Murray, 1999
Zingiber officinale	Ginger improves cholesterol levels by limiting cholesterol absorption and exhibits mild antiplatelet activity.	Taken as tea, with food, or as a standardized supplement	Bugarelli, 2002

Examination Board References

NPLEX (II): North American Board of Naturopathic Examiners
North American Board of Naturopathic Examiners (NABNE), Naturopathic Physician Licensing Examination Part II Blueprint and Study Guide. Portland, OR: NABNE, 2005.

USMLE (II): National Board of Medical Examiners
Bouchert A. USMLE Step 2 Secrets. Philadelphia, PA: Hanley & Belfus Inc., 2000.

MCCQE: Medical Council of Canada
Molckovsky A, Pirzada KS (eds.). Review for the Medical Council of Canada Qualification Examination. Toronto, ON: Toronto Notes Medical Publishing, 2004.

Related References

Anonymous. Dietary supplementation with n-3 polyunsaturated fatty acids and vitamin E after myocardial infarction: Results of the GISSI-Prevenzione trial. Gruppo Italiano per lo Studio della Sopravvivenza nell'Infarto miocardico. Lancet. 1999 Aug 7;354(9177):447-55.

Anonymous. Fish oil for the heart. Med lett Drugs Ther 1987;29(731):7-9.

Apple LJ, Moore TJ, Obarzanek E, et al. A clinical trial of the effects of dietary patterns on blood pressure. DASH Collaborative Research Group. N Engl J Med 1997;336:1117-24.

Ascerio A et al. 1999. Trans fatty acids and coronary heart disease. N Engl J Med 340:1994-98.

Ayback M et al. Effect of oral pyridoxine hydrochloride supplementation on arterial blood pressure in patients with essential hypertension. Arzneim Forsch 1995;45:1271-73.

Bugarelli R. Atherosclerosis – Complementary and Alternative Medicine Secrets. Kohatso W (ed.). Philadelphia, PA: Hanley & Belfus Inc., 2002.

Cappuccio FP et al. Does potassium supplementation lower blood pressure? J Hypertension 1991;9:465-73.

Cater NB, Garcia-Garcia AB, Vega GL, Grundy SM. Responsiveness of plasma lipids and lipoproteins to plant stanol esters. Am J Cardiol 2005 Jul 4;96(1A):23D-28D.

Compendium of Pharmaceuticals & Specialties (CPS). Toronto, ON: Canadian Pharmaceutical Association, 2005.

Despres JP, Lemieux I, Dagenais GR, Cantin B, Lamarche B. Evaluation and management of atherogenic dyslipidemia: Beyond low-density lipoprotein cholesterol. CMAJ 2001 Nov 13;165(10):1331-33.

Devaraj S, Jialal I, Vega-Lopez S. Plant sterol-fortified orange juice effectively lowers cholesterol levels in mildly hypercholesterolemic healthy individuals. Arterioscler Thromb Vasc Biol 2004 Mar;24(3):e25-8.

Digiesi V et al. Mechanism of action of Coenzyme Q10 in essential hypertension. Curr Ther Res 1992;51:668-72.

Ferrara L, Raimondi AS, d'Episcopo L, et al. Olive oil and reduced need for antihypertensive medications. Arch Intern Med 2000;160:837-42.

Ferri F. Ferri's Clinical Advisor Instant Diagnosis and Treatment. St. Louis, MO: Mosby Inc, 2004.

Fujita H et al. Effect of ACE: Inhibitory agent, katobishi oligopeptide in hypertensive and borderline hypertensive subjects. Nutr Res 2001;21:1149-58.

Grundy SM, Cleeman JI, Merz CN, Brewer HB Jr, Clark LT, Hunninghake DB, Pasternak RC, Smith SC Jr, Stone NJ; National Heart, Lung, and Blood Institute; American College of Cardiology Foundation; American Heart Association. Implications of recent clinical trials for the National Cholesterol Education Program Adult Treatment Panel III guidelines. Circulation 2004 Jul 13;110(2):227-39.

Gore SR et al. Soluble fiber and serum lipids: A literature review. J Am Diet Assoc 1994;94:425-468.

Hampton JR. ECG Made Easy. New York, NY: Churchill Livingstone, 2001.

Hanaki Y et al. Co-enzyme Q-10 and coronary artery disease. Clin Invest 1993;71(8):S112-S115.

Harper CR et al. The fats of life: The role of omega-3 fatty acids in prevention of coronary heart disease. Arch Intern Med 2001;161:2185-92.

Harris WS. n-3 fatty acids and serum lipoproteins: Human studies. Am J Clin Nutr 1997 May;65(5 Suppl):1645S-1654S.

Harrison. www.harrisonsonline.com

Heber D et al. Cholesterol-lowering effects of a proprietary Chinese red-yeast rice dietary supplement. Am J Clin Nutr 1999;69:231-36.

Hu FB, et al. Dietary fat intake and risk of CAD in women – The Nurses Health Study. N Engl J Med 1997;337:1491-99.

Jenkins DJ, Kendall CW, Faulkner D, Vidgen E, Trautwein EA, Parker TL, Marchie A, Koumbridis G, Lapsley KG, Josse RG, Leiter LA, Connelly PW. A dietary portfolio approach to cholesterol reduction: Combined effects of plant sterols, vegetable proteins, and viscous fibers in hypercholesterolemia. Metabolism 2002 Dec;51(12):1596-1604.

Jenkins DJ, Kendall CW, Marchie A, Faulkner DA, Wong JM, de Souza R, Emam A, Parker TL, Vidgen E, Lapsley KG, Trautwein EA, Josse RG, Leiter LA, Connelly PW. Effects of a dietary portfolio of cholesterol-lowering foods vs lovastatin on serum lipids and C-reactive protein. JAMA 2003 Jul 23;290(4):502-10.

Jenkins DJ, Kendall CW, Marchie A, Faulkner D, Vidgen E, Lapsley KG, Trautwein EA, Parker TL, Josse RG, Leiter LA, Connelly PW. The effect of combining plant sterols, soy protein, viscous fibers, and almonds in treating hypercholesterolemia. Metabolism 2003 Nov;52(11):1478-83.

Joint National Committee. Sixth report of the Joint National Committee on Prevention, Detection, Evaluation, and Treatment of High Blood Pressure (JNC VI). Arch Intern Med 1997;157:2413-2446.

Kamikawa T. Effects of coenzyme Q10 on exercise on exercise tolerance in chronic stable angina. AM J Cardiol. 1985;26:247.

Lakka HM, Tremblay A, Despres JP, Bouchard C. Effects of long-term negative energy balance with exercise on plasma lipid and lipoprotein levels in identical twins. Atherosclerosis 2004 Jan;172(1):127-33.

Lamarche B, Desroches S, Jenkins DJ, Kendall CW, Marchie A, Faulkner D, Vidgen E, Lapsley KG, Trautwein EA, Parker TL, Josse RG, Leiter LA, Connelly PW. Combined effects of a dietary portfolio of plant sterols, vegetable protein, viscous fibre and almonds on LDL particle size. Br J Nutr 2004 Oct;92(4):657-63.

Maciocia, Giovanni. The Foundations of Chinese Medicine. New York, NY: Churchill Livingstone, 2001.

Madigan C, Ryan M, Owens D, Collins P, Tomkin GH. Dietary unsaturated fatty acids in type 2 diabetes: Higher levels of postprandial lipoprotein on a linoleic acid-rich sunflower oil diet compared with an oleic acid-rich olive oil diet. Diabetes Care 2000 Oct;23(10):1472-77.

Maizes V. Hypertension. In: Kohatso W (ed.). Complementary and Alternative Medicine Secrets. Philadelphia, PA: Hanley & Belfus Inc., 2002.

Marz RB. Medical Nutrition from Marz. 2nd ed. Portland, OR: Omni-Press, 1999.

Mashour NH, Lin GI, Frishman WH. Herbal medicine for the treatment of cardiovascular disease. Arch Intern Med 1998;158:2225-34.

Mattson F et al. Comparison of effects of dietary saturated, monounsaturated and polyunsaturated fatty acids on plasma lipids and lipoprotein in man. J Lipid Res 1985;26:194-202.

Mills S. and Bone K. Principles and Practice of Phytotherapy: Modern Herbal Medicine. New York, NY: Churchill Livingstone, 2000.

Moore R. Hematology Laboratory Diagnosis. Guelph, ON: McMaster University Press, 2001.

Mortensen S. Long-term Coenzyme Q10 therapy: A major advance in the management of resistant myocardial failure. Drugs Exp Clin Res. 1985;11(8):581-93.

Patki PS. Efficacy of potassium and magnesium in essential hypertension. Brit J Med 1990;521-23; 301.

Perona JS, Canizares J, Montero E, Sanchez-Dominguez JM, Catala A, Ruiz-Gutierrez V. Virgin olive oil reduces blood pressure in hypertensive elderly subjects. Clin Nutr 2004 Oct;23(5):1113-21.

Pizzorno JE, Murray MT. Textbook of Natural Medicine. Vol. 1 and 2. 2nd ed. New York, NY: Churchill Livingstone, 1999.

Ripsin CM et al. Oat products and lipid lowering: A meta analysis. JAMA 1992;267:3317-25.

Saunders, PR. Herbal Remedies for Canadians. Toronto, ON: Prentice Hall, 2000.

Saynor R and Verel D. Fish oils & angina pectoris: Eskimos and their diets. Lancet 1983;1:1335.

Silagy CA, Neil HA. A meta-analysis of the effect of garlic on blood pressure. J Hypertens 1994;12:463-68.

Simon JA. 1992. Vitamin C and cardiovascular disease: A review. J Am Coll Nutr 1992;11:107-25.

Sirtori CR, Crepaldi G, Manzato E, Mancini M, Rivellese A, Paoletti R, Pazzucconi F, Pamparana F, Stragliotto E. One-year treatment with ethyl esters of n-3 fatty acids in patients with hypertriglyceridemia and glucose intolerance: Reduced triglyceridemia, total cholesterol and increased HDL-C without glycemic alterations. Atherosclerosis 1998 Apr;137(2):419-27.

Stamler R, Stamler J, Grimm R, et al. 1987. Nutritional therapy for high blood pressure: Final report of a four-year randomized controlled trial – the hypertension control program. JAMA 1987;257:1484-90.

Stark KD, Park EJ, Maines VA, Holub BJ. Effect of a fish-oil concentrate on serum lipids in postmenopausal women receiving and not receiving hormone replacement therapy in a placebo-controlled, double-blind trial. Am J Clin Nutr 2000 Aug;72(2):389-94.

St-Onge MP, Lamarche B, Mauger JF, Jones PJ. Consumption of a functional oil rich in phytosterols and medium-chain triglyceride oil improves plasma lipid profiles in men. J Nutr 2003 Jun;133(6):1815-20.

Studer M, Briel M, Leimenstoll B, Glass TR, Bucher HC. Effect of different antilipidemic agents and diets on mortality: A systematic review. Arch Intern Med 2005 Apr 11;165(7):725-30.

Ubbink JB et al. Hyperhomcystenemia and the response to vitamin supplementation. Clinic Invest 1993;71:993-998.

Varady KA, Jones PJ. Combination diet and exercise interventions for the treatment of dyslipidemia: An effective preliminary strategy to lower cholesterol levels? J Nutr 2005 Aug;135(8):1829-35.

Wester P and Dyckner T. Intracellular electrolytes in cardiac failure. Act Med Scand 1986; 707:33-36.

Winer N, Linas SL. Hypertension. In Mladenovic J (ed.). Primary Care Secrets. Philadelphia PA.: Hanely & Belfus, 2004.

Wolfret AL and Eckel. Abnormalities of Lipids. In: Mladenovic J. (ed.) Primary Care Secrets. Philadelphia, PA: Hanley & Belfus, 2004.

Wong ND, Ming, S, Zhou HY, Black HR. A comparison of Chinese traditional and Western medical approaches for the treatment of mild hypertension. Yale J Biol Med 1991;64:79-87.

EAR, NOSE & THROAT

FACIAL NERVE PARALYSIS

HEARING LOSS

OTITIS MEDIA

SINUSITIS

STREP THROAT

FACIAL NERVE PARALYSIS

Source

NPLEX
MCCQE
USMLE

1. What is lower motor neuron (LMN) facial nerve paralysis?

Facial Nerve Paralysis: lower motor neuron (LMN) lesion of the facial nerve causes unilateral paresis or paralyses of the whole side of the face. Lower quarter paralysis is associated with Upper Motor Neuron (UMN) lesion. Bell's palsy is the most common LMN lesion of the facial nerve. Other etiologies are viral or ischemic.

Signs and Symptoms:
- Facial paresis or paralysis
- Hyperacusis (paralysis of the stapedius → increased sense of hearing)

Causes:
- Herpes infection: sometimes causes VII + VIII cranial nerve paralysis + vesicles inside ear canal or on the pinna + meningitis.
- Lyme disease: causes bilateral facial nerve palsy.
- Stroke (history of TIA is usually present)
- Middle ear or mastoid infection
- Meningitis (from any cause)
- Temporal bone fracture (for example, baseball bat hit that leads to bleeding from the ear = battle's sign)
- Tumors in the cerebellopontine space: acoustic neuroma, neurofibromatosis, and glomus vulgare.
- Occasionally follows upper respiratory tact infections, although causal association is not established.

Treatment:
- Maintain lubrication to the paralyzed eye (tear drops and taping at night) to avoid corneal dryness, which causes inflammation, opacities, and ulceration.
- Almost all causes will resolve spontaneously in about 1 month, but some patients will have permanent sequelae. Although experimental studies are pending, supportive naturopathic measures, especially acupuncture and homeopathy, are promising in bettering the odds of developing permanent disability.
- If the cause is not apparent and the medical history and neurological signs are concerning, request CT scan or MRI of the head.

HEARING LOSS

Source

NPLEX
MCCQE
USMLE

2. What is presbyacusis? When would you suspect other causes of hearing loss?

Presbyacusis: a gradual and progressive hearing loss that occurs as part of the normal aging process (compare presbiopia = age related vision loss).

Diagnosis: In young patients presenting with hearing loss, the following conditions should be ruled out:
■ Exposure to prolonged and intense loud noise.
■ Congenital TORCH infection: **T**oxoplasmosis, **R**ubella, **C**ytomegalovirus, and **H**erpes.
■ Meniere's disease: deafness + severe vertigo + tinnitus + nausea/vomiting.
■ Acoustic neuroma: progressive space occupying lesion manifestations.
■ Labyrinthitis: may follow otitis media or meningitis.
■ Side effects of drugs, such as aminoglycosides (gentamicin and streptomycin), aspirin, quinidine (class I anti-arrhythmic for NPLEX), loop diuretics, and cisplatin.
■ Chronic diseases that lead to healing loss: diabetes, hypothyroidism, multiple sclerosis, and sarcoidosis.

Source

NPLEX
MCCQE
USMLE

3. What is the most common cause of acute onset deafness?

Acute Onset Deafness Causes: viral infection (mumps, measles, influenza, or chicken pox) constitutes the most common cause of endolymphatic labyrinthis, which manifests as relatively sudden onset sensorineural deafness. This is a self-limiting condition that usually resolves within 2 weeks.

Source

NPLEX
MCCQE
USMLE

4. What is the definition of otosclerosis and presbyacusis?

Otosclerosis: refers to otic bones fixation, which leads to hearing impairment. It is the most common cause of progressive conductive hearing loss in adults.

Presbyacusis: the most common sensorineural hearing loss in adults.

Treatment: for both presentations, supportive hearing aid.

Source

NPLEX
MCCQE
USMLE

5. What is the Weber test used to evaluate?

Weber Test: compares bone conduction in both ears. The normal response is to hear the vibration in the middle (or equally in both ears).
■ Patients with conductive hearing loss will hear the vibration best in the affected ear.
■ In contrast, patients with conductive hearing loss will hear the vibration best in the unaffected ear. Therefore, another test is required to investigate any perceived inequality in hearing.

Source

NPLEX
MCCQE
USMLE

6. What is the Rinne test used to evaluate?

Rinne Test: compares air conduction to bone conduction.
■ Normally air conduction is 2X greater than bone conduction (AC>BC). It follows that patients with

conductive hearing will hear the vibration over the mastoid, but not next to the auditory meatus (AC<BC).

■ In sensorineural hearing loss, both air and bone conduction is impaired, but the normal ratio is preserved (i.e., AC>BC)

7. What are the most common causes of vertigo?

Source

NPLEX
MCCQE
USMLE

Vertigo Causes: the following conditions can cause VII cranial nerve damage and are the most common causes of vertigo:

■ Meniere's disease
■ Tumors
■ Diabetes infections
■ Multiple sclerosis

Benign Positional Vertigo: Vertigo that is associated with certain head positions, accompanied by nystagmus, and not associated with hearing loss is termed Benign Positional Vertigo. BPV is a self-limiting condition.

OTITIS MEDIA

8. What is otitis media?

Source

NPLEX
MCCQE
USMLE

Otitis Media: inflammation of the middle ear. OM is extremely common in pediatric patients; in fact, it is the most common reason for pediatric (up to 15 years of age) primary care visits. This is largely due to the anatomy of the pediatric eustachian tube. Studies have found no bacterial etiology in approximately 60% of OM cases. However, the remaining of OM patients exhibit bacterial pathogens (*Haemophilus influenza, Streptococcus pneumonia & Brahnamella catarrhalis*).

Signs and Symptoms:

Pizzorno, 1999

■ Earache
■ Fever, nausea, and vomiting
■ Erythematous and bulging tympanic membrane
■ No pain on manipulation of the auricle (this is a feature of otitis externa)
■ Children who cannot talk may 'tell' you that their ear hurts by tugging on the ear.

Prognosis:
Prognosis is excellent with the following common factors present:

Shapiro, 2002

■ Well appearance of child
■ Mild pain
■ Mild or no fever
■ Unilateral inflammation
■ Little or no bulge in tympanic membrane
■ Little or no erythema of tympanic membrane
·■ No perforation of tympanic membrane
■ Presence of some movement of tympanic membrane with insufflation

Source

NPLEX
MCCQE
USMLE

9. What are the complications of bacterial otitis media? How are they avoided?

OM Complications:
- Tympanic membrane rupture (from impeded drainage of fluid)
- Mastoiditis
- Meningitis
- Labyrinthitis
- Cranial nerve palsies
- Cerebral abscess
- Lateral sinus thrombosis
- Chronic otitis media
- Regardless of the cause, recurrent OM (> 4 episodes per year) is also reason for concern because it can cause hearing loss, which, in a child, leads to developmental problems in speech and cognition.

Treatment:
- Prudent approach is to implement naturopathic treatment with frequent monitoring of all pediatric presentations for any sign of exacerbation.
- In cases of recurrent OM, consider tympanostomy or prophylaxis to avoid permanent neural damage.

Source

Shapiro,
2002

10. Does breast-feeding decrease the risk of acute OM?

Breast-feeding: Breast-feeding for over 4 months significantly decreases the risk of acute OM (even in day-care settings or in later years).
- The reasons for these findings are proposed to be the ingestion of lactoferrin and IgA (immune enhancers/modulators in breast milk) and the absence the more allergenic cow's milk (which is the basis of most infant formulae).
- Infants in day-care settings who are formula-fed are twice as likely to develop acute OM.

Source

NPLEX

11. What is the first-line naturopathic treatment of OM?

Naturopathic Treatment for Otitis Media

Approach: The naturopathic approach is patient-centered and aims to address the underlying nutritional, dietary, and immunologic balances, while simultaneously providing for symptomatic relief.

Shapiro,
2002

Pizzorno,
1999

1. Dietary measures
- Diet high in bioflavonoids helps decrease allergic and inflammatory responses (like mucous buildup and subsequent plugging of normal anatomic drainage).
- Allergy rotation or elimination diets are important in managing chronic OM presentations. The most common food allergies include wheat, cow's milk, soy, corn, and strawberries.
- Recommended diet: high in fresh fruits, vegetables, whole grains, beans, lean meats, and fish. Avoid mucous forming sources, such as wheat, dairy, and orange juice.

2. Lifestyle changes
- Parental or caregiver smoking is strongly associated with increased risk of upper respiratory conditions and OM in children.

■ Pacifier use is associated with increased risk of upper respiratory tract infections and OM.

3. Botanical medicine (with infants, safety is as desired as efficacy)

■ *Matricaria chamomila* (or *recutita*): a safe and effective antiviral, anti-inflammatory, and vulnerary that is used extensively in the treatment of OM. Strong infusions are considered excellent first-line approaches for acute or chronic OM. Chamomile is contraindicated for patients who are allergic to asters and chrysanthemums.

Shapiro, 2002

■ *Echinacea angustifolia* and *purpurea*: well-studied botanical remedies for the prevention and treatment of colds and flu. Also safe and effective in the treatment of both acute and serous OM. Glycerinates are available for infants. Echinacea is contraindicated for patients with autoimmune disease (e.g., SLE)

Pizzorno, 1999

■ *Althea officinalis, Ulmus fulva,* and *Verbascum thapsus:* used to loosen and moisten any thick mucous that is blocking the eustachian tube. Mucilages are generally given as teas or lozenges, but tinctures and glycerinate are also effective.

■ *Sambucus nigra* or *canadensis:* a potent immune stimulator that appears to be very promising in the treatment of OM, when mucous, allergies, sinusitis, or upper respiratory tract infects are present. Elder flower is taken as a tea, tincture, or even syrup.

■ *Zingiber officinalis:* also indicated in OM accompanying a cold with clear clear + watery mucous. Ginger is best combined with other botanicals in tea or syrup.

■ *Astragalus membranaceus:* relatively safe inducer of natural killer cytotoxicity (similar to alpha interferon), interleukin-2 production, and macrophage activity. Astragalus is usually given as a tincture or decoction.

4. Homeopathy

The following homeopathic remedies are most commonly chosen for acute otitis media:

■ *Ferrum Phosphoricum:* the most commonly used remedy for early OM. Indications include gradual onset of symptoms, flushed face, dislike of noise or stimulation, and desire to lie still.

Freise et al, 1996

■ *Belladonna:* recommended in right ear OM, flushed face, fever, restlessness, scant thirst, and sensitivity to noise or light.

■ *Chamomilia:* indicated for OM in irritable and cranky children who cannot be appeased for a long time; one cheek is red while other is pale; and aggravation by heat.

■ *Kali muriaticum:* recommended when patients experience fullness and congestion in the ear, impaired hearing, and popping or crackling sounds on swallowing. This remedy is commonly used to clear the eustachian tubes when serous fluid persists after acute OM.

■ *Pulsatilla:* usually used for earaches that are accompanied with white nasal discharge, thirstlessness, and throbbing pain in the ear that is aggravated by heat. Also indicated in the treatment of OM when the child exhibits changing moods (clingy, weepy, fidgety) with a need to be consoled.

5. Acupuncture

The World Health Organization (WHO) approves acupuncture for the treatment of acute OM. In China, acupuncture is considered a component of first-line treatment for all presentations of OM. Assessment and point prescription should follow traditional Chinese medicine doctrine (at least until experimental studies suggest significant variation). Acupressure (by hand or seeds) and laser acupuncture may be more appropriate for younger children who are particularly concerned about being needled.

Shapiro, 2002

SINUSITIS

Source

NPLEX
MCCQE
USMLE

12. What is acute sinusitis?

Acute Sinusitis: an inflammation and infection of one or more of the paranasal sinuses. It is usually preceded by a URTI.

Signs and Symptoms:
- Headache
- Tenderness over affected sinuses
- Fatigue
- Purulent postnasal rhinorrhea
- Bouts of cold that last longer than 10 days is characteristic of acute sinusitis

Cause: Sinusitis is often caused by *Streptococcus spp.*, *Staphylococcus spp.*, and *H. influenza*.

Source

NPLEX
MCCQE
USMLE

13. What is chronic sinusitis?

Chronic Sinusitis: the persistent or recurrent infection and/or inflammation of one or more sinus cavities. According to the Center for Disease Control and the National Center for Health Statistics, chronic sinusitis is the most common chronic disease in the United States. Prevalence is approximately 15% in North America (that is, one in seven people in the population has chronic sinusitis).

Ivker, 2002

Sub-types:
1. Type 1: persistent low-grade infection with periodic flare-ups of acute sinusitis.
2. Type 2: recurrent (at least 3 episodes within a 6 month period) sinus infection.
3. Type 3: chronic inflammation with little or no infection.

Causes and Risk Factors:
- Common cold
- Dental infection
- GERD
- Immunodeficiency
- Nasal polyps, cysts, or deviated septum
- Emotional stress
- Air pollution
- Smoking
- Certain occupations, such auto mechanics, construction workers, painters and beauticians
- Allergies and sensitivities to pollen, animal dander, mold, dairy, and wheat
- Dry-cold air

Diagnosis: Although a definitive diagnosis sometimes requires a CT scan of the sinuses, in primary care settings a good history and the clinical presentation suffice for reliable diagnosis.

14. What is the first-line naturopathic treatment for sinusitis?

Source

NPLEX

Ivker, 2002

Naturopathic Treatment for Sinusitis

1. Environmental factors
- Address air pollution, the first risk factor for this condition. A thorough cleaning of living spaces (especially carpets) and heating/cooling systems (furnace, humidifier, air conditioner), installing filters on ventilation systems, using negative ion generators, and encouraging indoor plants all help to improve breathable air.
- Saline nasal spray q3h or steam inhalation b.i.d. appears to sooth inflamed mucous membranes of the nasal passages.
- Increase fluid consumption (e.g., chicken soup, ginger tea with honey and lemon). Hot showers and baths are practical hydrating methods.

2. Dietary and lifestyle measures
- Avoid dairy products, eggs, wheat, chocolate, oranges, refined sugars, and caffeine.
- Explore food sensitivities.
- Gradually progressive exercise is of great benefit in improving sinusitis, as well as preventing relapse.
- Ensure adequate periods of rest and sleep (lack of sleep leads ultimately to immune suppression).

3. Clinical nutrition
- Vitamin C: 500 mg q.i.d. (or to bowel tolerance if not contraindicated)
- Vitamin E: 400 mg (mixed tocopherols are preferred) q.d.
- Zinc picolinate: 30 mg b.i.d.
- NAC (N-acetyl cysteine): 500 mg t.i.d. (mucolytic + antioxidant)
- Flaxseed oil or fish oil: 2 tbsp q.d.

Pizzorno, 2002

4. Botanical medicine
- Grapefruit seed extract: 100 mg or 10 gtts t.i.d.
- Garlic extract or equivalent: 1200 mg q.d.
- *Echinacea spp.:* 6:1 standardized (3.5% echinacoside) solid extract: 150-300 mg t.i.d.

OTHER COMMON CONDITIONS

Source

NPLEX
MCCQE
USMLE

15. How does myringitis present?

Myringitis: infectious inflammation of the tympanic membrane. Myringitis is diagnosed when otoscopy reveals vesicles + erythema on the tympanic membrane.

Cause: Infectious myringitis is most commonly caused by *Mycoplasma, streptococcus pneumoniae*, or viruses.

Treatment: The recommended treatment is topical antimicrobials (botanicals and/or drugs).

Source

NPLEX
MCCQE
USMLE

16. What causes parotid gland swelling?

Parotid Gland Swelling: The classic example is mumps, but it may be due to neoplasms (pleomorphic adenoma), Sjogren syndrome, sialolithiasis (stone in the parotid duct), sarcoidosis, and alcoholism.

STREP THROAT

Source

NPLEX
MCCQE
USMLE

RSNC
manual

17. What is pediatric pharyngitis? How is it best managed?

Pediatric Pharyngitis: refers to the inflammation of nasopharynx, oropharynx, and tonsils. The classic strepthroat is a subcategory of pharyngitis, which in pediatric patients may lead to rheumatic fever.

Signs and Symptoms of Strep Throat:
- Acute onset
- Red swollen tonsils
- Purulent exudates on tonsils
- High fever
- Lymphadenopathy

Management:
1. Perform a rapid strep screen on suspected cases. If positive, then antimicrobials are required.
2. If negative, do culture and sensitivity (C&S) on a throat swab. If C&S indicate *Streptococcus pyogenes* infection, then antimicrobials are required.
3. While waiting for C&S results (which take at least 3 days), initiate naturopathic treatment for pharyngitis (see below). If treatment is successful in 1 week, then antimicrobials are not indicated.
4. Be prepared to refer or prescribe penicillin if pharyngitis is refractory to 1 week of naturopathic treatment.
5. Rule out rheumatic fever. The prevalence of rheumatic fever has plummeted since the introduction of penicillin. However, in underdeveloped countries, the threat of rheumatic fever remains unchanged. When it occurs, rheumatic fever affects children 5 to 15 years of age after untreated

and complicated strep throat (Group A beta-hemolytic *Streptococcus pyogenes*) infections. Rheumatic fever is antibody mediated due to antibody cross reactivity between *strep* antigens and cardiac antigens. This autoimmune attack causes myocarditis and leads to valvular heart disease in susceptible patients. The extent of permanent and irreversible valve damage depends on how many times this autoimmune reaction occurs (frequency of strep throats). Unfortunately, once a patient has developed an episode of rheumatic fever, they are susceptible to recurrent bouts.

Six Major Manifestations of Rheumatic Fever (Jones Criteria):
1. Fever
2. Myocarditis
3. Arthritis
4. Chorea (uncontrolled dance-like movements occur 2-3 weeks after throat infection)
5. Subcutaneous nodules (rubbery nodules)
6. Erythema marginatum rash

18. What is the first-line naturopathic treatment for pediatric pharyngitis?

Source

NPLEX

IPizzorno, 1999

Naturopathic Treatment for Pediatric Pharyngitis

1. General recommendations
- Avoid most common food allergens for 2 to 3 weeks. Oligoantigenic diet (also refered to as elimination or hypoallergenic diet) may be tried.
- Increase fluid consumption (e.g., chicken soup, ginger tea with honey and lemon). Hot showers and baths are practical hydrating methods.
- Topical: gargle with salt water (1 tbsp salt/240ml of warm water) b.i:d.
- Hydrotherapy: cold water towel over the throat covered with a dry towel for 20 minutes b.i.d.

2. Clinical nutrition
- Make sure the dose is safe for your pediatric patient 'by weight'.
- Vitamin C: 500 mg q.i.d. (or to bowel tolerance if not contraindicated)
- Vitamin A: 25,000 IU b.i.d. for 1 week; or beta-carotene 200,000 IU q.d. (Caution: vitamin A at this dose is contraindicated in women of reproductive potential.)
- Bioflavonoids: 1000 mg q.d.
- Zinc picolinate lozenges: 30 mg b.i.d.
- Thymus extract: 120 mg pure polypeptide equivalent q.d.

3. Botanical medicine
- *Echinacea spp.*: 2-4 ml 1:1 fluid extract t.i.d.
- *Hydrastis canadensis:* 2-4 ml 1:1 fluid extract, or 500 mg (4:1) powdered extract standardized to 8% to 12% alkaloid content t.i.d.
- *Althea officinalis* and *Ulmus fulva* (throat-coat tea) may be used to soothe the throat and moisten any presenting thick mucous. Mucilages are generally given as teas or lozenges, but tinctures and glycerinate are also effective.

Examination Board References

NPLEX (II): North American Board of Naturopathic Examiners
North American Board of Naturopathic Examiners (NABNE), Naturopathic Physician Licensing Examination Part II Blueprint and Study Guide. Portland, OR: NABNE, 2005.

USMLE (II): National Board of Medical Examiners
Bouchert A. USMLE Step 2 Secrets. Philadelphia, PA: Hanley & Belfus Inc., 2000.

MCCQE: Medical Council of Canada
Molckovsky A, Pirzada KS (eds.). Review for the Medical Council of Canada Qualification Examination. Toronto, ON: Toronto Notes Medical Publishing, 2004.

Related References

Dains J, Baumann L, Scheibel P. Advanced Health Assessment & Clinical Diagnosis in Primary Care. 2nd ed. St. Louis, MI: Mosby Inc, 2003.

Freise KH et al. Acute Otitis Media in Children: Comparison of Conventional and Homeopathic Treatment. Berlin, Germany: Hals-Nasen-Ohren, 1996:426-66.

Ivker R. Sinusitis: Complementary and Alternative Medicine Secrets. Philadelphia, PA: Hanley & Belfus Inc., 2002.

Pizzorno JE, Murray MT. Textbook of Natural Medicine. Vol. 1 and 2. 2nd ed. New York, NY: Churchill Livingstone, 1999.

Pizzorno JE, Murray MT, Joiner-Bey H. The Clinician's Handbook of Natural Medicine. New York, NY: Churchill Livingstone, 2002.

Robert Schad Naturopathic Clinic. Policy and Procedures Manual. Toronto, ON: The Canadian College of Naturopathic Medicine, 2004.

Shapiro M. 2002. Otitis Media. In: Kohatso W (ed.). Complementary and Alternative Medicine Secrets. Philadelphia, PA: Hanley & Belfus Inc., 2002.

ENDOCRINOLOGY

Diabetes

DIABETES

1. What is the definition of diabetes mellitus?

Diabetes mellitus: a chronic disorder of carbohydrate, fat, and protein metabolism.

Characteristics:
- Diabetes manifests when there is a defect in insulin secretion, insulin action, or both.
- Diabetes is characterized by chronic hyperglycemia.
- Diabetes increases the risk of:
  - Myocardial infarction
  - Stroke
  - Peripheral vascular disease
  - Retinopathy
  - Neuropathy
  - Nephropathy
  - Early mortality

Clinical Definition: If a patient has classic symptoms of diabetes, one of the following three tests is sufficient to establish the diagnosis. In asymptomatic patients, the test should be repeated.
- Random plasma glucose level > 11.1 mmol/L (or > 200 mg/dL for NPLEX)
- 8-hour fasting plasma glucose (FPG) > 6.9 mmol/L (or > 126 mg/dL for NPLEX)
- 2-hour Oral Glucose Tolerance Test (OGTT) > 11.1 mmol/L, where plasma glucose is measured 2 hours after ingestion of a 75 g of glucose dissolved in water. This is the standard glucose load as defined by the WHO. This test is recommended only in the following situations:
  - To make sure a diagnosis has not been missed in patients exhibiting impaired fasting glucose (IFG), which is defined as borderline FPG values between 6.1-6.9 mmol/L.
  - To define positive urine glucose in a pregnant female as glucosuria may be perfectly normal in pregnancy (i.e., OGTT screens for gestational diabetes).

2. What are the recommendations for diabetes screening?

Diabetes Screening:
- Universal screening is *not* supported by randomized trials.
- The American Diabetes Association (ADA) recommends screening every 3 years beginning at age 45 years.
- Screening for diabetes in pregnancy is mandatory.
- Testing at a younger age should be considered in patients who exhibit any of following conditions, lifestyle factors, or genetic risks:
  1. Overweight
  2. First-degree relative with diabetes
  3. Belong to high-risk ethnic group
  4. Hypertensive

5. HDL< 0.9 mmol/L (or 35mg/dL), TG > 2.82 mmol/L (or 250 mg/dL)
6. Polycystic ovarian syndrome
7. Acanthosis nigricans
8. Vascular disease

Source

NPLEX
MCCQE
USMLE

3. What are the differences between type 1 and type 2 DM?

TYPE 1 VS. TYPE 2 DIABETES

Diabetes Type	Type 1	Type 2
Age at onset	Most commonly < 30 years of age	Most commonly > 40 years of age
Weight	Low	Normal or high
Onset	Rapid	Slow
Development of ketoacidosis	Yes	No
Development of Hyperosmolar State	No	Yes
Level of endogenous insulin	Low or none Due to destruction of islet "B" cells	Normal or high Due to insulin resistance
Human leukocytic antigen (HLA) association	Yes	No
Islet antibody	Yes (at time of diagnosis)	No
Genetic association	Weak genetic association	Strong genetic association
Environmental factors	Post viral and possibly post toxic exposure	Obesity + inactivity
Risk for diabetic complications	Yes	Yes

Source

NPLEX

4. What is syndrome X? How is it diagnosed?

Syndrome X: This insulin resistance syndrome is known by many names: obesity dyslipidemia syndrome, syndrome X, and metabolic syndrome.

NCEP, 2001

Diagnosis: The National Cholesterol Education Program (NCEP) publishes the following diagnostic criteria for syndrome X. Three or more need to be present:
1. Abdominal obesity, which is defined as waist circumference > 40 inches in men and > 35 inches in women.

2. Hypertension or even high-normal BP ≥ 130/85 mmHg.

3. FPG > 6.1 mmol/L or 110 mg/dL.

4. Dyslipidemia:
   - HDL Cholesterol < 1.0 mmol/L (40 mg/dL) for men, and < 1.3mmol/L (50 mg/dL) for women.
   - Triglycerides ≥ 150 mg/dL.

5. What are the goals of management of diabetes in terms of glucose levels?

Source

MCCQE
USMLE

Management Goals:
- The goal of any approach to diabetes is to maintain postprandial (or after-meal) glucose level <11.1 mmol/L (200 mg/dL) and fasting glucose level < 6.9 mmol/L (126 mg/dL).
- Remember that the defect in diabetes also places the patient at a greater risk for hypoglycemia, which is defined as FPG < 2.5 mmol/L or 46 mg/dL. Thus, management should also maintain FPG above hypoglycemic levels.

6. What is a good measure of long-term diabetes control or compliance with treatment?

Source

NPLEX
MCCQE
USMLE

Control and Compliance:
- Hemoglobin A1C (also known as glycosylated hemoglobin) reflects average control of plasma glucose level over the previous 2 to 3 months.
- It is recommended that hemoglobin A1C levels be monitored every 6 to 12 months for patients exhibiting good glycemic control, and every 3 months for patients with poor glycemic control.
- Rule of thumb: if you multiply the HA1C levels by 100, you will get the average blood glucose levels in mmol (multiply by 200 for mg scale).

7. What is diabetic ketoacidosis (DKA)?

Source

NPLEX
MCCQE
USMLE

Ketoacidosis: without adequate insulin administration, this condition occurs in type 1 diabetics. Absolute lack of insulin causes cellular glucose deprivation (glucose cannot enter cells without insulin) and triggers compensatory lipolysis and muscle proteolysis, which produce ketones sufficient to cause metabolic acidosis, hyperosmolar state, and ultimately coma.
- DKA is a serious emergency condition that leads to coma and death in type 1 diabetics (mortality of DKA is 10%).
- The cause is usually non-compliance with insulin therapy.

Clinical Signs and Symptoms:
- Kussmaul breathing (deep and rapid respirations)
- Dehydration
- Hyperglycemia
- Acidosis (since ketones are acidic)
- Increased ketones in the serum (causes fruity or alcohol breath odor) and urine (smells like acetone or nail polish remover)

Treatment: Acutely, this condition is treated by:
- Intravenous fluids (rehydration of DKA is probably the most effective advance in modern medicine)
- Insulin
- Electrolyte replacement

Source

NPLEX
USMLE

8. What is hyperosmolar non-ketotic state (HONK)?

Hyperosmolar Non-Ketotic State: occurs in type 2 diabetics without adequate blood sugar control.
- HONK is an emergency condition that leads to coma and death of type 2 diabetics. If HONK presents with mental status changes, its mortality rate approaches 50%.
- Hyperglycemia and increased serum osmolality are present in absence of ketones or acidoses.
- First treatment is 'fluids, fluids, and some more fluids' and electrolytes.

Source

MCCQE
USMLE

9. What is lactic acidotic coma (LA)?

Lactic Acidotic Coma: LA has nothing to do with diabetes, but it presents very similarly to DKA in the emergency department.
- LA type I causes coma in hypoxic patients (as in shock trauma).
- LA type II is caused by impaired metabolism of lactate in the liver.

Source

MCCQE
USMLE

10. If a patient urinates, drinks, and eats a lot, what is the likely diagnosis?

New-Onset Diabetes:
- Classic presentation of new-onset diabetes is the triad:
  - Polyuria
  - Polydipsia
  - Polyphagia
- In practice, however, suspect diabetes in any patient with frank candidal infections, weight loss, or blurry vision.
- A spontaneous improvement in vision of a geriatric patient should also sound an alarm.

Source

MCCQE
USMLE

11. What is the recommended evaluation strategy for every patient with a diagnosis of diabetes?

Diabetes Evaluation Strategy: Considering the significantly increased risk for myocardial infarction, stroke, peripheral vascular disease, retinopathy, neuropathy, nephropathy, and early mortality, diabetic patients should be adequately screened for atherosclerotic disease:
1. Careful history-taking and review of systems, focusing on cardiovascular symptoms (i.e., chest pain, SOB, exertional dyspnea, and claudications).
2. Physical examination of feet (sensations, ulcers, abnormal skin or nails), carotid bruit, and peripheral pulses.
3. Dipstick (or Spot) urinalysis for albumin-to-creatinine ratio (if positive confirm with 24-hour urine collection) to screen for diabetic nephropathy.
4. Lipid profile.
5. ECG if > 40 years of age.

12. What are the common long-term complications of diabetes mellitus?

Source

NPLEX
MCCQE
USMLE

LONG-TERM COMPLICATIONS OF DIABETES MELLITUS

Condition	Facts
Atherosclerosis, CAD, and MI	Diabetics often have silent heart attacks due to autonomic neuropathy.
Retinopathy	Diabetes is the number one cause of blindness for people under 50 years of age.
Peripheral vascular disease	Diabetes is the number one cause of limb amputations in the absence of trauma. It also leads to intermittent claudication and erectile dysfunction.
Nephropathy	Diabetes is the number one cause of end-stage renal failure.
Peripheral neuropathy	Diabetes causes numbness of feet and silent heart attacks.
Increased risk of infections	WBCs lose function in hyperglycemic environments, but the real issue is clogged arteries (further reducing WBC presence) and inability to sense pain in uncontrolled diabetes.

■ All of these grim complications can be prevented or delayed indefinitely by controlling blood glucose levels.

13. How serious is peripheral neuropathy?

Source

NPLEX
MCCQE
USMLE

Peripheral Neuropathy Complications: Peripheral neuropathy causes far more serious complications than just numb feet. These complications are:
1. Early satiety and vomiting because the stomach does not empty well
2. Erectile dysfunction
3. Cranial nerve palsies of CNIII, CNIV, and CNVI
4. Orthostatic hypotension
5. Charcot joints (refer to Rheumatology module)
6. Pressure ulcers in the feet that may progress into gangrene

14. What is the first-line naturopathic treatment for diabetes mellitus?

Naturopathic Treatment for Diabetes

Approach: Dietary modifications are fundamental to the success of therapy in type 1 and type 2 DM. Although type 1 diabetics will always require insulin supplementation, better outcomes are strongly correlated with high-fiber/low-refined carbohydrate diet. Diabetic patients exhibit increased need for many nutrients and vitamins. The goal of treatment for either type is centered on improving blood sugar control, preventing or ameliorating long-term complications, and improving overall health status.

1. Dietary measures

The patient must be willing to improve lifestyle since required dietary changes are demanding, to say the least. The cornerstone of therapy is the high complex-carbohydrate diet, frequent small meals, and observance of the following:

- Eliminate simple sugars, as well as processed and concentrated carbohydrates.
- Encourage high-fiber foods, legumes, onions, and garlic.
- Avoid or eliminate saturated fats.
- Reduce weight in overweight patients (a modest 10 lb reduction in weight significantly improves metabolic control, and, in some cases, induces remission of diabetes).

2. Clinical nutrition

- Chromium picolinate (or polynicotinate): 500 mcg b.i.d. Increases cell sensitivity to insulin via unknown mechanism. This dose is 350 times less than the suspected toxic dose.
- Magnesium citrate (or aspartate): 500 mg q.d. Magnesium deficiency is common in patients with DM and contributes somewhat to the development of most diabetic complications.
- Fiber (in order of preference: defatted fenugreek seeds > guar > pectin > oat bran): 20-30 g q.d. *Trigonella foenum gracum* seed fiber has been shown in clinical studies to control post-prandial plasma glucose by inhibiting intestinal absorption of glucose because of a suspected alpha-glucosidase inhibitor effect.
- Alpha-lipoic acid: 300-600 mg q.d. Potent antioxidant and aldose reductase inhibitor. Reduces numbness and pain in patients with peripheral neuropathy)
- Pyridoxine, biotin, and selenium. Ensure adequate intake.

3. Botanical medicine

The use of botanicals needs to be strictly controlled by the naturopathic physician so as not to precipitate hypoglycemia (especially when patient is on oral hypoglycemic drugs).

- *Mamordica charantia:* 30-60 ml fresh juice or 100-200 mg (5.1% triterpenes acids) t.i.d. Bitter melon is hypoglycemic and lowers both fasting plasma glucose and hemoglobin A1C.
- *Gymnema sylvestre:* 400-600 mcg (25% gymnemic acids) q.d. This is a potent oral hypoglycemic agent and alpha-glucosidase inhibitor that lowers plasma glucose and hemoglobin A1C and may stimulate regeneration of pancreatic insulin-secreting cells.
- *Vaccinuim myrtillus:* 80-160 mg (25% anthocyanidin content) t.i.d. This botanical is also beneficial for diabetic retinopathy.

Source

- *Ginkgo biloba* extract: 40 mg (24% ginkgo flavoglycosides) t.i.d. Excellent for improving CNS manifestations due to peripheral vascular disease.
- *Panax ginseng:* 100 mg (5% ginsenosides) t.i.d. Reduces fasting glucose levels and helps reduce body weight in type 2 diabetes.

4. Exercise

Recommend an aerobic exercise program that elevates heart rate to 60-70 HRMAX for 30 minutes three to four times per week.

- Advise patients with well-controlled diabetes to ingest 15-30 g of carbohydrates (juice or glucose tablets) 15-30 minutes prior to beginning their exercise and every 30 minutes of exercise time to avoid exercise-induced hypoglycemia.
- Recommend complex carbohydrate snacks after completion of exercise to prevent glycogen repletion induced hypoglycemia.
- For patients on insulin, plasma glucose should be measured before, during, and after exercise.

La Valle, 2001

15. What are the oral hypoglycemic medications used in the treatment of diabetes mellitus 2?

Source

NPLEX
MCCQE
USMLE
CPS

Oral Hypoglycemic Medications: Six classes of drugs are used in DM type 2 therapy. Choice depends on the individual patient and the medical presentation.

- Sulfonylureas
- Nonsulfonylureas
- Thiazolidinediones
- Biguanides
- Alpha-glucosidase inhibitors
- Combinations

ORAL HYPOGLYCEMIC MEDICATIONS

Class and Examples	Mechanism of Action	Facts and Side Effects
Sulfonylurea secretagogues: Glyburide (DiaBeta) Micronized glyburide (Glynase) Gliclazide (Diamicron) Glipizide (Glucotrol)	Widely used; stimulate pancreas to secrete insulin and somewhat increases insulin sensitivity; used alone, and with other oral agents, or insulin.	Well tolerated; taken q.d. or b.i.d.; lowers FPG by 20%. S/E: Hypoglycemia, nausea, skin sensitivity, abnormal LFTs.
Nonsulfonylureas secretagogues: Repaglinide (GlucoNorm) Nateglinide (Starlix)	Stimulate pancreas to secrete insulin; used alone and with metformin.	Taken t.i.d. or q.i.d.; selectively lowers postprandial plasma glucose. S/E: Hypoglycemia, weight gain.

Class and Examples	Mechanism of Action	Facts and Side Effects
Thiazolidinediones: Rosiglitazone (Avandia) Pioglitazone (Actos)	Enhance insulin sensitivity in muscle, liver, and adipose tissue by unknown mechanism; used alone and with sulfonylureas, metformin, or insulin.	Taken q.d.; long duration of action (days to weeks); can reduce HbA1C triglycerides and LDL. S/E: Dose-related weight gain, fluid retention, heart failure.
Biguanides: Metformin (Glucophage, Glucophage XR)	Insulin sensitizer; decrease glycogenolysis as well as gluconeogenesis; increase peripheral glucose utilization.	Taken q.d. to t.i.d.; lowers FPG by 20%; also lowers serum triglycerides. S/E: Metallic taste, mild anorexia, nausea, abdominal pain, bloating, diarrhea, reduced vitamin B-12 absorption (in up to 30% of patients)
Alpha-Glucosidase inhibitors: Acarbose (Precose) Miglitol (Glyset)	Inhibit enzymes that convert polysaccharides into monosaccharides, thus limiting postprandial glucose absorption.	Taken with meals; lowers HbA1C, LDL and possibly elevates HDL. S/E: Hypoglycemia, abdominal pain, flatulence, diarrhea.
Combinations: Metformin-glyburide (Glucovance)	Combines insulin sensitization with secretion induction, leading to more insulin sensitivity, as well as production.	Practical combination; taken b.i.d.; lowers FPG by 20%; also lowers serum triglycerides. S/E: Hypoglycemia, abdominal pain, flatulence, weight gain.

Source

MCCQE
USMLE

16. What is the treatment for proliferative diabetic retinopathy?

Diabetic Retinopathy Treatment:
- Besides controlling blood sugar, proliferative retinopathy in diabetic patients (usually seen in type 1 DM) requires panretinal laser photocoagulation to prevent progression into blindness.
- Focal laser photocoagulation is used in non-proliferative retinopathy with macular edema.

Source

NPLEX
MCCQE

17. What is the definition and cause of hypoglycemia?

Clinical Hypoglycemia: occurs when blood sugar level dips below 2.5 mmol/L (which is a value that normal people would not achieve even with prolonged fasting).

Causes: The cause for hypoglycemia is usually diabetes, but endocrine defects, liver cirrhosis, and inborn metabolic defects are also factors. Addison's disease, alcoholism, and sepsis frequently exhibit fasting hypoglycemia.

Signs and Symptoms:
- Aggression
- Sweating
- Tachycardia
- Nausea
- Weakness
- Mental status changes

Treatments:
- Acute treatment: immediate glucose administration.
- Chronic treatment: identifying and circumventing the cause best addresses chronic cases.
- Blood glucose control is the desired outcome of successful treatment.

18. What are the indications for insulin?

Source

NPLEX
MCCQE
USMLE

Indications for Insulin Use:
- Type 1 DM
- Type 2 DM, where glycemic control is poor desepite naturopathic and drug intervention.

19. What are some of the adverse effects of insulin therapy?

Source

NPLEX
MCCQE

Adverse Effects of Insulin Therapy:
- Hypoglycemia
- Hypokalemia (which causes cardiac arrhythmias and neuromuscular disturbances)

20. What are the different types of insulin preparations?

Source

NPLEX
USMLE

INSULIN PREPARATIONS

Preparation	Class and Trade Names	Pharmacokinetics (in hours)		
		Onset	Peak	Duration
1. Regular insulin	Short acting (Novolin Toronto, Humulin-N)	0.5-1	2-4	5-8
2. Semilente insulin		1-2	2-8	12-6
3. Neutral protamine hagedorn (NPH)	Intermediate acting (Novolin, NPH, Humulin-L)	1-2	4-12	18-24
4. Lente insulin		1-3	6-14	18-24
5. Protamine zinc insulin	Long acting (Humulin-V, Lantus, Humalong)	4-8	14-20	24-36
6. Ultralente insulin		4-8	12-24	36-40

Source

21. What is the Somogyi effect and the Dawn phenomenon?

MCCQE
USMLE

Somogyi effect: the body's natural reaction to hypoglycemia. If *too much NPH insulin* is given at din-nertime, the glucose level at 3 a.m. will be in hypoglycemic range. The body reacts to this condition (which occurs during sleep) by secreting glucagon, which causes a high glucose level at 7 a.m.

Dawn phenomenon: hyperglycemia caused by *too little NPH insulin* at dinnertime. The glucose level will be normal or high at 3 a.m., but will be high at 7 a.m.

Source

22. What is the concern with beta-blockers and diabetes?

NPLEX
MCCQE
USMLE

Beta-blocker Risks: Generally contraindicated in diabetes because they mask the alarm symptoms of hypoglycemia (tachycardia and sweating).

Source

23. What is the best single treatment for type 2 DM?

NPLEX
USMLE

Best Treatment: The bulk of published evidence indicates that weight loss alone may eliminate type 2 DM diabetes completely. It markedly reduces insulin resistance, thus circumventing the primary deficit.

Examination Board References

NPLEX (II): North American Board of Naturopathic Examiners
North American Board of Naturopathic Examiners (NABNE), Naturopathic Physician Licensing Examination Part II Blueprint and Study Guide. Portland, OR: NABNE, 2005.

USMLE (II): National Board of Medical Examiners
Bouchert A. USMLE Step 2 Secrets. Philadelphia, PA: Hanley & Belfus Inc., 2000.

MCCQE: Medical Council of Canada
Molckovsky A, Pirzada KS (eds.). Review for the Medical Council of Canada Qualification Examination. Toronto, ON: Toronto Notes Medical Publishing, 2004.

Related References

American Diabetes Association. Standards of medical care for patients with diabetes mellitus. Diabetes Care 2003;26(supp 1):S50-S55.

Anderson RA, et al. Elevated intake of supplemental chromium improve glucose and insulin variables in individuals with type 2 diabetes. Diabetes 1997;46:1786-91.

Compendium of Pharmaceuticals & Specialties (CPS). Toronto, ON: Canadian Pharmaceutical Association, 2005.

Dains J, Baumann L, Scheibel P. Advanced Health Assessment & Clinical Diagnosis in Primary Care. 2nd ed. Philadelphia, PA: Mosby C.V. Co. Ltd., 2003.

Head K. Natural Treatments for Diabetes. Roseville, CA: Prima, 2000.

Jonathan PC, et al. Diabetes Mellitus. In: Mladenovic J. (ed.). Primary Care Secrets. Philadelphia, PA: Hanley & Belfus Inc., 2004.

La Valle JB, et al. Natural Therapeutics Pocket Guide. Hudson, OH: Lexi-Comp, 2001.

Marz RB. Medical Nutrition form Marz. 2nd ed. Portland, OR: Omni-Press, 1999.

Morelli V, Zoorob R. Alternative therapies. Part I: Depression, diabetes, obesity. Am Fam Physician 2000;62(5):1051-60.

NCEP: National Cholesterol Education Program. Third Report of the NCEP Expert Panel on Detection, Evaluation, and Treatment of High Blood Cholesterol in Adults (Adult Treatment Panel III). JAMA 2001;285:2486-97.

Pizzorno JE, Murray MT. Diabetes mellitus. In: Textbook of Natural Medicine. New York, NY: Churchill Livingstone, 1999.

Saunders, PR. Herbal Remedies for Canadians. Toronto, ON: Prentice Hall, 2000.

GASTROENTEROLOGY

GASTROESOPHAGEAL REFLUX DISEASE

ESOPHAGEAL DISEASE

PEPTIC ULCER DISEASE

ACHLORHYDRIA

GASTRIC BLEEDING

DIARRHEA

CONSTIPATION

IRRITABLE BOWEL SYNDROME

INFLAMMATORY BOWEL DISEASE

LIVER DISEASE

HEPATITIS

AUTOSOMAL DISEASES

BILARY TRACT CONDITIONS

PANCREATITIS

PEDIATRIC CONDITIONS

GASTROESOPHAGEAL REFLUX DISEASE

1. What is gastroesophageal reflux disease (GERD)?

GERD: simply means that stomach acid is refluxing into the esophagus.

Signs and Symptoms: Patient presents with heartburn, abdominal discomfort, or chest pain that is often related to eating and/or lying down.
- Heartburn
- Bloating
- Belching
- Indigestion
- Regurgitation
- Acid reflux
- Bitter taste in the mouth
- Cardiac-like pain. To differentiate GERD from MI or angina pectoris, remember that MI pain is generally made worse by movement. See the Cardiology module for guidelines.

Causes: It occurs mainly due to inappropriate relaxation of the lower esophageal sphincter (LES) and/or delayed gastric emptying.

Prevalence: The prevalence in North America is about 20% in adults. The incidence is increased significantly in patients with hiatal hernia.

2. What are the sequelae of GERD?

Sequelae of GERD:
- Esophagitis
- Esophageal stricture (which may mimic esophageal cancer)
- Esophageal ulcer
- Hemorrhage
- Barrett's metaplasia (columnar metaplasia of esophageal squamous epithelium), which often leads to esophageal adenocarcinoma

3. What is the role of stomach acid levels in GERD?

Stomach Acid Level: Both extremes (excess and deficiency) in stomach acid production may cause GERD.
- When acid is produced in excess (e.g., in response to *Helicobacter pylori* infection, alcohol, spicy foods, or coffee), there is a higher chance for regurgitation.
- Conversely, when stomach acid production is deficient, gastric emptying is prolonged (i.e., longer

churning time is needed when acid levels are low), which in turn leads to GERD.

■ Insufficient production of digestive enzymes and environmental/ food sensitivities may also play a role in GERD etiology.

Source

NPLEX

Shapiro, 2002

4. What tests measure stomach acid levels?

Stomach Acid Levels Tests:

1. Direct measurement of postprandial stomach acid after a standard meal. This is the least refuted and most invasive method for evaluating stomach acid production.

2. Direct measurement of fasting stomach pH after a standard challenge (e.g., pH sensitive telemetry capsule or GastroTest). This method is better tolerated, but its analytical sensitivity (the ability of a test method to measure what it claims to measure – postprandial versus fasting), reliability (reproducibility), and sensitivity (propensity for high false positives) remains to be seen.

3. Indirect evaluation by supplementing with betaine hydrochloride (see below) with meals and monitoring the symptoms. If GERD symptoms improve, the patient may be deficient. If the symptoms exacerbate, then stomach acid is either excessive or normal (and the supplementation is stopped).

Source

NPLEX
MCCQU
USMLE

5. What is the first-line naturopathic treatment for GERD?

Pizzorno & Murray, 1999

Marz, 1999

Naturopathic Treatment for GERD

Recommendations	Rationale	Details
1. Avoid foods that commonly cause GERD symptoms.	Coffee, alcohol, tobacco, spicy and fatty foods, and chocolate decrease lower esophageal sphincter (LES) tone and significantly stimulate HC1 production.	Trial of 1-2 months
2. Relax while eating.	Relaxation favors the parasympathetic system. Have the patient sit down while eating slowly and deliberately. Prohibit television, reading, excessive chatter, or other distracting activities during meals. Focusing on chewing helps.	Always
3. Eat small meals with low fat content.	High fat content has a long transit time. This increases intra-abdominal pressure and decreases the lower esophageal sphincter tone.	4-5 small meals per day
4. Increase fiber intake.	Appears to decrease overall intra-abdominal pressure.	Depends on dietary intake
5. Avoid medications that aggravate the situation.	Anticholinergic drugs, botanicals, and aspirin tend to decrease peristalsis and relax the LES.	Always

Recommendations	Rationale	Details
6. Take bitters.	Bitter herbs, such as gentian, hops, angelica, and horehound, stimulate acid production and possibly increase LES tone.	1 ml of tincture or 1 oz of bitter tonics 20-30 minutes before meals
7. Take demulcents.	Recommend demulcents, such as *Althea officinalis* or *Ulmus fulva*, to alleviate epigastric discomfort	With two cups of water (as needed)
8. **Supplement with choline and lecithin.**	Anecdotal evidence of increased LES pressure. Safe in pregnancy.	Phosphatidyl choline: 500 mg q.d.

- If this approach fails, evaluate the possibility of gallstones and *H. pylori* infection.
- Then try H2 blockers and proton pump inhibitors.
- Nissen fundoplication, a surgical operation, is reserved for extreme non-responsive cases.

6. Can HCl supplementation be used to manage GERD?

Source

Pizzorno & Murray, 1999

Shapiro, 2002

HC1 Supplementation: Supplementing with betaine HCl (HCl bound to the amino acid betaine) is a documented naturopathic protocol that not only can ascertain the cause of GERD, but may even resolve the presentation altogether. Although the mechanism of action is not known, this protocol seems to restore proper stomach acid regulation.

Standard Trial HC1Protocol:
1. The initial dose consists of one capsule containing 300-600 mg betaine HCl (often with 5-10 mg pepsin) with each meal.
2. If symptoms exacerbate, the trial is stopped.
3. If symptoms remain the same or improve, the dose is gradually increased by increments of one capsule every 2 days until the patient experiences heartburn (epigastric discomfort, heartburn, or warmth).
4. The dose is then reduced to the previously tolerated level. One capsule less than the dose that produces heartburn = therapeutic dose.
5. When the therapeutic dose starts to cause epigastric discomfort, the number of capsules per meal is again reduced by 1 capsule.
6. This protocol is continued until the initial dose starts to cause heartburn. At this point, supplementation is stopped.
7. This outcome often occurs after weeks or months of betaine HCl supplementation and indicates that stomach acid auto-regulation is achieved.

ESOPHAGEAL DISEASE

Source

USMLE

7. What are the signs of esophageal disease?

Esophageal Disease Signs:
- Difficulty in swallowing (dysphagia) and/or painful swallowing (odynophagia)
- Tendency for atypical chest pains

8. What are hiatal hernia and paraesophageal hernia?

Hiatal Hernia: a sliding hernia, where the whole gastroesophageal junction moves above the diaphragm. This common and benign finding (seen on a barium study) may predispose to GERD.

Paraesophageal Hernia: a herniation of a portion of the stomach, where the gastroesophageal junction remains below the diaphragm. This is an uncommon but serious condition because the herniated portion may become strangulated. A surgical solution is recommended.

Source

**NPLEX
USMLE**

9. What causes achalasia? How is it diagnosed and treated?

Achalasia Causes: Incomplete relation of a hypertensive lower esophageal sphincter (LES) and loss of peristalsis causes achalasia. It is usually idiopathic or due to CHAGAS disease (tick born *Trypanosoma cruzi* endemic to South America).

Signs and Symptoms:
- Intermittent dysphagia without heartburn.
- Barium swallow reveals a dilated esophagus with "bird-beak" narrowing.

Treatment: Magnesium citrate and/or calcium channel blockers and pneumatic balloon dilatation. Surgical myotomy represents a last resort solution.

Source

**NPLEX
MCCQE
USMLE**

10. What are the causes of esophageal spasm? How is it treated?

Esophageal Spasm Causes: Irregular, forceful, and painful esophageal contractions that cause intermittent chest pain.

Diagnosis: Esophageal manometry.

Treatment: Magnesium citrate and/or calcium channel blockers and pneumatic balloon dilatation. Surgical myotomy represents a last resort solution.

Source

**NPLEX
MCCQE
USMLE**

11. What clues suggest that scleroderma is causing esophageal complaints?

Scleroderma: (the pathogenesis of which is poorly understood) may cause aperistalsis due to esophageal muscular fibrosis. The LES becomes incompetent, and most patients will have heartburn (this is the opposite of achalasia).

Signs and Symptoms:

- Positive anti-nuclear antibody (ANA)
- Mask-like facies
- CREST syndrome = **C**alcinosis, **R**aynaud's phenomenon, **E**sophageal dysmotility, **S**clerodactyly, and **T**elangectasia

12. What are the basic clinical facts about esophageal cancer?

Source

NPLEX
MCCQE
USMLE

Esophageal Cancer Facts:

- Usually caused by alcohol and tobacco.
- Classically seen in black men more than 40 years of age.
- Patients complain of weight loss (ominous cancer sign) and solid food "sticking" in their throat.
- Most common type is squamous cell carcinoma.

PEPTIC ULCER DISEASE

13. When are the signs and symptoms of peptic ulcer disease (PUD)?

Source

NPLEX
MCCQE
USMLE

Peptic Ulcer Disease Signs and Symptoms:

- Chronic
- Intermittent epigastric distress (burning, gnawing, or aching pain localized and often relieved by antacids or milk)
- Epigastric tenderness on P/E
- Occult blood in stool
- Nausea and vomiting
- PUD is more common in men

14. What are the differences between duodenal and gastric ulcers?

Source

NPLEX
MCCQE
USMLE

DUODENAL VS. GASTRIC ULCERS

Differential Feature	Duodenal Ulcers	Gastric Ulcers
% of cases	75	25
Acid secretion	Normal to high	Normal to low
Common cause	*Helicobacter pylori*	NSAIDs
Peak age	40s	50s
Ingestion of food	Initially ameliorates, then gets worse 2-3 hours after meals.	Pain is not relieved or aggravated noticeably.

Source

NPLEX
MCCQE
USMLE

15. How can you confirm a suspected diagnosis of PUD?

PUD Tests:
- Endoscopy is the most sensitive evaluation (includes biopsy), but an upper GI barium study is less expensive.
- Empiric treatment may be tried in the absence diagnostic studies if the symptoms are typical.

Source

NPLEX
MCCQE
USMLE

16. What is the most worrisome complication of PUD?

PUD Complications:
- Perforation: Look for peritoneal signs, history of PUD, and free air on abdominal radiograph. Refer for antibiotic treatment and laparotomy with repair of the perforation.
- Gastrinoma: If ulcers are severe, atypical (e.g., located in the jejunum), or resistant to treatment, consider testing gastrin levels for Zollinger –Ellison syndrome (gastrinoma) or referring for a stomach biopsy (cancer).

Source

MCCQE
USMLE

Pizzorno &
Murray,
1999

Marz, 1999

17. What is the first-line naturopathic treatment for PUD?

Naturopathic Treatment for Peptic Ulcer Disease

1. Dietary measures
- Eliminate cigarette smoking, coffee, alcohol, NSAIDs, spicy and fatty foods, and chocolate for 1-2 months.

2. Clinical nutrition
- Bismuth subcitrate: 240 mg b.i.d. before meals
- Glutamine: 500 mg t.i.d.
- Add supportive measures: Vitamins A, C, E, zinc, and flavonoids if indicated

3. Botanical medicine
- Deglycerrhizinated licorice root (DGL): 380-760 mg dissolved in mouth before meals t.i.d. for 8-16 weeks

If this regimen fails (uncommon) after a 2-month trial, then recommend triple therapy (usually amoxicillin, metronidazole, and bismuth) with proton-pump inhibitors.

Source

MCCQE
USMLE

18. What are the surgical options for ulcer treatment?

Surgical Options:
Surgical options may be considered after failure of naturopathic and medical treatment or when complications develop (perforations, bleeding). Common surgical procedures include:
- Antrectomy
- Vagotomy
- Billroth I or II

ACHLORHYDRIA

Source

NPLEX
MCCQE
USMLE

19. What is achlorhydria? What causes it?

Achlorhydria Definition: the *absence* of hydrochloric acid secretion from gastric parietal cells. It is estimated that one-third of the population more than 60 years of age are achlorhydric.

Causes:
- Most commonly due to pernicious anemia, in which antiparietal cell antibodies destroy acid-secreting parietal cells, thus causing achlorhydria and vitamin B-12 deficiency.
- Often a sign of other endocrine autoimmune disorders (e.g., hypothyroidism, vitiligo, diabetes, hypoadrenalism).
- Gastric resection.

GASTRIC BLEEDING

20. What are the diagnostic differences between upper and lower gastrointestinal (GI) bleeding?

Source

NPLEX
MCCQE
USMLE

UPPER VS. LOWER GI BLEEDING

Differential Feature	Upper GI Bleeding	Lower GI Bleeding
Location	Esophagus, stomach, or proximal small bowel	Distal small bowel, large bowel, or rectum
Common causes	Gastritis, ulcers, varices, and esophagitis	Vascular ectasia, diverticulosis, colon cancer, colitis, inflammatory bowel disease, and hemorrhoids
Stool	Tarry, black stool (melena)	Bright red blood seen in stool (hematochezia)

21. What radiological imaging studies can be done to localize a GI bleed?

Source

NPLEX
USMLE

Radiological Imaging Studies:
- Radionuclide scans: valuable for detecting slow or intermittent bleeds if the source cannot be found with endoscopy.
- Angiography: can detect more rapid bleeds (embolization of bleeding vessels can be done during the procedure).

Source

NPLEX
MCCQE
USMLE

22. How is gastric bleeding treated?

Gastric Bleeding Treatment Protocol:

1. Make sure the patient is stable (ABCs, intravenous fluids, and blood if needed) before attempting to diagnose.
2. Recommend hospitalization because a nasogastric tube (NGT) aspirate needs to be obtained to determine whether you are dealing with upper or lower GI bleeding.
3. Endoscopy should follow (upper or lower depends on NGT study). Traditionally, barium x-ray studies are performed, but endoscopy is more sensitive. Endoscopically treatable conditions include vascular tears or ectasias, polyps, and varices.
4. These procedures should not be performed in an outpatient facility.

Surgery: Recommended for severe or resistant bleeds. Usually involves resection of the affected bowel (usually colon).

Source

NPLEX
MCCQE
USMLE

23. What is diverticulosis? What are its complications?

Diverticulosis: sac-like mucosal projections through the muscular layer of the colon or rectum. It is extremely common, and the incidence increases with age. The patient is usually unaware of any ill effects unless complications occur.

Causes: In part, by a low-fiber + high-fat diet.

Complications:

- GI bleeding (common cause of painless lower GI bleeding)
- Diverticulitis (inflammation of the diverticula). Signs of diverticulitis include:
  - LLQ pain
  - Fever
  - Diarrhea or constipation
  - Leucocytosis

DIARRHEA

24. How is diarrhea categorized according to etiology?

Diarrhea Etiology:
- Systemic
- Osmotic
- Secretory
- Malabsorptive
- Infectious
- Exudative
- Functional or altered intestinal transit

Source

NPLEX

25. What is systemic diarrhea?

Systemic Diarrhea: any illness can cause diarrhea as a systemic symptom, especially in children (e.g., otitis media).

Source

NPLEX

26. What is osmotic diarrhea? How can a diagnosis be made?

Osmotic Diarrhea: occurs when non-absorbable solutes remain in the intestines (water flows down its osmotic gradient through the semi-permeable intestinal wall). Examples include lactose or other sugar intolerances and olestra in potato chips.
Diagnosis: When the patient stops ingesting the offending substance (e.g., avoidance of milk or a trial fasting), the diarrhea stops – an easy diagnosis.

Source

NPLEX
MCCQE

27. What is secretory diarrhea?

Secretory Diarrhea: involves too much intestinal secretion of fluid. This is an active process due to one of the following:
1. Bacterial toxins (*Vibrio cholera* and pathogenic *Escherichia coli*)
2. VIPoma (pancreatic islet tumor that secretes vasoactive intestinal peptide)
3. Bile acids after ileal resection

Diagnosis: Secretory diarrhea continues after the patient stops eating – another easy diagnosis – but remember to monitor the patient's hydration status prudently. Oral rehydration fluids are life-savers.

Source

NPLEX
MCCQE
USMLE

28. What are some common causes of malabsorption diarrhea?

Malabsorption Diarrhea Causes:
1. Celiac sprue (look for dermatitis herpetiforms and avoid gluten in diet)
2. Crohn's disease (due to depletion of brush-border enzymes)
3. Post-gastroenteritis (also due to depletion of brush-border enzymes)

Source

NPLEX
MCCQE
USMLE

Source

NPLEX
MCCQE
USMLE

29. What are the common signs and symptoms of infectious diarrhea?

Infectious Diarrhea Signs and Symptoms:

1. Fever
2. Leucocytes in stool analysis with invasive bacteria like: *Shigella* → bacillary dysentery; *Salmonella* → food poisoning; *Yersinia* → gastroenteritis; and *Campylobacter* → food poisoning in children. Leucocytes are not found in infections of toxigenic bacteria (see above).

Causes:

■ Travel history: Hikers and campers drinking from lakes and streams may have *Giardia lamblia* infection. This protozoal infection usually presents with steatorrhea (fatty, greasy, malodorous stools that float) due to small intestinal involvement.

■ History of antibiotic use (especially clindamycin): Consider *Clostridium difficile* → pseudomembranous enterocolitis. Test the stool for *C. difficile* toxin.

Source

NPLEX
MCCQE
USMLE

30. What causes exudative diarrhea?

Exudative Diarrhea Causes: Inflammation of the intestinal wall causing seepage of fluid. Mucosal inflammation is due to either IBD or cancer.

Diagnosis: As in infectious diarrhea, patients usually have fever and white blood cells in the stool, but the chronicity of symptoms and the non-bowel symptoms (see below) are clues.

Source

NPLEX
MCCQE
USMLE

31. What is the management protocol for a case of diarrhea?

Management: Diarrhea is a common and preventable cause of death in under-developed countries. To manage a case of diarrhea:

■ Obtain a good health history (BM, diet, medication history, laxative use, and recent changes).
■ Watch for dehydration and electrolyte disturbances, especially metabolic acidosis and hypokalemia.
■ Look for occult blood in stool.
■ Examine stool for bacteria, ova, parasites, fat content, and white blood cells.

Source

NPLEX
MCCQE
USMLE

32. What should you watch for in children after a bout of diarrhea?

Pediatric Caution: After bacterial diarrhea in children, there is a chance of them developing hemolytic uremic syndrome.

Diagnosis: Test for hemolytic anemia (evident on CBC and blood smear), thrombocytopenia (CBC), and acute renal failure (BUN and creatinine clearance).

Treatment: Treatment is supportive (in a hospital) because patients may need dialysis or transfusions.

CONSTIPATION

33. How is constipation defined?

Source

NPLEX

Pizzorno &
Murray,
1999

Constipation Subjective Definition: patient complains of infrequent BM and stools that are hard and difficult to expel. Symptoms of constipation include bloated-uncomfortable feeling and sluggishness.

Objective Definition: While the concept of ideal bowel movement frequency is a topic of debate in naturopathic circles, the objective signs of clinical constipation are clear:
1. Less than 3 bowel movements per week
2. More than 3 days without a bowel movement
3. If average daily stools weigh less than 35 gm on an adequate diet

34. What is the work-up for constipation?

Source

NPLEX
MCCQE
USMLE

Constipation Work-up:
1. Obtain a good health history (BM pattern, diet, medication history, laxative use) and inquire about any contributing lifestyle changes.
2. Assess dietary intake and composition.
3. Physical exam: check for weight loss, assess abdomen; do a rectal exam and anoscopy (to rule out fecal impaction, anal fissures, and/or hemorrhoids).
4. If the this strategy is unproductive, run the following tests:
    * Fecal occult blood or hem screen (to rule out colon cancer)
    * Sensitive TSH (to rule out hypothyroidism)
    * CBC (to rule out diverticulitis)

35. What are the common causes of constipation?

Source

NPLEX
MCCQE
USMLE

Constipation Causes:
- Not enough fiber in the diet. The most common reason by far is a diet typically low in vegetables, fruits, and whole grains and high in fats found in cheese, eggs, and meats.
- Not enough liquids and/or lack of exercise.
- Medications, such as calcium channel blocker and codeine containing drugs.
- Medical conditions, such as colon cancer (causing bowel obstruction), rectal fissures, hypothyroidism, diverticulitis, and irritable bowel syndrome.
- Changes in life or routine, such as pregnancy, older age, and travel.
- Abuse of laxatives. If patients are accustomed to laxatives (natural or otherwise), they will be adaptively constipated without them.
- Ignoring the urge to have a bowel movement (common in children).
- As sequelae of CNS conditions, such as stroke (common).

Source

NPLEX

Pizzorno &
Murray,
1999

36. What is the first-line naturopathic treatment for constipation?

Naturopathic Treatment for Constipation

Approach: Treatment will vary according to causative factors. However, the following generalizations are recommended for lifestyle/dietary induced and chronic idiopathic constipation.

1. Dietary measures
- Increase vegetable, fruit, and fiber (flaxseed, oat bran, guar gum, and pectin) intake.
- Avoid saturated fats, cholesterol, sugar, animal protein, and fried foods.
- Experiment with elimination diet for 3 weeks.
- Ensure adequate hydration: 2 liters of water daily.

2. Lifestyle changes
- In younger patients, recommend an aerobically adequate exercise program.
- For older patients, a daily leisurely walk should be adequate.

3. Clinical nutrition
- Vitamin B complex, high potency formulation: 100 mg q.d.
- Vitamin C: 1000 mg t.i.d. or to bowel tolerance
- Bulk forming laxatives: To help produce a bowel movement within 12 to 24 hours:
  - 5 g q.d. of combination fiber (guar gum+ pectin+ psyllium+ oat bran) in three divided doses with meals OR
  - 3-4 g q.d. of glucomannan (water-soluble dietary fiber that is derived from konjac root)

4. Botanical medicine (adjunctive short-term stimulant laxatives)
- *Cascara sagrada:* 20-30 mg of cascarosides q.d. for < 8-10 days. C/I pregnancy, Crohn's disease, and appendicitis.
- *Aloe vera:* 50-200 mg of latex q.d. for < 10 days. C/I pregnancy, breast-feeding, and IBD.
- *Cassia senna:* 20-60 mg of sennosides OR 1-5 ml of 1:5 tincture q.d. < 10 days. C/I first trimester of pregnancy.

IRRITABLE BOWEL SYNDROME

37. What are the signs and symptoms of irritable bowel syndrome (IBS)?

Source

NPLEX
MCCQE
USMLE

IBS Signs and Symptoms: Irritable bowel syndrome is considered a common psychosomatic GI complaint:
- Anxiety
- History of diarrhea (also bloating, abdominal pain, and/or mucus in stool) aggravated by stress
- Relieved by defecation

Diagnosis:
- Look for psychological stressors in the history and negative findings in physical exam and lab tests.
- IBS is diagnosis of exclusion: basic lab tests, rectal exam, stool exam, and sigmoidoscopy can be ordered. It is the most likely diagnosis if all of these tests give you negative results, especially in young adults.
- There is a 3:1 female to male incidence ratio.

38. What is the first-line naturopathic treatment for IBS?

Source

Pizzorno &
Murray,
1999

Naturopathic Treatment for IBS

1. Dietary measures
- Increase fiber-rich foods.
- Implement hypoallergenic diet.
- Avoid refined sugars.

2. Clinical Nutrition
- Lactobacillus acidophilus: 1-2 billion eq. per day.
- Enteric-coated volatile oil preparations (peppermint/caraway): 0.2-0.4 ml b.i.d. between meals.

3. Lifestyle: Leisurely walks, 20 minutes daily.

4. Counseling
- Stress reduction program
- Biofeedback

INFLAMMATORY BOWEL DISEASE

Source

NPLEX
MCCQE
USMLE

39. What are the classic differences between Crohn's disease and ulcerative colitis?

CROHN'S DISEASE VS. ULCERATIVE COLITIS

Differential Feature	Crohn's Disease (CD)	Ulcerative Colitis (UC)
Origin of lesion	Distal ileum and proximal colon	Rectum
Extent of inflammation	Transmural (throughout)	Limited to mucosa and submucosa
Progression	Irregular (skip-lesions)	Continuous (no skip-lesions)
Location	From mouth to anus	Only involves the colon, rarely extends into ileum
Bowel habit changes	Obstruction and abdominal pain	Bloody diarrhea
Classic lesions	Fistulas/abscesses, cobblestoning, and string sign (on barium x-ray)	Pseudopolyps, lead-pipe colon (on barium x-ray), and toxic megacolon
Colon cancer risk	Somewhat increased	Significantly increased
Surgery	Not recommended (may make it worse)	Recommended (proctocolectomy, ileoanal anastomosis, and pouch formation)
Common signs and symptoms	Fever; profuse, constant loose stools; anorexia; apathy; prostration; abdominal signs are normal; distended abdomen; and possibly rebound tenderness.	

Source

NPLEX
MCCQE
USMLE

40. What are the extra-gastrointestinal manifestations of IBD?

Systemic IBD Manifestations: Both CD and UC can cause:

- Uveitis
- Arthritis
- Ankylosing spondylitis
- Erythema nodosum or multiforme, primary sclerosing cholangitis
- Failure to thrive in children
- Toxic megacolon (markedly distended colon, common in UC)
- Anemia
- Fever

41. How is IBD treated conventionally?

Source

NPLEX
MCCQE
USMLE

Conventional Treatment:
- Emergency treatment and hospitalization in some patients. The goal is to achieve remission, which, once attained, can be maintained by conservative therapy.
- 5-aminosalicylic acid with or without a sulfa drug (e.g, sulfasalazine) when stable.
- Steroids during severe flare-ups.

42. What is the first-line naturopathic treatment for IBD?

Source

NPLEX

Pizzorno &
Murray,
1999

Naturopathic Treatment for IBD

Approach: First-line treatment starts with comprehensive dietary modifications.

1. Dietary measures
- Eliminate all possible food sensitivities (wheat, corn, dairy, carrageenan-containing foods)
- Provide a diet high in complex carbohydrates and fiber, low in sugar and other refined carbohydrates.
- Elemental diet (e.g., Peptamen, Nutren, Mediclear) is a proven effective alternative to corticosteroids to induce remission of acute IBD.
- Hypoallergenic (oligoantigenic) diet usually maintains remission once attained.

2. Clinical nutrition
- Glutamine: 500 mg t.i.d.
- Modified Robert's Formula (Bastyr's formula): 2-3 '00' capsules (or equivalent in tincture) t.i.d. with meals
- Quercetin: 400 mg t.i.d. 20 minutes before meals
- Evaluate and correct deficiencies in vitamins A and E, magnesium, and zinc.

43. What is a toxic megacolon?

Source

NPLEX
MCCQE
USMLE

Toxic Megacolon: may be precipitated by the use of motility suppressor antidiarrheal medications (e.g., Imodium-loperamide hydrochloride). This is classically seen with IBD and infectious colitis, especially *Clostridium difficile*. That is why antidiarrheal medications for any diarrhea with fever (infectious diarrhea) should not be recommended.
- Patients present with a high fever, leukocytosis, abdominal pain, rebound tenderness, and a dilated segment of colon (by palpation and radiograph).
- This is an emergency condition requiring prompt hospitalization. Instruct the patient not to eat. → Send to ER.

LIVER DISEASE

Source

NPLEX
MCCQE
USMLE

44. What are the signs and symptoms of acute liver disease?

Acute Liver Disease Signs and Symptoms:
- ↑ Liver Function Tests (LFTs): AST (SGOT for NPLEX), ALT (SGPT for NPLEX), bilirubin, ALP, prothrombin time or international normalized ratio (INR)
- Jaundice
- Nausea and vomiting
- RUQ tenderness
- Hepatomegaly (liver span)

Source

NPLEX
MCCQE
USMLE

45. What are the common causes of acute liver disease?

Common Causes of Acute Liver Disease:
- Alcohol
- Medications
- Infection (hepatitis)
- Reye's syndrome
- Biliary tract disease

46. What are the common causes of chronic liver disease?

Chronic Liver Disease Causes:
- Alcohol use
- Hepatitis
- Metabolic disease

Stigmata:
- Gynecomastia
- Testicular atrophy
- Palmar erythema
- Spider angiomas
- Ascites

47. What metabolic disorders result from liver failure?

Source

NPLEX
MCCQE
USMLE

METABOLIC DISORDERS RESULTING FROM LIVER FAILURE

Metabolic Disorders	Rationale
1. **Coagulopathy:** PT (prothrombin time) or even PTT (partial thromboplastin time) are prolonged.	The liver is responsible for synthesis of coagulation factors. Vitamin K is useless because the liver cannot utilize it in its failed state. Symptomatic patients must be given fresh frozen plasma to survive.
2. **Jaundice/ hyperbilirubinemia:** Elevated conjugated and unconjugated bilirubin.	Liver is responsible for the metabolism of both by-products of hemoglobin degradation (DDx with biliary tract disease).
3. **Hypoalbuminemia**	Liver makes albumin.
4. **Portal Hypertension**	Always seen with cirrhosis or chronic liver disease. This leads to hemorrhoids, varices, and caput medusae.
5. **Ascites**	You add portal-hypertension to hypoalbuminemia; the result is always ascites. On physical exam, shifting dullness and fluid wave.
6. **Hyperammonemia**	The liver detoxifies ammonia into uric acid. Treat with decreased protein intake and a substance that decreases ammonia absorption (lactulose).
7. **Hepatic Encephalopathy**	High bilirubin and ammonia in turn cause irritation of brain tissue. Look for coarse tremor (asterixis) and mental status changes.
8. **Hepatorenal Syndrome**	Idiopathic causality relationship, where liver failure induces kidney failure.
9. **Hypoglycemia**	Glycogen is stored in the liver.
10. **Disseminated Intravascular Coagulation (DIC)**	Normal liver cells usually remove activated clotting factors. In liver failure, this is not done, leading to this end-stage emergent condition.

HEPATITIS

48. What is the classic abnormality on LFTs in patients with alcoholic hepatitis?

Alcoholic Hepatitis Abnormality:
- ↑ AST (SGOT) that is more than twice the value of ALT (SGPT), although both maybe elevated.

49. What clues suggest hepatitis A?

Hepatitis A Signs and Symptoms:
- Anti-hepatitis A immunoglobulin (IgM) is positive during or shortly after jaundice episode.
- No significant long-term sequelae of infection with the exception of rare cases of acute liver failure.
- Transmission is through fecal contamination (e.g., day-care center or restaurant food).

50. How is hepatitis B acquired and prevented?

Hepatitis B Infection Sources:
- Shared needles
- Sexual contact
- Perinatal transmission (mother to baby)
- Transfused blood (a risk factor in the past but all blood banks now test for HBV and HCV)

Prevention: Best treatment is preventive vaccination, community education, condoms, etc.

Risk: 10% of patients will develop chronicity that predisposes to hepatobiliary cirrhosis and hepatocellular cancer.

51. What is the serology of hepatitis B infection?

Hepatitis B Serology:
- Hepatitis B surface antigen (HBsAg) is positive only with unresolved acute or chronic infection.
- Hepatitis B surface antibody (HBsAb) is positive when patient is immune (recovered or vaccinated). It never appears if the patient has chronic hepatitis.
- Hepatitis B 'e' antigen (HBeAg) is a marker for infectivity, which means that if a patient exhibits anti-hepatitis B 'e' antibody (HBeAb), the likelihood of them spreading the disease is low.
- The first antibody to appear is the IgM hepatitis B core antibody (HBcAb) during the "window phase" when both HBsAg and HBsAb are negative.

52. What are possible sequelae of chronic hepatitis B or C?

Chronic Hepatitis B and C Sequelae:
- Cirrhosis
- Hepatobiliary cancer

53. What should be administered to individuals exposed to hepatitis B?

Source

NPLEX
MCCQE
USMLE

Hepatitis B Treatment: Hepatitis B immunoglobulin should be given to individuals exposed to hepatitis within 48 to 72 hours of exposure. Examples include newborn babies, whose mothers are HepB positive, and healthcare workers after a needle-stick injury (even if they are vaccinated, unless their HBsAb titer is known).

54. What are the sources, risk factors, and prevention for hepatitis C?

Source

NPLEX
MCCQE
USMLE

Hepatitis C Infection Cause:
- Post-transfusion hepatitis (most likely cause). Screening for HCV was developed recently.
- Positive hepatitis C antibody means that the patient has had an infection in the past, but does not mean the infection has been cleared.

Risk Factor: Hepatitis C is 8 times more likely than hepatitis B to progress into chronicity, cirrhosis, and cancer.

Prevention: Treatment is not usually successful; thus, prevention is paramount.

55. When is hepatitis D seen?

Source

NPLEX
MCCQE
USMLE

Hepatitis D Presentation:
- Hepatitis D is seen only in patients with hepatitis B. Not only does it piggyback on it, but also the co-infection may become chronic.
- Transmission is similar to HBV.
- IgM antibodies to hepatitis D antigen indicate resolution of a recent infection.
- Positive hepatitis D antigen indicates chronicity.

56. How is hepatitis E transmitted?

Source

MCCQE
USMLE

Hepatitis E Transmission:
- Via fecal contamination of food sources, like HAV.
- Uniquely, there is no chronic state.
- It is often fatal in pregnant women.

57. Which drugs may cause drug-induced hepatitis?

Source

MCCQE
USMLE

Drug-induced Hepatitis

- Acetaminophen
- Tuberculosis drugs: isoniazid, rifampin, and pyrazinamide
- Halothane (anesthetic)
- Carbon tetrachloride
- Tetracycline
- HMG-CoA reductase inhibitors (e.g., cholesterol lowering agents, such as Lipitor)

Source

NPLEX
MCCQE
USMLE

Pizzorno &
Murray,
1999

58. What is the conventional treatment for acute viral hepatitis?

Conventional Treatment:

Acute viral hepatitis is extremely debilitating (fever, headaches, GI discomfort, nausea and vomiting, diarrhea, arthralgia, drowsiness, malaise, and itching) requiring bed-rest and 9 to 16 weeks for recovery.

■ Supportive treatment, bed-rest.

■ Limited use of interferon alpha-2a or alhpa-2b in chronic cases of HBV or HCV.

■ Avoid contact with others during contagious phase (3 weeks before and after onset of acute symptoms).

59. What is the first-line naturopathic medical treatment for acute viral hepatitis?

Naturopathic Treatment for Acute Viral Hepatitis

1. Dietary measures

■ Avoid alcohol and hepatotoxic medications.

■ Acute:
  • Replace fluids (vegetable broth, diluted vegetable juices, herbal teas).
  • Restrict solid food intake to brown rice, steamed vegetables, and lean protein.

■ Chronic:
  • Avoid saturated fats, simple carbohydrates, oxidized fatty acids, and animal fat.
  • Recommend a calorically adequate diet that is primarily vegetarian.

2. Clinical nutrition

■ Vitamin C: to bowel tolerance and maintain 1000 mg t.i.d. in chronic cases

■ Bovine liver and thymus extracts (received some favorable literature review thus far)

3. Botanical medicine

■ *Glycyrrhiza glabra* (standardized to 5% glycyrrhetinic acid): 250-500 mg t.i.d. for 9-16 weeks (with increased potassium-rich foods and weekly monitoring for possible hypertension side effect)

■ *Silybum marianum* (standardized to silymarin content): 140-210 mg silymarin t.i.d. for 9-16 weeks

Source

NPLEX
MCCQE
USMLE

60. When should you suspect idiopathic autoimmune hepatitis?

Idiopathic Autoimmune Hepatitis: classically seen in 20- to 40-year-old women with anti-smooth muscle or anti-nuclear antibodies, and no risk factors or lab markers for other causes of hepatitis.
Treatment: Corticosteroid therapy.

AUTOSOMAL DISEASES

61. What is hemochromatosis? How do you recognize it?

Primary Hemochromatosis: an autosomal recessive trait, where excessive iron is deposited in the liver, pancreas, heart, skin, and joints (see Hematology module).

Signs and Symptoms:
- Iron deposition leads to cirrhosis and/or hepatocellular carcinoma, diabetes, dilated cardiomyopathy, "bronze diabetes" skin pigmentation, and arthritis.
- Men are symptomatic earlier and more often than women due to menstrual loss of iron.

Treatment: Phlebotomy: weekly or biweekly removal of 500 ml of blood until iron levels return to normal.

Secondary Hemochromatosis: caused by iron overload, which is classically due to ineffective erythropoiesis (e.g., thalassemia), hemolysis, and excessive iron intake.

62. What is Wilson's disease? How do you recognize it?

Wilson's Disease (hepatolenticular degeneration): another autosomal recessive disease, where excessive copper is deposited mainly in the liver and to some extent in the CNS.
- Serum ceruloplasmin (copper binding protein) is low, but serum copper may be normal. Liver biopsy is confirmatory and will show excessive copper deposition in the liver.
- Think of Wilson's disease in patients with liver disease, CNS manifestations (tremor), psychiatric manifestations (psychosis), and Kayser-Fleischer rings in the iris.

Treatment: Copper chelation with penicillamine or other copper chelating agents.

63. What are the clues to diagnosing alpha-1 antitrypsin deficiency?

Alpha-1 Antitrypsin Deficiency Diagnosis: Young adult with cirrhosis and emphysema without risk factors for either. This is another rare autosomal recessive disease (i.e., look for an autosomal recessive family history because it skips generations).

Source

NPLEX
MCCQE
USMLE

BILIARY TRACT CONDITIONS

Source

MCCQE
USMLE

64. What signs and symptoms favor biliary tract obstruction as a cause of jaundice?

Biliary Tract Obstruction Signs and Symptoms:

- Very high ALP
- Elevated conjugated bilirubin (more than unconjugated bilirubin because the liver still functions normally)
- Pruritus
- Clay-colored stool
- "Coca cola" dark urine (unconjugated bilirubin is never excreted in urine because it is tightly bound to albumin)

Source

MCCQE
USMLE

65. What are the common types of biliary tract obstruction?

Types of Biliary Tract Obstruction:

- Bile duct obstruction
- Cholestasis
- Cholangitis
- Primary biliary cirrhosis
- Primary sclerosing cholangitis

66. What are the two major causes of common bile duct obstruction?

Causes of Common Bile Duct Obstruction:

Gallstone (Choledocholithiasis)

- This is the most common cause. Look for the five Fs: female, forty, fertile, fair complexion, and obese.
- Most gallstones are silent until they either produce cholecystitis or common bile duct obstruction.
- Ultrasound is often diagnostic, if not, endoscopic retrograde cholangio-pancreatography (ERCP) is recommended.

Pancreatic Cancer

- Clinical diagnosis is delayed because in most cases the symptoms are non-specific.
- Look for weight loss; dull abdominal pain; jaundice; palpably enlarged gall bladder (Courvoisier sign); and migratory thrombophlebitis (Trousseau syndrome).
- The etiology of pancreatic cancer is unknown, and to complicate matters, there is no satisfactory prevention or treatment. CT or ultrasound is often diagnostic.

67. What is first-line naturopathic treatment of gallstones?

Source

NPLEX

Pizzorno & Murray 1999

Naturopathic Treatment for Gallstones

Approach: Treatment varies slightly based on gallstone composition (80% are mixed, 20% are exclusively mineral). However, the following generalizations are adequate for both types:

1. Dietary measures
- Increase vegetable, fruit, and fiber (flaxseed, oat bran, guar gum, and pectin) intake.
- Avoid saturated fats, cholesterol, sugar, animal protein, and fried foods.
- Use elimination diet for 12 weeks.
- Ensure adequate hydration: 2 liters of water daily.

2. Clinical nutrition
- Phosphatidylcholine: 500 mg q.d.
- L-Methionine: 1 g q.d.
- Combination fiber (guar gum+ pectin+ psyllium+ oat bran): 5 g q.d. in three divided doses with meals

3. Botanical medicine
Duration of treatment should be no less than 12 weeks:
- *Taraxicum officinalis* (4:1): 250-500 mg t.i.d.
- *Peumus boldo:* (1:1) 0.5-1.0 ml t.i.d.
- *Silybum marianum* (standardized to silymarin content): 140-210 mg silymarin t.i.d.

68. What are the most common causes of cholestasis?

Source

MCCQE
USMLE

Cholestasis Common Causes:
- Birth control pills
- Pregnancy

69. What clues suggest primary biliary cirrhosis?

Source

NPLEX
MCCQE
USMLE

Primary Biliary Cirrhosis Signs and Symptoms:
- Seen in middle-aged women with no risk factors for liver or biliary disease.
- Marked pruritus, jaundice, and positive antimitochondrial antibodies. The rest of the work-up will be negative.
- Unfortunately, the only treatment recommended is liver transplantation.

Source

MCCQE
USMLE

70. What is cholangitis?

Cholangitis: inflammation of the bile duct that is usually caused by gallstone dislodgment in the common bile duct.

Primary Sclerosing Cholangitis: occurs in young adults with IBD (usually UC). It presents like regular cholangitis.

Symptoms and Diagnosis: Fever + RUQ pain + jaundice = Charcot's triad (diagnostic signs).

Treatment: Recommended treatment is surgical excision and antimicrobial treatment.

PANCREATITIS

Source

NPLEX
MCCQE
USMLE

71. What causes acute pancreatitis?

Acute Pancreatitis Causes:
- >80% are due to alcohol and gallstones.
- Less common causes include:
  - Hypertriglyceridemia
  - Mumps
  - Trauma
  - Hypercalcemia
  - Steroid medications
  - Scorpion bites

Source

NPLEX
MCCQE
USMLE

72. How do you recognize acute pancreatitis?

Acute Pancreatitis Signs and Symptoms:
- Epigastric abdominal pain that radiates to the back
- Nausea and vomiting without relief of pain
- Leucocytosis
- Elevated levels of serum Amylase and Lipase
- Cullen's sign – blue-black umbilicus; and/or Grey Turner's sign – blue-black flanks. These patients need to be hospitalized.
- Perforated ulcers are also associated with elevated serum amylase. However, patients usually have free air on abdominal radiographs and history of PUD.

73. What are the complications of acute pancreatitis?

Source

NPLEX
USMLE

Acute Pancreatitis Complications:
- Pseudocyst formation
- Abscess formation
- Infection
- Chronic pancreatitis

74. What causes chronic pancreatitis?

Source

NPLEX
USMLE

Chronic Pancreatitis Causes: Chronic pancreatitis is almost always caused by alcoholism and repeated acute pancreatitis. Gallstones do not cause chronic pancreatitis (only acute).

Treatment: Recommended treatment is alcohol abstention, oral pancreatic enzymes, and fat-soluble vitamins (i.e., A, D, E, and K).

PEDIATRIC CONDITIONS

75. What GI congenital malformations are common in children?

GI CONGENITAL MALFORMATIONS IN CHILDREN

Condition	Age of Onset	Vomit Description	Findings
Pyloric stenosis	0-2 months	Projectile nonbilious	Incidence in males > females; palpable olive shaped mass in epigastrium; low serum Cl and K; metabolic alkalosis.
Intestinal atresia	0-1 week	Bilious	Common in Down syndrome.
Tracheoesophageal fistula	0-2 weeks	Food regurgitation	Respiratory distress during feedings; aspiration pneumonia; and gastric distention with air.
Hirschsprung's disease	0-2 years	Feculent	Abdominal distension; and obstipation. Males > females.
Anal atresia	0-1 week	Late and feculent	Detected on initial nursing examination after delivery; males > females.
Choanal atresia	0-1 week	None	There is cyanosis with feeding relieved by crying. These infants cannot breath simultaneously while feeding due to nasal obstruction.

- Surgical repair is the treatment of choice for all of the above conditions.

76. What are other common pediatric GI conditions?

OTHER COMMON PEDIATRIC GI CONDITIONS

Condition	Age of Onset	Vomit Description	Findings
Intussusception	4 months-2 years	Bilious	Currant-jelly stools (blood and mucus mixed with stool); palpable sausage-shaped mass. Barium enema is diagnostic and commonly therapeutic.
Volvulus	0-2 years	Bilious	Sudden onset of pain; distention, rectal bleeding, peritonitis. Emergency surgical intervention is the only treatment for this condition.
Necrotizing enterocolitis	0-2 months	Bilious	Common in premature infants; fever; rectal bleeding. Refer to children's hospital for NGT, IV fluids, and antimicrobials.
Meconium ileus	0-2 weeks	Late & feculent	This is a manifestation of cystic fibrosis along with rectal prolapse.
Meckel's diverticulum	0-2 years	Varies	2% of population is affected; a 2-inch-long remnant of omphalomesenteric duct at the ileocolic junction. This condition may lead to intussusception, obstruction, or volvulus.
Strangulated hernia	Any age	Bilious	Palpation reveals intestinal loops in an inguinal hernia; there is also fever, distress and borborygmi.

Source

NPLEX
USMLE

77. What is the most common cause of diarrhea in children?

Causes of Diarrhea in Children:
- Viral gastroenteritis (e.g., Norwalk virus) is usually the culprit. It presents as fever, vomiting, diarrhea (check if other children in the daycare or school have similar symptoms).
- Diarrhea may be a sign of systemic illness.

Source

NPLEX
USMLE

78. Do you ever see IBS in children?

IBS in Children: Irritable bowel syndrome is possible in children with these presentations:
- Separation anxiety (e.g., not wanting to go to school)
- Depression
- Child abuse
- Other psychiatric presentations

79. How do you manage a case of yellow-infant?

Source

NPLEX
MCCQE
USMLE

Yellow-infant Management:
- Work-up of neonatal jaundice is to figure out whether it is physiologic or pathologic.
- Measure total, direct, indirect bilirubin, and microalbumin.
- There may be a concern that this infant will develop kernicterus (encephalopathy secondary to high levels of unconjugated bilirubin with seizures, flaccidity, opisthotonos, and irregular breathing).

80. What causes physiologic neonatal jaundice?

Source

NPLEX
MCCQE
USMLE

Physiologic Neonatal Jaundice Causes:
- Approximately 50% of normal infants will have physiologic jaundice. It is caused by degradation of fetal hemoglobin (and its replacement by adult hemoglobin).
- In addition, the liver functions aren't developed yet. That is why bilirubin will be mostly unconjugated.

Bilirubin Levels:
- In full-term infants, physiologic bilirubin rise is <12 mg/dl and returns to normal by 2 weeks of age.
- In premature babies, physiologic bilirubin rise is <15 mg/dl and returns to normal by 3 weeks of age.

81. How do you recognize pediatric pathologic jaundice?

Source

NPLEX
MCCQE
USMLE

Common Presentations of Pediatric Pathologic Jaundice:
- Jaundice presents at birth and/or bilirubin levels are above the levels mentioned above. In this case, send the patient to the emergency ward at a specialized children's hospital.
- Breast-milk jaundice: Occurs in breast fed infants with peak bilirubin level of 10-20 mg/dl at 2-3 weeks of age. Recommend temporary cessation of breast-feeding until jaundice resolves.
- Biliary atresia: Clay- or gray-colored stools and high levels of conjugated bilirubin. Refer for surgical intervention.
- Medication induced: SULFA drugs displace bilirubin from albumin.
- Illness: Infection or sepsis, hypothyroidism, liver disease, and cystic fibrosis may prolong physiologic jaundice, as well as lower the threshold for developing kernicterus.
- Metabolic disorders: Examples include Crigler's-Najjar disease (severe unconjugated hyperbilirubinemia); Gilbert's disease (mild unconjugated hyperbilirubinemia); and Dubin-Johnson disease (conjugated hyperbilirubinemia).

82. How is pathologic jaundice treated?

Pathologic Jaundice Treatments:
- Primary treatment is phototherapy to convert unconjugated bilirubin into a water-soluble form.
- If the unconjugated hyperbilirubinemia is >20 mg/dl, exchange transfusion may be performed.

Examination Board References

NPLEX (II): North American Board of Naturopathic Examiners
North American Board of Naturopathic Examiners (NABNE), Naturopathic Physician Licensing Examination Part II Blueprint and Study Guide. Portland, OR: NABNE, 2005.

USMLE (II): National Board of Medical Examiners
Bouchert A. USMLE Step 2 Secrets. Philadelphia, PA: Hanley & Belfus Inc., 2000.

MCCQE: Medical Council of Canada
Molckovsky A, Pirzada KS (eds.). Review for the Medical Council of Canada Qualification Examination. Toronto, ON: Toronto Notes Medical Publishing, 2004.

Related References

Cutler P. Problem Solving in Clinical Medicine: From Data to Diagnosis. 3rd ed. Baltimore, MD: Lippincott Williams & Wilkins, 1998.

Ferri F. Ferri's Clinical Advisor Instant Diagnosis and Treatment. New York, NY: Mosby Inc, 2003.

Marz RB. Medical Nutrition form Marz. 2nd ed. Portland, OR: Omni-Press, 1999.

Murray M. Encyclopedia of Nutritional Supplements. Rocklin, CA: Prima Publishing, 1996.

Pitchford P. Healing with Whole Foods. Asian Traditions and Modern Nutrition. 3rd ed. Berkley, CA: North Atlantic Books, 2002.

Pizzorno JE, Murray MT. Textbook of Natural Medicine. Vol. 1 and 2. 2nd ed. New York, NY: Churchill Livingstone, 1999.

Shapiro M. Gastroesophageal Reflux. In: Kohatso W (ed.). Complementary and Alternative Medicine Secrets. Philadelphia, PA: Hanley & Belfus Inc., 2002.

HEMATOLOGY

ANEMIA

BLEEDING DISORDERS

MONONUCLEOSIS

1. What are the diagnostic criteria, signs, and symptoms of anemia?

Source

NPLEX
USMLE

Anemia: a decrease in number of RBCs or Hb content caused by blood loss, deficient erythropoiesis, excessive hemolysis, or a combination of these changes. The term anemia denotes a complex of signs and symptoms, rather than a diagnosis.

Diagnostic criteria: Call it anemia only if CBC indicates the following:
■ Men: RBC < 4.5 million/µL, Hb < 14 g/dL, *or* Hct < 42%
■ Women: RBC < 4 million/µL, Hb < 12 g/dL, *or* Hct < 37%

Symptoms:
■ Fatigue
■ DOE (dyspnea on exertion)
■ Light-headedness, dizziness
■ Syncope
■ Palpitations
■ Angina
■ Claudications

Signs:
■ Pallor (better seen in palpebral conjunctiva and mucous membranes)
■ Tachycardia (compensation)
■ Systolic ejection murmurs (compensation)
■ Clues to underlying pathology (e.g., jaundice in hemolytic anemia)

2. What causes anemia?

Source

NPLEX
MCCQE
USMLE

Anemia Causes: There are several categories of anemia, the majority of which are due to blood loss, excessive red blood cell destruction, and deficient red blood cell production.
■ The most common anemias fall into the category of deficient red blood cell production.
■ In most cases seen in clinical practice, anemia presents as sign of blood loss (through menses or gastrointestinal bleeding) or nutrient deficiency (e.g., iron, folate, and/or B-12).
■ Iron deficiency is by far the most common nutritional cause of anemia.

3. What should you inquire about when faced with a case of anemia?

Source

NPLEX
MCCQE
USMLE

Anemia Diagnostic History: When diagnosing a possible case of anemia, inquire about the following history:
■ Blood loss: trauma, surgery, melena, hematemesis, and menorrhagia
■ Chronic diseases

- Family history: hemophilia, thalassemia, sickle cell disease, glucose-6-phosphatase deficiency (G6PD)
- Alcoholism: may lead to iron, folate, and B-12 deficiencies, as well as GI bleeds
- Medications

Source

NPLEX
MCCQE
USMLE

4. Which medications can cause anemia? What is the mechanism?

Medications that Cause Anemia: Many medications can cause anemia as a side effect. While the etiological mechanisms vary considerably, the following generalizations can be made:

Drug	Rationale
Methyl dopa Penicillins	Induce production of RBC antibodies, which leads to hemolysis.
Sulfa drugs	Induce production of RBC antibodies, which leads to hemolysis. Sulfa drugs are known to cause hemolysis in patients with G6PD.
Chloroquine	Induce production of RBC antibodies, which leads to hemolysis. This antimalarial drug is also known to cause hemolysis in patients with G6PD.
Phenytoin (Dilantin)	This anti-seizure medication interferes with folate metabolism, leading to megaloblastic anemia.
Chloramphenicol	This antibacterial drug inhibits formation of peptide bonds, thus temporarily causing bone marrow suppression (myelosuppression, neutropenia, and thrombocytopenia).
Chemotherapy agents	Anti-neoplastic drugs generally cause bone marrow suppression (chemotherapeutic agents preferentially target cells with fast mitotic activity, such as the bone marrow).
Zidovudine (AZT)	This reverse transcriptase inhibitor (used for the management of symptomatic and asymptomatic HIV infections) suppresses myeloid and erythroid progenitor cells.

Source

MCCQE
USMLE

Pizzorno
et al, 1999

5. What tests should be ordered first to work-up the cause of anemia?

Tests for Anemia:
- Complete blood count (CBC) with red blood cell indices:
  1. First, the hemoglobin and/or hematocrit must be below normal.
  2. Second, the mean corpuscular volume (MCV) indicates whether the anemia is Microcytic (MCV <80), Normocytic (MCV =80-100), or Macrocytic (MCV >100).
  3. Third, the reticulocyte count is elevated in hemolysis because the bone marrow tries to compensate for RBC loss. Conversely, it is decreased when the bone marrow is not responding properly.
- CBC interpretation: A peripheral blood smear is performed whenever the CBC or RBC indices return an abnormal result. Look for classic findings of specific diagnoses:

Blood Smear Results and Interpretations:

Findings	Interpretation	Findings	Interpretation
Sickeled cells	Sickle cell	Howell-Jolly bodies	Sickle cell disease or asplenia
Hyper-segmented neutrophils	Folate/B-12 deficiency	Teardrop-shaped RBCs	Myelofibrosis
Hypochromic microcytic RBCs	Iron deficiency	Schistocytes, helmet cells, and fragmented RBCs	Intra-vascular hemolysis
Parasites in RBCs	Malaria or babesiosis	Spherocytes and elliptocytes	Hereditary spherocytosis and elliptocytosis
Heinz bodies	G6PD	Acanthocytes and spur cells	Abetalipoproteinemia
Bite Cells	G6PD or other hemolytic anemias	Target cells	Thalassemia or liver disease
Iron inclusions in RBCs	Sideroblastic anemia	Polychromasia and reticulocytosis	Hemolysis
Basophilic stippling	Lead poisoning	Burr cells or echinocytes	Uremia; chronic renal failure

6. What are the causes of microcytic, normocytic, and microcytic anemia?

Source

NPLEX
MCCQE
USMLE

ANEMIA CAUSES:

Category	With low reticulocyte count	With normal or elevated reticulocyte count
Microcytic	Lead poisoning Sideroblastic anemia Anemia of chronic disease Iron deficiency	Thalassemia Hemoglobinopathy Sickle cell disease
Normocytic	Cancer or dysplasia Acute leukemia Bone marrow suppression Medications (bone marrow suppressors) Anemia of chronic disease Aplastic anemia Endocrine (thyroid or pituitary failure) Renal failure	Acute blood loss Hemolysis (multiple of causes) Medications (inducers of anti-RBC antibodies, see above)
Macrocytic	Folate deficiency Vitamin B-12 deficiency Medications (e.g., methotrexate, phenytoin)	None

Source

NPLEX
MCCQE
USMLE

7. What is iron deficiency anemia?

Iron Deficiency Anemia: the most common cause of anemia in North America, associated with the following symptoms and circumstances:

- Women of reproductive age due to menstrual blood loss.
- Children, pregnant, or breast-feeding women due to increased requirements.
- Asymptomatic chronic cases are often related to colon cancer.
- Often presents as fatigue, dyspnea on exertion, dizziness, and palpitations.
- Rarely, patients with iron deficiency anemia develop craving for ice or dirt (pica).

Diagnosis:

- Low iron
- Low ferritin level
- Increased total iron binding capacity (TIBC or transferrin)
- Low TIBC saturation
- In menstruating women, a presumptive diagnosis of menstrual blood loss can be made.
- In all patients more than 40 years of age (men and post menopausal women), rule out colon cancer as a cause of chronic, asymptomatic blood loss. A stool occult blood test should be performed. If the test returns a positive result or there is family history of colon cancer, seriously consider a colonoscopy.
- In postnatal care, recommend iron supplements or iron-containing formula for all infants (4 to 6 months), except full-term infants, who are exclusively breast-fed.

Source

NPLEX
MCCQE
USMLE

8. What is Plummer-Vinson syndrome?

Plummer-Vinson syndrome: a triad of esophageal web (leading to dysphagia), iron deficiency anemia, and glossitis.

- Plummer-Vinson syndrome is of unknown etiology.

Source

NPLEX
MCCQE
USMLE

Pizzorno
et al, 1999

9. What is the first-line naturopathic treatment for iron deficiency?

Naturopathic Treatment for Iron Deficiency

Approach: The cause of any presenting anemia should always be explored first.

1. Dietary measures
- Encourage liberal consumption of green leafy vegetables and/or other dietary sources of iron.

2. Clinical nutrition
- Hydrolyzed (liquid) liver extract: 500-1500 mg t.i.d. before meals as a rich source of heme iron, as well as folic acid and vitamin B-12; or ingestion of 4-6 oz of calf liver q.d.
- Iron succinate (or iron fumarate): 30 mg b.i.d. between meals. If abdominal discomfort occurs, change posology to 30 mg t.i.d. with meals.

- Follow these treatment protocols for 3 to 6 months to replete body iron stores.
- Monitor CBC monthly to determine when values normalize.

10. What causes folate deficiency?

Source

NPLEX
MCCQE
USMLE

Folate deficiency: commonly seen in alcoholics and pregnant women. Since folate deficiency causes congenital neural tube defects, women of reproductive age should take folate-containing supplements.

Causes:
- Poor diet
- Malabsorption
- Chronic use of some medications, including Methotrexate, sulfa drugs (trimethoprim sulfamethoxazole "TMP"); and phenytoin

Diagnostic Tests:
- The laboratory studies will show macrocytes and hyper-segmented neutrophils *without* neurologic signs (i.e., loss of sensation and position sense, paresthesia, ataxia, spasticity, hyperreflexia, positive Babinski sign, and dementia), which suggest B-12 deficiency.
- Confirm with serum or RBC folate assay.

11. What is the first-line naturopathic treatment for folate deficiency?

Naturopathic Treatment for Folate Deficiency

1. Address the cause of the deficiency
- Stop or change medications.
- Correct deficient diet.

2. Clinical nutrition
- Hydrolyzed (liquid) liver extract: 500-1500 mg t.i.d. before meals as a rich source of heme iron, as well as folic acid and vitamin B-12; or ingestion of 4-6 oz of calf liver q.d.
- Folic acid: 800-1200 mcg t.i.d.
- Vitamin B-12: 1000 mcg q.d. orally. It is always necessary to complement vitamin B-12 with folic acid to prevent the folate from masking a B-12 deficiency.

- Follow this treatment protocol for 3 months.
- Monitor CBC monthly to determine when values normalize.

12. What causes vitamin B-12 deficiency anemia?

Source

NPLEX

Pizzorno
et al, 1999

Vitamin B-12 Deficiency Anemia: subtype of megaloblastic anemias.

Causes:
- Pernicious anemia (most common cause)
- Gastrectomy
- Terminal ileum resection
- Crohn's disease
- Strict vegan diet
- Chronic pancreatitis

Diagnostic Tests:

- The peripheral smear looks exactly the same as in folate deficiency (macrocytes, hypersegmented neutrophils), but patients will have neurologic deficiencies (e.g., loss of sensation and position sense, paresthesia, ataxia, spasticity, hyperreflexia, positive Babinski sign, and dementia).
- Achlorhydria is a diagnostic feature of pernicious anemia.
- Confirm diagnosis with serum B-12 assessment and/or the Schilling test.

Source

Pizzorno et al, 1999

13. What is the first-line naturopathic treatment for vitamin B-12 deficiency anemia?

Naturopathic Treatment for Vitamin B-12 Deficiency Anemia

Clinical nutrition

- Hydrolyzed (liquid) liver extract: 500-1500 mg t.i.d. before meals as a rich source of heme iron, as well as folic acid and vitamin B-12; or ingestion of 4-6 oz of calf liver q.d.
- Oral vitamin B-12: 1000 mcg (sublingual methylcobalamin is preferred over cyanocobalamin) b.i.d. for 1 month followed by a maintenance dose of 1000 mcg q.d. Although it is popular to inject vitamin B-12, oral administration of an appropriate dose, even in the absence of intrinsic factor, is effective in achieving therapeutic elevation of serum B-12 levels.
- Alternative: Intramuscular vitamin B-12: 1000 mcg injection weekly for 8 weeks, followed by a maintenance dose of 1000 mcg once a month.
- Monitor CBC monthly until values normalize.

Source

NPLEX
MCCQE
USMLE

14. How is thalassemia differentiated from iron deficiency anemia?

Thalassemia and Iron Deficiency Anemia:

- Iron levels are normal in thalassemia, whereas in iron deficiency anemia the iron levels are low.
- Both presentations should be differentiated because they both lead to microcytic hypochromic anemia. In thalassemia, hemoglobin A2 levels will also be elevated.
- Remember that iron supplementation is contraindicated in thalassemia because it causes iron overload and subsequent hemochromatosis.

Source

NPLEX
MCCQE
USMLE

15. What lab test is positive in patients with autoimmune anemia?

Autoimmune anemia: Coombs test is positive in most cases of autoimmune anemia (e.g., secondary to SLE, lymphoma, leukemia, or long term of some prescription medications)

16. What clues point to lead toxicity as a cause of anemia?

Source

Marz, 1999

NPLEX
MCCQE
USMLE

Lead Toxicity: The human body can tolerate approximately 1 mg of lead per day without succumbing to deleterious side effects. In urban environments, the average intake of lead is about 2.5 mg per week. The World Health Organization estimates that 10% of ingested lead is absorbed by adults. However, recent research has demonstrated that children absorb and retain much higher amounts of lead than adults.

Acute (high-level exposure): Acute lead toxicity presents with vomiting, ataxia, colicky abdominal pains, irritability, aggression, behavioral regression, encephalopathy, cerebral edema, and/or seizures. Screen with serum lead assay.

Chronic (low-level exposure): Lead poisoning exhibits hypochromic microcytic anemia (CBC) and basophilic stippling (smear), as well as elevated free protoporphyrin. This presentation occurs almost always in children. Usually, lead toxicity is chronic and low-level with minimal nonspecific symptoms. Notwithstanding, chronic lead exposure has been linked to hyperactivity, attention deficit disorder (with or without hyperactivity), and behavioral disorders. Screen with CBC and blood, urine, or hair mineral analysis.

Risk factors for lead toxicity:

- Residence in old buildings that may have chipping or unstable lead-containing paint (building codes now prohibit lead based paints).
- Residence near lead-smelting or battery-recycling plants.
- Family members who work in lead-smelting or battery-recycling plants.
- Supplementation with oyster shell calcium, dolomite, and bone meal products (unless lead levels are stated on label).
- In underdeveloped countries still utilizing leaded fuels, living near highways or heavy traffic is a risk factor.
- In some underdeveloped countries, building codes do not prohibit lead pipes to be used in plumbing.

Screening:

- It is prudent to screen for lead toxicity in asymptomatic children at 1 and 2 years of age because chronic low-level exposure may lead to permanent neurologic damage.
- Screening of children with risk factors should be done even earlier at 6 month of age.

Source

Pizzorno
et al 1999

17. What is the first-line naturopathic treatment for lead toxicity?

Naturopathic Treatment Approach for Lead Toxicity

1. Address the cause
- Find the cause (environmental, dietary, or lifestyle).
- Decrease exposure.

2. First-line conservative chelation
- Vitamin C: 3 g q.d.
- Apple pectin
- Seaweed alginate
- Methionine
- Cysteine
- Cystine
- Encourage specific foods, such as beans, onions, and garlic

3. Acute toxicity
- For acute toxicity or in cases where laboratory evidence of improvement is not noted within 1 month of above treatment plan, consider the following lead-chelation measures:
  - Children: recommend Succimer (lead chelator). Add ethylenediamine tetraacetic acid (EDTA) in severe cases.
  - Adults: recommend Dimercaprol (lead chelator). Add EDTA in severe cases.

Source

NPLEX
MCCQE
USMLE

18. How do you recognize and manage anemia of chronic disease?

Anemia of Chronic Disease: can be either normocytic or microcytic.

Signs and Symptoms:
- Serum iron is low.
- Decreased total iron binding capacity (this is increased in iron deficiency anemia – an easy differential diagnosis).
- Serum ferritin will also be elevated.

Management:
- Treat the cause. Obviously, you should do your best to determine the disease that is causing this anemia (e.g., rheumatoid arthritis, SLE, cancer, or tuberculosis).
- Remember that chronic (often asymptomatic) renal disease causes normocytic anemia with reduced reticulocyte count due to decreased erythropoietin secretion.
- Refrain from prescribing iron supplementation.

19. What is sickle cell disease? How is it diagnosed and treated?

Source

NPLEX
MCCQE
USMLE

Sickle Cell Disease: 80% of African Americans are heterozygous for sickle cell trait.

Diagnosis:
- Diagnosis is established via peripheral blood smear exhibiting characteristic sickled erythrocytes; Howell-Jolly bodies in RBCs (nuclear remnants in erythrocytes); and elevated reticulocytes >8% to 10%.
- Diagnosis is confirmed via hemoglobin electrophoresis (screening is done at birth in Canada and the United States).

Clinical manifestations:
- Acute chest syndrome (presents like pneumonia)
- Bone pain (due to microinfarcts which may lead to avascular necrosis of femoral head)
- Dactylitis (hand-foot syndrome in children)
- Priapism
- Tendency for strokes
- Patients are also susceptible to pigment cholelithiasis; *Pneumococcus*, *Hemophilus*, and *Niesseria* infections; and aplastic crisis after parvovirus infection.

Management Guidelines:
- Folate supplementation
- Prophylaxis against infectious diseases
- Early and aggressive treatment of infections
- Proper hydration
- Severe presentations are termed "sickle cell crisis" and require hospitalization, oxygen administration, intravenous fluids, and analgesics (the pain is so severe that narcotic analgesics are the mainstay of pain management in hospitals).
- If all these measure fail in alleviating the sickle cell crisis, blood transfusion is considered

20. How do you recognize G6PD in your clinical practice?

Source

NPLEX
MCCQE
USMLE

Glucose-6-phosphatase deficiency: an X-linked recessive disorder, affecting males. It is most common in African American and Mediterranean populations. These patients are susceptible to sudden hemolytic episodes after exposure to fava beans, certain drugs (e.g., antimalarials, salicylates, sulfa drugs), infections, or DKA (diabetic ketoacidosis).

Diagnosis: RBC enzyme assay.

Treatment: Avoidance of inducers is the key to managing patients with G6PD.

BLEEDING DISORDERS

Source

NPLEX
MCCQE
USMLE

21. What is disseminated intravascular coagulation (DIC)?

Disseminated Intravascular Coagulation: a severe emergent condition, where thrombosis engages clotting factors, leading to their deficiency in circulating blood. DIC does not usually present to out-patient facilities. However, it should be suspected with bleeding disorders that prolong prothrombin time and partial thromboplastin time, as well as bleeding time.

Causes:
■ Pregnancy and obstetric complications (50%)
■ Malignancy (33%)
■ Sepsis
■ Trauma
■ Prostate surgery
■ Snake bites

Source

NPLEX
MCCQE
USMLE

22. What conditions may lead to eosinophilia?

Eosinophilia: an increase in the amount of circulating eosinophils.

Common Causes:
■ Atopic conditions (such as allergy, eczema, angioedema)
■ Parasitic infections
■ Autoimmune disease (e.g., SLE and rheumatoid arthritis)
■ Drug reaction
■ Adrenal insufficiency
■ Blood dyscrasias (such as lymphoma)

Source

NPLEX
MCCQE
USMLE

23. What do clotting tests measure?

Clotting Tests:
■ Prothrombin Time (PT) = extrinsic clotting pathway; prolonged by Warfarin (Coumadin or dicumarol).
■ Activated Partial Thromboplastin Time (PTT) = intrinsic clotting pathway; prolonged by Heparin.
■ Bleeding Time (BT) = platelet function; prolonged by Aspirin.

24. What conditions prolong and differentiate coagulation tests?

CONDITIONS PROLONGING AND DIFFERENTIATING COAGULATION TESTS:

Condition	PT	PTT	BT	Platelets	RBCs	Facts
Hemophilia A or B (deficiency in factor VIII or IX, respectively)	Normal	High	Normal	Normal	Normal	Mostly men are affected since it is X-linked. Common. Look for positive family history.
von Willebrand factor deficiency	Normal	High	High	Normal	Normal	Autosomal dominant inheritance. Common. (vWF deficiency) Look for positive family history.
Liver failure	High	High	High	Low	Normal or low	Look for stigmata of liver disease.
Vitamin K deficiency	High	Normal	Normal or High	Normal	Normal	Seen in malabsorption, alcoholism and prolonged antibiotic use.
Vitamin C deficiency (scurvy)	Normal	Normal	Normal	Normal	Normal	Easy bleeding from fingernails and gums.
Idiopathic thrombocytopenic purpura (ITP)	Normal	Normal	High	Low	Normal	May follow upper respiratory tract infections.
Thrombotic thrombocytopenic purpura (TTP)	Normal	Normal	High	Low	Low	Characteristics of hemolysis is usually present in peripheral smear.
Disseminated intravascular coagulation	High	High	High	Low	Low	Diagnosed largely from the presenting history (see above).

Source

NPLEX
MCCQE
USMLE

25. What causes thrombocytopenia?

Thrombocytopenia: bleeding from thrombocytopenia occurs as petechiae, nosebleeds, and easy bruising.

Common Causes of Low Platelet Count:
- Purpura (ITP or TTP)
- Hemolytic uremic syndrome (HUS)
- Disseminated intravascular necrosis (DIC)
- HIV
- Medications (especially heparin, quinidine, and sulfa drugs)
- Autoimmune disease
- Alcoholism

Source

NPLEX
MCCQE
USMLE

26. What causes petechiae in the absence of thrombocytopenia?

Petechiae Causes:
- Vitamin C deficiency (from poor dietary habits) is the main factor that causes splinter and gum hemorrhages (due to connective tissue 'collagen' instability rather than thrombocytopenia), myalgia, arthralgia, and capillary fragility.
- Chronic steroid use also leads to capillary fragility due to poor collagen formation.
- Less common causes are uremia (chronic renal failure), inherited connective tissue disease (this will also manifest as weak joint capsules, joint hypermobility, hemorrhoids, and/or varicose veins), Marfan's syndrome, and osteogenesis imperfecta.

Examination Board References

NPLEX (II): North American Board of Naturopathic Examiners
North American Board of Naturopathic Examiners (NABNE), Naturopathic Physician Licensing Examination Part II Blueprint and Study Guide. Portland, OR: NABNE, 2005.

USMLE (II): National Board of Medical Examiners
Bouchert A. USMLE Step 2 Secrets. Philadelphia, PA: Hanley & Belfus Inc., 2000.

MCCQE: Medical Council of Canada
Molckovsky A, Pirzada KS (eds.). Review for the Medical Council of Canada Qualification Examination. Toronto, ON: Toronto Notes Medical Publishing, 2004.

Related References

Dawson J, Taylor M, Reide P. Crash Course Pharmacology. 2nd ed. Philadelphia, PA: Mosby Inc, 2002.

Lederly F. Oral Cobalamin for pernicious anemia: Medicine's best kept secret. JAMA 1991;265:94-95.

Marz RB. Medical Nutrition from Marz. 2nd ed. Portland, OR: Omni-Press, 1999.

Murray M. Encyclopedia of Nutritional Supplements. New York, NY: Prima Publishing, Random House Inc., 1996.

Pizzorno JE, Murray MT. Textbook of Natural Medicine. Vol. 1 and 2. 2nd ed. New York, NY: Churchill Livingstone, 1999.

IMMUNOLOGY AND GENETICS

HYPERSENSITIVITY

IMMUNODEFICIENCY DISORDERS

GENETIC DISORDERS

HYPERSENSITIVITY

1. What are the four types of hypersensitivity reactions?

Four Types of Hypersensitivity Reactions:
1. Anaphylactic (type 1)
2. Cytotoxic (type II)
3. Immune complex-mediated (type III)
4. Cell-mediated/delayed (type IV)

2. What is the definition of type I hypersensitivity?

Type I Hypersensitivity: true anaphylactic hypersensitivity is due to preformed immunoglobulin type E (IgE) that binds with its target, leading to the release of vasoactive amines (like histamine and leukotrienes) from mast cells and basophils. Symptoms of this type of hypersensitivity depend on the extent and tissue location of mast cells.

Signs and Symptoms:
- Anaphylaxis
- Atopy
- Hay fever
- Urticaria
- Allergic rhinitis
- Asthma
- True food allergies (e.g., peanut or shellfish)
- Bee sting allergy
- Medication allergy (e.g., penicillins and sulfa drugs)
- Rubber glove allergy

Diagnosis:
- Eosinophilia
- Elevated IgE levels
- Positive family history of allergies, seasonal exacerbations
- Shiners (i.e., bilateral infraorbital edema)
- Bluish edematous nasal mucosa

3. What type of testing can identify an allergen if it is not obvious?

Allergen Tests:
- Allergins that react with preformed IgE are identified clinically by cutaneous scratch antigen test battery or intradermal antigen testing.
- Blood testing via radioallergosorbent test (RAST) quantify specific levels of preformed IgE as well as IgG.

Source

NPLEX
MCCQE
USMLE

4. What type of hypersensitivity explains food sensitivities?

Food Sensitivities: 20% of food reactions exhibit IgE-mediated (type I) immediate allergy symptoms toward food antigens. However, the most common food reactions (food sensitivities) are IgG and IgG complex mediated (type III).

Source

NPLEX
MCCQE
USMLE

5. What causes type II hypersensitivity?

Type II Cytotoxic Hypersensitivity: due to preformed IgG and IgM that bind to cell-bound antigens (or parts of a cell) leading to secondary inflammation. Examples include:

- Hyperacute transplant rejection
- Cytopenias caused by antibodies (e.g., idiopathic thrombocytopenic purpura)
- Transfusion reactions
- Erthythroblastosis fetalis (due to Rh incompatibility between parents)
- Goodpasture's syndrome
- Myasthenia gravis
- Graves' disease
- Pernicious anemia
- Pemphigus
- Autoimmune hemolytic anemia (e.g., due to exposure to methyldopa, penicillin, or sulfa)

Source

NPLEX
USMLE

6. What type of test is positive with hypersensitivity induced anemia?

Hypersensitivity Induced Anemia Test: Coomb's test (usually direct Coomb's test).

Source

NPLEX
MCCQE
USMLE

7. What causes type III hypersensitivity?

Type III Hypersensitivity Causes: Immune-complex-mediated hypersensitivity is due to antigen-antibody complexes that are deposited in tissues and/or vascular endothelium leading to a delayed inflammatory response. Examples include:

- Food sensitivities
- Serum sickness
- Lupus erythematosus
- Rheumatoid arthritis
- Glomerulonephritis (some types).
- Polyarteritis nodosa

Source

NPLEX
MCCQE
USMLE

8. What causes type IV hypersensitivity?

Type IV Hypersensitivity Causes: Cell-mediated/delayed sensitivity is due to sensitized T-lymphocytes that release inflammatory mediators. Examples include:

- Chronic transplant rejection
- Granulomas (such as tuberculous Ghon's focus, syphilitic gumma, and sarcoidosis)
- Contact dermatitis (poison ivy, nickel earrings, cosmetics, and medications)

IMMUNODEFICIENCY DISORDERS

9. What is the most common primary immunodeficiency?

Source

MCCQE
USMLE

Primary Immunodeficiency: IgA deficiency, which causes recurrent respiratory and gastrointestinal infections. IgA levels are always low (as well as IgG2).

10. What sexually transmitted disease should you consider when a patient presents with sore throat and mononucleosis-like syndrome?

Source

NPLEX
MCCQE
USMLE

Human Immunodeficiency Virus (HIV) Infection: HIV often initially presents to primary care providers as fever, malaise, pharyngitis, rash and/or lymphadenopathy. You need to distinguish HIV from a diagnosis of infectious mononucleosis.

11. How is HIV diagnosed as positive?

Source

NPLEX
MCCQE
USMLE

HIV Diagnosis:
- Established with enzyme-linked immunosorbent assay (ELISA), which, if positive, should be confirmed with retesting and Western blot test.
- Because it takes at least 1 month for HIV antibodies to develop, if a patient wants testing because of a recent unprotected sex encounter, the test should be repeated in 6 months if the initial test is negative.

12. What are the signs and symptoms of infectious mononucleosis?

Source

NPLEX
MCCQE
USMLE

Infectious mononucleosis: affectionately called the kissing disease, mononucleosis is caused by the Epstein-Barr virus.

Signs and Symptoms:
- Low-grade fever
- Malaise
- Pharyngitis
- Lymphadenopathy

Diagnosis:
- Lymphocytosis is diagnostic for this infectious disease.
- Diagnosis is confirmed by the specific Monospot test.

13. What usually causes hereditary angioedema?

Source

MCCQE
USMLE

Hereditary Angioedema Cause: A deficiency in C1 esterase inhibitor (complement enzyme) is the usual cause of hereditary angioedema. This term denotes some form of facial swelling.

Diagnosis:

- Patients exhibit diffuse swelling of the lips, eyelids, and possibly the airway, *unrelated* to allergen exposure.
- Look for positive family history because this disease is autosomal dominant.
- Laboratory investigations will show decreased levels of C4 complement levels.

Treatment: Acute treatment is the same as for anaphylaxis. Androgens are used for long-term management because they increase liver production of C1 esterase inhibitor.

Source

MCCQE
USMLE

14. What type of immune deficiency do recurrent Neisseria infections suggest?

Neisseria Infections: Complement deficiencies of C5 through C9 cause recurrent *Neisseria* sp. infections.

Source

NPLEX
MCCQE
USMLE

15. What is chronic mucocutaneous candidiasis?

Chronic Mucocutaneous Candidiasis: a cellular immunodeficiency specific for candidal infection.

Diagnosis:

- Patients have oral thrush and other candidal infections of the scalp, skin, and nails.
- Skin testing will confirm if it displays no reaction toward *Candida* sp. This is a peculiar finding since everyone in Canada and the United States is exposed and should exhibit a positive result.
- Consider this condition if a patient exhibits susceptibility to candidal infections without any other immune function disorders (i.e., susceptibility to other types of infections).
- Often this condition is associated with hypothyroidism.

Source

16. What naturopathic botanical remedies are commonly used as immune modulators or stimulants?

Naturopathic Immune Modulating and Stimulating Botanicals:

Yarnell,
2000

- *Astragulus membranaceus*
- *Boswella serrata*
- *Echinacea spp.*
- *Ganoderma lucidum*

Saunders,
2000

- *Lentinus edodes*
- *Thuja occidentali*
- *Withania somnifera*
- *Spilanthes acmella*
- *Uncaria tomentosa*

GENETIC DISORDERS

17. What are the patterns of inheritance of common genetically transmitted disorders?

PATTERNS OF INHERITANCE OF GENETICALLY TRANSMITTED DISORDERS

Pattern of inheritance	Genetically Transmitted Disorders		
Autosomal Dominant (no generations are skipped)	Von Willebrand's hemophilia	Neurofibromatosis	Hereditary spherocytosis
	Achondroplasia (dwarfism)	Huntington's chorea	Marfan's syndrome
	Adult polycystic kidney disease	Familial hypercholesterolemia	Familial polyposis coli
	Myotonic dystrophy	Multiple endocrine neoplasia syndrome (MEN I/II)	
Autosomal Recessive (generations are skipped)	Glycogen storage diseases	Tay-Sachs sphingolipidosis	Cystic fibrosis
	Galactosemia	Amino acid disorders (e.g., phenylketonuria or PKU)	Sickle cell disease
	Children polycystic kidney disease	Wilson's disease	Hemochromatosis (usually)
	Ambiguous genitalia due to Androgenital Syndrome (e.g., 21-hydroxylase deficiency)		
X-Linked Recessive	Hemophilia	Glucose-6-phosphate-deficiency	Bruton's agammaglobulinemia
	Fragile X syndrome	Duchenne's muscular dystrophy	
Chromosomal	Down syndrome (trisomy 21)	Edward's syndrome (trisomy 18)	Patau's syndrome (trisomy 13)
	Turner's Syndrome (XO)		
Polygenic	Pyloric stenosis	Cleft lip/palate	Type II diabetes
	Obesity	Neural tube defects	Schizophrenia
	Bipolar disorder (I/II)	Ischemic heart disease	Alcoholism

Source

NPLEX
MCCQE
USMLE

18. What is the likelihood of a woman's autosomal dominant condition being passed to her child?

Autosomal Dominant Transmission: Assuming that the father does not have the disease (a proper deduction since autosomal dominant conditions express themselves in carries), the likelihood is 50%, unless the patient was told that she was homozygous for the gene defect, which is extremely rare.

Source

NPLEX
MCCQE
USMLE

19. If both parents are carriers of an autosomal recessive condition, what are the odds that their child will develop the condition?

Autosomal Recessive Transmission: The easy way to navigate autosomal genetic counseling questions is by applying binomial statistics (there are only two genes per parent). Thus, in this example you would multiply both parents' genetic factor (0.5 X 0.5 = 0.25). Therefore, you can confidently answer this question by saying that the child has a 25% chance of developing the condition, a 50% chance of being a carrier, and a 25% chance of not inheriting the trait at all.

Source

NPLEX
MCCQE
USMLE

20. If a father has an X-linked recessive disorder, what are the odds that his child will be affected if the mother is not a carrier?

X-linked Recessive Disorder (male): Obviously, if his child is male, there will be no chance of him inheriting the trait (as the father would have only contributed the Y chromosome to his son). If the child is female, the X chromosome will always be passed, but since this a recessive disorder, there will be no chance that his daughter will develop the condition (i.e., she will only be a carrier for the trait).

Source

NPLEX
MCCQE
USMLE

21. If a mother is a carrier of an X-linked recessive disorder and the father is healthy, what are the odds that their son or daughter will develop the disease?

X-linked Recessive Disorder (female):
There is a 50% chance for a son and no chance for a daughter to develop the disorder. However, there is a 50% chance that she will be a carrier.

Source

NPLEX
MCCQE
USMLE

22. How do you recognize Down syndrome?

Down Syndrome: occurrence of three genetic alleles (trisomy) on chromosome # 21 leads to Down syndrome, which is the most common cause of mental retardation in North America.

Signs and Symptoms:
- At birth there is hypotonia, transverse palmar crease, and characteristic facies.
- Congenital cardiac defects, such as ventricular septal defect (VSD), increased risk of leukemia, duodenal atresia, and early Alzheimer's disease are also common.

Risk Factors: The major risk factor appears to be maternal age (1 in 1500 of 16-year-old mothers compared to 1 in 25 of 45-year-old mothers).

23. What is fragile X syndrome?

Source

NPLEX
MCCQE
USMLE

Fragile-X syndrome: the second most common cause of inherited mental retardation after Down syndrome, this syndrome is X-linked recessive.
- Affected males often exhibit large testicles.

24. What is Patau's syndrome?

Source

MCCQE
USMLE

Patau's Syndrome: another trisomy on chromosome # 13 (i.e., trisomy 13) that causes mental retardation.

Signs and Symptoms:
- Apnea
- Deafness
- Fusion of cerebral hemispheres (holoprosencephaly)
- Myelomeningocele
- Cardiovascular abnormalities

25. How do you recognize Turner's syndrome?

Source

NPLEX
MCCQE
USMLE

Turner's Syndrome: occurs in females who exhibit XO instead of XX.

Signs and Symptoms:
- Short stature
- Webbed neck
- Widely spaced nipples
- Amenorrhea
- Lack of appropriate breast development (due to primary ovarian failure)
- Infertility
- Coarctation of the aorta
- Horse-shoe kidneys or cystic hygroma

Diagnosis: Established through karyotyping and absence of Barr bodies on a buccal smear.

26. What is Klinefelter's syndrome?

Source

NPLEX
MCCQE
USMLE

Klinefelter's Syndrome: occurs in males who exhibit XXY instead of XY.

Signs and Symptoms:
- Tall stature
- Small testicles
- Gynecomastia
- Infertility
- Slightly decreased IQ

Source

NPLEX
MCCQE
USMLE

27. What is Marfan's syndrome?

Marfan's Syndrome: an autosomal dominant connective tissue disorder.

Signs and Symptoms:
- Positive family history
- Tall stature
- Arachnodactyly (long, thin fingers)
- Hyperextensible joints
- Mitral valve prolapse
- Dislocation of the ocular lens
- High risk for thoracic aortic aneurysm (i.e., aortic dissection)

Source

MCCQE
USMLE

28. What is cri-du-chat syndrome?

Cri-du-chat (or cry of the cat) Syndrome: appropriately named after the propensity of affected infants to emit a high-pitched cry, which sounds similar to a cat's cry.
- Caused by the deletion of the short arm of chromosome 5.
- Leads to severe mental retardation.

Source

NPLEX
MCCQE
USMLE

29. When would you suspect galactosemia in an infant?

Galactosemia: an autosomal recessive inherited disorder that manifests as elevated levels of galactose in the blood, congenital cataracts, and neonatal sepsis.
- These infants are born with a congenital inability to metabolize galactose and lactose. Affected infants should avoid all foods containing galactose or lactose.
- The affected newborn will consistently vomit after breast-feeding, leading to failure to thrive.

Examination Board References

NPLEX (II): North American Board of Naturopathic Examiners
North American Board of Naturopathic Examiners (NABNE), Naturopathic Physician Licensing Examination Part II Blueprint and Study Guide. Portland, OR: NABNE, 2005.

USMLE (II): National Board of Medical Examiners
Bouchert A. USMLE Step 2 Secrets. Philadelphia, PA: Hanley & Belfus Inc., 2000.

MCCQE: Medical Council of Canada
Molckovsky A, Pirzada KS (eds.). Review for the Medical Council of Canada Qualification Examination. Toronto, ON: Toronto Notes Medical Publishing, 2004.

Related References

Dains J, Baumann L, Scheibel P. Advanced Health Assessment & Clinical Diagnosis in Primary Care. 2nd ed. City, St. Louis: Missouri: Mosby Inc, 2003.

Pizzorno JE, Murray MT. Textbook of Natural Medicine, Vol. 1 and 2. 2nd ed. New York, NY: Churchill Livingstone, 1999.

Pizzorno JE, Murray MT, Joiner-Bey H. The Clinician's Handbook of Natural Medicine. New York, NY: Churchill Livingstone, 2002.

INFECTIOUS DISEASES

INFECTIOUS DISEASE REPORTNG

FEVER

MICROBIAL INFECTIONS

INFECTIOUS DISEASE REPORTING

1. Which infectious conditions are naturopathic physicians obligated to report to public health officials?

Public Health Reporting: The list of reportable diseases varies somewhat depending on provincial or state regulations. In the Province of Ontario, for example, the following infectious diseases are to be reported to the local medical officer of health according to Ontario Regulation 559/91 and amendments under the Health Protection and Promotion Act. For all other jurisdictions, contact your local medical officer of health. Note that there are usually penalties for not reporting indicate disease to your local public health office.

■ If you suspect one of these diagnoses but are unable to ascertain the etiology because of lack of experience and/or when confirmatory work-up is unavailable, the prudent approach is to report the condition as 'possible' and consult with another practitioner who can ascertain the diagnosis.

Infectious Disease Reporting:

Immediate reporting required	*Reporting by next working day required*
■ Acquired Immunodeficiency Syndrome (AIDS)	■ Amebiasis
■ Anthrax	■ Brucellosis
■ Botulism	■ Campylobacter enteritis
■ Cholera	■ Chancroid
■ Diphtheria	■ Chickenpox (Varicella)
■ Food poisoning (all causes)	■ Chlamydia trachomatis
■ Gastroenteritis, institutional outbreaks	■ Cryptosporidiosis
■ Group A Streptococcal infections, invasive	■ Cytomegalovirus, congenital (CMV)
■ Haemophilus influenza B disease, invasive	■ Encephalitis
■ Hemorrhagic fevers (e.g., Ebola, Marbug, and other viral causes)	■ Giardiasis, except asymptomatic cases
■ Hepatitis A	■ Gonorrhea
■ Lassa fever	■ Group B Streptococcal infections, neonatal
■ Measles	■ Hepatitis B, C, D
■ Meningococcal disease, invasive	■ Influenza
■ Paratyphoid fever	■ Legionellosis
■ Plague	■ Leprosy
■ Poliomyelitis	■ Listeriosis
■ Rabies	■ Lyme disease
■ Shigellosis	■ Malaria
■ Typhoid fever	■ Meningitis, acute
	■ Mumps

Immediate reporting required	*Reporting by next working day required*
■ Verotoxin-producing E. Coli, causing Hemolytic Uremic Syndrome (HUS) ■ Yellow fever	■ Ophthalmia neonatorum ■ Pertussis (whooping cough) ■ Psittacosis / Ornithosis ■ Q fever ■ Rubella, congenital syndrome ■ Salmonellosis ■ Syphilis ■ Tetanus ■ Trichinosis ■ Tuberculosis ■ Tularemia ■ Yersiniosis

FEVER

Source

Dains,
2003

2. What is the etiology of fever?

Fever: a persistent elevation of body temperature above the normal daily variation.

Causes: Fever can be caused by three distinct pathophysiological processes:
1. Hypothalamic set point elevation: infections, collagen disease, vascular disease, and malignancy trigger the hypothalamus to reset core body temperature. Subsequently, there is elevation of T-lymphocytes and increased effectiveness of interferons.
2. Excessive heat production despite normal heat loss: hyperthyroidism, hyperthermia, and aspirin overdose usually lead to elevation of basal metabolic rate beyond the normal capacity of heat-loss mechanisms. Antipyretic agents are not effective in managing this type of fever.
3. Defective heat loss despite normal heat production: burns, heat stroke, overbundling a child, anticholinergic overdose, and ectodermal dysplasia often lead to decreased efficiency of heat-loss mechanisms. Again, antipyretic agents would not be effective in managing this type of fever.

Source

NPLEX

Bickley,
2003

Dains,
2003

3. What is normal body temperature?

Normal Body Temperature: Because body temperature follows a normal daily variation, instead of referring to the usually quoted 37C or 98.9F absolute as a measure of normal, practitioners need to be aware of the following normal ranges:
1. Oral temperature: 35.8 to 37.3C (96.4 to 99.1F)
2. Rectal temperature: 36.3 to 37.8C (97.2 to 99.9F)
3. Tympanic temperature: 36.6 to 38.1C (97.7 to 100.4F)
4. Axillary temperature: 34.8 to 36.3C (94.8 to 97.5F)

Measurement Methods:
- In infants under 3 months of age, rectal temperatures are required. Pediatric clinical guidelines unanimously use rectal temperature ranges.
- Axillary and thermal-tape skin temperatures are not considered accurate enough for clinical management.
- Tympanic (auditory canal) and temporal artery temperature are gaining acceptance as quick and comfortable methods of recording body temperature for children and adolescents.
- Remember to follow the appropriate reference range of your method of choice.

4. What are clinically important facts about pyrexia?

Source

NPLEX
MCCQE
USMLE

Pyrexia Facts:
- Body temperature greater than 41.1C (106F) almost always indicates central nervous system disease or heat illness (over bundling) with or without infectious etiology.
- Infectious diseases in neonates, immune-compromised patients, patients with chronic renal insufficiency, and elderly patients usually do not present as febrile conditions.

In Children:
- Fevers in infants under 2 months of age are *rare* and should be viewed as serious until proven otherwise.
- During early childhood, fevers up to 40C (104F) are common, even with minor infections.
- All febrile infants < 3 months of age are considered to have sepsis or meningitis until proven otherwise.
- Toxic appearing febrile infants < 3 months old have 17% chance of bacterial infections, 11% chance of bacteremia, and 4% chance of meningitis.
- Non-toxic appearing febrile infants < 3 months have 8.6% chance of bacterial infections, 2% chance of bacteremia, and 1% chance of meningitis.
- Febrile children between 3 and 36 months have a 4.3% chance of bacteremia.
- The risk for bacteremia is directly related to the age of patient and elevation of the WBC count (leucocytosis).

5. Which localizing symptoms indicate the source of fever?

Source

NPLEX

Dains,
2003

Fever Signs and Symptoms: Specifically inquire about the presence (or absence) of these symptoms during your evaluation of febrile presentations:
- Headache or sinus pain
- Purulent nasal discharge
- Ear pain
- Toothache
- Sore throat
- Chest pain
- Dyspnea
- Cough
- Breast tenderness
- Abdominal pain
- Flank pain
- Dysuria
- Pelvic pain

- Vaginal discharge
- Rectal pain
- Testicular pain
- Calf pain
- Neck stiffness
- Joint swelling or stiffness
- Localized pain or heat
- Focal neurological deficits

Source

NPLEX
MCCQE
USMLE

6. What are the signs and symptoms that indicate serious febrile diseases?

Febrile Diseases: infectious diseases typically present as a febrile condition; however, in neonates, immune-compromised patients, patients with chronic renal insufficiency, and elderly patients, infectious diseases usually do not present as a febrile condition.

Serious Febrile Presentations:
- Progressive acute fever > 38.9C/102F (oral)
- Persistent fever for 3 weeks or longer
- Toxic appearance of patient (especially in pediatric presentations), altered consciousness, persistent vomiting, diarrhea with tenesmus, convulsions, lethargy, anorexia, or poor feeding, as well as the signs of sepsis (e.g., respiratory distress, temperature instability, jaundice, and apnea)
- Significant increases in WBC counts (e.g., leucocytosis, lymphocytosis)
- Infants:
  - Bulging or tightness of anterior fontanelle
  - Nuchal rigidity, Brudzinski's, or Kernig's signs

Source

MCCQE
USMLE

Dains,
2003

7. How do you manage fever without identifiable source (FWS) in children?

Fever without Identifiable Source: When patients present with FWS, take a complete history and conduct a physical exam.

History:
- Onset, duration, and pattern of fever
- Alertness
- Hydration status
- Illness in other household members
- Immunizations, blood transfusions, HIV
- Exposure to animals
- Heat exposure
- Last Tylenol given
- History of febrile seizures
- Birth, family, and past medical history
- Child's social and home environment

Physical Exam:
- Vital signs
- Use standard evaluation scales, such as the Yale Observation Scale

- Nuchal rigidity (which is common in meningitis in infants under 3 months old)
- Check eyes for conjunctivitis (watch for bilateral injection in Kawasaki Disease)
- Examine ears, nose, throat, and sinuses
- Check for lymphadenopathy
- Skin exam (watch for roseola between 6 and 36 months)
- Assess lungs and heart
- Assess for suprapubic and CVA tenderness
- Rule out UTI
- Rule out arthritis, osteomyelitis and meningitis

8. What naturopathic botanical remedies are commonly used as antipyretics or diaphoretics?

Source

Yarnell, 2000

Saunders, 2000

Naturopathic Antipyretics and Diaphoretic Botanicals:
- *Achilia millefolium*
- *Eupatorium perfoliatum*
- *Filipendula ulmaria*
- *Pimpinella anisum*
- *Populus tremloides*
- *Salix alba/nigra*
- *Tilia europa*

MICROBIAL INFECTIONS

9. What principles guide antimicrobial therapy?

Source

NPLEX
MCCQE
USMLE

Assessment of Benefit and Risk: Selection of antibiotics should be guided by comparing the potential harms from the presenting illness versus those of the pharmacological agent.
- Like most pharmacological agents, antimicrobials may have various side effects.
- The severity of the illness, immune status of the host, previous adverse reactions, allergies, pregnancy or breast-feeding status, and other medications the patient is taking must also be considered.
- Clinicians should identify the causative organism (through culture and sensitivity testing) of infectious presentations to improve the outcome of treatment.
- However, in outpatient settings, it may not be practical to wait for C&S results before implementing time-sensitive treatment. A prudent approach is to start addressing infectious diseases by using antimicrobial agents that are empirically recommended for particular conditions, and then refine the selection based on C&S results.

10. What are the antimicrobial drugs of choice for treating bacterial pathogens?

ANTIMICROBIAL DRUGS:

Condition	Usual Causative Organism(s)	Antimicrobial(s) of choice	Alternatives	Background Information
Typical Pneumonia	*Streptococcus pneumoniae*	Penicillin	Cephalosporin (1st or 3rd gen) Erythromycin Vancomycin	Some S. *pneumoniae* are penicillin resistant; 30% of H. *influenza* is aminopenicillin resistant. Erythromycin is only used in mild infections. Vancomycin is reserved for serious infections.
	Haemophilus influenzae	Ampicillin or Amoxicillin		
Atypical Pneumonia	*Mycoplasma Chlamydia pneumoniae trachomatis*	Erythromycin	Tetracycline Cephalosporin (3rd generation)	Although tetracycline is as effective as macrolides (erythromycin), the latter covers *Pneumococcus*, which mimics *Mycoplasma*.
AIDS Pneumonia	*Pneumocystis carinii (PCP)*	TMP-SMZ	Pentamidine	In AIDS (i.e., HIV +ve patient with CD4 < 200). PCP is the most common opportunistic infection.
	Cytomegalovirus (CMV)	Ganciclovir	Foscarnet	
Tuberculosis	*Mycobacterium tuberculosis*	Isoniazid + Rifampicin + Ethambutol	Streptomycin Flouroquinolone Cycloserine Clarithromycin Capreomycin	Isoniazid and rifampin should be given for 6-12 months duration. Add ethambutol in immune-compromised patients. Isoniazid is used for preventive therapy.
Bacterial Bronchitis	*Mycoplasma pneumoniae Haemophilus influenzae*	Amoxicillin or Erythromycin	Cephalosporin (3rd generation) Cholramphenicol	Although tetracycline is as effective as the macrolides (erythromycin), the latter covers *Pneumococcus*, which mimics *Mycoplasma*.

Condition	Usual Causative Organism(s)	Antimicrobial(s) of choice	Alternatives	Background Information
Urinary Tract Infection	*Escherichia coli*	TMP-SMZ (supersulfa) or Nitrofurantoin	Ciprofloxacin Gentamicin	Beta-lactam antibiotics (penicillins and cephalosporins) are less effective than TMP-SMZ, nitrofurantoin, and ciprofloxacin.
Osteomyelitis	*Staphylococcus aureus* *Salmonella sp.*	Antistaphylo-coccal penicillin (e.g., Methicillin)	Cephalosporin (1st generation) Vancomycin	Vancomycin is required for Methicillin-resistant *Staph. aureus* (MRSA).
Cellulitis	*Staphylococcus aureus* *Streptococcus pneumoniae*	Antistaphylo-coccal Penicillin	Cephalosporin (1st generation) Vancomycin	Antistaphylococcal penicillins, such as flucloxacillin, target both causative organisms.
Meningitis (in neonates)	*Streptococcus B* *Escherichia coli* *Listeria monocytogenes*	Ampicillin +Gentamicin	Vancomycin Cephalosporin (3rd generation)	Vancomycin is an alternative for ampicillin, but should still be combined with gentamicin.
Meningitis (children & adults)	*Streptococcus pneumoniae* *Neisseria meningitidis*	Amoxicillin+ Chloramphenicol	Penicillin Cephalosporin (3rd generation)	*Haemophilus influenzae* is the most likely cause of childhood meningitis, if there is no history of immunization.
Sepsis	*Enterococcus sp.* *Streptococci* *Staphylococci*	Penicillin or Ampicillin+ Streptomycin	Cephalosporin (3rd generation) + Gentamicin	There are some *Enterococci* sensitive to synergism with streptomycin, but not with gentamicin. Some strains are resistant to both types of aminoglycosides.
Septic arthritis	*Staphylococcus aureus* *Neisseria gonorrhea*	Antistaphylo-coccal Penicillin Cephalosporin (3rd generation)	Vancomycin (for MRSA) Ciprofloxacin	*Neisseria gonorrhea* should be suspected in any patient who is sexually promiscuous (especially younger adults).

Source

NPLEX
MCCQE
USMLE

Dain, 2003

11. What sputum characteristics are seen in cough presentations?

SPUTUM CHARACTERISTICS:

Characteristics	Common Etiology
Malodorous sputum	Anaerobic infection of the lungs and sinuses
Brown or black	Smoking
Very thick, dark sputum that is hard to expectorate.	Bronchiectasis
Cloudy thick sputum	Lower respiratory tract infection or sequelae of asthmatic process (i.e., due to manifesting esinophila)
Scanty mucopurulent sputum (less than 2 tbsp/day)	Viral or low grade bacterial bronchitis
Purulent sputum more than 2 tbsp/day	Bacterial bronchitis
Hemoptysis	Bacterial pneumonia, acute inflammatory bronchitis, cystic fibrosis, tumor, or foreign body.

12. What are the causative organisms for classic infections?

CLASSIC INFECTIONS:

Infection	Presentation	Probable Cause
Pneumonia	In a malnourished patient or in patients who exhibit silicosis. Also in immigrants or after recent ravel to a developing country.	Mycobacterium tuberculosis
	After recent travel to Southwest U.S.A. (Arizona, New Mexico, and southern California) and northern Mexico.	Coccidioides immitis
	In cave explorers (bird or bat droppings) or after recent travel to Midwest United States (Ohio and Mississippi River valleys)	Histoplasma capsulatum
	After exposure to parrots or exotic bird's droppings	Chlamydia psittaci
	After spending time in a low-budget centrally air-conditioned hotel	Legionella pneumophila

Infection	Presentation	Probable Cause
Acute Diarrhea	After hiking trips and drinking from streams	*Giardia lamblia*
	After travel to Mexico	Montezuma's revenge caused by *Escherichia coli*
	After antibiotics (especially clindamycin)	*Clostridium difficile*
	In young children	Norwalk virus
	Food poisoning after eating improperly stored meats or custard-filled pastries (profuse non-bloody diarrhea with cramping and vomiting)	*Staphylococcus aureus*
	Food poisoning after eating raw seafood	*Vibrio parahaemolyticus*
	Food poisoning after eating reheated rice	*Bacillus cereus*
	Food poisoning after ingestion of improperly preserved food, poultry or eggs (bloody diarrhea with cramping and vomiting)	*Salmonella sp.*
	Profuse painful & bloody diarrhea after ingesting contaminated water or food	*Entamoeba histolytica*
	Bloody diarrhea after anal sex (fecal-oral transmission)	*Shigella sp.*
	Bloody diarrhea in day care settings	*Shigella sp.*
	Profuse watery diarrhea that is painless; Rice-water diarrhea that occurs after ingestion of contaminated water or seafood.	*Vibrio cholera*
	Hemolytic uremic syndrome	*Escherichia coli* 0157:H7
Hemoptysis	After 'resolved' tuberculosis Cavitary lesion on CXR	*Aspergillus sp.*
Abscess	After getting stuck with a thorn	*Sporothrix schenckii*
Vesicular genital lesions	Without recent sexual activity (umbilicated)	*Molluscum contagiosum*

Infection	Presentation	Probable Cause
Cellulitis	After cat or dog bite	*Pasteurella multocida*
Pregnant woman	Lives with cats	*Toxoplasma gondii*
Aplastic crisis	In a patient with sickle cell disease	Parvovirus B19
Burn site infection	Purulent with blue/green color	*Pseudomonas arginosa*
Burn site infection	Purulent with yellow color	*Staphylococcus aureus*
UTI	With green urine	*Pseudomonas arginosa*
UTI	Without green urine	*Escherichia coli*
Reiter's Syndrome and Lympho-granuloma venereum		*Chlamydia trachomatis*

Source

NPLEX

Yarnell, 2000

Saunders, 2000

13. What are commonly used naturopathic botanical antimicrobials?

NATUROPATHIC ANTIMICROBIAL BOTANICALS:

Antibacterial	Antiviral	Antiparasitic	Antifungal
Allium sativum	*Allium sativum*	*Allium sativum*	*Berberis aquifolium*
Arctostaphylos uva ursi	*Astragalus membranaceus*	*Artemisia absinthium*	*Calendula officinalis*
Baptisia tinctoria	*Echinacea spp.*	*Artemisia annua*	*Chilopsis linearis*
Berberis aquifolium	*Glycyrrhiza glabra*	*Berberis aquifolium*	*Commiphora molmol*
Capsicum spp.	*Hypericum perforatum*	*Chenopodium ambrosoides*	*Melaleuca alternifolia*
Commiphora molmol	*Larrea tridentate*	*Cucurbita pepo*	*Tabebuia avellanedae*
Coptis chinensis	*Lentinus edodes*	*Dryopteris filix-mas*	*Thymus vulgaris*
Echinacea spp.	*Ligusticum porterii*	*Hydrastis canadensis*	*Usnea barbata*
Grapefruit seed extract	*Lomatium dissectum*	*Juglans nigra*	
Hydrastis Canadensis	*Melissa officinalis*	*Picrasma excelsa*	
Ligusticum porterii	*Phyllanthus spp.*	*Ricinus communis*	
Ligustrum lucidum	*Populus candicans*	*Tanacetum vulgare*	

Antibacterial	Antiviral	Antiparasitic	Antifungal
Lomatium dissectum	Salvia officinalis	Verbena spp.	
Rosmarinus officinalis	Silybum marianum	Zingiber officinalis	
Salvia officinalis	Tabebuia avellanedae		
Tabebuia avellanedae	Uncaria tomentosa		
Tussilago farfara	Zingiber officinalis		
Thymus vulgaris			
Uncaria guyanensis			
Usnea barbata			

14. What naturopathic botanical remedies are commonly used as anti-inflammatories?

Source

NPLEX

Yarnell, 2000

Saunders, 2000

Naturopathic Anti-inflammatory Botanicals:

Phytotherapeutic Agent	Background Information
Achillia millefolium	Gentle anti-inflammatory and antipyretic. Clinical trial showed that combination of 100 mg Filipendula + 90 mg Populus + 60 mg Achillia had the same efficacy as 400 mg Ibuprofen on severe OA (reported to have fewer S/E). Used in febrile condition and diarrheal presentations.
Boswella serrata	Inhibits 5- but not 12-lipoxygenase/cycloxygenase. Used in arthritis and ulcerative colitis.
Calendula officinalis	Anti-inflammatory and vulnerary. Used in proctitis, colitis, anal fistulas (with Echinacea and Commiphora), PUD, URI, and wound dressing.
Camellia sinensis	Antioxidant, stimulates B-cell regeneration. Used in atherosclerosis, hyperlipidemia, elevated liver enzymes, and dental caries.
Curcuma longa	Inhibits 5- and 12-lipoxygenase/cycloxygenase. Used primarily for musculoskeletal inflammation.
Filipendula ulmaria	Similar to Salix nigra. Used in febrile conditions, rheumatic disease, hyperchlorhydria, GERD, and diarrheal presentations.
Glycyrrhiza glabra	Anti-inflammatory, inhibits T-suppressor lymphocytes, inhibits endogenous cortisol degradation; bactericidal towards H. Pylori, and is an antioxidant. Used in inflammatory conditions in the GI, respiratory, or GU tract.

Phytotherapeutic Agent	Background Information
Larrea tridentata	Antimicrobial, anti-inflammatory. Used for skin injuries, PMS, rheumatic disease, and autoimmune diseases.
Matricaria recutita	Antispasmodic, anti-inflammatory, anxiolytic, and carminative. Used in oral mucositis, chronic GI inflammation (e.g., esophagitis, PUD, and IBD), stasis ulcers (with plantago lanceolata), wounds, and atopic dermatitis.
Salix alba/nigra	Antipyretic, analgesic. Used in febrile conditions, OA, RA, prostatitis, urethritis and cystitis.

Source

Morrison, 1998

15. What homeopathic remedies are commonly used in infectious diseases?

Homeopathic Remedies for Infectious Diseases: The following is a description of basic homeopathic prescribing criteria for some frequently encountered conditions:

Presentation	Remedy of Choice and Background Information
Pharyngitis and Tonsillitis	
Rapid onset of inflammation and burning sensation. Bright red swollen mucosa; with visible aphthae; strawberry tongue; high fever; flushed face; cold extremities.	*Belladonna:* the most commonly used remedy for acute tonsillitis with rapid onset. Also considered a remedy for peritonsillar abscess. Mainly right sided complaints.
Exquisite sharp throat pain, commonly described as splinters in the throat. There may be ulceration ion the throat; pain radiates to ears on swallowing.	*Hepar Sulphur:* used for more advanced pharyngitis and suppurative tonsillitis. One of the main remedies for peritonsillar abscess.
Tonsils are swollen, mucosa is deep red or purple; uvula is swollen; advanced cases exhibit ulceration, excoriation, and bleeding. Sensation of a lump or constriction in the throat. Mainly left-sided.	*Lachesis:* used for mild sore throats as well as serious inflammation and peritonsillar abscess. Mainly left-sided complaints.
Suppurative pharyngitis with offensive halitosis 'sick breath'; sensation of something lodged in the throat; metallic taste in the mouth; night sweats, and cervical lymphadenopathy.	*Mercurius Vivus:* used for suppurative pharyngitis, acute or recurring pharyngitis, or tonsillitis of any severity.
Urinary Tract Infections	
Intense burning with urination; each drop feels like scalding acid as it passes. The patient feels that emptying the bladder will bring relief.	*Cantharis:* used for mild or moderate urethritis and cystitis. This remedy is prescribed when pain is the main symptom.

Presentation	Remedy of Choice and Background Information
Constant urging and full sensation, but only small, non-satisfying amounts are passed.	*Nux Vomica:* used in renal colic, cystitis, and pyelonephritis. This remedy is prescribed when frequent urging is the main symptom.
Intense itching or tingling deep in the urethra; sudden intense urges to urinate; pain if the patient cannot void immediately.	*Petroselinum:* prescribed when urethral itching or irritation is the main symptom.
Sudden urges to void with no capacity to hold back the urine. Involuntary urination; pain increases every moment voiding is resisted.	*Pulsatilla:* prescribed when the pain is irregular, paroxysmal, or with spurting. Indicated when urine is copious, bloody, and mucousy.
Copious urination with marked burning pain at the end of micturition; pain occurs only with the last few drops.	*Sarsparilla:* prescribed when the main symptom is pain at the end of voiding.

Impetigo

Sores become crusted, cracked, and eventually thickened. Oozing of thin, smelly, or sometimes honey-like discharge.	*Antimonium Crudum:* the most commonly prescribed remedy for acute and recurring cases of impetigo. Location – face, corners of mouth, or nose.
Thick crusts, characteristic honey-like discharge, itching, and prompt suppuration.	*Graphites:* Location – intertriginous areas, mouth, or behind ears.
Moist eruptions or pustules over an erythematous base.	*Mercurius:* Location – scalp or face.
Moist eruptions (as opposed to the above dry and crusty variety), large coalescing pustules, surrounded by erythema, seen in neglected wounds or poor hygiene.	*Sulphur:* may be indicated in skin infections where the eruption itches or burns.

Fungal Infections

Patches of scaly dry skin that are somewhat itchy; tinea versicolor.	*Sepia:* the most commonly prescribed remedy for skin conditions exhibiting scaly round patches.
Ringworm on the scalp; tinea corporis	*Calcarea Carbonica, Dulcamara,* or *Radium bromatum*
Fungal infections of toenails; thick, hard, yellow, friable nails. Also a remedy for tinea pedis.	*Graphites:* used for moist, crusty eruption with thick borders.
Tinea pedis or cruris with excessive exudate. Burning athlete's foot infections.	*Sulphur:* used for markedly itchy tinea cruris, especially when intertriginous areas are erythematous.

Presentation	Remedy of Choice and Background Information
Abscesses	
Abscess continues to discharge for weeks after opening; creamy yellow discharge; fistula formation.	*Calacarea sulphurica:* recommended for chronic abscess formation and hydradenitis suppurativa.
Crops of slowly developing abscesses and indurated boils. Also used in bartholinitis; paronychia; and nape carbuncles.	*Silica:* indicated for abscesses developing around retained foreign bodies.
Recurring boils in patients with poor hygiene; yellow offensive discharge.	*Sulphur:* indicated for recurring boils anywhere in the body.
Painful abscess that is exquisitely sensitive to touch; recurring crops of abscesses with offensive discharge 'old cheese'.	*Hepar Sulphur:* the main remedy for paronychia and also recommended for hydradenitis.
Infectious Conjunctivitis	*Pulsatilla, Argenticum nitricum, Euphrasia,* or *Graphitus*
Acute Otitis Media	*Chamomilia, Belladonna, Ferrum phosphoricum, Hepar,* or *Mercurius*
Chronic Otitis Media	*Pulsatilla, Mercurius, Graphites, Calcarea carbonica,* or *Lycopodium*

Source

NPLEX

Yarnell, 2000

16. What is the role of probiotic therapy in managing infectious presentations?

Probiotic Therapy: Non-pathogenic symbiotic flora, known as probiotics, are touted for their protective effect on the tissues they colonize (e.g., GI, bladder, and vagina). Probiotics generally exhibit a dose-response relationship, where the observed effect depends of the dose administered (2.5-20 billion organisms per day) and is somewhat reversible. The bulk of published evidence suggests that the use of probiotics in management of infectious or inflammatory presentations is safe at any age and can be synergistically combined with herbal or pharmaceutical antimicrobial therapy.

Types of Probiotics: Several types of probiotics have been the subject of rigorous studies over the past few years:
- *Lactobacillus acidophilus*
- *L. sporogenes*
- *L. Casei, L. rhamnosus*
- *Bifidobacterium bifidus*
- *Saccharomyces boulardii*

Mechanism of Action: The actual mechanism of action appears to be a complex interplay between the following functions:
1. Spatial competition with pathogenic strains for adherence sites (crowding)
2. Resource competition with pathogenic strains for food (competitive inhibition)

3. Secretion of antimicrobial mediators (such as bacteriocins)
4. Gut-associated lymphoid tissue modulation (systemic immune response modification)
5. Inducing mucus secretion
6. Support intestinal integrity and permeability

17. What conditions are candidates for probiotic therapy?

Source

NPLEX

Yarnell, 2000

Conditions for Probiotic Therapy:

Condition	*Published Evidence*
Antibiotic-induced diarrhea	*Saccharomyces boulardii* was effective for treatment and prevention.
Pseudomembranous colitis	*Saccharomyces boulardii* was effective in prevention treatment of chronic and recurrent *Clostridium difficile* colitis. *Saccharomyces boulardii and Lactobacillus spp* better the outcome of treatment when combined with antibiotics.
Infectious diarrhea	*Lactobaccilus casei* was effective in viral (rotavirus) and vaccination-induced diarrhea. Positive evidence also exists for vancomycin-resistant *Enterococcus faecalis* infection, GI *Staphylococcal* infection, *Shigella*, Salmonella, pathogenic *Escherichia coli*, and *Campylobacter jejuni*.
Traveler's diarrhea	Mixed evidence; positive studies prevail.
Inflammatory bowel disease (IBD)	*Saccharomyces boulardii* was helpful in relieving chronic diarrhea in patients with Crohn's disease. Various other probiotics have induced and maintained remission in ulcerative colitis patients (e.g., non-pathiogenic *E. coli*).
Irritable bowel syndrome (IBS)	Mixed evidence; negative studies prevail.
Lactose intolerance	Negative studies with lactic acid bacteria (theoretical hypothesis).
Increase intestinal permeability	Probiotics have a normalizing effect on enterocyte permeability.
Aphthous ulcers	*Lactobacillus acidophilus* is promising.
Infectious vaginitis	Oral and topical probiotics have shown efficacy in treatment and prevention of bacterial vaginosis.
Hyperlipidemia	*Lactobacillus sporogenes, Enterococcus faecum,* and *Streptococcus thermophilus* may play a future role in LDL reduction.
Atopic dermatitis	Probiotics have reduced severity in infants.
Food allergy	Trials suggest that probiotics may decrease food allergies.

Condition	Published Evidence
Bladder cancer	Two studies suggest that *Lactobaccilus casei* can reduce the rate of recurrence of urinary bladder cancer.
Cystic fibrosis	Probiotics have reduced the incidence of pulmonary infection in one trial

- Probiotic efficacy and effective dosing appear to be condition-specific. Consult a protocol manual or review publications for appropriate use.
- Please note that some severely immune compromised patients have developed probiotic sepsis.

Examination Board References

NPLEX (II): North American Board of Naturopathic Examiners
North American Board of Naturopathic Examiners (NABNE), Naturopathic Physician Licensing Examination Part II Blueprint and Study Guide. Portland, OR: NABNE, 2005.

USMLE (II): National Board of Medical Examiners
Bouchert A. USMLE Step 2 Secrets. Philadelphia, PA: Hanley & Belfus Inc., 2000.

MCCQE: Medical Council of Canada
Molckovsky A, Pirzada KS (eds.). Review for the Medical Council of Canada Qualification Examination. Toronto, ON: Toronto Notes Medical Publishing, 2004.

Related References

Bickley LS, Szilagyi PG. Bates' Guide to Physical Examination & History Taking. Philadelphia, PA: Lippincott, Williams & Wilkins, 2003.

Canadian Pharmaceutical Association. Compendium of Pharmaceuticals & Specialties (CPS). Toronto, ON: Canadian Pharmaceutical Association, 2004.

Dains J, Baumann L, Scheibel P. 2003. Advanced Health Assessment & Clinical Diagnosis in Primary Care. 2nd ed. St. Louis, MI: Mosby C.V. Co. Ltd., 2003.

Dawson JS. Pharmacology. Crash Course Series. Philadelphia, PA. Mosby/Elsevier Science Ltd, 2002.

Morrison R. Desktop Companion to Physical Pathology. Nevada City, CA: Hahnemann Clinic Publishing, 1998.

Ontario Health Protection and Promotion Act. Regulation 559/91 and amendments.

Pizzorno JE, Murray MT. 1999. Textbook of Natural Medicine. Vol. 1and 2. 2nd ed. New York, NY: Churchill Livingstone, 1999.

Saunders, PR. Herbal Remedies for Canadians. Toronto, ON: Prentice Hall-Pearson Canada Inc., 2000.

Yarnell E. Naturopathic Gastroenterology. Scottsdale, AZ: Naturopathic Medical Press, 2000.

NEPHROLOGY

RENAL FAILURE

Source

1. What is the definition of renal failure?

NPLEX
USMLE

Renal Failure: loss of kidney function due to any number of reasons. Renal failure can be acute or chronic.

2. What is azotemia?

NPLEX
USMLE

Azotemia: excess blood urea (BUN) or nitrogenous waste (creatinine).

3. What is the definition of acute renal failure?

NPLEX
MCCQE
USMLE

Acute Renal Failure: rapid and progressive elevation of BUN with or without oliguria (oliguria =daily excretion of < 500 ml of urine). This condition is fatal in 40% of cases.

Signs and Symptoms:
- Edema, HTN, CHF
- Urine output may be completely arrested (anuria) or diminished (oliguria) or normal

Laboratory findings that warrant referral to emergency care:
1. Progressive rise in serum creatinine
2. Urinalysis: RBCs, WBCs, proteinuria, and casts
3. CBC: normochromic normocytic anemia

4. What are the three categories of renal failure?

NPLEX

Renal Failure Categories:
1. Prerenal
2. Renal/Intrarenal
3. Postrenal

5. What is prerenal failure?

NPLEX
MCCQE
USMLE

Prerenal Failure:
- Prerenal implies that the kidney is not adequately perfused. This occurs secondary to hypovolemia (dehydration or hemorrhage), sepsis, heart failure, liver failure, or renal artery stenosis.
- BUN: Creatinine ratio will be >15-20.
- There will also be systemic signs of hypovolemia = tachycardia, weak pulse, loss of skin turgor (tenting), and depressed fontanelle in infants.

Treatment: Address the cause:

- Rehydrate (IV fluids)
- Treat CHF
- Support the liver
- Balloon dilation of stenotic renal arteries if present (PCD review: renal artery bruit)

6. What is postrenal failure?

Source

NPLEX
MCCQE
USMLE

Postrenal Failure: urinary excretion is somehow blocked at the ureters, prostate, or urethra (i.e., distal to the kidneys).

Cause: The most common cause is benign prostatic hypertrophy (BPH). Nephrolithiasis will not produce postrenal failure unless stones exist bilaterally (rare).

Signs and Symptoms:

- Patient is male >50 years of age with hesitancy, frequency, and dribbling on urination.
- In men and women, diagnostic ultrasound will reveal bilateral hydronephrosis.

Treatment:

- Acute treatment involves catheterization to prevent further renal damage.
- Then, a more permanent solution needs to be sought (such as transurethral prostatic resection or naturopathic treatment).

7. What is the cause of intrarenal failure?

Source

NPLEX
USMLE

Intrarenal Failure Cause:

- Failure lies within the kidney.
- Basically, anything that causes tubular necrosis will lead to intrarenal failure.

8. What medications commonly cause renal insufficiency or failure?

Source

NPLEX
MCCQE
USMLE

Medication Causes:

- Chronic use of NSAIDs may cause papillary necrosis and thus chronic renal failure.
- Women are 3-5 times more likely to develop this side effect.
- Other drugs that are known for such complications are cyclosporin (immune suppressant used in psoriasis and rheumatoid arthritis) and aminoglycosides (antibiotics known for their nephrotoxicity).

9. What is the presentation of Goodpasture's syndrome?

Source

NPLEX
MCCQE
USMLE

Goodpasture's Syndrome Signs and Symptoms: A young man with hemoptysis, dyspnea, and hematuria (possibly renal failure, too).

Cause: Anti-glomerular basement membrane antibody. This antibody cross-reacts with lung and kidney parenchyma.

Treatment: Since the cause of this serious autoimmune condition is unknown, the recommended conventional treatment is cyclophosphamide + steroids.

10. What are the main causes of chronic renal failure (CRF)?

Source

NPLEX
MCCQE
USMLE

Chronic Renal Failure Cause: Any cause of acute renal failure may lead to chronic failure if the insult is severe or prolonged. The following are the main causes of CRF worldwide:

- 40%: Glomerulonephritis (you will see RBC casts in urinalysis)
- 10% to 16%: Chronic pyelonephritis (you will see WBC casts in urinalysis)
- 14%: Hypertension and coronary artery disease
- 7% to 8%: Polycystic kidney disease
- 7%: Diabetes
- In developed countries, the etiology of CRF shifts toward diabetes and then hypertension. Polycystic kidney disease contribution to CRF remains unchanged.
- Polycystic kidney disease (= hypertension, hematuria, palpable renal masses, multiple cysts in the kidneys, berry aneurysms in the circle of Willis, and cysts in the liver), an autosomal recessive disease, is almost always diagnosed in children.

11. What are the symptoms of chronic renal failure?

Source

NPLEX
MCCQE
USMLE

Chronic Renal Failure Symptoms:

Early	■ Nocturia, lassitude, fatigue, and decreased mental activity
Intermediate	■ Bad taste in mouth ■ Nausea and vomiting ■ Stomatitis and diarrhea ■ Muscle twitches and cramps ■ Peripheral neuropathies ■ Anorexia
Advanced	■ GI ulcers and bleeding ■ Yellow/brown skin ■ Generalized tissue wasting ■ Uremic frost on skin with pruritus ■ HTN, CHF, acidosis, and anemia
Labs	■ Azotemia ■ Metabolic acidosis ■ Hyperkalemia ■ Waxy casts ■ Anemia (due to lack of erythropoietin) ■ Hypocalcemia and hyperphosphatemia (due to impaired vitamin D production, which in turn leads to bone demineralization)

12. How is chronic renal failure treated?

Source

NPLEX
MCCQE
USMLE

Chronic Renal Failure Treatment: Regardless of the cause, the recommended treatment for CRF is as follows. This comprehensive and demanding regimen is usually adopted until kidney transplantation can be arranged.

1. Regular hemodialysis 3X per week
2. Water-soluble vitamin supplements (because they are lost in dialysis)
3. Phosphate restriction
4. Calcium supplementation
5. Erythropoietin administration
6. Hypertension treatment

NEPHROTIC SYNDROME

Source

NPLEX
MCCQE
USMLE

13. What is nephrotic syndrome? How is it diagnosed?

Nephrotic Syndrome: a descriptive term meaning: proteinuria >3.5gm/day + central edema + hypo-albuminemia + hyperlipidemia + lipiduria. It is a manifestation of glomerular disease, which may be immune mediated or metabolic.

Causes:
- In children, it is usually due to minimal change disease secondary to an infection.
- In adults, it is most commonly due to membranous nephropathy (idiopathic or secondary to hepatitis B or SLE), diabetes, and amyloidosis, or as a side effect of medications (e.g., penicil-lamine, captopril, or gold).

Diagnosis: Establish diagnoses by measuring 24-hour urine protein.

Source

NPLEX
MCCQE
USMLE

14. What is nephritic syndrome?

Nephritic Syndrome: a descriptive term meaning: oliguria + azotemia + hematuria + hypertension. It may be accompanied with proteinuria, but not in the nephrotic range (see above). It is a manifesta-tion of glomerulonephritis that is severe enough to obstruct glomerular capillaries, leading to renal hypoperfusion.

Causes:
- In children, it is usually due to acute post-streptococcal-glomerulonephritis.
- In adults, the causes are:
  - Goodpasture's syndrome (see above)
  - Wegener's granulomatosis (vasculitis that affects kidneys, nose, and lungs)
  - IgA nephropathy (see below)
  - SLE (refer to Rheumatology module)
  - Idiopathic

GLOMERULONEPHRITIS

15. What is the presentation of acute glomerulonephritis?

Source

NPLEX
MCCQE
USMLE

Acute Glomerulonephritis Signs and Symptoms: Typically patients are children with a history of upper respiratory tract infection 1 to 3 weeks before.

- Edema
- Hypervolemia
- Hypertension
- Hematuria
- Oliguria
- Microscopic urinalysis will show pathognomonic red blood cell casts.

16. What is the most common glomerular disease diagnosed in clinical practice worldwide?

Source

NPLEX
MCCQE
USMLE

IgA Nephropathy Disease: also known as Berger disease, this is the most commonly diagnosed glomerular disease worldwide. It is due to deposition of IgA around renal mesangial cells (no one knows why yet). This disease occurs most often in children and young adults. It is typically preceded by a mild respiratory, urinary, or gastrointestinal infection.

Signs and Symptoms: Clinical presentation is mild hematuria and proteinuria without systemic symptoms. However, despite this innocuous initial presentation, the disease is progressive, and approximately 50% of cases will ultimately develop end-stage kidney disease.

PYELONEPHRITIS

17. What is pyelonephritis?

Source

NPLEX
MCCQE
USMLE

Pyelonephritis: occurs as an ascending UTI caused by *E. coli* in >80% of the time.

Signs and Symptoms:
- High fever
- Shaking chills
- Flank pain
- With or without UTI symptoms

Diagnosis:
- Positive costovertebral angle tenderness (CVA tenderness) and urinalysis.
- Confirm diagnosis with urine and blood cultures.
- In life-threatening conditions, such as this one, empiric treatment should be started while waiting for culture results.
- Look for WBC casts in urinalysis – these are pathognomonic for pyelonephritis.

NEPHROLITHIASIS

18. What are the signs and symptoms of kidney stones (nephrolithiasis)?

Nephrolithiasis Signs and Symptoms:
- Severe, intermittent, loin-to-groin unilateral flank pain.
- Most stones (calcium salts type) will be visible on a KUB image (kidney and urinary bladder x-ray) if not request a renal ultrasound.

Tests: All passed stones should be collected and analyzed by the lab to determine the type and possible prophylactic measures.

19. What causes kidney stones?

Source

NPLEX
MCCQE
USMLE

Nephrolithiasis Causes: For the majority of cases, no single etiology may be found. However, some individuals (stone-formers) appear to be more susceptible than others. The following is a list of underlying disorders that may lead to nephrolithiasis:
- Hypercalcemia: This may be due to hyperparathyroidism or malignancy.
- *Proteus sp.* Infection: *Proteus sp.* are ammonia producing microorganisms associated with stag-horn calculi that fill the renal pelvis (also known on NPLEX boards as struvite stones).
- Hyperuricemia: This may be due to gout or leukemia chemotherapy.
- Cystinuria/aminoaciduria: This condition needs to be considered in stone-formers (recurrent nephrolithiasis). Diagnose by laboratory assessment of urine as well as any passed stones.

20. What is the first-line naturopathic treatment for kidney stones?

Source

NPLEX
MCCQE
USMLE

Naturopathic Treatment for Kidney Stones

Approach: Naturopathic treatment is effective, but varies according to stone type. Three distinct treatment guidelines exist for calcium, uric acid, or struvite (struvite is magnesium-ammonium-phosphate) stones. In refractive cases, lithotripsy, ultrasonic resonance dissolution, or endoscopic stone removal is recommended.

Calcium Stones
1. Dietary measures
- Reduce urinary calcium and oxalate; increase magnesium.
- Increase consumption of green leafy vegetables.
- Increase high Mg:Ca foods, such as bran, buckwheat, rye, soy, brown rice, avocado, coconut, and lima beans.
- If calcium oxalate is depositing, then it is prudent to also restrict consumption of oxalates (black tea, spinach, cranberry, or nuts).

Pizzorno,
1999

Hoffmann,
1996

2. Clinical nutrition
- Vitamin B-6: 25 mg q.d. Reduce production and increase excretion of oxalates.
- Magnesium: 600 mg q.d. Magnesium significantly increases solubility of calcium phosphate and oxalate.
- Calcium: 300-1000 mg q.d. With oxalate stones, calcium supplementation is preventive.

3. Botanical medicine: Empirical approach involves combination therapy using *Hydrangea arborescens, Eupatorium purpurium, Parietaria diffusia,* and *Aphanes arvensis.* It important to note that the anthraquinones in *Rubia tinctura, Rumex crispus,* and *Aloe vera,* in oral doses lower than laxative, bind calcium and act as a urinary crystal inhibiting factor.

Uric Acid Stones
1. Dietary measures
- Restrict consumption of red meat, fish, poultry, and yeast.
- Encourage more complex carbohydrates and green leafy vegetables.

2. Clinical nutrition
- Alkalinize urine using citrate or bicarbonate salts.

3. Botanical Medicine: Empirical approach involves combination therapy using *Hydrangea arborescens, Eupatorium purpurium, Parietaria diffusia,* and *Aphanes arvensis.*

Struvite Stones
- The critical factor in eliminating these stones is controlling the presenting infection by appropriate identification and tailored treatment. Follow-up assessment is required to ensure eradication.
- Empirically, clinicians recommend acidifying urine with ammonium (or potassium) chloride 100-200 mg t.i.d. and dietary approaches.

Source

Pizzorno, 1999

PEDIATRIC CONDITIONS

21. How do you differentiate among the common pediatric hematological disorders that affect the kidney?

COMMON PEDIATRIC HEMATOLOGICAL DISORDERS:

Disorder	Presentation	Key to DDx	Labs	Notes
IgA nephropathy	Children and young adults after URI	No systemic effects	Hematuria and proteinuria without systemic effects	Poorly understood, unknown etiology. Does not respond well to treatment.
Henoch-Shonlein Purpura (HSP)	Children after URI	Rash, abdominal pain, arthritis, and melena	Urine: hematuria CBC: normal	Treatment is supportive, but may need dialysis and/or transfusion in severe cases.
Hemolytic Uremic Syndrome (HUS)	Children after diarrhea (*E. coli*)	Hemolytic anemia and renal failure *without* neurologic symptoms	Acute renal failure Urine: hematuria CBC: low RBC count, low platelet count, peripheral smear shows hemolysis	Treatment is supportive.
Thrombotic Thrombocytopenic Purpura (TTP)	Young adult women	Hemolytic anemia and renal failure *with* neurologic symptoms	Acute renal failure Urine: proteinuria CBC: low RBC count, Low platelet count, peripheral smear shows hemolysis.	Recommended treatment is plasmapheresis, NSAIDs. If these patients need transfusion, platelets should be excluded (due to clot formation).

22. A marathon runner collapses after completing a race. Primary work-up suggests acute renal failure. What is the rationale of diagnosis?

Source

NPLEX
MCCQE
USMLE

Moore,
2001

Rhabdomyolysis: due to strenuous exercise (also occurs in burn victims, crush accident victims, and heat stroke), this acute condition produces cellular debris in the blood that plugs the renal filtration system.

Diagnostic Tests: Myoglobinuria (which is detected as hemoglobin in urinalysis) and elevated creatine phosphokinase (CPK) will establish diagnosis.

Treatment: IV hydration (watch the acid-base and electrolytes) and diuretics.

Examination Board References

NPLEX (II): North American Board of Naturopathic Examiners
North American Board of Naturopathic Examiners (NABNE), Naturopathic Physician Licensing Examination Part II Blueprint and Study Guide. Portland, OR: NABNE, 2005.

USMLE (II): National Board of Medical Examiners
Bouchert A. USMLE Step 2 Secrets. Philadelphia, PA: Hanley & Belfus Inc., 2000.

MCCQE: Medical Council of Canada
Molckovsky A, Pirzada KS (eds.). Review for the Medical Council of Canada Qualification Examination. Toronto, ON: Toronto Notes Medical Publishing, 2004.

Related References

Cutler P. Problem Solving in Clinical Medicine: From Data to Diagnosis. 3rd ed. Baltimore, MD: Lippincott, Williams & Wilkins Press, 1998

Dains J, Baumann L, Scheibel P. Advanced Health Assessment and Clinical Diagnosis in Primary Care. 2nd ed. St. Louis, MI: Mosby C.V. Co. Ltd, 2003.

Damjanov I, Conran PB, Goldblatt PJ. Pathology: Rypins' Intensive Reviews. Philadelphia, PA: Lippincott-Raven, 1998.

Hoffmann D. The Complete Illustrated Holistic Herbal. Boston, MA: Elements Books, 1996

Moore R. Hematology Laboratory Diagnosis. Guelph, ON: McMaster University Press, 2001.

Pizzorno JE, Murray MT, Joiner-Bey H. The Clinician's Handbook of Natural Medicine. New York, NY: Churchill Livingstone, 2002.

NEUROLOGY

MOTOR NEURON DISORDERS

HEADACHE

SYNCOPE AND SEIZURES

DEMENTIA

MOTOR NEURON DISORDERS

1. What are the characteristics of motor neuron lesions?

Source

NPLEX
MCCQE
USMLE

MOTOR NEURON LESION (MNL) CHARACTERISTICS:

Type	Lower MNL	Upper MNL
Causes	Peripheral motor neurons (corticospinal tract) are interrupted beyond the level of decussation	Due an interruption of the same corticospinal tract, but above the level of decussation (brain or cord lesion).
Presentation	Flaccid paralysis; decreased or no reflexes; fasciculations; and muscle atrophy.	Spastic paralysis; hyperreflexia; and clonus.
Babinski's sign	Negative	Positive

■ Electromyography (EMG) exhibits fasciculations or fibrillation in LMNL. In contrast, intrinsic muscle diseases exhibit no muscle activity at rest on EMG with decreased amplitude upon stimulation.

2. What are the characteristics of common neurological disorders?

Source

NPLEX
MCCQE
USMLE

PRIMARY NEUROLOGICAL DEFICIT:

Loss of motor functions	Loss of motor and sensory functions
Amyotrophic Lateral Sclerosis	Guillain-Barré syndrome
Botulism – descending paralysis	Multiple Sclerosis
Huntington's Chorea	Acute Poliomyelitis
Parkinson's Disease	Stroke
Polymyositis	Peripheral Neuropathies
Tick paralysis – ascending paralysis	

Source

NPLEX
MCCQE
USMLE

3. What is multiple sclerosis (MS)?

Multiple Sclerosis: an autoimmune demyelinating disease of the CNS.

Signs and Symptoms:
- Symmetric muscle weakness (legs > arms) and clumsiness (GAIT disturbances + trips a lot)
- Paresthesias
- Sudden radiating pain (especially after exposure to heat – showers and baths)
- Visual disturbances (diplopia, blurring, and scotomas)
- More common in white females 20-40 years of age
- Course exhibits characteristic exacerbations, followed by periods of remission
- Other manifestations: emotional lability, scanning speech, and a positive Babinski's sign

Diagnosis:
- Positive diagnosis is suspected when magnetic resonance imaging shows demyelination plaques (MRI is sensitive, but not specific to MS).
- Confirm with CSF analysis (if it shows high levels oligoclonal IgG levels, lymphocytes, and possibly myelin basic protein).

Treatment: Conventional treatment is not considered highly effective. These may include corticosteroids and interferons.

4. How can the history of common neurological symptoms lead to the correct diagnosis?

COMMON NEUROLOGICAL SYMPTOMS AND DIAGNOSIS:

Gradual and Progressive	Sudden or Insidious	Waxes and Wanes	Regressive
Amyotrophic Lateral Sclerosis	Guillain-Barré syndrome	Multiple Sclerosis	Guillain-Barré syndrome
Huntington's Chorea	Multiple Sclerosis Poliomyelitis Polymyositis Stroke Tick paralysis Meniere's disease	Myasthenia Gravis	Poliomyelitis

Source

NPLEX
MCCQE
USMLE

5. What is the classic presentation of Gullain-Barré syndrome (GBS)?

Guillain-Barré Syndrome Presentation:
- Usually presents as symmetric distal weakness or paralysis of the feet and legs (along with paresthesia) with loss of deep tendon reflexes.
- Ascending loss of motor function without significant sensory impairment, which usually occurs 1 week after mild respiratory infections (other infections are also implicated) or immunization.
- Although demyelination is ultimately observed (note that GBS and MS exhibit demyelination), the pathophysiology of this condition remains elusive.

Diagnosis:

- Taking a thorough history and performing a complete neurological assessment usually establish this diagnosis.
- Confirmatory tests include evoked nerve potential testing (nerve conduction velocity will be slowed) and CSF analysis (markedly increased protein).
- Be on the lookout for respiratory impairment (assess via spirometry), which may require intubation and assisted respiration.

Treatment:

- Plasmapheresis is of value in reducing the severity and overall duration of this self-limiting neurological syndrome.
- It is important to note that steroidal anti-inflammatory agents are contraindicated as they may exacerbate this condition.

6. What is the diagnostic protocol for myasthenia gravis (MG) ?

Source

NPLEX
MCCQE
USMLE

Myasthenia Gravis Signs and Symptoms:

- Loss of motor function (general muscle fatigability after steady or continued use, ptosis, and diplopia) without any loss of sensory function. The progressive motor impairment is due to autoimmune antibodies that destroy postsynaptic acetylcholine receptors.
- Incidence rates in women (between the ages of 20 and 40 years) are higher than in men (in their 50s).
- Symptoms in women often exacerbate prior to menses and during prenatal or postpartum periods.

Diagnosis:

- Tensilon test (administration of edrophonium, a short acting anticholinesterase inhibitor) establishes diagnosis if it improves the presenting muscle weakness.
- Nerve stimulation tests are also of value in confirming this diagnosis.
- MG patients are prone to developing thymomas and most improve after removal of the thymus, which is considered part of standard conventional treatment (along with long acting acetylcholinesterase inhibitors, such as neostigmine and pyridostigmine).

7. What is amyotrophic lateral sclerosis (ALS)?

Source

NPLEX
MCCQE
USMLE

Amyotrophic Lateral Sclerosis: an idiopathic degenerative disease of anterior horn cells. Previously called Lou Gehrig's disease.

Signs and Symptoms:

- ALS = LMNL + UMNL. In other words, you will see spasticity and hyperreflexia (which are characteristic of UMNL) in addition to fasciculations and muscle atrophy (features of LMNL).
- Whenever you are faced with both upper and lower motor neuron lesion signs and symptoms, think of ALS.
- More common in men (in their mid-50s).

Prognosis: The prognosis is poor because the course is progressive and, ultimately, leads to loss of all motor function without dementia or sensory deficits (50% of ALS patients die within 3 years of onset).

Source

NPLEX
USMLE

8. Which vitamin deficiencies present with neurologic manifestations?

VITAMIN DEFICIENCIES AND NEUROLOGICAL MANIFESTATIONS:

Deficiency	Manifestations
Vitamin B-12	Peripheral neuropathy; loss of vibration sense; loss of position sense; spasticity; ataxia; hyperreflexia; positive Babinski's sign; and dementia.
Vitamin B-6	Peripheral sensory neuropathy (often secondary to the use of isoniazid in anti-tuberculosis therapy).
Thiamine	Confusion; delirium; dementia; peripheral neuropathy; ophthalmoplegia; ataxia; and nystagmus ('dry' beriberi often seen in alcoholics).
Vitamin E	Loss of proprioception; loss of vibration sense; areflexia; ataxia; and gaze palsy.
Vitamin A	Vision loss (night blindness).

Source

NPLEX
MCCQE
USMLE

9. How would you describe the muscle weakness seen in botulism?

Botulism: sudden onset bilateral descending paralysis, common in infants who ingest raw honey or adults who consume home-canned foods. This condition is caused by the neurotoxin of *Clostridium botulinum* bacteria, which flourishes under anaerobic conditions.

Signs and Symptoms:
- In infants, the main presentation of botulism is that of a 'floppy' or 'flaccid' baby.
- In adults, there is usually a prodromal state (N&V, abdominal pain, diarrhea, diplopia, and dysphagia) that precedes frank paralysis.

Diagnosis: Confirmed by identifying *C. botulinum* or its toxin in the stool.

Treatment: This is an emergency condition that requires inpatient monitoring (for respiratory function) and often involves intubation and assisted respiration (otherwise patients die from respiratory muscle paralysis). This is a self-limiting condition that usually resolves within 1 week of onset with supportive care.

Source

NPLEX
MCCQE
USMLE

10. How would you describe the muscle weakness seen in tick paralysis?

Tick Paralysis: a paralytic syndrome caused by toxins from tick bites. History is the key to solving this condition. This presentation is most common in children who play in tick-infested areas.

Signs and Symptoms:
- Flaccid paralysis that progress from proximal to distal
- Areflexia
- Incoordination
- Anorexia
- Without sensory deficits

Treatment: This is a self-limiting condition that subsides approximately 2 days after removal of tick.

HEADACHE

11. What are the various types of headache? How are they diagnosed?

Types of Headaches: The majority of headaches are classified as benign or primary (i.e., migraine, tension, and cluster). Serious or secondary headaches are manifestations of underlying pathology (i.e., meningitis, temporal arteritis, increased intracranial pressure, tumor, or abscess).

Diagnosis: A systematic approach that involves a thorough history, followed by complaint-oriented physical examination, is paramount to differentiate among the types as well as causes of headaches. Rule out serious and potentially fatal pathologies that may manifest in headaches.

Serious Headache Signs and Symptoms:
- New onset headache
- Patient describes it as the 'worst headache ever'
- Different and more severe than ever experienced
- Sudden onset of maximal intensity
- Fever, nausea, and vomiting
- Altered level of consciousness
- Focal neurological symptoms
- Recent head injury
- Optic disc edema
- Signs of meningeal irritation
- Progressively worsening headache (crescendo headache)

Red Flags in Headache	Clinical Response
Headaches that occur daily with nausea and projectile vomiting, mental status changes, and papilledema.	Beware: these are the signs of intracranial hypertension → Request a CT/MR scan promptly.
Headaches with fever, positive Brudzinski's and/or Kernig's sign	Be concerned: these are the signs of meningeal irritation. → Request lumbar tap (for CSF analysis).
The worst headaches in a patient's life with sudden onset of maximal intensity and/or history of trauma	STAT: these are typical manifestations of subarachnoid hemorrhage. → Request a CT/MR scan and lumbar tap.
Severe temporal headaches with palpatory tenderness over temple and scalp and sudden painless loss of vision	Suspect temporal arteritis (Giant cell arteritis): this is more common in women with history of polymyalgia rheumatica (PMR). If untreated, it leads to blindness in 20% to 25% of cases. → Request ESR, CRP, and temporal artery biopsy.

Source

NPLEX
MCCQE
USMLE

12. How are migraine, cluster, and tension headaches differentiated?

CHARACTERISTICS OF MIGRAINE, CLUSTER, AND TENSION HEADACHES:

Migraine
- Classic migraine headaches are associated with an aura (peculiar sensation – noise, smell, or flash of light) that announces to the patient that a migraine is coming.
- Presentation: photophobia, nausea, vomiting, and positive family history. Age of onset is usually between 10 and 30 years of age.

Cluster
- These unilateral excruciating headaches occur in clusters (i.e., few frequent episodes for a week and then none for couple of months).
- Presentation: no prodrome, flushing, diaphoresis, or lacrimation.

Tension
- These 'garden-variety' (most common) headaches usually manifest as bilateral frontal or occipital tenderness.
- Presentation: long history of headaches and stress; feeling of tightness or stiffness; better with stress reduction activities.

13. What are the causes of tension headaches?

Tension Headache Causes:
- Eye pain due to optic neuritis; eye strain; refractive errors; glaucoma; and iritis.
- Middle ear pain due to otitis media or mastoiditis
- Sinus pain due to sinusitis or allergic rhinitis
- Herpes zoster infection affecting cranial nerves
- Toothache or oral cavity pain
- Illness or general malaise from any cause
- Food sensitivities: caffeine withdrawal; tyramine; nitrites; MSG; red wine.
- Stress
- Fasting
- Menstruation
- Ovulation

SYNCOPE AND SEIZURES

Source

NPLEX
MCCQE
USMLE

14. When is syncope a cause for concern?

Syncope: most common cause of 'passing-out'. Vasovagal syncope usually follows situations of stress or fear. Be concerned if you suspect other more serious causes:

- If you suspect cardiac arrhythmias or other cardiac pathology (check ECG).
- If you suspect transient ischemic attacks or carotid stenosis (refer for carotid ultrasound/duplex scan).
- If you suspect neurological disorders especially seizures or intracranial lesion (request an electroencephalogram 'EEG' and/or CT/MR scan).

15. What are the common types of seizures?

COMMON TYPES OF SEIZURES:

General Type	Characteristics and Management
Simple partial	<ul><li>Most commonly occur in older children and adults.</li><li>Consciousness is never impaired.</li><li>Paroxysmal functional disturbances of sensory, motor, or autonomic systems.</li><li>Motor or 'Jacksonian seizure' is most common.</li><li>Hallucinations, cognitive, and affective variants exist.</li></ul> *Treatment:* <ul><li>Rule out focal neurological disease (EEG + CT/MR scan).</li><li>Conventional treatment = phenytoin, valproate, or carbamazepine.</li></ul>
Complex partial **'Focal Cortical'**	<ul><li>Similar to simple partial characteristics, but is followed by loss of consciousness</li><li>Patients often perform purposeless movements (e.g., staring, chewing movements, smacking, and unintelligible noises) and may become aggressive if restrained.</li></ul> *Treatment:* <ul><li>Recommended first-line therapy is carbamazepine.</li></ul>
Absence seizure **'Petit Mal'**	<ul><li>Patients are always younger than 20 years of age.</li><li>Main manifestation is loss of awareness (but not consciousness) for 10 to 30 seconds with eye or muscle fluttering.</li><li>The 'petit' child usually stares into the void for a while and then resumes prior activity (looks like abrupt daydreaming). This scenario can occur up to 100X per day.</li></ul> *Treatment:* <ul><li>Recommended first-line therapy is ethosuximide.</li></ul>

General Type	Characteristics and Management
Tonic-clonic seizure **'Grand Mal'**	■ Primary epilepsy of adulthood, where tonic muscle contraction is followed by clonic contractions. ■ Lasts 2 to 3 minutes with loss of consciousness. ■ Sometimes there is an aura; incontinence; and tongue lacerations. ■ This is followed by a postictal state, during which patient feels headachy, drowsy, confused and sore. *Treatment:* ■ Conventional treatment = phenytoin, valproate, or carbamazepine.
Febrile seizure	■ Infants and children (<6 years of age) may get seizures during febrile conditions. ■ Assume organic cause until proven otherwise (i.e., rule out meningitis, tumors, or other serious causes of seizures). *Treatment:* ■ These children do not have epilepsy, and as such should not receive antiepileptics. ■ Treat the cause of the fever and provide supportive measures.
Secondary seizure	■ Occur secondary to organic causes (e.g., tumor, meningitis, encephalitis, toxoplasmosis, cysticercosis, hemorrhage, hypoglycemia, PKU, hyponatremia, lead/cocaine/carbon monoxide poisoning, substance withdrawal, severe hypertension, pheochromocytoma, eclampsia, trauma, and stroke). *Treatment:* ■ A full work-up is essential in determining the best course of action.

DEMENTIA

Source

NPLEX
MCCQE
USMLE

16. What is the definition of dementia?

Dementia: memory loss with impairment of at least one of the following cognitive capacities:
1. Language ability
2. Orientation
3. Attention or ability to concentrate
4. Frontal executive function (like judgment and problem solving)
5. Apraxia (inability to perform acquired motor skills)
6. Activity of daily living

Diagnosis: To qualify for the diagnosis, the impairment must be at a level that interferes with social or occupational functioning. Major depression can present similarly, but due to lack of motivation (to recall or learn) rather than ability. This is termed pseudodementia. Delirium, psychiatric disorders, mental retardation, and mild cognitive impairment can also be mistaken for dementia.

Causes:
■ Alzheimer's disease (leading cause)
■ Severe depression

- Cerebrovascular disease (multi-infarct dementia)
- Parkinson's disease
- Hypothyroidism
- Multiple medications
- Substance abuse
- Carbon monoxide, organophosphates, solvent inhalation
- Vitamin B-12 deficiency
- Brain tumor
- Liver or kidney failure

17. How can you distinguish delirium from dementia?

CHARACTERISTICS OF DELIRIUM AND DEMENTIA:

Delirium

Dementia

Delirium is state of confusion that occurs abruptly and is usually associated with precipitating causes, such infections, acid/base imbalance, electrolyte imbalance, and cardiac events (in fact it, can be viewed as a marker for them).

Dementia is a slower progressive decline of cognitive function that may be exacerbated by social stressors, such as bereavement, unfamiliar environment, and high stress social functions.

Decreased attention span is a presenting feature.

Decreased attention span is a late feature.

Waxing and waning in the level of consciousness.

Level of consciousness is usually not affected.

Waxing and waning in the level of arousal.

Level of arousal is normal.

Examination Board References

NPLEX (II): North American Board of Naturopathic Examiners
North American Board of Naturopathic Examiners (NABNE), Naturopathic Physician Licensing Examination Part II Blueprint and Study Guide. Portland, OR: NABNE, 2005.

USMLE (II): National Board of Medical Examiners
Bouchert A. USMLE Step 2 Secrets. Philadelphia, PA: Hanley & Belfus Inc., 2000.

MCCQE: Medical Council of Canada
Molckovsky A, Pirzada KS (eds.). Review for the Medical Council of Canada Qualification Examination. Toronto, ON: Toronto Notes Medical Publishing, 2004.

Related References

Dains J, Baumann L, Scheibel P. Advanced Health Assessment & Clinical Diagnosis in Primary Care. 2nd ed. St. Louis, MI: Mosby C.V. Co. Ltd., 2003.

Pizzorno JE, Murray MT. Textbook of Natural Medicine. Vol. 1 and 2. 2nd ed. New York, NY: Churchill Livingstone, 1999.

Pizzorno JE, Murray MT, Joiner-Bey H. The Clinician's Handbook of Natural Medicine. New York, NY: Churchill Livingstone, 2002.

ORTHOPEDICS

Musculoskeletal Pain

Disk Herniation

Hip Disorders

1. What is the best protocol for diagnosing and managing pain conditions?

History taking: Nothing beats good history taking skills in managing pain conditions. In fact, it has been argued that a good history will indicate an accurate diagnosis without resorting to batteries of diagnostic tests in approximately 70% of primary care presentations.

2. What features of musculoskeletal pain help to identify the underlying cause?

Source

NPLEX
MCCQE
USMLE

Musculoskeletal Pain Diagnostic Characteristics:

Musculoskeletal pain differentials	Etiology or contributing factors	Musculoskeletal pain differentials	Etiology or contributing factors
Dull and aching with diminished passive ROM	Joint capsule	Cramping, dull, and aching	Muscle pain
Sharp, shooting	Nerve root	Sharp, non-shooting	Peripheral nerve
Sharp, intolerable, and always present	Fracture	Deep, nagging, dull,	Bone pain
Throbbing, diffuse	Vascular compromise	Burning, aching, pressure-like, or stinging	Sympathetic nerve irritation
Pain that improves with activity	Chronic inflammation causing edema	Pain that worsens with activity	Vascular insufficiency; muscular or articular pathology
Pain that is not affected by activity	Bone pain, tumors, and visceral referral	Pain that worsens at night	Peripheral nerve entrapment; thoracic outlet syndrome
Intermittent claudications	Vascular insufficiency or spinal stenosis	Severe pain at night	Serious organic pathology (tumor)
Pain that worsens by sitting or bending	Inter-vertebral disc	Pain that improves by sitting or bending	Lumbar facet joint inflammation

3. What are the most clinically important orthopedic tests?

ORTHOPEDIC TESTS:

Test	Performance	Interpretation
Cervical spine compression	Push down on seated patient's head – repeat with bilateral lateral bending	Pain = inter-vertebral nerve root compression
Cervical spine distraction	Traction head upwards via occiput	Relief = nerve root impingement Pain = ligament or joint capsule pathology
Adson's	Take radial pulse with arms internally rotated and abducted 45 degrees – ask patient to rotate and extend neck to each side	Disappearance of pulse indicates thoracic outlet syndrome, cervical rib syndrome, or tight anterior scalene
Drop arm test	Patient seated with arms at the side – slowly abduct arm and hold at maximal abduction	Arm drop = rotator cuff tear
Apprehension test	Place hand of affected arm on opposite shoulder – push posteriorly on the elbow of the affected arm	Pain in shoulder = anterior dislocation of shoulder
Lippmann's test	Forearm is flexed to 90 degrees – palpate biceps tendon 2.5 inches distal to shoulder	Sharp pain = bicipital tendonitis
Allen's test	Compress both arteries of the wrist – ask patient to flex and extend digits until palm turns pale – release one side (repeat, but release the other)	Non patent radial or ulnar artery
Phalen's test	Place dorsae of hands together – press both wrists into significant flexion for 30 to 60 seconds.	Pain during test or upon release = carpal tunnel syndrome
Tinel's tess	Tap over middle of flexor wrist retinaculum.	Pain over the distribution of the median nerve = carpal tunnel syndrome
Straight leg raise	Patient is supine – passively raise leg to tolerable range of hip motion	Shooting pain at 35 degrees = disc herniation Pain at 70 degrees = SI pathology
Kemp's test	Rotate and extend torso to both sides, then press anteriorly on lumbar spinal processes	DDx facet joint irritation, lumbar strain, and disc herniation

Test	Performance	Interpretation
Valsalva	Patient is seated – patient takes deep breath and blows out with a pursed mouth	Pain in the back or neck = space occupying lesion (disc herniation) anywhere along the spinal canal
Ely's test	Patient is prone – flex patient knee to maximum tolerance	Ipsilateral hip flexion = tight rectus femoris
Gaenslen's test	Patient is supine – bring knee of affected side (of lumbar pain) to chest	Pain in the sacroiliac area = SI pathology or nerve root lesion
Ober's test	Patient is lying on their side – abduct supported limb – extend hip slightly then lower the limb in a supported fall	Leg remains abducted and doesn't fall below table level = iliotibial tract syndrome (tightness)
FABER Patrick's test	Patient is supine – flex, abduct, and externally rotate hip – then extend the hip	Hip pain = bursitis, arthritis, ligament strain, or tight capsule in the hip joint
Thomas' test	Patient is supine – bring knee to chest	Contralateral limb comes off the table = tight iliopsoas
Pelvic rock	Patient is supine – compress iliac crests bilaterally toward midline	Pain = SI lesion
McMurray's test	Patient is supine – flex hip and knee – then externally and internally rotate knee (change angle of knee flexion and repeat)	Snap or click sound = meniscus tear in knee joint
Patellar bulge	Patient is seated – milk medial side of patella superiorly – keep medial pressure – then milk inferiorly on the lateral side	Fluid wave = minor knee joint effusion, and patellofemoral syndrome
Patellar ballottement	Patient is supine – compress patella into patellofemoral groove then rapidly release	Click = major patellar effusion, and patellofemoral syndrome
Kernig's test	Patient is supine – flex knee and hip to 90 degrees – then attempt to extend knee while keeping the hip in flexion	Attempt to extend knee is significantly resisted = meningeal irritation (meningitis, herniated disc, cauda equina syndrome)
Brudzinski's test	Patient is supine – examiner passively flexes the neck	Involuntary hip flexion = ominous sign of meningitis

Source

NPLEX
MCCQE
USMLE

4. What is a compartment syndrome?

Compartment Syndrome: since the deep fascia that surrounds muscular compartments is non-elastic, any condition that causes swelling inside a muscle compartment will cause some degree of nerve compression. This manifestation is seen in the extremities when edema or hemorrhage cases swelling inside the affected muscle compartment (e.g., anterior compartment syndrome of the leg or shin splints). This mechanism is considered to be protective since it invariably leads to the cessation of the offending activity (e.g., running), but sometimes the pain is tolerated (or the patient resorts to potent analgesics) so that compartmental pressure progressively rises, causing more severe nerve dysfunction (it can even lead to permanent nerve damage).

Signs and Symptoms:
- Severe pain (even on passive movement)
- Firm-feeling muscle compartment
- Signs of nerve compression: decreased sensation; decreased two-point discrimination; paresthesia; formications; numbness; or hypesthesia
- Decreased distal pulse amplitude (since arterial supply is also compressed)
- Cyanosis or pallor
- Paralysis and absence of peripheral pulses (late, ominous signs)

Exercise-induced Compartment Syndrome:
- Mild presentations that are caused by excessive (often novel sports activity that the patient is not used to) muscular exercise can be addressed with rest, massage, hydrotherapy, and supportive physical therapy.

Non-exercise Induced Compartment Syndrome:
- Fractures (mid-shaft tibial fractures in adults and supracondylar humeral fractures in children)
- Burns (especially electrical burns of sufficient magnitude leading to soft tissue edema)
- Vascular compromise (this offsets the balance of interstitial fluid formation and drainage → edema)

Emergency Care:
- Surgical intervention is warranted for severe non-remitting presentations to avoid any permanent neurological damage.
- A compartment syndrome presentation of such magnitude is an emergency that requires prompt fasciotomy.

Source

NPLEX
USMLE

5. What are the main motor and sensory functions of the cardinal peripheral nerves?

Cardinal Peripheral Nerve Functions:

Nerve	Motor	Sensory
Radial	Wrist extension Palsy manifests in 'wrist drop'	Back of forearm and hand (first three digits)
Ulnar	Finger abduction. Palsy manifests in 'claw hand deformity'	Front and back of last two digits

Nerve	Motor	Sensory
Median	Forearm pronation and thumb opposition. Usually affected in carpal tunnel syndrome	Palmar surface of hand and front of the first three digits
Axillary	Abduction and lateral rotation of arm (football throwing stance)	Lateral shoulder
Fibular (Peroneal)	Dorsiflexion and eversion of foot Palsy manifests in foot drop	Lateral aspect of leg and dorsum of foot

6. How do you test the cruciate ligaments of the knee joint?

Source

NPLEX
USMLE

Cruciate Ligaments: Anterior and posterior drawer tests are specific orthopedic tests that assess the anterior and posterior cruciate ligament, respectively.

7. What fracture is likely after a fall on an outstretched arm?

Source

NPLEX
USMLE

Scaphoid Bone Fracture: Presents clinically as palpatory tenderness in the anatomical snuff-box along with other signs of wrist fracture.

DISK HERNIATION

8. What are the most common locations for intervertebral disk herniation?

Source

NPLEX
MCCQE

Intervertebral Disk Herniation: lumbar disk herniation is a common and often correctable cause of low back pain.

L5-S1 Disk Herniation Signs and Symptoms: The most likely location of herniation is the L5-S1 disc, which leads to nerve compression of the S1 nerve root. Features of this presentation include:
- History of lumbar trauma or strain
- Sciatica with positive straight leg raise (SLR) finding
- Decreased ankle jerk
- Weakness of plantar flexors of the foot

L4-L5 Disk Herniation Signs and Symptoms: The second most common location for herniation is L4-L5 disc, which leads to nerve compression of the L5 nerve root. Features of this presentation include:
- Pain in the hip or groin
- Decreased biceps femoris reflex
- Weakness of the extensors of the foot

C6-C7 Disk Herniation Signs and Symptoms: Although less common, the third most common site of herniation is the C6-C7 disc, which affects the C7 nerve root. Features of this presentation include:

- Neck pain
- Decreased biceps and triceps reflexes
- Weakness of forearm extension

Diagnosis: Definitive diagnosis is established via computed tomography (CT) or magnetic resonance imaging (MRI).

Treatment: Treatment of these conditions should always start as a conservative approach – bed rest and pain management. If such approach fails in reducing the symptoms, surgical intervention may be considered.

Source

NPLEX
USMLE

9. Which bacteria are the most common cause of septic arthritis?

Septic arthritis: redness + pain + swelling + joint dysfunction.

Causes: Most commonly caused by *Staphylococcus aureus* (gram negative cocci). In patients who exhibit high-risk sexual activity, *Neisseria gonorrhea* should also be ruled out.

Diagnosis: Definitive diagnosis and treatment require CBC + differential white cell count + joint fluid culture and gram stain.

Source

NPLEX
USMLE

10. What are the most common type of bone tumors?

Bone Tumors: The most common tumors are metastatic from:

- Breast cancer
- Prostate cancer
- Lung neoplasia

HIP DISORDERS

Source

NPLEX
USMLE

11. To what site is pain from hip inflammation or dislocation commonly referred?

Hip Inflammation: the knee is a common site of referred pain form hip pathology (especially in children).

12. What is the presentation of the most common pediatric hip disorders?

Source

NPLEX
USMLE

PEDIATRIC HIP DISORDERS:

Disorder	Onset	Epidemiology	Presentation	Treatment
Congenital Hip Dysplasia	At birth	Female, first born, breech delivery	Positive Ortolani's and Barlow's signs	Harness
Legg Calve-Perthes Disease	4-10 years	Short male with delayed bone age	Knee, thigh, and groin pain + limp	Orthoses
Slipped Capital Femoral Epiphysis	9-13 year	Overweight male adolescent	Knee, thigh, and groin pain + limp	Surgery

13. What is Osgood-Schlatter disease? How is it recognized and treated?

Source

NPLEX
USMLE

Osgood-Schlatter Disease: results from osteochondritis of the tibial tubercle. It usually occurs bilaterally in boys 10 to 15 years of age. The patient will exhibit knee pain (referred – no palpatory tenderness or knee swelling), as well as pain and swelling of the tibial tubercles.

Treatment: Since most cases resolve spontaneously, the treatment of this condition always starts as conservative:
■ Rest
■ Activity restriction (no jumping down stairs)
■ Anti-inflammatory approaches

14. How do you assess functional and structural scoliosis?

Source

NPLEX
USMLE

Scoliosis Diagnosis: The most reliable assessment of scoliosis is having the patient bend forward while the doctor evaluates the alignment of the vertebral column:
■ Functional scoliosis (listing) will exist in the upright position, but disappear in the bent forward position (this is not true for structural).
■ Structural scoliosis is idiopathic and disproportionately affects pre-pubertal girls.

Treatment:
■ Functional scoliosis is treated by addressing thecauses for listing (knee or foot problems).
■ Structural scoliosis is usually correctable via vertebral column braces. Surgery is reserved for severe presentations.

Examination Board References

NPLEX (II): North American Board of Naturopathic Examiners
North American Board of Naturopathic Examiners (NABNE), Naturopathic Physician Licensing Examination Part II Blueprint and Study Guide. Portland, OR: NABNE, 2005.

USMLE (II): National Board of Medical Examiners
Bouchert A. USMLE Step 2 Secrets. Philadelphia, PA: Hanley & Belfus Inc., 2000.

MCCQE: Medical Council of Canada
Molckovsky A, Pirzada KS (eds.). Review for the Medical Council of Canada Qualification Examination. Toronto, ON: Toronto Notes Medical Publishing, 2004.

Related References

Dains J, Baumann L, Scheibel P. Advanced Health Assessment & Clinical Diagnosis in Primary Care. 2nd ed. St. Louis, MI: Mosby C.V. Co. Ltd., 2003.

Damjanov I, Conran PB, Goldblatt PJ. Pathology: Rypins' Intensive Reviews. Philadelphia, PA: Lippincott-Raven, 1998.

Pizzorno JE, Murray MT. Textbook of Natural Medicine. Vol. 1 and 2. 2nd ed. New York, NY: Churchill Livingstone, 1999.

PSYCHIATRY

SCHIZOPHRENIA

DEPRESSION

MANIA

ANXIETY

PERSONALITY DISORDERS

PEDIATRIC CONDITIONS

SCHIZOPHRENIA

1. What is the prevalence of schizophrenia?

Source

NPLEX
MCCQE
USMLE

Schizophrenia Prevalence: The World Health Organization estimates that 1% of the population of almost every country has schizophrenia. It is also estimated that 10% of this population (diagnosed or not) eventually commit suicide.

■ It is perhaps more worrisome that an even greater percentage exhibit functional disability (i.e., they can't do what they aspire to do), and constitute a significant burden on their social support group (partners, friends, or family, if any).

■ Whether you are concerned with quantity or quality of life, and regardless of your modality of interest, these staggering statistics compel us as primary healthcare providers to screen, treat, educate as well as cooperate with other healthcare providers.

2. What are the five main diagnostic criteria for schizophrenia?

Source

NPLEX
MCCQE
USMLE
DSM IV

Schizophrenia Diagnostic Criteria: These are the same five criteria that describe psychotic behavior, according to the *Diagnostic and Statistical Manual* (DSM).

1. Delusions: These are non-bizarre observations that could potentially happen, but generally don't. For example: "*The guy on* Days of Our Lives *is talking trash about me all the time*" or "*My husband has been adding rat poison to my morning coffee.*"
2. Hallucinations: These are bizarre observations that 'to the best of your knowledge' could not potentially happen. For example: "*I avoid air travel because customs officers steal body parts when you pass through their scanners.*"
3. Disorganized speech: Using words out of their intended context (be cautious with people whose mother tongue is not the same as yours), mixing words, creating new ones, or simply not making sense.
4. Grossly disorganized or catatonic behavior: Movements such as swatting at the air or repetitive movements that are clearly out of context.
5. Negative symptoms: Negative behavior, such as flat affect and poor attention.

Clinical Reasoning: The same clinical reasoning that you employ in establishing non-psychiatric diagnoses holds true for psychiatric disease. That is, a clinical reasoning that is based on preponderance of evidence rather than isolated features of any presentation. For example, while any person may experience any of the five manifestations of schizophrenia (under stressful conditions beyond the person's tolerance threshold), that person would definitely not be diagnosable with schizophrenia.

3. Why is the duration of psychotic behavior a crucial factor in establishing a diagnosis?

Source

NPLEX
MCCQE
USMLE
DSM IV

Duration of Psychotic Behavior: According to the DSM, a patient with the same psychotic symptoms is given one of three different diagnoses based only on the duration of symptoms. The following is the differential list for psychotic disorders:

1. Acute Psychotic Disorder: lasts at least 1 day but < 1 month
2. Schizophreniform Disorder: lasts 1 to 6 months
3. Schizophrenia: lasts > 6 months

4. What are the positive and negative symptoms of schizophrenia?

Source

NPLEX
MCCQE
USMLE

Schizophrenia Symptoms:

Positive	*Negative*
Delusions	Flat affect (no good days or bad days)
Hallucinations	Anhedonia (loss of pleasure in previously pleasurable activities)
Bizarre Behavior	Avolition (apathy)
Thought disorder (e.g., tangentiality and clanging)	Poor attention
	Alogia (loss of speech)

5. What is the difference in age of onset for schizophrenia in males and females?

Source

NPLEX
MCCQE
USMLE

Age Onset of Schizophrenia: The typical age of onset is 15 to 25 years of age for males (the cue is behavioral and academic deterioration in high school or college), but 25 to 35 years of age for females.

6. What is the etiology of schizophrenia?

Source

NPLEX
MCCQE
USMLE

Schizophrenia Etiology: The manifestations of psychotic disorders, including schizophrenia, are multifactorial:
- Genetic predisposition
- Environmental factors
- Sustained excessive stressors

Hypotheses: Several hypotheses have been posited to account for the causes and course of schizophrenia:

Hoffer,
1998

- Adrenaline Hypothesis: Dr Abram Hoffer argues that psychotic behavior is, in part, a biochemical result of sustained increased secretion of adrenaline (due to severe and prolonged stress). It follows that catecholamine derivatives, such as adrenochrome and adrenolutin, are implicated in the toxic psychosis known as schizophrenia. These derivatives are metabolized first by phenolases, then by secondary pathways, such as monoamine oxidase, catechol-O-methyl transferase, and phenol sulfo-

Pfieiffer,
1975

transferase. The result is a net increase in circulating indolic catechols (toxic free radicals) and orthoquinones. Accordingly, the two main components of the biochemical treatment of schizophrenia must be to decrease the biochemical effects of stress and to use ample amounts of antioxidants.

Horrobin,
1996

- Other Hypotheses: Researchers have implicated abnormal circulating histamine levels (histapenia and histadilia), depletion of zinc + vitamin B-6, and altered membrane phospholipid metabolism in the pathogenesis of schizophrenia.

7. What is the conventional treatment for schizophrenia?

Source

NPLEX
MCCQE
USMLE

Conventional Treatment: Conventional approaches to managing schizophrenia revolve around the use of antipsychotic drugs (prototypes include haloperidol, chlorpromazine, and clozapine) with secondary utilization of psychosocial treatment.

DRUG TREATMENTS:

Characteristics	High Potency	Low Potency	Atypical
Prototype drug	Haloperidol	Chloropromazine	Clozapine
Incidence of extra pyramidal system side effects – dystonia, akathisia, Parkinsonism, and tardive dyskinesia	High	Low	Low
Incidence of autonomic side effects – dry mouth, urinary retention, orthostatic hypotension, and sedation	Low	High	Medium
Therapeutic efficacy for positive symptoms	Effective	Effective	Effective
Therapeutic efficacy for negative symptoms	Poor	Poor	Effective

8. What is the first-line naturopathic treatment for schizophrenia?

Source

Naturopathic Treatment for Schizophrenia

Approach: Naturopathic approaches range from complementary to alternative. However, following the well-documented Hoffer model, the following generalizations can be made:

Pizzorno,
1999

1. Reduce biochemical stress
- Prescribe anxiolytics or botanical alternatives.
- Avoid hallucinogenic and recreational drugs.
- Avoid exposure to allergens.
- Address food sensitivities if present.
- Avoid infections.
- Employ psychosocial or cognitive behavioral treatments.

2. Antioxidants: Antioxidants (ascorbic acid, vitamin E, and vitamin B-3) are valuable in protecting against the toxic effects of the chrome indoles on the brain.

Hoffer
1998

Source

Hoffer
1998

3 Clinical nutrition (Hoffer's recommended treatment plan)

■ Niacinamide: 1-12 g q.d. The dose is increased gradually and over a long period of time to allow the patient to adjust to the peculiar effects of vitamin B-3 at this dose. Due to possible but rare liver toxicity, monitoring of liver function markers (ALP, AST, ALT & Bilirubin) is recommended at 1, 3, and 6 months of treatment.

■ Vitamin C: 3 g q.d. (or to bowel tolerance)

■ Vitamin B-6: 250-1000 mg q.d.

■ Zinc: 25-100 mg q.d.

■ Calcium and magnesium supplementation: 1:1 or 2:1 ratio

DEPRESSION

Source

NPLEX
MCCQE
USMLE
DSM IV

9. What is a major depressive episode?

Major Depressive Episode: The terms major depressive episode, major depression, and clinical depression refer to the same condition. The lay term 'depression' usually refers to depressed mood, one of many criteria for diagnosing a depressive episode, according to the *Diagnostic and Statistical Manual* (DSM).

■ A major depressive episode is a period of > 2 weeks that exhibits at least five of the following nine signs/symptoms:
   1. Depressed mood
   2. Diminished interest in previously pleasurable activites
   3. Weight loss or gain
   4. Psychomotor agitation or retardation
   5. Insomnia or hypersomnia
   6. Fatigue
   7. Feelings of worthlessness or guilt
   8. Cognitive difficulty
   9. Suicidal ideation

Diagnosis: To be diagnosed with major depressive disorder, patients must exhibit two or more major depressive episodes. These episodes must be at least 2 months apart.

10. What is adjustment disorder?

Adjustment Disorder: occurs when something 'bad' happens in our life (relationship break-up, failing at school, or loosing a job, for example) and we don't take it so well.

■ Although we may feel 'down' and 'good for nothing', we would not fulfill the criteria (quantitative or periodic) of major depression.

11. How do you distinguish between normal grief and pathologic grief?

Normal Grief: follows the passing of a loved one.
- Often manifests like major depression and lasts up to 1 year.
- Experiencing hallucinations about the deceased – and even searching for the deceased years after their death – is considered part of normal grief.

Pathological Grief: exhibits other features of major depression.
- Feelings of worthlessness
- Psychomotor retardation
- Suicidal ideation

12. What is the definition of dysthymia?

Dysthymia: simply refers to depressed mood (on most days) for more than 2 years *without* episodes of major depression, mania, hypomania, or psychosis.

13. What are the major risk factors for suicide?

Source

NPLEX
MCCQE

Major Risk Factors for Suicide:
- Age > 45 years
- Recent loss or separation
- Single, widowed, or divorced status
- Alcohol or substance abuse
- Loss of health (recent disability)
- Unemployed or retired
- History of rage or violence
- History of psychiatric disease
- History of suicide attempts
- Being male (three time more successful suicides than women; but women attempt suicide four times more than men)
- Although suicide rates are on the rise in 15 to 24 year olds, the highest rate still belongs to people over the age of 65.

14. What are the limitations of conventional treatments for major depressive disorder?

Conventional Treatment Limitations: Current epidemiological studies indicate that inadequately treated mood disorders account for 60% to 75% of suicide cases.
- A recent National Institute of Mental Health survey suggests that approximately 70% of depressed people go without conventional pharmacological treatment.
- Another recent study showed that over 50% of patients receiving treatment with selective serotonin reuptake inhibitors (SSRIs) or tri-cyclic antidepressants (TCAs) discontinue treatment after 6 weeks.
- The reason for under treatment is suspected to be fear of social stigma (the implication of a mental disease label), as well as worry regarding the side effects of conventional treatment (for example, the sexual side effects of SSRIs).

Source

NPLEX

Pizzorno,
1999

Schnider,
2002

Schnider,
2002

Pizzorno,
1999

Schnider,
2002

15. What is the first-line naturopathic treatment for depression?

Naturopathic Treatment for Depression

Approach: Naturopathic approach to depression is patient-centered and focuses on modulating factors that contribute to the individual patient's condition; optimizing overall nutrition; utilizing safe and effective botanicals; and counseling patients to develop positive mental attitudes.

1. Dietary modifications
- Encourage eating of vegetables, grains, legumes, cold-water fish, raw nuts, and seeds.
- Avoid caffeine, nicotine, alcohol, and sugar.
- Identify and control food sensitivities.

2. Lifestyle changes
- Counsel patient (e.g., cognitive behavioral counseling) with the goals of:
  - Developing an unconditionally positive mental attitude
  - Helping the patient set realistic goals
  - Avoiding negative behavioral patterns
  - Finding ways to include laughter and humor into the patient's life
- Since regular exercise has been shown to be as effective as antidepressants and psychotherapy, attention should be dedicated to motivating the patient to include exercise as part of daily health regime.

3. Clinical nutrition
- Enteric-coated S-adenosylmethionine (SAM-e): 200 mg q.d. to be gradually increased over 1-2 weeks to 800 mg b.i.d. Has been shown to be an effective and well-tolerated antidepressant in a number of randomized controlled trials; most patients respond within 1 week of treatment; useful in major depression; contraindicated in bipolar disorders.
- Folic acid and vitamin B-12: 800 mcg q.d.
- Omega-3 fatty acids: Evidence of efficacy exists for depression and bipolar disorders; recommend food sources, as well as flaxseed or fish oil supplements.

4. Botanical medicine
- *Hypericum perforatum:* 300 mg or equivalent t.i.d. Recommended and proven to be effective for mild to moderately severe depression; well tolerated. Possible mild form of serotonin syndrome when combined with SSRI, or MOAI.
- *Griffonia simplifica:* 100-200 mg t.i.d. A natural source of 5-HTP; indicated in combination with *Hypericum* for severe depression.
- *Ginkgo biloba:* 80 mg t.i.d. Indicated for older patients, who also exhibit signs of cerebrovascular insufficiency.

5. Acupuncture:
Numerous controlled and uncontrolled trials indicate that acupuncture is promising in the treatment of depression. Two randomized trials indicate that electro-acupuncture is as effective as amitriptyline (a TCA) in the treatment of major depression; the same observation holds true for preventing recurrence. Diagnose and treat based on the patient's overall TCM presentation.

MANIA

16. What is the definition of mania? What is a hypomanic episode?

Source

NPLEX
MCCQE
USMLE

Manic Episode: a distinct period (>1 week) of abnormally and persistently elevated or irritable mood, which exhibits the following symptoms:
- Decreased need for sleep
- Pressured speech; talkative with flight of ideas
- Exaggerated self-importance or delusions of grandeur
- Seeking high-risk pleasurable activity (sexual promiscuity, driving against traffic, etc.)

Hypomania: essentially mania, but not to the level that impedes social or occupational function.

17. What is the definition of bipolar disorder I and bipolar II disorder?

Source

NPLEX
USMLE

Bipolar Disorder: bipolar (used to be called manic-depressive) patients exhibit at least one manic episode and at least one major depressive episode.

Bipolar II Disorder: somewhat milder than Bipolar I Disorder. The patient exhibits at least one period of hypomania and major depression.

18. What is cyclothymia or cyclothymic disorder?

Source

NPLEX
USMLE

Cyclothymia: at least 2 years of hypomania alternating with depressed mood. These patients do not experience mania or major depression.

ANXIETY

19. What are anxiety disorders?

Source

NPLEX
MCCQE
USMLE
DSM

Anxiety Disorders: encompass a number of conditions marked by irrational and involuntary thoughts and behavior. Again, the etiology seems to be a network of genetic, environmental, biochemical, and experiential factors. The defining characteristic of anxiety disorders is disruption of personal, social, and/or occupational activities by overt distress.

Prevalence: The 13.3% prevalence of anxiety disorders in North America ranks them as the most common mental disorder (ever). To complicate matters, this condition is clearly under-diagnosed in primary care practices. (Comparing prevalence and frequency of diagnosis is how you determine whether primary care facilities are doing their mandated job or not.)

ANXIETY DISORDERS CLASSIFICATIONS:

Class	Criteria of Diagnosis	Other Characteristics
General Anxiety Disorder (GAD)	Intense worrying (about everything – career, family, future, money, relationship); occurs on most days for > 6 continuous months + three of the following symptoms: easy fatigability, difficulty in concentrating, irritability, muscle tension, restlessness, and sleep disturbance.	Patients usually complain of physical symptoms, with no awareness that their condition may be related to a mental disorder.
Panic Disorder	Discrete, unprovoked episodes of intense fear + four of the following symptoms: chest pains, chills, hot flushes, derealization, diaphoresis, dizziness, trembling, unsteadiness, fear of losing control, fear of dying, nausea, palpitation, paresthesia, and sensation of choking.	Patients are so worried about having another episode or the implications of panic that they start avoid seemingly tolerable situations.
Phobias	Irrational fears of a specific entity or situation. The most common phobias are agoraphobia, social phobia, snakes, spiders, heights, and flying.	Social phobia is the fear of being humiliated in public. This fear usually leads to avoidance of ordinary events, such as birthdays or professional gatherings.
Post-Traumatic Stress (PTSD)	This is a typical set of symptoms that develop after a person sees, gets involved in, or hears an extreme stressor.	The person persistently starts to relive the event, either in its entirety (visions/illusions/fear) or partially (fear and helplessness).

Source

Lee, 2002

20. What is the first-line naturopathic treatment for anxiety?

Naturopathic Treatment for Anxiety

1. Botanical medicine
- *Piper mythesticum* (kava): perhaps the most effective botanical for these conditions. It has been proven in seven clinical trials to be safe and effective in the treatment of mild to moderate anxiety disorders. However, case reports from Germany/Switzerland raised suspicion of hepatotoxicity. Because of these reports, the marketing of kava is under evaluation in Germany. In the United States, the FDA has decided to monitor the situation closely. *In Canada, a health advisory notice has been issued advising against the public use of kava*. It is important to note that the American Botanical Council continues to recommend kava for anxiety disorders (except in alcoholics or patients with liver disease).
- *Valeriana officinalis, Melissa officinalis, Nepeta cataria, Passiflora officinalis, Scutellaria lateriflora, Cypripedium pubescens, Datura stramonium, Vinca major, Viscum album* and *Luctica virosa* should be prescribed based on specific presenting symptoms.

2. Mind-Body techniques
- Meditation results in remarkable improvement in people with anxiety. The challenge is to motivate the patient to start a formal or informal meditation (both equally effective) program.
- Biofeedback has also been shown to be effective (for children, too).
- Guided imagery
- Hypnosis
- Progressive muscle relaxation is also gaining acceptance.

3. Counseling
- Cognitive behavioral therapy has been shown to alleviate anxiety in a number of clinical studies.
- Also consider other successful techniques, such as flooding and systematic desensitization in the treatment of phobias.

4. Exercise
- Similar to its effect on depression, regular exercise (aerobic or anaerobic) is particularly effective in reducing anxiety.

5. Diet
- Avoidance of stimulants (coffee, tobacco, tea, colas, soft drinks), alcohol, and refined sugars constitutes a crucial cornerstone in the effective management of anxiety disorders.

6. Clinical nutrition
- Niacinamide: 1-12 g q.d. The dose is increased gradually and over a long period of time to allow the patient to adjust to the peculiar effects of vitamin B-3 at this dose. Due to possible but rare liver toxicity, monitoring of liver function markers (ALP, AST, ALT & Bilirubin) is recommended at 1, 3, and 6 months of treatment.
- Vitamin C: 3 g q.d. (gradual increase, not to exceed bowel tolerance)
- Vitamin B-6: 250-1000 mg q.d.

PERSONALITY DISORDERS

Source

NPLEX
MCCQE
USMLE
DSM IV

21. What is the definition of a personality disorder?

Personality Disorder: according to DSM-IV criteria, personality disorders are defined as "enduring subjective experiences and behavior that deviates from cultural standards, are rigidly pervasive, have onset in adolescence or early childhood, are stable through time, and lead to unhappiness and impairment." The classification of subtypes depends upon the predominant symptoms and their severity. Personality disorders can be considered a matrix for some of the more severe psychiatric problems – for example, schizotypal, relating to schizophrenia, and avoidance types, relating to some anxiety disorders.

Diagnosis:
- Long history dating back to childhood or adolescence
- Recurrent maladaptive behavior
- Low self-esteem and lack of confidence
- Minimal introspective ability with a tendency to blame others for all problems
- Major difficulties with interpersonal relationships or society
- Depression with anxiety when maladaptive behavior fails

Source

NPLEX
USMLE
DSM IV

22. What characterizes each subtype of personality disorder?

PERSONALITY DISORDER CLASSIFICATIONS:

Paranoid	Believe that everyone is out to get them; they tend to pursue legal proceedings against accountancies.
Schizoid	Loners who have no friends and no interest in having any.
Schizotypal	Bizarre beliefs (e.g., cults, superstition, illusion) without psychosis.
Avoidant	Social inhibition, feelings of inadequacy, hypersensitive to negative criticism. Have no friends, but have interest in forming friendships. Avoid others out of fear of rejection or criticism.
Histrionic	Over dramatic, attention seekers (often seductive) who must be the center of attention.
Narcissistic	Egocentric, need excessive admiration, lack empathy, and use others for their own gain.
Antisocial	Long criminal record, liar, aggressive, torture animals. History of pediatric conduct disorder. Do not uphold their responsibilities. Severe presentations usually make the news because of their lack of remorse.

PERSONALITY DISORDER CLASSIFICATIONS:

Borderline   Lack of own identity, with rapid changes in mood, intense unstable interpersonal
relationships, marked impulsivity, instablility of affect, and instability in self image.

Other   features include: suicide attempts, micropsychotic episodes, and in constant crisis.

Dependent   Pervasive and excessive need to be taken care of. Cannot be or do anything alone.
Difficulty making everyday decisions.

Obsessive   Rules are more important than objectives; inflexible, stubborn; excessively orderly;
Compulsive   perfectionist (leads to difficulty in completing tasks); and overly controlling.
Exclusion of leisure activities due to work preoccupation is a main feature.

23. What is the definition of obsessive compulsive disorder (OCD)?

Obsessive Compulsive Disorder: characterized by anxiety surrounding recurrent thoughts, behaviors, or impulses that lead to marked dysfunction in inter-personal or occupational realms.

Signs and Symptoms: Patients may present with washing (hands, objects) or checking (doors, locks) rituals that occur > 30 times per day. These repetitive behaviors or mental acts are aimed at reducing distress.

Source

NPLEX
USMLE
DSM IV

PEDIATRIC CONDITIONS

24. What are the common causes of mental retardation?

Mental Retardation Causes:
- Usually the cause is idiopathic.
- Pathologic causes include fetal alcohol syndrome, cerebral palsy, Down syndrome, and fragile-X syndrome.
- Approximately 85% of diagnosed cases with mental retardation are mild, with a considerable level of independence (assistance may be required during periods of stress).

Source

NPLEX
MCCQE
USMLE

25. How do you recognize autism in children?

Autism Signs and Symptoms:
- First sign is usually impaired social interaction (i.e., isolated as if temporarily deaf, blind, and mute) in a child who is less than 3 years of age.
- Also impaired verbal (babbling, strange words, repetition) or nonverbal (eye contact, head-banging, strange movements) communication.

Source

NPLEX
USMLE
DSM IV

26. What is conduct disorder?

Conduct Disorder: the pediatric form of antisocial personality disorder. The affected child manifests aggressive and cruel behavior, such as setting fires, animal abuse, cheating, stealing, and fighting.

Source

NPLEX
USMLE
DSM IV

Diagnosis: The prudent approach to assessment in such presentations is to consider the child's motive, if any. This manifestation is often associated with child abuse or dysfunctional family units (but don't make any assumptions, since conduct disorder can occur without motives).

Source

NPLEX
DSM IV

27. What behavior characterizes oppositional defiant disorder?

Oppositional Defiant Disorder:
- Child is hostile (but never cruel) toward authority figures.
- Behaves normally with other children.

Source

NPLEX
USMLE
DSM IV

28. Is bed-wetting in a 4-year-old boy normal?

Enuresis and Encopresis:
- From a behavioral and neurological perspective, enuresis is considered normal up to 5 years of age, while encopresis is normal up to 4 year of age.
- From a naturopathic perspective, a prudent approach is to reassure the mother and child while ruling out organic etiologies (such as UTIs).

Source

NPLEX
USMLE
DSM IV

29. What are the diagnostic criteria for anorexia?

Anorexia: a serious and potentially fatal condition that can lead to starvation, electrolyte imbalance, infections, and arrhythmias. Statistics show that 10% to 15% of anorexics die from sequelae of starvation; 50% of patients exhibit bulimia.

Diagnostic Criteria:
- Body weight > 15% below normal
- Intense fear of gaining weight or 'feeling fat' despite emaciation
- Amenorrhea

Source

NPLEX
USMLE
DSM IV

30. How does bulimia manifest?

Bulimia: common in females who want to lose weight but cannot control their desire for food.

Signs and Symptoms:
- Bulimic patients often lose control, gorge themselves, and then engage in purging behavior (vomiting, laxatives, exercise, fasting).
- The typical patient is adolescent with normal or above average weight.
- Classic findings include tooth enamel erosion and eroded skin over knuckles from purging.

ASSOCIATED CONDITIONS

31. What are somatoform disorder, factitious disorder, and malingering?

Source

NPLEX
MCCQE
USMLE

Somatoform Disorder: somatoform disorder (or somatization) refers to psychiatric stress that manifests itself in the form of physical symptoms. This is an unconscious process where the patient does not intend for the manifestations to occur.

Factitous Disorder: in factitious disorder (or Münchausen syndrome), a patient intentionally feigns symptoms to assume the sick role.

Malingering: a patient intentionally feigns symptoms for economic gain or to avoid responsibilities (legal or vocational).

32. What is the prognosis of Tourette's syndrome?

Source

NPLEX
MCCQE
USMLE

Tourette's Syndrome: motor tic disorder (e.g., repetitive blinking, throat-clearing, grimacing, swearing)
- Tends to be a life-long problem.
- Remits during periods of low stress.
- Males are affected more than females.

33. What symptoms are associated with cocaine dependency and amphetamine intoxication?

Source

NPLEX
USMLE
DSM

Cocaine Dependency: Cocaine is a sympathetic stimulant that causes hyper-alertness, tachycardia, insomnia, hypertension, aggression, paranoia, psychosis, and formications.
- Overdose often causes arrhythmia, MI, seizure, or stroke.
- Withdrawal invariably leads to sleepiness, hunger, depression, and irritability.
- Cocaine use by pregnant females causes congenital vascular disruption in the fetus.
- While cocaine withdrawal is not considered dangerous, the cravings are so severe that some form of support is required for long-term compliance.

Amphetamine Intoxication: effects are similar to those of cocaine, but more psychotic manifestations prevail.

34. What is opioid toxicity?

Source

NPLEX
USMLE
DSM

Opioid Toxicity: Recreational use of heroin (and other opioids) leads to euphoria, drowsiness, analgesia, constipation, and CNS depression.
- Overdose causes respiratory depression and secondary apnea.
- Since the delivery method is often intravenous with shared needles, think HIV, endocarditis, and cellulitis.
- Although heroin withdrawal is not considered life threatening, the patient almost always perceives it to be so.

Source

NPLEX
MCCQE
USMLE

35. What are the features of 'mushroom' or lysergic acid diethylamide (LSD) intoxication?

'Mushroom' or LSD intoxication: Features include visual hallucinations, tachycardia, and mood disturbances.
- Although overdose is not considered dangerous, there are rare reports of dangerous behavior that occurs secondary to visual hallucinations.
- Users may experience 'bad trips' while intoxicated and 'flashbacks' months or years later.

Source

NPLEX
MCCQE
USMLE

36. What are the risks of benzodiazepine (tranquilizer) and barbiturate (sleeping pill) dependency?

Benzodiazepine and Barbiturate Dependency: Both are sedatives that cause drowsiness and disinhibition.
- Can be particularly dangerous when combined with alcohol because of CNS and respiratory depression.
- Abrupt withdrawal from either (after a long periods of dependency) is considered to be life threatening because patients often experience seizures and cardiovascular collapse.
- Gradual withdrawal over several days is recommended (at inpatient withdrawal facilities).

Examination Board References

NPLEX (II): North American Board of Naturopathic Examiners
North American Board of Naturopathic Examiners (NABNE), Naturopathic Physician Licensing Examination Part II Blueprint and Study Guide. Portland, OR: NABNE, 2005.

USMLE (II): National Board of Medical Examiners
Bouchert A. USMLE Step 2 Secrets. Philadelphia, PA: Hanley & Belfus Inc., 2000.

MCCQE: Medical Council of Canada
Molckovsky A, Pirzada KS (eds.). Review for the Medical Council of Canada Qualification Examination. Toronto, ON: Toronto Notes Medical Publishing, 2004.

Related References

American Psychiatric Association. Diagnostic and Statistical Manual of Mental Disorders. 4th ed., Primary Care Version. Washington, DC: American Psychiatric Association, 1995.

Dains J, Baumann L, Scheibel P. Advanced Health Assessment & Clinical Diagnosis in Primary Care. 2nd ed. St. Louis, MI: Mosby C.V. Co. Ltd., 2003.

Diagnostic and Statistical Manual of Mental Disorders. 4th ed. Primary Care Version. Washington, DC, American Psychiatric Association, 1995.

Hoffer A. Vitamin B-3 & Schizophrenia: Discovery, Recovery, Controversy. Kingston, ON: Quarry Press, 1998.

Horrobin D. Schizophrenia as a membrane lipid disorder which is expressed throughout the body. *Psychiatry Res.* 1996;63(2-3):133-42.

Lee R. Anxiety. Complementary and Alternative Medicine Secrets. Philadelphia, PA: Hanley & Belfus Inc, 2002.

National Institutes of Health. www.nimh.nih.gov

Pfeiffer C. The schizophrenias: At least three types. Mental and Elemental Nutrients. New Canaan, CT: Keats Publishing, 1975:396-421.

Pizzorno JE, Murray MT. Textbook of Natural Medicine. Vol. 1 and 2. 2nd ed. New York, NY: Churchill Livingstone, 1999.

Schnider C. Depression. Complementary and Alternative Medicine Secrets. Philadelphia, PA: Hanley & Belfus Inc, 2002.

Sherman J. The Complete Botanical Prescriber. 3rd ed. Corvallis, OR: The National College of Naturopathic Medicine, 1979.

PULMONOLOGY

Source

NPLEX
MCCQE
USMLE

1. How important is the skill of interpreting lung sounds in clinical practice?

Lung Sounds: The art of documenting and interpreting lung sounds is like riding a bike – once achieved it requires minimal refresher training. It is good practice to be systematic, comparative, and unhurried while auscultating lung fields. This skill is fundamental in diagnosing pulmonary conditions. It is also tested on naturopathic medical board examinations.

2. How are lung sounds used to diagnose pulmonary disease?

Source

NPLEX
MCCQE
USMLE

INTERPRETING LUNG SOUNDS:

Auscultation	Lung Sound	Context
Late inspiratory crackles (rales) in the dependent portions of both lungs. Normal vesicular lung sound over lung fields.	*Crackles or rales:* Discontinuous 'taps' heard on inspiration.	**Left-sided heart failure**: leads to pulmonary congestion and alveolar edema.
Localized late inspiratory crackles. Localized abnormal bronchial lung sounds over affected area.	*Bronchial sounds:* Indicate consolidation = high pitch expiration note lasts longer than inspiration note (compare to vesicular below)	**Consolidation:** leads to increased conductance of sound – bronchophony, egophony, and whispered pectoriloquy.
Low pitch inspiration tone lasts 3X longer than expiration tone. Occasional transient inspiratory crackles at the bases of the lungs.	*Vesicular sounds:* The normally predominant lung sound	**Normal:** transient crackles disappear after asking the patient to cough (compare to persistent crackles above).
Normal vesicular sounds + scattered persistent crackles + rhonchi or wheeze.	*Rhonchi:* The most musical of lung sounds (low pitched continuous, like a snore); cough may clear	**Chronic Bronchitis:** absent bronchophony, egophony, and whispered pectoriloquy.
Markedly decreased breath sounds, but normal vesicular sounds predominate.	*Clear:* COPD lung fields are 'clear' except when the etiology is chronic bronchitis	**COPD:** decreased tactile fremitus and transmitted lung sounds.
Obscured lung sound due to predominance of wheeze.	*Wheeze:* High pitched, continuous, musical, squeaking sounds	**Asthma:** also exhibits resonant or hyperresonant percussion note.

Source

NPLEX
MCCQE
USMLE

3. What are the differences between obstructive and restrictive pulmonary disease on spirometry?

Obstructive Lung Disease (e.g., chronic obstructive pulmonary disease 'COPD' = chronic bronchitis + emphysema, asthma). Patients can inhale normally, but can't expire adequately; thus, total lung capacity (FVC) will be normal, while forced expiratory volume in one second (FEV_1) divided by the total forced expiratory volume (FEV) will be decreased (i.e., $\downarrow FEV_1/FEV$).

Restrictive Lung Disease (e.g., muscular dystrophy, parenchymal disease, pneumothorax). Patients can't inhale normally, but expire quite well; thus, total lung capacity (FVC) will be reduced, while FEV_1/FEV will be normal. FEV_1 may be equal in both conditions, but the ratio will always tell you what is going on.

BRONCHITIS

Source

NPLEX
MCCQE
USMLE

4. What is acute bronchitis? What are the causes?

Acute Bronchitis: inflammation of the trachea and large bronchi. It is usually caused by bacterial or viral infection, but it can be triggered by allergic reactions. Progression: runny nose + fever + dry cough → productive cough with clear sputum → productive cough with yellow sputum. Acute bronchitis is usually self limiting and responds to conservative treatment, but in some cases it may progress to pneumonia (see below).

Signs and Symptoms:
- Cough
- Coryza
- Fatigue
- Myalgia
- Pyrexia
- Pharyngitis
- Chest pain
- Dyspnea

Auscultation:
- Scattered rhonchi
- Wheezing
- Rare crackles (rales)
- Forced expiration > 4 seconds

Etiology:
- Bacterial, viral, or allergic
- Most common in the winter after upper respiratory tract Infection (URI)
- Air pollution
- Cold climate
- Malnutrition
- Chronic sinusitis

5. What is the first-line naturopathic treatment for acute bronchitis?

Source

NPLEX

Pizzorno, 1999

Naturopathic Treatment for Acute Bronchitis

1. Dietary measures
- Avoid food allergens for 2 to 3 weeks (first eliminate milk products, then try grains, especially wheat).
- Try hypoallergenic diet for 2 to 3 weeks.
- Increase fluid consumption (e.g., chicken soup, ginger tea with honey and lemon).
- Hot showers and baths are practical bronchial soothing methods.

2. Clinical nutrition
- Vitamin C: 500 mg q.i.d. (or to bowel tolerance if not contraindicated)
- Vitamin A: 25,000 IU b.i.d.
- Zinc picolinate: 30 mg b.i.d.
- NAC (N-acetyl cysteine) 500 mg t.i.d. (mucolytic + antioxidant)

3. Botanical medicine
- Formulation depends on patient's TCM presentation; drying herbs for wind cold invasion or cooling and drying herbs in wind heat invasion.
- Bot Φ of *Lobelia, Echinacea, Zingiber and Glycyrrhiza* in equal parts: 35 gtts in hot water 4-5 times per day
- Specific herbs, such as *Inula helenium & Marrubium vulgare,* are also indicated.

6. How do you recognize and manage sinusitis?

Source

NPLEX
MCCQE
USMLE

Sinusitis Signs and Symptoms:
- Purulent 'yellow/green' nasal discharge
- Tender sinus palpation
- Localized headache that is worse when patient leans over
- Toothache in maxillary sinusitis
- Negative transillumination

Treatment: Same approach as acute bronchitis (above), substituting antimicrobial botanicals instead of cough formula.

CHRONIC OBSTRUCTIVE PULMONARY DISEASE

Source

NPLEX
MCCQE
USMLE

7. What is chronic obstructive pulmonary disease (COPD)?

COPD: characterized by the presence of recurrent airflow obstruction that is irreversible or minimally reversible. COPD is a descriptive term that denotes:
1. Chronic cough >3 months
2. Dyspnea
3. Progressive reduction in expiratory air flow (i.e., diminishing FEV_1 on spirometry)

Subtypes: Based on additional predominant symptoms, signs, and sequelae, COPD is further classified into:
1. Chronic bronchitis
2. Emphysema
3. Mixed

Prevalence:
- In the Unites States, approximately 16 million people are affected, with >80,000 deaths per year; 500,000 hospitalizations; and > $18 billion in direct healthcare costs.
- In Canada, approximately 2 million people are affected, with 12,000 deaths per year; 70,000 hospitalizations; $4 billion in estimated healthcare costs.

Prognosis:
- 5-year survival:
  - FEV_1 < 1.0 L = 50%
  - FEV_1 < 0.75 L = 33%
- Average decline in FEV_1: 75 mL/year for COPD (versus 25 mL/year for healthy individuals)
- Cause of death: usually related to hypoxemia and cor pulmonale (right ventricular failure RVF).

8. What are the risk factors for COPD?

COPD Risk Factors:
- Cigarette smoking is the most important risk factor (10% to15% of smokers develop COPD)
- Environmental factors
  - Air pollution
  - Occupational exposure to pulmonary toxins (e.g., talcum powder, cadmium)
  - IV drug abuse
- Demographic factors
  - Age > 40
  - Family history
  - Male sex

- Recurrent childhood respiratory infections
- Low socioeconomic status
- Treatable factors
  - Low BMI
  - α-1 antitrypsin deficiency (rare <1% of COPD patients)
  - Bronchial hyperactivity (asthmatic bronchitis)

9. What is the pathophysiology of COPD?

Source

NPLEX
MCCQE
USMLE

COPD Pathophysiology:

1. Inflammatory cytokines → Narrowing of bronchioles → Wheeze + decreased FEV.
2. Release of lysosomal enzymes → Proteolytic digestion of connective tissue framework of the lung → Decreased parenchymal tethering of airways.
3. Loss of alveolar surface area and capillary bed → Loss of functional respiratory membrane.
4. Loss of lung elasticity (recoil) → Lung hyperinflation.
5. Reduced pulmonary ventilation triggers corrective vasoconstriction in the remaining capillaries → Increased pulmonary vascular resistance (leading to pulmonary hypertension and RVF).

10. What is the clinical presentation of COPD?

Source

NPLEX
MCCQE
USMLE

Ferri,
2004

COPD CLINICAL PRESENTATION:

Type	Symptoms	Signs	Complications
Chronic Bronchitis 'Blue Bloater'	■ Mild dyspnea ■ Productive cough ■ Purulent sputum ■ Hemoptysis	■ Rhonchi 'noisy' chest and crackles that are reducible by coughing ■ Cyanotic (secondary to hypoxemia and hypercapnia) ■ Peripheral edema (due to RVF) ■ Frequently obese	■ Secondary polycythemia ■ Pulmonary HTN ■ RVF
Emphysema 'Pink Puffer'	■ Significant dyspnea (+/- exercise) ■ Minimal cough ■ Tachypnea	■ Pink skin ■ Pursed-lip breathing ■ Cachectic appearance (due to increased work of breathing + anorexia) ■ Barrel chest ■ Hyperresonant percussion ■ Decreased breath sounds ■ Decreased diaphragmatic excursion	■ Pneumothorax due to formation/ rupture of bullae ■ Weight loss due to more mechanical work exerted in breathing
Mixed	■ Although pure *blue-bloater* and *pink-puffer* presentations exist, chronic bronchitis and emphysema typically coexist within the same patients. ■ In these cases, you will be faced with a combination of the above symptoms, signs, and complications. ■ In end-stage patients, it is difficult to differentiate between the two.		

Source

NPLEX
MCCQE
USMLE

11. How do you evaluate a case of suspected COPD?

COPD Differential Diagnosis: Because several conditions may mimic the presentation of COPD, begin with a differential diagnosis to rule out these conditions:

- CHF
- Asthma
- Respiratory infections
- Bronchiectasis
- Cystic fibrosis
- Neoplasm
- Pulmonary embolism
- Obstructive sleep apnea
- Hypothyroidism

Evaluation Strategy: To narrow down the list of differentials or to confirm your clinical suspicion, the following evaluation strategy is recommended:

1. Chest x-ray (CXR): *Look for:*
   - Hyperinflation with flattened diaphragm
   - Tending of diaphragm at rib margin
   - Increased retrosternal space
   - Predominant chronic bronchitis
     - Thickened bronchial markings
     - Enlarged right side of the heart
   - Predominant emphysema
     - Decreased vascular markings
     - Bullae formation

2. Complete Blood Count (CBC): *Look for*
   - Leucocytosis during acute exacerbations

3. Pulmonary Function Testing (PFTs): *Look for*
   - Simple Spirometry
     - Increased total lung capacity
     - Increased residual volume
     - Reduction of FEV_1
   - Diffusion capacity for carbon monoxide (DLCO)
     - Predominant chronic bronchitis exhibits abnormal diffusion capacity
     - Predominant emphysema exhibits normal diffusion capacity

4. Arterial Blood Gases (ABGs): *Look for*
   - Normocapnia
   - Mild to moderate hypoxemia

12. What are common non-pharmacologic treatments for COPD?

Source

NPLEX
MCCQE
USMLE

Ferri,
2004

Non-Pharmacologic Treatments for COPD:
- Patient education: allows patient to modify progression and improves compliance.
- Smoking cessation and elimination of air pollutants: reduces annual decline of FEV_1, cough, and sputum.
- Exercise rehabilitation: improves physical endurance.
- Nutritional counseling: poor nutrition is associated with increased mortality of COPD patients.
- Intermittent mechanical ventilation: relieves dyspnea and allows respiratory muscles to rest.
- Supplemental oxygen therapy: shown to decrease COPD complications such as cor pulmonale and improve survival.

13. What is the first-line naturopathic treatment for chronic bronchitis?

Source

NPLEX

Pizzorno,
1999

Ferri,
2004

Naturopathic Treatment for Chronic Bronchitis

1. Dietary measures
- Implement hypoallergenic diet.
- Increase fluid consumption (e.g., chicken soup, ginger tea with honey and lemon).
- Hot showers and baths are also practical bronchial soothing methods.

2. Clinical nutrition
COPD:
- Vitamin C: 500 mg t.i.d.
- Zinc picolinate: 30 mg b.i.d.
- Beta- carotene: 200,000 IU q.d.

Predominant Chronic Bronchitis: *Add*
- Magnesium citrate: 300 mg b.i.d.
- NAC (N-acetyl cysteine): 500 mg t.i.d. (mucolytic + antioxidant)

Predominant Emphysema: *Add*
- Lecithin: 1200 mg t.i.d. Improves surfactant section by pneumocytes.
- Vitamin E: 400 IU t.i.d.
- Fish oil or flax oil: 2 tbs q.d.

3. Botanical medicine
- Bot Φ of *Trigonella foenum-graecum*, *Grindellia robusta*, *Boswella serrata*, and *Tussilago farfara* in equal parts: 1 tsp t.i.d.
- General respiratory tonics, such as *Inula helenium*, *Thymus vulgaris*, *Marrubium vulgare*, and *Verbascum thapsus*, are also indicated.

Source

NPLEX
USMLE

Ferri,
2004

14. What is the conventional pharmacologic approach to treatment of COPD?

COPD Conventional Drug Treatment:

- Bronchodilators (mainstay of drug therapy): increase airflow and reduce dyspnea.
  - Inhaled B2-agonists (salbutamol, salmeterol): fast onset of action, but significant side effects at high doses (hypokalemia).
  - Inhaled anticholinergics (ipratropium bromide): slow onset of action, more effective, and fewer side effects than B2-agonists.
- Methylxanthines (theophylline): increase strength of respiratory muscles, collateral ventilation, and mucociliary clearance.
- Corticosteroids (beclomethasone, flunisolide): although COPD involves inflamed airways, it is usually not responsive to steroids.
- Nicotine replacement (gum or patch): may aid in smoking cessation.
- Antibiotics (azithromycin, levofloxacin): warranted with febrile bacterial exacerbations.
- Diuretics (furosemide): used in patients with RVF.
- α-1 antitrypsin replacement: for documented deficiency. Evidence of efficacy is lacking and treatment is very expensive.

Source

MCCQE
USMLE

Ferri,
2004

15. What are the surgical approaches to treatment of COPD?

Surgery for COPD:

- Lung volume reduction therapy (LVRS): experimental intervention. Evidence suggests a transient improvement in clinical symptoms. Unknown effect on survival.
- Lung transplantation: rarely considered due to confounding factors, but is an option for severe presentations in young patients.

Source

NPLEX
MCCQE
USMLE

16. What is bronchiectasis?

Bronchiectasis: a common complication of chronic bronchitis, uncontrolled asthma, or cystic fibrosis. Chronic bronchiolar suppurative infection → abnormal and irreversible dilation of bronchioles due to changes in elastic and muscle layers.

- Patient complains of long standing cough and copious foul-smelling sputum that gets worse over the years.
- This type of cough almost always occurs in exhaustive bouts on rising or with typical regularity.

Complications: Respiratory failure and cor pulmonale are the most important complications, followed by general sepsis with subsequent abscess formation.

Treatment: Treat aggressively to avoid progression of respiratory deficit.

PNEUMONIA

17. What are the characteristics of pneumonia?

Source

NPLEX
MCCQE
USMLE

Pizzorno,
1999

Pneumonia: the 5th leading cause of death in the United States. Pneumonia is especially dangerous in the elderly, infants, immune compromised, and alcoholics (due to aspiration and ineffectual cough reflex).

Signs and Symptoms:
- Cough, malaise, pyrexia, tachypnea, and pleuritic pain
- CBC shows leucocytosis
- Chest x-ray (CXR) abnormal and consistent with pneumonia
- Rusty-brown purulent sputum is typical

Auscultation:
- Crackles (rales), especially in base of affected lung and friction rubs (due to pleuritis)

Etiology:
- Bacterial, viral, or fungal
- Most common in the winter after influenza URI
- Smoking
- Hospitalization
- Malnutrition
- Chronic debilitating disease

18. What is the difference between typical and atypical pneumonia?

Source

NPLEX
MCCQE
USMLE

TYPICAL VS. ATYPICAL PNEUMONIA:

Characteristic	Typical Pneumonia	Atypical Pneumonia
URI Prodrome	< 2 days	> 3 days + headache, malaise, and body aches
Fever	High > 39 C	Low < 39 C
Age	> 40 years of age	< 40 years of
CXR	One distinct lobe is involved	Diffuse or multiple lobes involved
Causative organism	*Streptococcus pneumonia*	*Hemophilus influenza, Mycoplasma, Chlamydia,* etc.
Empiric antibiotic	Penicillin or cephalosporin	Erythromycin

Source

NPLEX
MCCQE
USMLE

19. What are the classic clinical clues for the causative organisms in pneumonia?

Pneumonia Causative Organisms:
- College student: *Mycoplasma* (look for cold agglutinins) or *Chlamydia* (positive DNA probe)
- HIV/AIDS: *Pneumocystis carinii* or *cytomegalovirus*
- Child < 1 year: RSV
- Child > 1 year: Parainfluenza (croup)
- Cystic fibrosis: Pseudomonas or *Staphylococcus aureus*
- COPD: *Hemophilus influenza*
- Immigrant from developing country: TB
- TB with pulmonary cavitation: *Aspergillus sp.*
- Exposure to central air conditioners: *Legionella sp.*
- Exposure to bird droppings: *Chlamydia psittaci* or histoplasmosis
- Alcoholics: *Klebsiella* (i.e., 'currant jelly' sputum) or *Staph. aureus*

Source

Ferri,
2004

20. What is the conventional drug treatment for pneumonia?

Pneumonia Medications: Pneumonia is serious condition with potentially lethal sequelae.
- A prompt prescription for erythromycin (pneumococci and mycoplasma), co-trimoxazole (trimethoprim + sulfamethoxazole), or penicillin (G/V 500 mg q.i.d.) will provide substantial clinical improvement within a few days.
- Empiric antimicrobials are usually prescribed after sputum culture and sensitivity (C&S) studies.

Source

Pizzorno,
1999

21. What is the first-line naturopathic treatment for pneumonia?

Naturopathic Treatment for Pneumonia

Approach: Naturopathic treatment is recommended as adjunctive treatment.

1. Dietary measures
- Because the main concern is adequate protein and caloric intake, a protein mixture (e.g., whey or rice) or meal replacement shakes are required.
- Increase fluid consumption (e.g., chicken soup, ginger tea with honey and lemon).
- Hot showers and baths are practical hydrating methods.

2. Clinical nutrition
- Vitamin C: 500 mg q.2h. Watch for osmotic diarrhea.
- Vitamin A: 50,000 IU q.d. for 1 week. C/I in women with reproductive potential because dosage may be teratogenic.
- Vitamin E: 200 IU q.d.
- Zinc picolinate: 30 mg b.i.d.
- Thymus extract (pure polypeptide fraction): 120 mg q.d.

3. Botanical medicine
- *Lobelia inflata:* 15-30 gtts of tincture t.i.d.
- *Echinacea sp.:* 150-300 mg of 3.5% echinacoside standardized solid extract (6.5:1) t.i.d.
- *Hydrastis canadensis*: 250-500 mg of 12% alkaloid standardized solid extract (4:1) t.i.d.
- Antimicrobial botanicals (see Infectious Diseases module)

4. Physical medicine
- Diathermy to chest and back 30 minutes q.d.
- Teach partner/parent to perform lymphatic massage and aid in postural drainage t.i.d.

ASTHMA

22. What is the conventional treatment for asthma?

Source

NPLEX
MCCQE
USMLE

Conventional Treatment for Asthma:
- Involves B2 agonists (e.g., Ventolin, salbutamol, or albuterol) in acute settings.
- Other measures include cromolyn sodium (mast cell stabilizer used only for prophylaxis) and corticosteroids.
- Beta-blockers are contraindicated in asthma and COPD because they produce bronchoconstriction.

23. What is the first-line naturopathic treatment for asthma?

Source

NPLEX
MCCQE
USMLE

Naturopathic Treatment for Asthma

Approach: Involves a systematic process to determine defect allowing for sensitization; to address the metabolic condition causing excessive inflammation; to avoid triggering allergens; to modulate inflammatory process; and to treat for bronchoconstriction.

1. Environment
- Minimize exposure to air-borne allergens (pollen, dander, and dust mites).
- Avoid cats, dogs, upholstery.
- Allergen proof the bedroom.
- Install air purification filters (HEPA=high efficiency particulate arresting filters) to central heating or air-conditioning systems.

Mark,
2002

Pizzorno,
1999

2. Dietary measures
- Identify and eliminate food allergens.
- Use 4-day rotation diet, hypoallergenic diet, or vegan diet.
- Eat cold-water ocean fish.

3. Clinical nutrition (adult dosage is provided)
- Vitamin B-6: 25 mg b.i.d.
- Vitamin B-12: 1000 ug oral q.d. or weekly IM injection. Re-evaluate after 6 weeks.
- Antioxidant cocktail = vitamin C 10-30 mg/kg body weight in divided doses; vitamin E 200-400 IU q.d.; and selenium 200 ug q.d.
- Magnesium citrate: 200-400 mg t.i.d. Bronchodilator - calcium channel blocker.
- Quercetin: 400 mg t.i.d. before meals. Natural mast cell stabilizer.

Mark,
2002

4. Botanical medicine: (specific botanicals need to be considered)

- *Glycyrrhiza glabra:* 250-500 mg t.i.d. Inhibits phospholipase A2 and subsequent ecosanoid synthesis + expectorant.
- *Tylophora asthmatica:* 200 mg leaves or 40 mg dry extract b.i.d. Histamine receptor blocker, antispasmodic, inhibits mast cell degranulation.
- *Coleus fosrkohlii:* 50 mg (18% forskolin) b.i.d. or t.i.d. Side effects include nausea, decreased taste for salt, and slight oral soreness.

5. Counseling: Especially important for young patients with behavioral problems, as well as adults for whom asthma attacks are precipitated by emotional crisis.

LUNG CANCER

Source

NPLEX
MCCQE
USMLE

24. What is the typical presentation of lung cancer?

Lung Cancer Signs and Symptoms:

- Cough; hemoptysis; dyspnea; chest pain; increased sputum production; hoarseness; and weight loss in advanced cases.
- On percussion, there may be atelectasis, consolidation, or abnormalities in auscultation.
- Prudent management plan of such a patient would involve imaging, ruling out other causes for chronic cough (see above), then referral for bronchoscopy/biopsy.

ADULT RESPIRATORY DISTRESS SYNDROME

Source

NPLEX
MCCQE
USMLE

25. How do you recognize and treat adult respiratory distress syndrome (ARDS)?

ARDS Signs and Symptoms:

- Rapid onset respiratory insufficiency = severe dyspnea + cyanosis + intercostals retractions + hypoxia that is refractory to oxygen therapy.
- Results from noncardiogenic pulmonary edema secondary to alveolar injury (sepsis, inhalation of irritants, pancreatitis, shock, near drowning, and drug overdose). It usually occurs 24-48 hours after the initial insult.

Treatment: This patient needs positive end expiratory pressure (PEEP) ventilation. Call an ambulance while trying high concentration oxygen ventilation in your office.

PEDIATRIC CONDITIONS

26. What are the most common causes of epistaxis in children?

Source

NPLEX
MCCQE
USMLE

Epistaxis Causes in Children:
- Nose-picking
- Trauma
- Platelet problems, like leukemia or idiopathic thrombocytopenic purpura (idiopathic because no one knows why it often occurs after URIs)
- Clotting factor deficiency, like hemophilia

27. What is infant respiratory distress syndrome (IRDS)?

Source

NPLEX
MCCQE
USMLE

IRDS: a feature of premature infants and those of diabetic mothers.

Signs and Symptoms:
- Breathing fast, hard, and labored
- Substernal retractions
- Cyanotic
- Grunting
- Nasal flaring

Treatment: This infant requires intubation, oxygen, and surfactant as soon as possible.

28. In pediatric settings, when would you suspect diaphragmatic hernia?

Source

NPLEX
MCCQE
USMLE

Diaphragmatic Hernia: a defect in the diaphragm allows for bowel herniation into chest. It sounds much worse than it really is. This herniation commonly leads to respiratory problems by restricting lung inflation (atelectasis) and development (lung hypoplasia).

Diagnosis:
- Bowel sound heard in chest
- Scaphoid (concave) abdomen
- CXR

29. What is a common cause of wheezing in children under the age of 2?

Source

NPLEX
MCCQE
USMLE

Respiratory Syncytial Virus: usually occurs in winter and causes an acute febrile condition with marked wheezing.

Asthma: the second common cause of wheezing, but a chronic history is the key to diagnosis. Classic presentation is 'chronic wheezing in allergic children' with a family history of asthma or allergies.

CYSTIC FIBROSIS

Source

NPLEX
MCCQE
USMLE

30. What is cystic fibrosis (CF)?

Cystic Fibrosis: the most lethal genetic disease in Caucasians, this autosomal recessive disorder affects 1 in 2,500 newborn white babies.

- Viscous secretions accumulate (and block the flow) in the glandular lumen of the pancreas, bronchi, and gastrointestinal system.
- Subsequently, there is pancreatic fibrosis, deficiency in digestive enzymes, malabsorption, multiple nutritional deficiencies, and bronchiectasis with recurrent bouts of pneumonia.

Signs and Symptoms: The classical board examination example is a mother who claims that her baby is 'salty-tasting'. Clinically, however, suspect CF in pediatric patients with these symptoms:

- Rectal prolapse
- Meconium ileus
- Esophageal varices
- Recurrent pulmonary infections
- Failure to thrive

Treatment: Any pulmonary infection in these patients requires aggressive treatment to avoid additional irreversible damage.

- Chest physical therapy (i.e., postural drainage, lymphatic pump)
- Fat-soluble vitamins (vitamin A,D,E,K)
- Pancreatic enzyme supplementation

Source

NPLEX
MCCQE
USMLE

31. A patient presents with chronic cough of more than 3-month duration. CXR shows a solitary pulmonary nodule. What is the management protocol?

Solitary Pulmonary Nodule Management: A systematic process is required to identify the cause before secondary care can be initiated.

Presentation	*Probable Cause*
Immigrant; recent residence in developing country; tree-planting; malnourished.	Suspect tuberculosis. Request a PPD skin test and culture sputum if positive.
Recent travel to Southwest United States (Arizona, New Mexico, and Southern California) and northern Mexico.	Suspect *Coccidioides immitis* fungal infection. Request coccidioidin skin test.
Cave explorers; exposure to bird droppings; recent travel to Midwest United States (Ohio and Mississippi River valleys)	Suspect *Histoplasmosis* fungal infection. Request a histoplasmin skin test.

Presentation	Probable Cause
Smoker over the age of 50	Consider lung cancer. Request bronchoscopy and biopsy.
Person under age 40	Consider hamartoma (normal cells are arranged abnormally – i.e., a nevi is an abnormally arranged cluster of normal melanocytes)

Examination Board References

NPLEX (II): North American Board of Naturopathic Examiners
North American Board of Naturopathic Examiners (NABNE), Naturopathic Physician Licensing Examination Part II Blueprint and Study Guide. Portland, OR: NABNE, 2005.

USMLE (II): National Board of Medical Examiners
Bouchert A. USMLE Step 2 Secrets. Philadelphia, PA: Hanley & Belfus Inc., 2000.

MCCQE: Medical Council of Canada
Molckovsky A, Pirzada KS (eds.). Review for the Medical Council of Canada Qualification Examination. Toronto, ON: Toronto Notes Medical Publishing, 2004.

Related References

Dains J, Baumann L, Scheibel P. Advanced Health Assessment & Clinical Diagnosis in Primary Care. 2nd ed. St. Louis, MI: Mosby C.V. Co. Ltd, 2003.

Damjanov I, Conran PB, Goldblatt PJ. Pathology: Rypins' Intensive Reviews. Philadelphia, PA: Lippincott-Raven, 1998.

Ferri F. Ferri's Clinical Advisor: Instant Diagnosis and Treatment. St. Louis, MI: Mosby Inc, 2004.

Mark JD. Asthma. Complementary and Alternative Medicine Secrets. Philadelphia, PA: Hanley & Belfus Inc, 2002.

Marz RB. 1999. Medical Nutrition from Marz. 2nd ed. Portland, OR: Omni-Press, 1999.

Mills S, Bone K. Principles and Practice of Phytotherapy: Modern Herbal Medicine. New York, NY: Churchill Livingstone, 2000.

Moore R. Hematology Laboratory Diagnosis. Guelph, ON: McMaster University Press, 2001.

Pizzorno JE, Murray MT. Textbook of Natural Medicine. Vol. 1 and 2. 2nd ed. New York, NY: Churchill Livingstone, 1999.

Saunders, PR. 2000. Herbal Remedies for Canadians. Toronto, ON: Prentice Hall-Pearson, 2000.

Sherman J. The Complete Botanical Prescriber. 3rd ed. Corvallis, OR: National College of Naturopathic Medicine, 1979.

Skidmore, LR. Mosby's Handbook of Herbs & Natural Supplements. St. Louis, MI: Mosby Inc, 2001.

RHEUMATOLOGY

OSTEOARTHRITIS

GOUT

RHEUMATOID ARTHRITIS

RHEUMATIC FEVER

ASSOCIATED CONDITIONS

OSTEOARTHRITIS

1. What is the most common form of arthritis?

Source

NPLEX
MCCQE
USMLE

Osteoarthritis: accounts for more than 75% of arthritis cases. OA is a degenerative joint disease, also called 'old age' or 'wear-and-tear' arthritis. OA first appears asymptomatically at age 20, then by age 40 almost all people will exhibit some characteristic pathologic changes in weight bearing joints.

2. What clues point to a diagnosis of osteoarthritis?

Osteoarthritis Signs and Symptoms:
- Mild early morning stiffness
- Stiffness following periods of rest
- Pain that worsens on joint use
- Loss of joint function
- Physical examination: OA exhibits few signs of inflammation without the hot, red, tender joints seen in rheumatoid, gout, pseudogout, and septic arthritis. Look for Heberden's nodes at the DIPs and Bouchard nodes at the PIPs.
- X-ray findings: While not essential in clear presentations, radiographs will show narrowed joint space, osteophytes, increased density of subchondral bone, subchondral sclerosis, bony cysts, and periarticular swelling.

3. What is the first-line naturopathic treatment for OA?

Source

NPLEX

Shaver,
2002

Pizzorno
et al,
1999

Naturopathic Treatment for Osteoarthritis

Approach:
- Reduce weight because this is a weight-bearing manifestation.
- Reduce joint stress.
- Promote collagen repair and eliminate foods and other factors that inhibit collagen repair.
- Control predisposing factors (obstacles to healing).
- Minimize or eliminate need for NSAIDs (while valuable in relieving pain and inflammation, they often inhibit collagen matrix synthesis and accelerate cartilage destruction).

1. Dietary measures
- Avoid simple, processed, and refined carbohydrates.
- Emphasize complex-carbohydrates and high-fiber foods.
- Minimize fats.
- Encourage flavonoid-rich berries or extracts (e.g., blue berries).
- Determine sensitivity to night shades (e.g., tomatoes, potatoes, eggplant, peppers) via a trial elimination diet because this group of plants contain an alkaloid that may aggravate symptoms of OA.

Shaver, 2002

Pizzorno et al, 1999

2. Clinical nutrition

- Glucosamine sulfate: 500 mg t.i.d.
- Niacinamide: 800 mg t.i.d. Establish a baseline liver enzyme profile and then monitor appropriately.
- Ensure adequate intake of vitamins A, C, B-5, and B-6.
- Ensure adequate intake of boron, zinc, and copper.
- S-Adenosyl-Methionine (SAMe): 400 mg. Significantly better alternative to NSAIDs: increases cartilage formation in 91% of cases; tolerance is very good in 87% of cases; and is a mild analgesic anti-inflammatory agent.

3. Botanical medicine

- *Medicago sativa* (alfalfa tonic): equivalent to 5-10 g crude herb q.d.
- *Harpagophytum procumbens:* 5 ml tincture or 400 mg solid extract t.i.d
- *Boswella serrata:* 400 mg boswellic acids t.i.d.

4. Physical medicine

- Monitored daily non-impact exercise is highly recommended (e.g., swimming and isometric exercise).
- Short wave diathermy and hydrotherapy are important because they improve joint perfusion.

GOUT

Source

NPLEX
MCCQE
USMLE

4. What is gout?

Gout: an inherited disorder of purine metabolism with 95% of cases occuring in male patients. Joint affected is usually either a big toe, MTP of foot, or knee. Alcohol- and protein-rich foods may precipitate an attack.

Signs and Symptoms:
- Acute onset
- Frequently nocturnal
- Typically monoarticular joint pain with asymptomatic periods between attacks
- Joint is red, hot and swollen
- Elevated serum uric acid

5. What is the first-line naturopathic treatment for gout?

Source

NPLEX

Pozzorno
et al, 1999

Naturopathic Treatment for Gout

1. Dietary measures
- Eliminate alcohol.
- Implement low-purine diet.
- Increase complex-carbohydrates.
- Minimize fats.
- Limit protein intake (0.8g/kg body weight).
- Increase pure water consumption.
- Encourage consumption of 0.25 kg flavonoid-rich berries per day or equivalent supplementation (e.g., blue berries, cherries).
- Monitor compliance with 24-hour urine uric acid on a monthly basis.

2. Clinical nutrition
- Eicosapentanoic acid (EPA): 1.8 g q.d. Anti-inflammatory, inhibits synthesis of leukotrienes.
- Vitamin E: 400-800 IU q.d. Antioxidant, lowers leukotriene levels.
- Folic acid: 10-40 mg q.d. Inhibits xanthine oxidase, thus uric acid production.
- Bromelain: 125-250 mg t.i.d. Anecdotal evidence of effective anti-inflammatory activity.
- Quercetin: 125-250 mg t.i.d. Alternative to allopurinol, inhibits xanthine oxidase, leukotriene release, and neutrophil aggregation.

3. Botanical medicine
- *Harpagophytum procumbens:* 5 ml tincture or 400 mg solid extract t.i.d.
- *Vaccinium myrtillus:* equivalent to 80 mg anthocyanoside q.d.

RHEUMATOID ARTHRITIS

Source

NPLEX
MCCQE
USMLE

6. What is the presentation of rheumatoid arthritis (RA)?

Rheumatoid Arthritis Signs and Symptoms:
- Prolonged morning stiffness
- Vague joint pain preceding visible swelling
- Joint stiffness that is ameliorated by motion (compare to OA)
- Progressive joint involvement

Diagnosis:
- Key to diagnosis is systemic symptoms (fever, malaise, subcutaneous nodules, uveitis, pericarditis, or pleural effusion).
- Look for ulnar deviation, swan neck, and Boutonnière deformities during your physical examination.

X-ray Findings:
- Bilaterally symmetrical soft tissue swelling, pannus formation, erosion of cartilage margin, and joint space narrowing.

Lab Tests:
- Rheumatoid factor (RF) is present in most adult patients, but absent in children.
- Antinuclear antibodies (ANA) are elevated in 20% to 60% of patients.

Source

NPLEX
MCCQE
USMLE

7. Can psoriasis cause arthritis similar to RA?

Psoriasis: can cause arthritis in the hands and feet that resembles RA. However, RF is almost always negative in psoriatic arthritis.

Diagnosis: Key to diagnosis is observing psoriatic skin lesions on physical examination.

Source

NPLEX
MCCQE
USMLE

8. What are the hallmarks of ankylosing spondylitis (AS)?

AS Signs and Symptoms:
- Typically, a 20- to 40-year-old man with positive family history complaining of back pain and morning stiffness.
- The SI joints are primarily affected.
- Since this is an autoimmune disorder, you would expect a low-grade fever as well as microcytic anemia.

X-ray findings:
- 'Bamboo spine'
- Syndesmophytes

Lab Tests:
- Positive human leukocyte antigen B27 (HLA-B27)
- Elevated ESR
- High C-reactive protein

9. How do you recognize Reiter's syndrome as a cause of arthritis?

Source

NPLEX
MCCQE
USMLE

Reiter's Syndrome: linked to the mnemonic "can't see, can't pee, can't dance with me" by generations of healthcare providers.

Signs and Symptoms:
- Conjunctivitis
- Urethritis (due to chlamydial infection)
- Arthritis
- Superficial oral and penile ulcers (possible)

Lab Tests:
- Reiter's syndrome is HLA-B27 positive (which is not required for diagnosis).

Treatment:
- This condition follows bacterial infections (STDs or, rarely, enteric pathogens). Therefore, the target of treatment is the causative organism.
- Also treat the patient's sexual partner where applicable.

10. Can hemophilia cause arthritis?

Source

NPLEX
MCCQE
USMLE

Hemophilia Risk Factor:
This condition can cause arthritis, but the patient would know about the condition long before hemarthrosis causes debilitating arthritis – an easy diagnosis.

11. Can Lyme disease cause arthritis?

Source

NPLEX
MCCQE
USMLE

Lyme Disease: The tick-borne *Borrelia burgdorferi* causes erythema chronicum migrans 'bulls-eye lesion' and late onset migratory arthritis. Lyme disease can cause myriad manifestations (similar to meningitis or cranial nerve palsies), but the bulls-eye is the tell-tale sign.

Diagnosis: ELISA or western blot test.

12. Sickle cell patients are susceptible to what kind of joint pain?

Source

NPLEX
MCCQE
USMLE

Ischemic arthralgia: due to sickle cell crisis, which is usually a manifestation of avascular necrosis of the femoral head. Refer to the Hematology module for diagnosis of sickle-cell anemia.

R H E U M A T I C   F E V E R

Source

NPLEX
MCCQE
USMLE

13. What is rheumatic fever?

Rheumatic Fever: prevalence has plummeted after the introduction of penicillin; however, in under-developed countries, the threat of rheumatic fever remains. When it occurs, rheumatic fever affects children 5 to 15 years of age after untreated and complicated strep throat (Group A beta-hemolytic *Streptococcus pyogenes*, or GABS) infections. Rheumatic fever is antibody mediated due to antibody cross reactivity between *strep* antigens and cardiac antigens.

Complications: This autoimmune attack causes myocarditis and leads to valvular heart disease in susceptible patients. The extent of permanent and irreversible valve damage depends on how many times this autoimmune reaction occurred (frequency of strep throats). Unfortunately, once patients have developed an episode of rheumatic fever, they are susceptible to recurrent bouts.

Strep Throat Manifestations:
- Acute onset
- Red swollen tonsils
- Purulent exudates on tonsils
- High fever
- Lymphadenopathy

Major Manifestations of Rheumatic Fever (Jones criteria):
- Fever
- Myocarditis
- Arthritis
- Chorea (uncontrolled dance-like movements occurs 2-3 weeks after throat infection)
- Subcutaneous nodules (rubbery nodules)
- Erythema marginatum rash

Managing Pharyngitis in Children:
1. Perform a rapid strep screen on suspected cases.
2. If positive, then antimicrobials are required.
3. If negative, do culture and sensitivity (C&S) on a throat swab. If C&S indicates *Streptococcus pyogenes* infection, then antimicrobials are required.
4. While waiting for C&S results (which takes at least 3 days), initiate naturopathic treatment for pharyngitis. If treatment is successful in 1 week, then antimicrobials are not indicated.
5. Be prepared to refer or prescribe penicillin if pharyngitis is refractory to 1 week of naturopathic treatment. There is published evidence that shows a decline of in incidence of GABS induced rheumatic complications if therapy is successful in the first 9 days of being infected.

ASSOCIATED CONDITIONS

14. What are Charcot joints?

Source

NPLEX
MCCQE
USMLE

Charcot Joint: lack of sensation causes abuse of joints, which, in turn, leads to joint deformity and pain.
- Seen in diabetics and other patients with neuropathies.
- The best treatment is prevention and treatment of the cause of neuropathy.

15. What generalized systemic signs of inflammation suggest autoimmune disorders?

Source

NPLEX
MCCQE
USMLE

Autoimmune Disorder Signs:
- Elevated ESR and C-reactive protein
- Fever
- Anemia of chronic disease (microcytic)
- Fatigue
- Weight loss
- Incidence of autoimmune disease is significantly higher in women of reproductive age.

16. How would you recognize systemic lupus erythematosus (SLE)?

Source

NPLEX
MCCQE
USMLE

SLE Signs and Symptoms:
- Well demarcated rash (malar or discoid)
- Photosensitivity
- Kidney damage
- Poly-arthritis (more than one joint is involved)
- Possible pericarditis/pleuritis
- Oral ulcers
- Neurological disturbances (depression, psychosis, and seizures)

Diagnosis: It is a difficult diagnosis in early stages before the classical clinical presentation is recognized.
- Use Anti-Nuclear Antibody (ANA) titer as a screening test.
- Confirm with Anti-Smith antibody test.
- CBC disorders (thrombocytopenia, leukopenia, anemia, or pancytopenia).

17. What are the hallmarks of scleroderma?

Source

NPLEX
MCCQE
USMLE

Scleroderma Signs and Symptoms:
- Classically presents with CREST symptoms:
  - **C**alcinosis
  - **R**aynaud's phenomenon
  - **E**sophageal dysmotility with dysphagia
  - **S**clerodactyly
  - **T**elangectasia + heartburn and mask-like leathery face

Lab Tests:
1. Use ANA titer as a screening test.
2. If positive, perform anticentromere antibody test (this is positive in CREST patients).
3. If positive, perform antitopoisomerase antibody test (a positive result here indicates full blown scleroderma).

Source

NPLEX
MCCQE
USMLE

18. What is the presentation of Sjogren syndrome?

Sjogren Syndrome Signs and Symptoms:
- Causes keratoconjunctivitis sicca (dry eyes) and xerostomia (dry mouth).
- Often a feature of autoimmune diseases.

Source

NPLEX
MCCQE
USMLE

19. What characterizes fibromyalgia, polymyositis, and polymyalgia rheumatica?

FIBROMYALGIA, POLYMYOSITIS, AND POLYMYALGIA DIFFERENTIATION:

Differential Feature	Fibromyalgia	Polymyositis	Polymyalgia Rheumatica
Class age/sex	Young adult women	Female 40-60 years of age	Female >50 years of age
Location	Various	Weakness and stiffness of proximal muscles	Severe pain and stiffness in pectoral and pelvic girdles; neck is usually involved.
ESR	Normal	Elevated	Markedly elevated
Electromyography and/or biopsy	Normal	Abnormal	Normal
Classic findings	Anxiety, stress, point tenderness over affected muscles	Elevated creatine phosphokinase (CPK)	Temporal arteritis, gelling phenomenon (stiffness after inactivity), malaise, fever, depression, and weight loss).

Source

NPLEX
MCCQE
USMLE

Black-welder, 2002

20. How do you recognize and treat chronic fatigue syndrome (CFS)?

Chronic Fatigue Syndrome: suspected when there is profound fatigue that disrupts daily activities in absence of identifiable pathology.

Signs and Symptoms:
- Hypotension
- Mild fever
- Recurrent sore throat
- Painful lymphadenopathy
- Muscle weakness, muscle pain
- Prolonged fatigue after exercise

- Recurrent headaches
- Migratory joint pain
- Depression
- Hypersomnia or insomnia

21. What is the first-line naturopathic treatment for CFS?

Source

Pizzorno et al, 1999

Naturopathic Treatment for Chronic Fatigue Syndrome

Approach: The first-line naturopathic approach is aimed at identifying underlying factors (e.g., food sensitivities), restoring hepatic detoxification, and supporting proper GI and immune functions.

1. Dietary measures
- Identify and control food allergies, increase water consumption, and eliminate caffeine and alcohol.
- Encourage consumption of whole organic foods and regular healthy small meals.
- Control hypoglycemia (if suspected) by eliminating sugar and refined foods.
- Support detoxification through the use of oligoantigenic diets.

2. Lifestyle modification
- Encourage regular low intensity aerobic exercise (>3X per week).
- Involve patient in meditation and/or progressive relaxation activities.
- Counsel to support mental-emotional well-being.

3. Clinical nutrition
- Vitamin C: 500-1000 mg t.i.d.
- Vitamin E: 200-400 IU q.d.
- Pantothenic acid: 250 mg q.d. Valuable in treating associated depression.
- Magnesium citrate and/or malate: 200-300 g t.i.d. Deficiency in Mg causes symptoms similar to CFS.

4. Botanical medicine
- *Eleutherococcus senticosus:* 200 mg solid extract t.i.d. Supports adrenals, adaptogen, increases T-helper cells and NK activity, published evidence of efficacy in treatment of CFS.
- *Glycyrrhiza glabra:* 250-500 mg t.i.d. Antiviral and glucocorticoid potentiating properties. Monitor blood pressure on monthly basis since prolonged use may produce hypertension.
- *Hypericum perfoliatum* 300 mg eq. t.i.d. May also be indicated in cases presenting with moderate depression. Immune support; suspected SSRI activity; published evidence of efficacy in mild-moderate depression; C/I with SSRIs, MAOI, and tricyclic antidepressants.

Source

NPLEX
MCCQE
USMLE

22. What are the signs of juvenile rheumatoid arthritis in a pediatric patient?

Juvenile Rheumatoid Arthritis Signs and Symptoms:
- Uvetis
- Arthritis
- Negative rheumatoid factor

Source

NPLEX
MCCQE
USMLE

23. What is Paget's disease?

Paget's Disease: usually occurs in men >40 years of age. Patients often complain of bone pain, arthritis, nerve deafness, and paraplegia. Classic cases involve the pelvis and the skull. These patients may tell you that they had to buy larger hats to accommodate their growing head. The risk of osteosarcoma is increased in affected bones.

Lab Tests: Markedly elevated Alkaline Phosphatase (ALP) indicating increased bone remodeling.

X-ray Findings: Cortex thickening, blade of grass sign, frontal bossing, and coarse bizarre trabeculae (once you have seen a Pagetoid skull you will not confuse it with anything else).

Examination Board References

NPLEX (II): North American Board of Naturopathic Examiners
North American Board of Naturopathic Examiners (NABNE), Naturopathic Physician Licensing Examination Part II Blueprint and Study Guide. Portland, OR: NABNE, 2005.

USMLE (II): National Board of Medical Examiners
Bouchert A. USMLE Step 2 Secrets. Philadelphia, PA: Hanley & Belfus Inc., 2000.

MCCQE: Medical Council of Canada
Molckovsky A, Pirzada KS (eds.). Review for the Medical Council of Canada Qualification Examination. Toronto, ON: Toronto Notes Medical Publishing, 2004.

Related References

Blackwelder R. Chronic Pain Syndrome. Complementary and Alternative Medicine Secrets. Philadelphia, PA: Hanley & Belfus Inc, 2002.

Damjanov I, Conran PB, Goldblatt PJ. Pathology: Rypins' Intensive Reviews. Philadelphia, PA: Lippincott-Raven, 1998.

Mills S, Bone K. Principles and Practice of Phytotherapy: Modern Herbal Medicine. New York, NY: Churchill Livingstone, 2000.

Moore R. Hematology Laboratory Diagnosis. Guelph, ON: McMaster University Press, 2001.

Pizzorno JE, Murray MT. Textbook of Natural Medicine. Vol. 1 and 2. 2nd ed. New York, NY: Churchill Livingstone, 1999.

Saunders, P. Herbal Remedies for Canadians. Toronto, ON: Prentice Hall-Pearson Canada Inc., 2000.

Shaver SL. Osteoarthritis. Complementary and Alternative Medicine Secrets. Philadelphia, PA: Hanley & Belfus Inc, 2002.

UROLOGY

Male Conditions

Urinary Tract Infections

Sexually Transmitted Diseases

MALE CONDITIONS

1. What are the reasons for conducting a male urogenital examination?

Urogenital Examination: Conduct an examination if the following signs and symptoms are present:
- Penile discharge
- Dysuria
- Lesions reported by patient
- Pain (abdominal or pelvic)
- Hernias
- Dermatological disease (e.g., redness and excoriation)

Prepuce Retraction: Retract the prepuce during routine male genital to detect chancres and carcinomas.

Penile discharge: If a patient presents with penile discharge, the most prudent approach is to conduct a male genital examination, followed by Gram stain and culture of any urethral discharge.

2. What are the differences in presentation between testicular torsion and epididymitis?

TESTICULAR TORSION VS. EPIDIDYMITIS:

Characteristics	*Testicular Torsion*	*Epididymitis*
Age of onset	< 30 years of age	> 30 years of age
Appearance	There is notable testicular swelling. Testes may be elevated into the inguinal canal.	Swollen testes; scrotal erythema; urethral discharge; urethritis; and possible prostatitis.
Prehn's sign	Pain is not alleviated by testicular elevation	Pain decreases upon testicular elevation.
Treatment	This is an emergency condition because immediate surgical intervention is required to prevent irreversible damage to the testes.	Naturopathic supportive treatments, as well as antimicrobial botanicals, are recommended.

Source

NPLEX
MCCQE
USMLE

3. How does testicular cancer usually present? What are the major risk factors?

Testicular Cancer: usually presents as a painless (often firm) mass in young men (20 to 40 years of age). The main risk factor is cryptorchidism (undescended testes).

Diagnosis:
■ Confirmed via testicular ultrasound, biopsy, and tumor marker assay – for example, Alfa-fetoprotien (AFP) and human chorionic gonadotropin.

Treatment:
■ Because testicular cancer is one of the most aggressive cancers (this is true for all germ-cell tumors), the recommended treatment is radiation and orchiectomy (for refractive tumors).
■ For metastatic presentations, antineoplastic chemotherapy is the mainstay of treatment.

4. What causes orchitis? Does it affect fertility?

Orchitis: presents as a painful and swollen testis. Mumps is touted for its propensity to cause orchitis (in post-pubertal males). Orchitis will rarely cause infertility.

Source

NPLEX
MCCQE
USMLE

5. What is benign prostatic hypertrophy (BPH)?

Benign Prostate Hypertrophy: as men age, BPH is extremely common, affecting 5% to10% of men at age 30 and more than 90% of men over age 85.

Ferri, 2004

Symptoms and Sequelae of BPH:
■ Increased progressive urinary frequency, especially at night (nocturia)
■ Weak urine stream
■ Straining and dribbling on urination
■ Feeling that the bladder cannot be completely emptied
■ Urine of abnormal color
■ Impotence
■ Burning on urination

Pizzorno
et al, 2002

Risk Factors:
1. Aging
2. Inadequate zinc intake. Zinc inhibits the activity of 5-alpha reductase enzyme (the enzyme that converts testosterone to dihydrotestosterone 'DHT') and prolactin secretion by the pituitary gland.
3. Regular beer consumption. Hops increases circulating prolactin levels (prolactin increases the prostatic uptake of testosterone).
4. Stress. Considerable and excessive stress physiologically induces both thyroid hormones, as well as prolactin.
5. Low protein diet (70% carbohydrate; 10% protein; 20% fat) has been shown to stimulate 5-alpha reductase.
6. Alcohol consumption of >740ml per month (especially wine and sake) is associated with increased incidence of BPH.
7. Smoking (even second-hand) is major source of cadmium, which is an antagonist of zinc.

Diagnostic Procedure:

- The most effective work-up is accomplished by screening symptomatic patients via a digital rectal examination (DRE) and/or transrectal prostatic ultrasound, along with a serum prostate specific antigen (PSA) assay to rule out prostatic carcinoma. Because symptoms of BPH and prostate cancer can be similar, the PSA test is added to this work-up.
- In men over 50 years of age with an immediate relative diagnosed with prostate cancer, a yearly DRE, as well as a PSA test, are highly recommended (combined will identify 90% of prostate cancers).
- Normal value for PSA is < 4ng/ml; a level >10ng/ml is highly suggestive of prostatic carcinoma.

6. What is the first-line naturopathic treatment for BPH?

Source

NPLEX

Pizzorno et al, 2002

Naturopathic Treatment for Benign Prostate Hypertrophy

1. Prevention
- Limit alcohol consumption.
- Avoid smoking (first-hand and second-hand smoke).
- Increase consumption of soy foods (genistein and daidzein in soy compete for estrogen receptors).
- Avoid pesticides (inducers of 5-alpha reductase) in the environment, as well as in foods.
- Increase consumption of omega-3 EFA-containing foods, such as cold-water fish, nuts, and seeds (e.g., flaxseed and walnuts).
- Maintain healthy cholesterol levels.

2. Dietary measures
- Encourage a high-protein diet (40% protein) of nuts, seeds, fresh vegetables, whole grains, legumes, and liberal amounts of soy products.

3. Clinical nutrition
- Zinc: 45-60 mg q.d.
- Flaxseed oil or fish oil: 1 tbsp q.d.
- Glycine, glutamic acid, and alanine: 200 mg q.d. In controlled studies, this combination of amino acids provided significant symptomatic relief for men with BPH.

4. Botanical medicine
- *Serenoa repens:* 160 mg of standardized (85% to 95% fatty acids and sterols) extract b.i.d. Clinical studies indicate that saw palmetto is 90% effective in diminishing all major symptoms of BPH. The effect is similar (and demonstrably faster in action) to the drug finasteride (e.g., Proscar, an anti-androgenic drug).
- *Pygeum africanum:* 100 mg of standardized (14% triterpenes) extract b.i.d. When combined with saw palmetto, the net synergistic effect is marked reduction of the presenting symptoms, as well as the clinical signs of BPH.
- Other complementary phytotherapeutics, include Cernilton (flower pollen) and *Urtica dioica*.

7. What are the common conventional treatments for BPH?

Conventional Treatment: Conventional approaches are recommended for severe cases (significant urinary retention of > 150ml residual urine volume after voiding):
■ Alpha-1 blockers: e.g., prazosin (Cardura) and terazosin (Hytrin).
■ Gonadotropin releasing hormone analogs: e.g., flutamide and finasteride (Proscar).
Transurethral resection of the prostate (TURP) is reserved for even more advanced cases, especially with recurrent urinary tract infections.

8. What are the common causes of erectile dysfunction (ED)?

Source

NPLEX
MCCQE
USMLE

Erectile Dysfunction: history often indicates the etiology in cases of psychogenic-erectile-dysfunction, which is a common presentation in general practice.

Signs and Symptoms:
■ Patients will present with a normal pattern of nocturnal erections.
■ In addition, they will exhibit some level of selective dysfunction – for example, where the patient has normal erections on masturbation, but not with his sexual partner.
■ Other cues include stress, anxiety, and fear.

Organic Causes:
■ Vascular insufficiency secondary to atherosclerosis and diabetes.
■ Uncontrolled diabetes can also cause ED through diabetic autonomic neuropathy (see Diabetes module).
■ Some prescription medications (antihypertensives and antidepressants) are known to cause ED as a side effect.

9. How do you distinguish between a hydrocele and a varicocele?

Source

NPLEX
MCCQE
USMLE

Hydroceles: will transilluminate, generally cause no symptoms, and do not require treatment.

Varicoceles: will not transilluminate; on palpation feel like a 'bag of worms' (more common over the left testis); disappear in the supine position; and may cause pain and/or infertility.

10. What is cryptorchidism?

Source

NPLEX
MCCQE
USMLE

Cryptorchidism: arrested descent of the testes from their embryological place of origin (renal area) to the scrotum. It is common in premature infants. Most cases of cryptorchidism eventually resolve within the first year of life (warm sitz baths may encourage descent). After 1 year of age, if the testis is showing no sign of descent, surgical orchiopexy is considered to preserve fertility.

Risk Factor: Cryptorchidism is a major risk factor for testicular cancer; it increases the incidence of this cancer up to 40 times the normal rate. Note that while surgical reduction of cryptorchidism improves fertility, it does not reduce testicular cancer risk significantly.

11. What are epispadias and hypospadias?

Source

NPLEX
MCCQE
USMLE

Epispadias and Hypospadias: both are congenital penile defects. As the name implies, epispadias refers to a urethra that opens on the top-side of the penis, while hypospadias refers to a urethra that opens on the bottom-side of the penis (the non-anatomical terms 'top' and 'bottom' are chosen so as to avoid any spatial confusion).

Treatment: Surgical intervention is recommended to ensure both functions (urination and ejaculation) and to circumvent the resulting susceptibility to UTIs.

URINARY TRACT INFECTIONS

12. Can urethral discharge be considered normal?

Urethral Discharge: absence of urethral discharge is generally considered the norm for males as well as females. In fact, scanty white or clear urethral discharge is a common sign of non-gonococcal urethritis and requires gram stain and culture to rule out infectious etiology.

13. How are urinary tract infections (UTIs) classified?

Source

NPLEX
MCCQE
USMLE

Upper Urinary Tract Infection: The convention is to call the renal nephron, pelvis, and ureter the upper urinary tract.

Lower Urinary Tract: Anything below the ureter is termed the lower urinary tract (i.e, bladder, prostate, and urethra).

14. What are the characteristics and causes of UTIs?

Source

NPLEX
MCCQE
USMLE

UTI Signs and Symptoms:
- Urgency
- Dysuria
- Distorted stream (in females)
- Suprapubic pain (both genders) and/or low back pain (more common in males when prostate is inflamed)

Causes: In > 75% of cases, UTIs are caused by *Escherichia coli*. Other causes include *Staphylococcus saprophyticus, Proteus, Pseudomonas, Klebsiella, Enterobacter,* and *Enterococcus.*

15. What factors increase the likelihood of UTIs?

Source

NPLEX
MCCQE
USMLE

Predisposing Factors for UTI:
- Females are more susceptible because of their short urethra: 90% of cases occur in women; 10% to 20% of all women have UTIs at least once a year.
- Any condition that promotes urinary stasis (BPH, pregnancy, stones, neurogenic bladder,

vesicourethral reflux) or bacterial colonization (indwelling catheters without proper maintenance, fecal incontinence, urethral trauma).

■ Diabetes predisposes to infections, including UTIs (rule it out if recurrent).

■ Ureteric valve incompetence causes urine reflux into ureter and is a leading cause of recurrent UTIs (but you will most likely catch it in children).

■ Some females acquire recurrent lower UTIs from sexual intercourse (treat prophylactically and encourage urination after intercourse).

■ Recurrent kidney infection secondary to UTIs is associated with progressive damage of renal tissue, leading to scarring and, rarely, kidney failure.

Source

NPLEX
MCCQE
USMLE

16. How do you diagnose UTIs?

UTI Diagnosis:

1. Definitive diagnosis constitutes clean-catch urinalysis showing WBCs, positive leukocyte esterase, and/or positive nitrite; with urine microscopy exhibiting > 100,000 colony-forming units (CFU) of a specific kind of bacteria per ml of urine.

2. If urine culture exhibits >100,000 Colony-forming Units (CFU)/ml of 'mixed flora', then sample was contaminated with vaginal flora or otherwise and should not be used to diagnose or treat the condition.

3. If the signs and symptoms are typical of uncomplicated UTI, a urine dipstick test showing positive leukocyte esterase and/or positive nitrite will suffice.

4. However, if urine dipstick test is negative for leukocyte esterase, urine microscopy and culture should still be performed.

5. Approximately 40% of women with classic symptoms of UTI do not exhibit a significant level of bacteruria. Some references recommend treatment of classic presentations even without definitive laboratory evidence.

Source

NPLEX
MCCQE
USMLE

17. Why are UTIs in infants and children a special concern?

UTI in Infants: Infants can't tell you exactly what is going. To complicate matters, the presentation of UTIs in infants is atypical and elusive, accounting for most cases of fever without source (FWS = febrile condition without identifiable origin).

Diagnostic Procedure:

1. For any FWS in an infant, the first action should be to obtain a urine sample for urinalysis.
2. If positive for infection, treat.
3. If urinalysis is negative and you suspect UTI, the gold standard is a clean-catch urine culture.

UTI in Children: In children less than 5 year of age, a UTI may be the presenting symptom of genitourinary malformations (such as vesicourethral reflux or posterior urethral valves). The alarm should sound when UTI occurs recurrently in a patient < 6 years of age.

Treatment: Refer or consult with urologist because you will require a voiding cystourethrogram to ascertain your hypothesis.

18. Should asymptomatic bacteruria be treated?

Source

NPLEX
MCCQE
USMLE

Hoffman,
1996

Saunders,
2000

Asymptomatic Bacteruria Management: In general, do not treat. Bacteria may exist in urine without causing malice (remember that urine is not a sterile medium). However, you should treat asymptomatic bacteruria in pregnant females because of lowered immunity and high risk of progression to pyelonephritis.

Treatment:
- Use only botanical and nutritional agents that are safe in pregnancy, such as *Arctostaphylos uva-ursi* (Bearberry), *Agropyron repens* (Couchgrass), *Agathosma betulina* (Buchu), *Hydrangea arborescense* (Hydrangea), and *Zea mays* (Cornsilk).
- There are also a select few antibiotics considered safe for use during pregnancy (e.g., penicillin, amoxicillin, and erythromycin).

19. What is the first-line naturopathic treatment of UTIs?

Source

NPLEX

Bhat-
tacharya
2002

Pizzorno
et al, 2002

Naturopathic Treatment for Urinary Tract Infection

1. Adjust urinary pH: A significant amount of controversy continues regarding the role of urinary pH in the treatment of UTIs. On the one hand, low urinary pH is considered protective against *Proteus* & *Klebsiella* (both are urease producers that like alkaline environments). On the other, alkalinization has long been the cornerstone for successful naturopathic treatment and prophylaxis of UTIs. In addition, many of the herbs used to treat UTIs work better in an alkaline environment.

2. Dietary and lifestyle measures
- Consider food sensitivities.
- Avoid consumption of simple sugars, refined carbohydrates, and concentrated fruit juices.
- Encourage ingestion of watermelon (natural diuretic) and liberal amounts of garlic and onion.
- Advise patient to drink plenty of filtered water and cranberry or blueberry juice, which prevents *E. coli* adhesion to the endothelial cells of the bladder.

3. Clinical nutrition
- Vitamin C: 500 mg q.2h. for the first day of infection (or until bowel tolerance), then reduce dose.
- Bioflavonoids: 1000 mg q.d.
- Vitamin A: 25,000 IU q.d. May not be safe during pregnancy.
- Zinc: 30 mg q.d.
- Choline: 1000 mg q.d.

4. Botanical medicine
- *Hydrastis canadensis*: Berberine works better in alkaline environment; specific antimicrobial spectrum against *E. coli, Staphylococcus, Proteus, Pseudomonas, Klebsiella,* and *Enterobacter.* May not be safe during pregnancy.

Source

- *Arctostaphylos uva ursi*: Arbutin is hydrolyzed into hydroquinone, which alkalinizes the urine; crude plant is more effective than isolated arbutin; recent clinical trials established efficacy in treatment of recurrent cystitis; narrow therapeutic window; toxic signs include tinnitus, N/V, and shortness of breath.
- Traditional herbalists recommend a mixture of *Arctostaphylos uva-ursi* (bearberry), *Agropyron repens* (couchgrass), & *Achillea millefolium* (yarrow) in equal parts as a tea: 1 cup q.2h. until condition improves, then t.i.d. for a week or two for total cure.

Hoffman, 1996

Saunders, 2000

- Other beneficial herbs in the treatment of UTIs include *Juniperus communis* (juniper berries), *Agathosma betulina* (buchu), *Hydrangea arborescense* (hydrangea), and *Zea mays* (cornsilk).
- Note that of the above mentioned herbs, the following are not considered safe for use during pregnancy: *Hydrastis canadensis* (goldenseal), *Achillea millefolium* (yarrow), and *Juniperus communis* (juniper berries).

Morrison, 1998

5. Acute Homeopathic Remedies: Most homeopaths recommend giving the constitutional remedy in a 12C or 30C strength, especially if the remedy covers urinary tract disorders.

- *Cantharis*: indicated for intense dysuria when every drop feels like scalding acid as it passes + feeling that emptying bladder would bring relief + pain is the primary symptom.
- *Nux Vomica*: indicated for constant urging and full sensation, but only small, unsatisfying amounts are passed + frequent urging is the main symptom.
- *Petroselinum*: indicated for intense itching or tingling deep in urethra or neck of bladder + itch or irritation is the main symptom.
- *Pulsatilla*: indicated for pain that increases every moment the urge is postponed + pain is irregular, paroxysmal or with spurting.
- *Sarsaparilla*: indicated for copious urination with marked burning pain at the end of urination.
- *Staphysagria*: indicated for post-coital and honeymoon cystitis + burning and tenesmus + unsatisfied after urination.

Ferri, 2004

Conventional Treatment: Antimicrobial treatment should be considered for any patient with persistently positive urine cultures or recurrent infections despite naturopathic treatment.

Source

NPLEX
MCCQE

20. What is chronic interstitial cystitis (IC)?

Chronic Interstitial Cystitis: a peculiar presentation of a severe bladder disorder of at least 12 months duration that causes chronic suprapubic pain, urinary frequency, and nocturia. Routine urine cultures are negative, and symptoms do not respond to antimicrobials.

Bhat-tacharya, 2002

Causes: Possible causes include:
- Autoimmune reaction toward bladder antigens
- Deficiency of glycosaminoglycan (GAG) mucosal layer
- Mast cell infiltration of bladder interstitium
- Food sensitivities

Diagnosis:
- Common differentials of cystitis must first be ruled out before diagnosing this condition.
- Consider bladder tumors, bladder calculi, and side effects of medications in chronic presentations.

Treatment:
- Although clinical studies are pending, conservative naturopathic treatments, including a trial oligoantigenic (elimination) diet and acupuncture, as well as the herb *Centella asiatica* or gotu kola (contraindicated during pregnancy), have been shown to be effective in the treatment of IC.

Source

Pizzorno et al, 2002

Bhat-tacharya, 2002

SEXUALLY TRANSMITTED DISEASES

21. What are the risk factors for sexually transmitted disease?

STD Risk Factors:
1. Promiscuous sexual practices
2. Multiple sexual partners
3. Homosexual men or bisexual men or women
4. New sexual partner
5. Use of injection drugs
6. Not using condoms

Source

NPLEX
MCCQE
USMLE

22. What are the most common non-genital manifestations of sexually transmitted disease?

Systemic STD Signs and Symptoms:
- Sore throat
- Diarrhea
- Rectal bleeding
- Anal itching
- Proctitis
- Uveitis
- Arthritis

Source

NPLEX
MCCQE
USMLE

Examination Board References

NPLEX (II): North American Board of Naturopathic Examiners
North American Board of Naturopathic Examiners (NABNE), Naturopathic Physician Licensing Examination Part II Blueprint and Study Guide. Portland, OR: NABNE, 2005.

USMLE (II): National Board of Medical Examiners
Bouchert A. USMLE Step 2 Secrets. Philadelphia, PA: Hanley & Belfus Inc., 2000.

MCCQE: Medical Council of Canada
Molckovsky A, Pirzada KS (eds.). Review for the Medical Council of Canada Qualification Examination. Toronto, ON: Toronto Notes Medical Publishing, 2004.

Related References

Bhattacharya B. Urinary Tract Infection. Complementary and Alternative Medicine Secrets. Philadelphia, PA: Hanley & Belfus Inc, 2002.

Cutler P. Problem Solving in Clinical Medicine: From Data to Diagnosis. 3rd ed. Baltimore, MD: Lippincott, Williams & Wilkins Press, 1998

Dains J, Baumann L, Scheibel P. Advanced Health Assessment and Clinical Diagnosis in Primary Care. 2nd ed. St. Louis, MI: Mosby C.V. Co. Ltd, 2003.

Damjanov I, Conran PB, Goldblatt PJ. Pathology: Rypins' Intensive Reviews. Philadelphia, PA: Lippincott-Raven, 1998.

Ferri F. Ferri's Clinical Advisor: Instant Diagnosis and Treatment. St. Louis, MI: Mosby Inc, 2004.

Hoffmann D. The Complete Illustrated Holistic Herbal. Boston, MA: Element Books Ltd, 1996.

Moore R. Hematology Laboratory Diagnosis. Guelph, ON: McMaster University Press, 2001.

Morrison R. Desktop Companion to Physical Pathology. Nevada City, CA: Hahnemann Clinic Publishing, 1998.

Pizzorno JE, Murray MT, Joiner-Bey H. The Clinician's Handbook of Natural Medicine. New York, NY: Churchill Livingstone, 2002.

Saunders, P. Herbal Remedies for Canadians. Toronto, ON: Prentice Hall-Pearson Canada Inc., 2000.

CASE-BASED
REVIEW QUESTIONS

The following sample questions are included to illustrate the interplay of the clinical knowledge and reasoning skills required to pass Primary Care objective-structured clinical evaluation examinations. These multiple choice questions simulate concepts and criteria tested by the North American Board of Naturopathic Examiners (NABNE). The following questions offer a realistic 'look and feel' of the physical clinical diagnosis and laboratory diagnosis component of the Naturopathic Physician Licensing Examination (NPLEx).

Directions: Circle the ONE answer that BEST fulfills the objective of each question.

1. Which of the following is a feature of secretory diarrhea?

   a) Persistent diarrhea despite fasting
   b) Malodorous, often floating stools
   c) Blood and/or pus in the stools
   d) Elevated levels of leucocytes in stool

2. A 35-year-old female patient seeks your opinion regarding four episodes of chest pain that she experienced during the last month. She is anxious because her husband died of a heart attack 3 months ago and hands you a typed list of laboratory tests that her niece (second-year naturopathic student) recommends to rule out heart attacks. She has no family history of heart disease. Your physical examination reveals no abnormalities. What is your plan?

   a) Recommend avoidance of coffee, alcohol, spicy foods, and milk
   b) Send this patient to ER
   c) Tell this patient that the cause of her episodes is psychologic
   d) Order routine electrocardiography and serum creatine kinase

3. In a 5-year-long observational study published in a peer-reviewed journal, researchers documented an inverse relationship between average serum beta-carotene level and incidence of coronary artery disease (CAD). What can you confidently conclude from this study?

   a) B-carotene is an appropriate marker to screen for CAD
   b) B-carotene supplementation can be used to treat CAD
   c) Low serum B-carotene causes CAD
   d) None of the above

4. A 52-year-old healthy woman comes to your office for her annual check-up. Your usual intake is unremarkable as well as your age-specific laboratory screening tests. However, on her CBC report, hemoglobin level was slightly elevated. What do you do?

   a) Send patient to her family doctor, as this condition requires prescription medications
   b) Treat her polycythemia vera with proven antineoplastic botanical *Ganoderma lucidum*
   c) Nothing; monitor her CBC during her next visit
   d) Reassure patient that the test result does not indicate any abnormality

5. Abdominal pain of psychogenic origin can be distinguished from organic pain based on history. Which of the following reasoning criteria distinguish organic from functional pain?

   a) Psychological stress rules out organic pain
   a) Acute persistent pain rules out functional pain
   a) Abdominal pain that awakes patient strongly suggests organic etiology
   a) Anxiety, fever, and anemia strongly suggests functional etiology

6. A mother brings her 1-year-old infant with a chief complaint of abdominal colic, insomnia, and fussiness. She describes the stool as 'mucousy' and blood tinged. Your work-up is unremarkable, with the exception of a 1 cm x 3 cm palpable mass in the hypogastrum. You decide to send the patient to your local children's hospital for which of the following diagnostic procedures?

a) A blood sample for liver enzymes
b) Lower GI computed tomography scan
c) Lower GI radiological study with barium
d) Kidney and urinary bladder ultrasound scan

7. Which of the following is not a considered first-line naturopathic treatment of gallstones?

a) Phosphatidylcholine: 500 mg q.d.
b) Fiber supplementation: 2 g t.id.
c) Complete avoidance of saturated fat, animal protein, and fried foods
d) Drinking 1/2 cup of lemon juice t.i.d.

8. What precaution should be taken when complementing oral hypoglycemic drugs with botanicals?

a) None; oral hypoglycemic drugs and botanicals are contraindicated
b) Gradual introduction with daily glucometer journaling
c) Patient should take oral hypoglycemic agents before meals and botanicals afterwards
d) Dose of oral hypoglycemics should be reduced before starting naturopathic treatment

9. B. F. is a 16-year-old type 1 diabetic male who has been seeing you for adjunct naturopathic therapy. He tells you that his glucometer test shows high levels in the morning. What is your assessment?

a) He has been taking less insulin than required
b) He has been taking more insulin than required
c) His insulin dose is adequate but his diet is poor
d) It is impossible to determine appropriateness of insulin dose from data provided

10. Acute wheezing in pediatric presentations is most common with which of the following conditions?

a) Klebsiella pneumonia
b) RSV infection
c) Legionnaire's disease
d) Bronchial asthma

11. Detection of white blood cells in the stool is a sign of which of the following conditions?

    a) Colon cancer
    b) Ulcerative colitis
    c) Malabsorption syndrome
    d) Irritable bowel syndrome

12. A 12-year-old boy complains of aching knees and elbows, a fever, and loss of appetite. Physical examination reveals painless subcutaneous nodules near his hips and shoulders. What is the most important question to ask this child?

    a) "Did you fall down in the last week?"
    b) "Has your fever been getting worse?"
    c) "Have you had a sore throat recently?"
    d) "Do you have any skin irritation?"

13. A 36-year-old Mediterranean female is assigned to you at the clinic as a new patient. She complains of chronic low back pain that is "better after hot showers." Otherwise, she has an unremarkable medical history. Physical examination reveals decreased lordosis, tenderness on palpation, and decreased range of motion of low back and hips. Your laboratory work-up indicates an elevated ESR. Which of the following statements is correct regarding this patient?

    a) Presence of ANAs would strongly suggest rheumatoid arthritis
    b) Bilateral sacroiliitis on plain film radiology would strongly suggest ankylosing spondylitis
    c) Ameliorating factors indicate functional low back pain that is best treated by massage
    d) CT is required to confirm lumbar disk herniation, which is the most likely diagnosis

14. A 45-year-old Caucasian female presents with difficulty breathing due to progressive sharp pain in the left side of her chest. She tells you that she has tried some of her father's nitroglycerin to no avail, and then she came promptly to see you. Her medical history includes cholecystectomy at age 31. Pressure on the indicated point of pain causes it to worsen and radiate into her shoulder. Given a normal ECG and cardiac enzymes, what is your diagnosis?

a) Costochondritis
b) Myocardial infarction
c) GERD
d) Cholangitis

15. A 6-year-old girl complains of abdominal pain. Which of the following would be included in your differential diagnosis?

a) Gastroenteritis, musculoskeletal origin, strangulated hernia, UTI
b) Gastroenteritis, fibroids, strangulated hernia, UTI
c) Intussusception, strangulated hernia, constipation, hypothyroidism
d) Alcohol abuse, lactose intolerance, fibroids, hyperthyroidism

16. A 41-year-old female presents with nervousness and insomnia. She reports a significant increase in her appetite without weight gain. How would you proceed with this patient?

a) Order laboratory tests, then refer to the emergency department
b) Refer to a nearby hospital outpatient clinic
c) Order laboratory tests
d) Prescribe a nervine tincture of *Humulus lupulus* and *Valeriana officinalis*

17. The 2002 edition of the *Merck Manual* lists polydipsia, polyuria, polyphagia, fatigue, and weight loss as diagnostic criteria for diabetes mellitus. Why is progressive weight loss considered a feature of this disease given that obesity is an etiological factor?

a) Because catabolic metabolism maintains fasting hyperglycemia despite progressive glycosuria
b) Because there is a net gain in body stores of glycogen, fat, and protein
c) Because there is a net loss of body water; thus, the loss of weight represents dehydration in these cases
d) The *Merck Manual* is wrong; a naturopathic physician would not consider diabetes in a patient who is losing weight

18. Which of the following options is true? A patient with acute renal failure is likely to be _____, while a patient with chronic renal failure is likely to be _____.

    a) Afebrile; Febrile
    b) Symptomatic; Asymptomatic
    c) Polyuric; Anuric
    d) Jaundiced; Pale

19. This ECG tracing of a patient presenting with bouts of palpitation exhibits which of the following conditions?

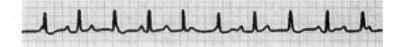

    a) Increasing PR interval until a QRS complex is dropped
    b) Multiple P waves but when beats are conducted PR intervals are unvarying
    c) Ventricular rhythm is regular while atrial rhythm is not
    d) ST segment is elevated

20. How is irritable bowel syndrome diagnosed?

    a) Air-fluid levels on abdominal plain films
    b) Through a process of exclusion
    c) History of stress
    d) Small intestinal biopsy

21. Recently, investigators working with your municipal health department collected the following cancer statistics. As of 31 December 2006: 1,000 cases of prostate cancer were counted, 200 of which were diagnosed since 01 January 2006. As of the same date, the adult population of the municipality was 100,000; 60% of whom are female. Based on the statistics provided, which of the following fractions correctly indicates the rate of incidence of prostate cancer in the municipality in the year 2006.

    a) 200/100,000
    b) 200/40,000
    c) 200/39,800
    d) 200/39,200

22. Sickle cell anemia patients are susceptible to what kind of joint pain?

    a) Ischemic arthralgia
    b) Osteoarthralgia
    c) Autoimmune arthralgia
    d) Hemarthrosis arthralgia

23. Which of the following laboratory tests reliably indicate autoimmune disorders?

    a) Decreased hematocrit
    b) Decreased erythrocyte sedimentation rate
    c) Increased C-reactive protein
    d) Increased serum alkaline phosphatase

24. CREST syndrome is described as calcinosis, Raynaud's phenomenon, esophageal dysmotility with dysphagia, and telangiectasia. This syndrome is a less severe manifestation of which of the following conditions?

    a) Systemic lupus erythematosus
    b) Scleroderma
    c) Sjogren's syndrome
    d) Reiter's syndrome

25. A 28 year-old female presents with a complaint of progressive fatigue. The following are the highlights of your chart: normal vitals; bilateral periorbital edema; no cyanosis; normal capillary refill; normal heart and lung examination; normal jugular venous pressure; negative kidney punch; bilateral ankle swelling; and grade 3 pitting edema of ankles. Your in-house urinalysis indicates marked proteinuria without hematuria. What is the most likely diagnosis?

    a) Nephrotic syndrome
    b) Nephritic syndrome
    c) Acute glomerulonephritis
    d) Chronic pyelonephritis

26. Persistent fever without identifiable etiology (FWS) in infants necessitates laboratory investigation to rule out which of the following conditions?

    a) Juvenile rheumatoid arthritis
    b) Upper urinary tract infection
    c) Upper respiratory tract infection
    d) Hemolytic uremic syndrome

27. A 60-year-old vegetarian male is referred to you for nutritional counseling. The CBC you ordered exhibits decreased Hct, low RBC count, increased MCV, and hyper-segmented neutrophils. What would you advise this patient to do?

    a) Increase his consumption of green leafy vegetables
    b) Avoid spicy and bitter foods
    c) Supplement with vitamin B-12 and folic acid
    d) Get retested during his next scheduled visit

28. A 48-year-old male has been seeing you regularly for annual checkups. As part of your work-up, you obtain a CBC and lipid profile. The CBC results are suggestive of iron deficiency anemia. Given the patient's exemplary dietary habits, you decide to perform a stool occult test, which returned a positive result. What would you do next?

    a) Retest during next annual check-up
    b) Advise patient to supplement with iron succinate 100 mg t.i.d.
    c) Refer patient for flexible colonoscopy
    d) Inquire about family history of sickle cell disease

29. With regards to microcytic hypochromic anemia, which of the following statements is incorrect?

    a) Elevated hemoglobin A2 level indicates thalassemia
    b) Basophilic stippling indicates lead poisoning
    c) Increased total iron binding capacity (TIBC) indicates anemia of chronic disease
    d) Elevated serum ferritin levels rule out iron deficiency anemia

30. A 14-year-old female patient tells you that she has been suffering from extreme tiredness for the last 3 days. You noted in your chart that the patient appears pale; temp 38.6C; BP 109/76; RR 14; generalized lymphadenopathy; pharynx is erythematous and tender w/o discharge. Which laboratory tests would you order to confirm your suspicions?

    a) CBC & Indirect Coombs test
    b) CBC & Schilling test
    c) CBC & transferrin
    d) CBC & Monospot test

31. Which of the following statements is not true with regards to penile discharge?

    a) Clear discharge is normal
    b) Yellow discharge occurs with gonococcal urethritis
    c) White discharge is common sign of non-gonococcal urethritis
    d) Scanty discharge is a common sign of chlamydial urethritis

32. Which finding in the prostate suggests prostatic cancer?

    a) Symmetrical smooth enlargement
    b) Diffuse hardness
    c) Extreme tenderness
    d) Boggy soft enlargement

33. Your attending supervisor inquires about the rationale for your decision to prescribe the antimicrobials *Hydrastis canadensis* and *Arctostaphylous uva-ursi* to a 26-year-old female who exhibits classical signs of lower urinary infection, but does not show laboratory evidence of bacterial colonization. What is your response?

    a) Mention that 15% of all women have UTIs at least once a year
    b) Accept his criticism and inform patient that she does not have a urinary tract infection
    c) State that 40% all UTIs do not exhibit a significant level of bacteruria
    d) Argue that the predictive value of urinalysis has not been established yet

34. What condition is suggested by the following presentation: headache that follows URIs; associated with pyrexia; anorexia; and neck rigidity?

    a) Subarachnoid hemorrhage
    b) Sinusitis
    c) Meningitis
    d) Intracranial hypertension

35. During an initial intake, your 22 year-old male patient appears to be detached from his surroundings; his behavior and speech are disorganized; and he tells you that your receptionist tried to "double swipe" his credit card and warns you to keep an eye on her. He is also concerned about the "racial practices" pervasive in his university program that resulted in his placement on academic probation for the last year or so. What is your most likely diagnosis?

    a) Paranoid personality disorder
    b) Acute psychotic disorder
    c) Schizophrenia
    d) Panic disorder

36. Which of the following behaviors does a manic episode not exhibit?

    a) Depressed mood
    b) Decreased need for sleep
    c) Talkative with flight of ideas
    d) Impedance of social or occupational functions

37. A 54-year-old man has become forgetful, preoccupied, withdrawn, irritable, and disheveled. His physical examination is unremarkable. This patient has been with his company for 22 years and was considered an excellent employee. Which of the following is the most likely diagnosis?

    a) Senile dementia
    b) Schizophrenia
    c) Alcoholism
    d) Major depression

38. A young mother is very focused on the health of her 8-month-old infant. She keeps her house immaculate for fear that dirt will harm her baby. She checks the locks on the door at least ten times before going to bed, and she has to get up and check that her child is still breathing at least three times a night. She knows that her fears are a bit irrational, but persists with these behaviors. Which of the following is the most likely diagnosis?

    a) Post-partum depression
    b) Obsessive compulsive disorder
    c) Generalized anxiety disorder
    d) Paranoid personality disorder

39. A 52-year-old man comes walking slowly into your office, stooped over, and holding his hand to his back. He complains of acute onset back-pain and bilateral leg pain. He is unable to void and has not had a bowel movement for 1 week. Examination reveals a lax anal sphincter and an absent cremasteric reflex. Which of the following is the most likely diagnosis?

    a) Upper motor neuron lesion
    b) Central disk herniation
    c) Benign prostatic hypertrophy with urinary obstruction
    d) Spondylolisthesis

40. You are called in to assess an acute presentation of leg pain in a 28-year-old male. The patient started getting these debilitating pains after starting an intensive running program in preparation for a marathon. Your physical examination reveals bilateral hypertonicity of lateral leg muscles; decreased posterior tibial and dorsalis pedis pulses; decreased pain, touch, and two-point discrimination over the dorsum of both feet. What is your diagnosis?

    a) Deep venous thrombosis
    b) Atherosclerosis
    c) Fibular nerve palsy
    d) Anterior compartment syndrome

41. What is the most common location for traumatic intervertebral disk herniation?

   a) L2-L3
   b) L3-L4
   c) L4-L5
   d) L5-S1

42. As you were conducting a screening physical examination on an 8-year-old female, you noted vertebral column listing suggestive of scoliosis. This finding seems to disappear when the patient bends forward. What would you do next?

   a) Recommend a vertebral column brace to address the structural scoliosis
   b) Recommend a vertebral column brace to alleviate the functional scoliosis
   c) Perform a complete musculoskeletal examination to find the cause of her scoliosis
   d) Nothing; scoliosis is a self-limiting finding in children of that age

43. A 42 year-old male presents with vertigo that occurs with particular head movements. On examination, you note that he experiences vertigo and nystagmus when his head is laterally bent and rotated toward the left side; there is no sign of conductive or sensorineural hearing loss. This condition started 2 weeks ago and has a steady course. What is the most likely diagnosis?

   a) Meniere's disease
   b) Labyrinthitis
   c) Multiple sclerosis
   d) Benign positional vertigo

44. How would you best evaluate a presentation of a firm non-tender testicular mass?

   a) Transilluminate, and request radioactive iodine uptake scan
   b) Transilluminate, and request PSA levels and local X-ray
   c) Transilluminate, and request ultrasound and biopsy
   d) Reevaluate in 3 weeks as condition will likely subside

45. A 3-year-old is brought to you with what appears to right ear pain. The girl cries incessantly and fusses with her right ear. The crying began last night. The parents report some clear discharge from the ear. Otoscopic examination reveals vesicles and erythema of the right tympanic membrane; the left ear is unaffected. What is the most likely diagnosis?

    a) Purulent otitis media
    b) Serous otitis media
    c) Infectious myringitis
    d) Acute mastoiditis

46. When should you recommend or prescribe IM penicillin for the management of pediatric streptococcal pharyngitis that is refractory to naturopathic treatment?

    a) 3 days
    b) 7 days
    c) 10 days
    d) 14 days

47. An expecting mother is a carrier of the X-linked recessive, glucose-6-phosphate-dehehydrogenase deficiency. Her family history reveals that both male siblings as well as her mother have the enzyme defect. Her husband never exhibited any symptoms suggestive of this condition. What are the odds of that their daughter will develop this condition?

    a) 75%
    b) 50%
    c) 25%
    d) 0%

48. A 53-year-old male patient presents to your office with localized weakness in his legs and feet. The condition has been getting worse over the past month or so and has begun to interfere with his ability to perform daily activities. Your neurological examination reveals: no paresis in the upper extremity in contrast to the lower; bilateral loss of ankle and knee tendon reflex; no sensory deficits in vibration, temperature, pain or two-point discrimination. How would you best confirm your diagnostic impression of this presentation?

a) CSF analysis & Evoked nerve potential testing
b) Tensilon test
c) Indirect Coomb's test & Electromyography
d) Spinal cord computed tomography (CT) scan

49. Plummer-Vinson syndrome is characterized by which of the following presentations?

a) Iron-deficiency anemia
b) Cerebellar ataxia
c) Ascending paralysis
d) Pernicious anemia

50. Senile tremors may resemble Parkinsonism, but senile tremors do not include which of the following presentations?

a) Nodding the head as if responding yes or no
b) Rigidity and weakness of voluntary movement
c) Tremor of the hands
d) Tongue protrusion

Answers

1.	a	11.	b	21.	d	31.	a	41.	d
2.	d	12.	c	22.	a	32.	b	42.	c
3.	d	13.	b	23.	c	33.	c	43.	d
4.	c	14.	a	24.	b	34.	c	44.	c
5.	c	15.	a	25.	a	35.	c	45.	c
6.	c	16.	c	26.	b	36.	a	46.	b
7.	d	17.	a	27.	c	37.	d	47.	d
8.	b	18.	b	28.	c	38.	b	48.	a
9.	d	19.	c	29.	c	39.	b	49.	a
10.	b	20.	b	30.	d	40.	d	50.	b

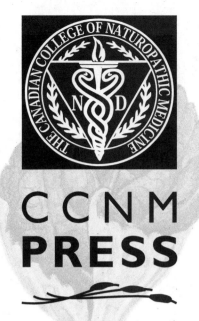

CCNM PRESS

CCNM Press is dedicated to publishing college texts, clinical reference materials, consumer health books, and corporate wellness guides in the field of naturopathic medicine to further the advancement of the profession of naturopathic medicine and to teach the principles of healthy living and preventive healthcare, enabling patients to participate in their healing process.

The Principles of Naturopathic Medicine
First, do no harm
Co-operate with the healing power of nature
Address the fundamental causes of disease
Heal the whole person through individualized treatment
Teach the principles of healthy living and preventive medicine

Distribution Partners
Login Brothers Canada, Health Management Books, Coutts Library Service, Nutri-Books, BMS Resources, SCB Distributors, Blackwell North America, Mathews Medical Books, J.A. Majors Company, Rittenhouse Book Distributors, Baker & Taylor Company, Ingram Book Company, NetLibrary.com, amazon.com, amazon.ca.

CCNM Press, 1255 Sheppard Avenue East, Toronto, Ontario, Canada M2K 1E2
Tel. 416-498-1255 Ext. 290   Fax: 416-498-3157
E-mail: ccnmpress@ccnm.edu Website: www.ccnmpress.com

Principles & Practices of Naturopathic Medicine Series

This 'principles and practices' series of college text and clinical reference books is designed primarily for the student and practitioner of naturopathic medicine. Thoroughly researched, well-illustrated, functional reference and teaching resources, these books will become standard texts in medical colleges. They cover the primary modalities of naturopathic medicine and meet the required therapeutic curriculum components established by the Council on Naturopathic Medical Education (CNME).

Publishing Program:

Principles & Practices of Naturopathic Clinical Nutrition
Principles & Practices of Naturopathic Botanical Medicine
Principles & Practices of Naturopathic Lifestyle Counseling
Principles & Practices of Naturopathic Physical Therapies
Principles & Practices of Naturopathic Homeopathic Medicine
Principles & Practices of Naturopathic Asian Medicine

Principles & Practices of Naturopathic Clinical Nutrition

by Jonathan Prousky, ND
Preface by Abram Hoffer, MD

Clinical nutrition is an integral part of naturopathic medicine with respect to the creation of a nutritious diet to achieve optimum health and the use of nutrient supplements to prevent and treat nutritional deficiencies, dependencies, disorders, and related diseases. This book focuses on the pathophysiology of these conditions and establishes diagnostic and therapeutic nutritional protocols for clinical practice, based on current medical research. Fully illustrated with up-to-date references and case studies. This book promises to become the standard text and clinical reference in this growing field of study, both in naturopathic and conventional medical colleges.

Jonathan Prousky, BPHE, BSc, ND, FRSH, is the Chief Naturopathic Medical Officer, the Associate Dean of Clinical Education, and an Associate Professor of Clinical Nutrition at The Canadian College of Naturopathic Medicine. He also coordinates the monthly Grand Rounds lecture series and supervises the post-graduate residency program in naturopathic medicine.

After receiving his ND degree from Bastyr University, he furthered his clinical training by completing a Family Practice Residency sponsored by the National College of Naturopathic Medicine. He has published in such medical journals as *Townsend Letter for Doctors & Patients, Journal of Orthomolecular Medicine,* and *BMC Clinical Pharmacology* on topics ranging from elderly malnutrition to gastric acid secretion. His current research focuses on the therapeutic aspects of vitamin B-3.

Abram Hoffer, MD, is a founding father of clinical nutrition therapy for common medical and psychiatric diseases and disorders. A graduate of the University of Toronto (MD) and the University of Minnesota (PhD), he has published more than 500 articles in medical journals and 15 books in the field of clinical nutrition.

Contents

Preface by Dr Abram Hoffer, MD

Principles of Naturopathic Clinical Nutrition
Biochemical Individuality
Orthomolecular Medicine
Energy Balance and Weight Control

**Diagnosing Nutritional Deficiencies,
Dependencies & Disorders**
Anthropometric Assessment Methods
Biochemical Assessment Methods
Clinical Examination
Toxicology of Commonly Used Supplements

**Nutritional Prevention & Treatment
of Common Diseases & Disorders**
Psychiatric and Behavioral Disorders
Neurologic Disorders
Endocrine Disorders
Integumentary Disorders
Cardiovascular Diseases
Respiratory Disorders
Renal Disorders
Liver Disorders
Ocular Disorders
Pancreatic Disorders
Inflammatory Bowel Disease
Infection and Immunodepression
Cancer
Uric Acid and Gout
Celiac Disease
Esophagus and Stomach Disorders
Short Bowel Syndrome and Small Bowel Diseases

References
Index

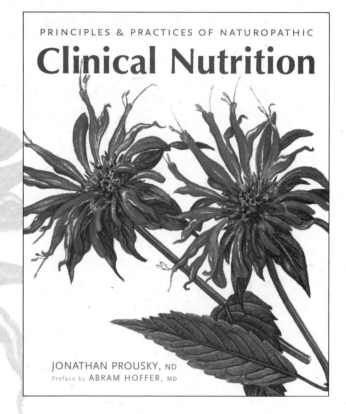

PRINCIPLES & PRACTICES OF NATUROPATHIC
Clinical Nutrition

JONATHAN PROUSKY, ND
Preface by ABRAM HOFFER, MD

400 pages, illustrated, 8 x 10 inches
BISAC: MED06000 HEA016000
ISBN 1-897025-04-1   HC $99.95 CDA/USA $79.95

Fundamentals of Naturopathic Medicine Series

This series of textbooks focuses on core CNME curriculum subjects and integrative clinical courses in the medical sciences taught at naturopathic and other complementary and alternative medical colleges in North America. These texts will also appeal to traditional medical colleges with natural medicine curriculum components and electives.

Publishing Program 2005-2008:

Fundamentals of Naturopathic Endocrinology
Fundamentals of Naturopathic Cardiology
Fundamentals of Naturopathic Gastroenterology
Fundamentals of Naturopathic Gynecology & Obstetrics
Fundamentals of Naturopathic Pediatrics
Fundamentals of Naturopathic Geriatrics

Fundamentals of Naturopathic Endocrinology

Complementary and Alternative Treatments
by Michael Friedman, ND
Preface by Denis Wilson, MD

This is an essential text for naturopathic medical students and clinical practitioners pursuing complementary and alternative treatments for endocrine disorders and imbalances — diabetes, hypothyroidism, adrenal exhaustion, impotence, menopause, and other metabolic disorders. The book features three sections: a textbook geared to medical college curriculum; a clinician's handbook of diagnostic and therapeutic protocols; and a selection of recent clinical studies and literature reviews by other renowned physicians, notably Alan R. Gaby (MD), John Lee (MD), Gregory Kelly (ND), Zoltan Rona (MD), Denis Wilson (MD), and Abram Hoffer (MD). This collaboration between leading medical and naturopathic doctors makes *Fundamentals of Naturopathic Endocrinology* uniquely valuable for all healthcare professionals. Fully illustrated, with extensive references, featuring case studies from Dr Friedman's medical files.

Michael Friedman, BSc, ND, is a graduate of The Canadian College of Naturopathic Medicine and a former Professor of Endocrinology at the University of Bridgeport (CT) who has published articles on diabetes and other endocrine disorders in leading consumer health and scholarly publications. He lives in Montpelier, Vermont.

Denis Wilson, MD, is an internationally renowned physician who developed the concept of Wilson 's Thyroid Syndrome in 1988 after observing people with symptoms of low thyroid and low body temperature who, nevertheless, had normal blood tests. He originated the use of T3 mixed with a sustained-release agent to treat this disorder. He is the author of *Wilson's Thyroid Syndrome: A Reversible Thyroid Problem* and the *Doctor's Manual for Wilson's Thyroid Syndrome.*

CONTENTS

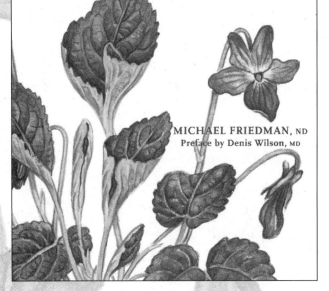

FUNDAMENTALS *of*
Naturopathic Endocrinology

MICHAEL FRIEDMAN, ND
Preface by Denis Wilson, MD

400 pages, illustrated, index, 8 x 10 inches
BISAC: MED027000 HEA016000
ISBN 1-897025-02-5   HC $99.95 CDA/USA $79.95

Naturopathic Grand Rounds Series

The Grand Rounds lectures provide DVD programs for viewing by naturopathic doctors and other medical practitioners. Guest speakers address a wide spectrum of specialties and subspecialties, introducing new research developments. The objective of the program is to update naturopathic doctors, naturopathic students, and other medical practitioners on developing trends and techniques in naturopathic medicine. Each DVD package includes a literature review of the most current evidence-based research on the topic. Ideal for required professional development units.

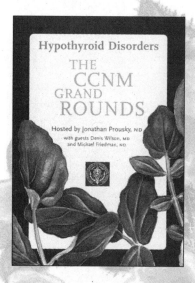

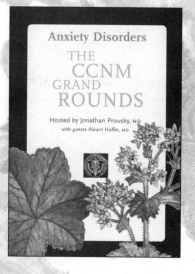

Hypothyroid Disorders Grand Rounds

Hosted by Jonathan Prousky (ND) with guests Denis Wilson (MD) and Michael Friedman (ND)

Dr Denis Wilson first diagnosed Wilson's thyroid syndrome and developed the WT3 therapy for this hypothyroid condition. He practices in Orlando, Florida. Dr Michael Friedman is author of *Fundamentals of Naturopathic Endocrinology.*

DVD, 1 hour, Reference Booklet
BISAC: MED02700 HEA016000
ISBN 1-897025-19-X $49.95 CDA/USA $39.95

Anxiety Disorders Grand Rounds

Hosted by Jonathan Prousky (ND) with guest Abram Hoffer (MD)

Dr Abram Hoffer developed the medical discipline of orthomolecular psychiatry for the nutritional therapy of psychiatric disorders and founded *The Journal of Orthomolecular Medicine.*

DVD, 1 hour, Reference Booklet
BISAC: MED10500 HEA016000
ISBN 1-897025-20-3 $49.95 CDA/USA $39.95